CLEAR AND PRESENT DANGER

The killing of three U.S. officials in Colombia ignites the American government's explosive, and top secret, response . . .

"A CRACKLING GOOD YARN."

—*Washington Post*

THE SUM OF ALL FEARS

The disappearance of an Israeli nuclear weapon threatens the balance of power in the Middle East—and around the world . . .

"CLANCY AT HIS BEST . . . NOT TO BE MISSED."

—*Dallas Morning News*

WITHOUT REMORSE

The Clancy epic fans have been waiting for. His code name is Mr. Clark. And his work for the CIA is brilliant, cold-blooded, and efficient . . . but who is he really?

"HIGHLY ENTERTAINING."

—*Wall Street Journal*

continued . . .

The bestselling novels of
TOM CLANCY

RAINBOW SIX

John Clark is used to doing the CIA's dirty work. Now he's taking on the world ...

"ACTION-PACKED."

—*New York Times Book Review*

EXECUTIVE ORDERS

The most devastating terrorist act in history leaves Jack Ryan as President of the United States ...

"UNDOUBTEDLY CLANCY'S BEST YET."

—*Atlanta Journal-Constitution*

DEBT OF HONOR

It begins with the murder of an American woman in the back streets of Tokyo. It ends in war ...

"A SHOCKER CLIMAX SO PLAUSIBLE YOU'LL WONDER WHY IT HASN'T YET HAPPENED!"

—*Entertainment Weekly*

THE HUNT FOR RED OCTOBER

The smash bestseller that launched Clancy's career—the incredible search for a Soviet defector and the nuclear submarine he commands ...

"BREATHLESSLY EXCITING."

—*Washington Post*

continued ...

RED STORM RISING

The ultimate scenario for World War III—the final battle for global control...

"THE ULTIMATE WAR GAME ... BRILLIANT."

—*Newsweek*

PATRIOT GAMES

CIA analyst Jack Ryan stops an assassination—and incurs the wrath of Irish terrorists...

"A HIGH PITCH OF EXCITEMENT."

—*Wall Street Journal*

THE CARDINAL OF THE KREMLIN

The superpowers race for the ultimate Star Wars missile defense system...

"*CARDINAL* EXCITES, ILLUMINATES ... A REAL PAGE-TURNER."

—*Los Angeles Daily News*

TOM CLANCY'S BESTSELLING NOVELS INCLUDE

The Hunt for Red October
Red Storm Rising
Patriot Games
The Cardinal of the Kremlin
Clear and Present Danger
The Sum of All Fears
Without Remorse
Debt of Honor
Executive Orders
Rainbow Six

CREATED BY TOM CLANCY AND STEVE PIECZENIK

Tom Clancy's Op-Center
Tom Clancy's Op-Center: Mirror Image
Tom Clancy's Op-Center: Games of State
Tom Clancy's Op-Center: Acts of War
Tom Clancy's Op-Center: Balance of Power
Tom Clancy's Op-Center: State of Siege
Tom Clancy's Net Force
Tom Clancy's Net Force: Hidden Agendas

CREATED BY TOM CLANCY AND MARTIN GREENBERG

Tom Clancy's Power Plays: Politika
Tom Clancy's Power Plays: ruthless.com

SSN: Strategies of Submarine Warfare

NONFICTION

Submarine:
A Guided Tour Inside a Nuclear Warship
Armored Cav:
A Guided Tour of an Armored Cavalry Regiment
Fighter Wing:
A Guided Tour of an Air Force Combat Wing
Marine:
A Guided Tour of a Marine Expeditionary Unit
Airborne:
A Guided Tour of an Airborne Task Force
Carrier:
A Guided Tour of an Aircraft Carrier

Into the Storm: A Study in Command

Tom Clancy's
NET FORCE™
HIDDEN AGENDAS

Created by
Tom Clancy and Steve Pieczenik

B
BERKLEY BOOKS, NEW YORK

This is a work of fiction. Names, characters, places, and incidents are either the product of the author's imagination or are used fictitiously, and any resemblance to actual persons, living or dead, business establishments, events or locales is entirely coincidental.

TOM CLANCY'S NET FORCE™: HIDDEN AGENDAS

A Berkley Book / published by arrangement with
Netco Partners

PRINTING HISTORY
Berkley edition / October 1999

All rights reserved.
Copyright © 1999 by Netco Partners.
NET FORCE is a trademark of Netco Partners, a partnership of
Big Entertainment, Inc., and CP Group.
This book may not be reproduced in whole or in part,
by mimeograph or any other means, without permission.
For information address: The Berkley Publishing Group,
a division of Penguin Putnam Inc.,
375 Hudson Street, New York, New York 10014.

The Penguin Putnam Inc. World Wide Web site address is
http://www.penguinputnam.com

ISBN: 0-425-17139-6

BERKLEY®
Berkley Books are published by The Berkley Publishing Group,
a division of Penguin Putnam Inc.,
375 Hudson Street, New York, New York 10014.
BERKLEY and the "B" logo
are trademarks belonging to Penguin Putnam Inc.

PRINTED IN THE UNITED STATES OF AMERICA

10 9 8 7 6 5 4 3 2 1

ACKNOWLEDGMENTS

We'd like to thank Steve Perry for his creative ideas and his invaluable contributions to the preparations of the manuscript. We would also like to acknowledge the assistance of Martin H. Greenberg, Larry Segriff, Denise Little, John Helfers, Robert Youdelman, Esq., Richard Heller, Esq., and Tom Mallon, Esq.; Mitchell Rubenstein and Laurie Silvers at BIG Entertainment; the wonderful people at Penguin Putnam Inc., including Phyllis Grann, David Shanks, and Tom Colgan; our producers on the ABC mini-series, Gil Cates and Dennis Doty; the brilliant screenwriter and director Rob Lieberman; and all the good people at ABC. As always, we would like to thank Robert Gottlieb of the William Morris Agency, our agent and friend, without whom this book would never have been conceived, as well as Jerry Katzman, Vice Chairman of the William Morris Agency, and his television colleagues. But most important, it is for you, our readers, to determine how successful our collective endeavor has been.

ACKNOWLEDGMENTS

"The greatest dangers to liberty lurk in insidious encroachment by men of zeal, well-meaning but without understanding."

—*Louis Brandeis*

"Nothing is secret that shall not be made manifest; neither any thing hid, that shall not be known and come abroad."

–*Luke, 8:17*

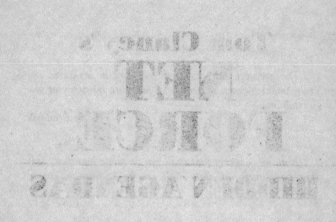

Tom Clancy's
NET
FORCE™

HIDDEN AGENDAS

PART ONE

A Little Knowledge

PROLOGUE

A cold and damp winter wind played around the windows of the building, a breeze not strong enough to rattle the still-pristine thermopane glass, but potent enough to tweak an occasional whistle from an art-deco protrusion, whistles that now and then came low enough to sound almost like moans.

Alone inside, the night watchman—watch*woman* in this case—pored over the laptop on the guard station's desk, adding a few personal notes to the text of Professor Jenkins's long and incredibly boring lecture on the strata of rock formations in southern New Zealand. The lecture was from his auditorium-sized class Introduction to Geology, her final science requirement, and she'd put it off as long as she could, but graduation was fast approaching and there was no way around it. She would have taken Astronomy, supposedly a walk, but the classes had been filled before she'd ever logged on to registration. Too bad. Stars were much more interesting than rocks.

Kathryn Brant sighed, leaned back in the creaky chair, and rubbed at her eyes. Geology. Bleh.

She leaned toward the desk again and got another nail-wrenched-from-wet-wood noise. Lord. Brand-new, and already the chair squeaked as if it had been left out in the Louisiana rain for a couple years. But that was what happened when you bought everything from the lowest bidder—a bid that had probably been the low one because the company had bribed somebody in the Contracts office. Bribery was a normal way of doing business around here. Kat had taken two semesters of political science at LSU, where she was, thankfully, a senior. Studying politics was almost a necessity in Louisiana, where people still spoke fondly of Huey Long, the governor-turned-senator who'd been assassinated in the main part of the capitol building, just up the hall there, more than seventy-five years past.

Huey had been one in a long list of rogues who had run the state, and with the public's blessing. After all, the big oil companies had paid for everything for decades, there hadn't been any income tax—no property tax to speak of—and if you were going to elect somebody, why not elect somebody colorful, especially if it didn't cost you anything? Her political science professor had once told the class that when he'd been a teenager, he and his friends would catch a bus to the capitol and sit in the gallery, watching the House in action. More interesting than going to a movie, he'd said. People came from all over the country to study Louisiana politics, and rightly so.

She grinned as the wind howled at the glass doors that opened out onto the capitol grounds. Huey was out there, in spirit and in bronze, just around the bend, the spotlight from the top of the tall and pointed building—once the tallest in the entire South, and still pretty much the tallest in the state—again shining down upon the populist martyr's huge statue. Every now and then, the state tightened its purse strings and decided to turn the spotlight off to save a few dollars, but they always turned it back on again. Tourists still came to see old Huey out there, pigeons and all.

Working your way through school as a guard at the state

capitol wasn't the best job in the world, but it left plenty of time to study, that was the main thing—

Her com buzzed. She grinned again and pulled the tiny unit from her belt. She knew who it was. Nobody else would be calling at this hour.

"Hey," she said.

"Hey, Kat," her husband said.

"How come you're still awake?" Kat asked. "You'll never make Lard Ass's class."

"Piss on him. I miss you. All alone here in this big, old bed. Naked under the covers. Full of lust for my new wife."

Kat laughed. "You all talk, goat-boy. If I came home right now, you'd whine about how you had to get some sleep."

"No, ma'am. You come home and I'll show you. I have a big surprise for you."

"Not so big as all that, honey chile. I'd say it was just an . . . *average* surprise."

"How would *you* know? Come on home and see. I've been lifting weights."

She laughed. "I *am* tempted—" she began.

She never finished the sentence. The compression shock wave blasted her so hard that if the investigators hadn't known who she was, they would never have been able to identify her, not even using dental records. When the various agencies finished combing the rubble—city and state police, fire department, ATF, FBI—they found in the bloody mush that had been Kat Brant only eight of her teeth still intact, none of which had ever been touched by a dentist's laser.

The only blessing was that she did not suffer. She never knew what hit her.

1

Alexander Michaels, Commander of the FBI's elite Net Force unit, fell on the floor, smack onto his butt. He hit harder than he expected; it knocked the wind out of him. Fortunately, the cheek that took most of the impact was the left one, and not the right where, two months ago, a bullet had exited after he'd been shot in the thigh. The wound was pretty much healed; it only twinged now and then.

The woman who had just slammed him to the floor was his chief deputy, Assistant Commander Antonella "Toni" Fiorella—all five feet five inches, one hundred and maybe ten pounds of her.

Before he could even try to recover his breath, Toni dropped to one knee next to him and threw a short right elbow at his face, slapping it with her left hand for emphasis—and to move her left hand into position for a follow-up wipe, did she deem it necessary.

It wasn't going to be necessary. Michaels had no plans to punch her. He could barely breathe. Smiling took everything he had.

Toni offered Michaels a hand, and he took it. She stood and helped him do the same.

"You okay?"

He managed to suck in enough air to say, "Yeah, fine." Holding the smile was one of the hardest things he'd done in a while, but he held it.

"Good. You see what I did?"

"I think so."

Generally, they practiced such takedowns on the nice, padded mat thoughtfully provided here by the FBI in the smaller of the two gyms in Net Force HQ. Now and again, however, they stepped off the mats onto the floor. Toni, who had been practicing this esoteric martial art since she was twelve, had explained why such training was necessary.

"If you practice on the mats all the time, you get used to that cushion. If you fall on the street or a sidewalk, it won't be quite so easy. And since a lot of fights end up on the ground, you need to know how it feels."

Yeah. Right.

He could understand it, though he wasn't sure he was going to ever learn the stuff so well he could hit the concrete and bounce like a rubber ball. But after a month of training five days a week, at least Michaels could finally get the name of the system right: *Pukulan Pentjak Silat*. Or *silat*, for short. It was, Toni had told him, a slimmed-down and simplified version of a more complex art that had come out of the Indonesian jungles less than a century ago. She had learned it from an old Dutch-Indonesian woman who'd lived across the street from the Fiorellas in the Bronx, after she had witnessed the old woman use the art against four gangbangers who had tried to run the granny off her door stoop. A big mistake, that.

Michaels had been impressed with what he'd seen Toni do. If this was the simple and easier stuff, he could wait on the really nasty moves.

"Okay, you try," she said.

"You gonna punch left or right?" he asked.

"Doesn't matter," she said. "If you control the center like you're supposed to, it'll work either way."

"In theory," he said.

She smiled at him. "In theory."

He nodded, then tried to relax and assume a neutral stance. That was supposed to be part of it too, Toni had said. It ought to work from whichever position you happened to be in if an attacker jumped you; otherwise—what was the point? You wouldn't have time to bow and get into your ready stance if the street thug decided to eat your lunch. It wasn't real likely a guy in an alley coming at you with a knife was going to allow you to run home to take off your shoes and put on your *gi* while he stood there waiting, maybe cleaning his nails with his blade. If a move wasn't practical, the Indonesian fighters didn't much like to pass it along. This wasn't a *do*, a spiritual "way." It was the distilled essence of anything-goes street-fighting. It was not an art of flashy, fancy moves, but an art of war. In *silat,* you didn't merely defeat an enemy, you destroyed him, and you used whatever you had at hand to do it: fists, feet, elbows, knives, clubs, guns—

Toni leaped at him.

You were supposed to block first, then step, and this defense was supposed to be a move to the outside of the attacker. Instead, Michaels, rattled, blocked and stepped to the inside of Toni's leading foot. In theory, as she'd said, it didn't matter, since anything that worked was the point.

His right thigh slid between Toni's legs and pressed against her pubis. His concentration on protecting himself just kind of . . . evaporated. He'd blocked the punch, but now he just stood there. He didn't follow up. He was very much aware of the warmth of her crotch astraddle his thigh, even through two sets of sweatpants.

Damn!

"Alex?"

"Sorry, I drew a blank."

Quickly, Michaels stepped back. He'd nearly been killed by

that assassin a couple of months ago; if it hadn't been for Toni, the killer would have gotten him, and it had seemed a good idea to learn more about how to protect himself, but right now this intimate martial contact with Toni might be bringing up more problems than it solved. It certainly was bringing up one problem in particular he could do without—

"Hey, Boss?"

Michaels shook off the erotic thoughts. Jay Gridley stood near the gym's entrance, looking at the two of them. The younger man was grinning.

"Jay. What's up?"

"You said you wanted to hear about that Louisiana thing as soon as it came in. I just downloaded the packet from the field team in Baton Rouge, got vid and reports. It's flagged in your incoming files."

Michaels nodded. "Thanks, Jay." He looked at Toni. "I need to check that out."

"We can pick up where we left off Monday," she said. "Unless you're working tomorrow?"

"I wish. I was hoping to work on the car, but I've got to bone up on financial stuff. I'm supposed to appear before Senator White's committee on Tuesday."

"You get all the fun," Toni said.

"Don't I just?"

They bowed to each other, the intricate *silat* beginning and ending salute, and Michaels headed for the dressing room.

Sheldon Gaynel Worsham was sixteen years old, a student at New Istrouma High School. He looked about twelve, was thin, and had black, oily hair slicked down all over, save for a wavy lock that dangled greasily over his left eye. He wore blue parachute pants and a black T-shirt with a putrid-green pulse-paint logo. The logo was a stylized badge with the word "GeeterBeeter" in jagged letters across it. Whatever that meant.

The kid slouched in a cheap chair next to a heavy castplast

table that was scratched and battered by years of abuse. Somebody had carved a heart with initials inside it on one corner, something of a surprise, since this was obviously a room where knives or other sharp objects were generally forbidden.

The man seated across the table from Worsham was heavyset, florid-faced, in a cheap, dark business suit, and he might as well have had "cop" flashing in neon over his head.

"So tell me about this bomb," the cop said.

Worsham nodded. "Yeah, okay, okay. So we're not talking semtex or C4 or crap like that, we're talking RQX-71, a topsecret chemical used in conventional missile warheads. It's an analog of some old stuff called PBX-9501. You want to know about anisotropic elastics or isotropic polymerics? Expansion rates or like that?"

"Why don't we just skip over that for now," the cop said. "Where did you get it, this explosive?"

The kid grinned. "I made it in the chem lab. Swiped a keycard from the janitor's desk and duped it, got the alarm codes, snuck in at night. Only took a week. Got a little tricky at one point, I thought I was gonna blow myself up, but it worked out okay."

"You made it. And took down a brand-new, three-story, steel-framed addition to the capitol with it."

The kid grinned wider. "Yeah. Something, huh?" Worsham sat up straighter in the plastic chair.

"And that blast killed a woman guard working her way through college."

"Yeah, well, I'm sorry about that part, but it's not really my fault. The coozers shouldn't have fired my dad, you pross?"

"Your father worked on the construction of the building."

"Until the stupid coozers fired him, yeah. I wanted to make a point, you pross?"

The cop nodded. "I guess you did that." He shifted in his chair. The thin plastic squeaked in protest. "And how did you

happen to come up with the top-secret formula for this—
RAQ?''

"RQX-71.'' Now the kid favored the cop with his biggest
grin yet. "That was the easy part. I scarfed it off the net.''

Michaels leaned back in the conference room chair and
glanced at Toni and Jay Gridley. Gridley touched a control
and the holoproj of the interrogation faded.

"Full of remorse about killing that young woman, isn't
he?'' Michaels said.

"Kids don't relate to death,'' Jay said. "Too much entcom,
too many vids, too much VR slaughter-rooming.''

Toni said, "And the formula?''

"Just like the little bastard said,'' Jay said. "Right in the
middle of a public net room. We pulled it as soon as we found
it, but it was posted anonymously. We're trying to backwalk
it, but it looks like it came from a recaster somewhere.''

"Who would do such a thing? Why?'' Toni said.

"And how did they *get* the formula to do it?'' Michaels
added.

Jay shrugged. He tapped at the portable and the image of
the destroyed building shimmered and came up on the holoproj. It basically looked like a pile of concrete and metal rubble, beams sticking out, shards of glass glittering under the
searchlights, and smoke still coming from sections of it.

"Jesus,'' Toni said.

"Yeah,'' Michaels said. "Only this one is in our lap and
not His. We've got to find whoever is responsible for putting
this formula onto the net where our sociopathic teener could
find it.''

"According to the counter, there were more than nine hundred hits on that file before we cleaned it off,'' Jay said. "We
better hope nobody else who downloaded that formula has a
grudge against somebody.''

Michaels shook his head. Nine hundred hits. Nine hundred
chances for someone to try to concoct this stuff. Nine hundred

chances for someone to succeed, and take out a building like that Worsham kid or—and this was maybe even worse—blow themselves and a whole school full of kids up in the process.

What kind of scum would do something like this? The Worsham boy was obviously bent, missing a few key neurons in his brain, but whoever posted the formula for the explosive was really sick. They needed to find him fast.

And Christmas was also fast approaching. The holidays would slow things around here to a crawl, and he had to go back to Idaho to see his daughter, Susie. And his ex-wife, Megan, too. A prospect that brought forth mixed emotions in Michaels, to be sure. At eight, Susie was the brightest spot in his life, but it was a long way from Washington, D.C., to Boise, and he didn't see her nearly as much as he wanted to. And Megan? Well, that was another whole can of worms that didn't bear opening just at this moment. The divorce had been final for more than a year, and if she called and asked him to come home right now . . . Up until recently, there hadn't been any question, he'd go. But the torch he'd been carrying had dimmed a little when he'd found out Megan was dating somebody. Being with another man. Enjoying it.

"Alex?"

He looked at Toni. "Sorry, I slipped into the void. What?"

"Joanna Winthrop is coming in at two-thirty."

Gridley snorted. "Lightweight Lite? What's she want?"

"Lieutenant Winthrop is going to be assisting us on this matter," Michaels said. "Colonel Howard has graciously allowed us to borrow her from the field. In fact, she will be working with you."

"What? I don't need her, Boss," Jay said. "I can run this dweebo to ground without some airhead sim-bimbo—"

"Jay." Michaels's tone was sharp.

"Sorry, Boss. But she's only gonna get in the way."

"As I recall, her grade-point average was higher than yours straight across the board," Toni said.

"Sure, where *she* went to school."

"MIT, wasn't it?"

"Yes, ma'am, but their standards have gone way down. CIT is acme now."

Alex just shook his head and said, "Jay, whatever your differences with Lieutenant Winthrop, you'll just have to find a way to get past them. We need all the help we can get on this mess." He waved at the holoproj.

Gridley nodded, but his jaw muscles flexed as he gritted his teeth.

Great, Michaels thought, one more brick on the load I don't need. A computer prima donna jealous of his territory. Just great.

His temporary secretary came into the conference room. "Commander, I have Director Carver on the phone."

Michaels stood. "I'll take it in my office." He waved at Jay and Toni. "Get busy, folks."

2

Friday, December 17th, 1:45 p.m.
Washington, D.C.

Thomas Hughes strode into the senatorial offices as if he owned them, the building they were in, *and* the city around them. He waved at the receptionist. "Bertha. Is he alone?"

"Yes, sir, Mr. Hughes."

Hughes nodded. He'd known Bertha for more than a dozen years. She'd been with Bob since his first term, but she still called him "Mr. Hughes," and he had not encouraged otherwise. He walked to the inner office door, rapped once, and pushed it open in the same motion.

Jason Robert White, fifty-six, the senior United States senator from the great state of Ohio, sat at his desk. He was playing a computer game. He looked up and started to frown at the interruption before he realized who had dared barge in.

"Hey, Tom." White did a fingerwave over the sensor on his handpad and the small-scale holoproj images froze. It looked like two guys in hand-to-hand combat, one of whom was green and scaly. Jesus.

"Bob. How'd the lunch with Hicks go?" Hughes moved to

the pale gray leather couch, sat, and looked at the man for whom he worked.

White appeared ten years younger than his actual age, with a deep chemical tan under his perfectly styled, artfully graying hair. He wore a dark-blue tailored Saigon suit, a pastel-pink silk shirt, and a striped regimental tie for a regiment that had never existed. Hughes couldn't see his feet, but the shoes were doubtless Italian or Australian, and handmade. Altogether, the outfit the senator wore offhandedly was worth what Hughes made in salary each month, easy. He was the image of a successful senator, handsome, fit, and comfortable in his custom clothes, no doubt about it. He could play a Viennese waltz on the piano, speak passable French and German, keep up with a so-so tennis pro, and break a hundred on a bad day at the country club golf course. A man who could walk the corridors of international power with ease.

Hughes, on the other hand, knew he looked every day of his fifty-two years. He was twenty pounds too heavy, wore a decent, but not expensive, Harris Tweed sport coat and gray wool slacks from Nordstrom, both off the rack, and his shoes were Nike dress casuals. Total cost of his outfit was maybe a twentieth that of White's.

White leaned back in his chair and waggled his left hand in a so-so gesture. "Well, Tom, you know Hicks. He never gives a nickel but what he wants a dime. If we want to get his support, the honorable senator from Florida wants to see the Naval Air Station remain a fixture in Pensacola from now until the end of time."

Hughes nodded. He had expected no less. "Fine. Give him what he wants. What do we care? He's a critical vote. We get him, we'll get Boudreaux and Mullins. We get them, we're out of committee and it's a lock on the floor."

White smiled at his chief of staff. "Probably won't hurt us with Admiral Pierce either."

"Exactly." Hughes glanced at his watch, a gold Rolex that White had given him on the eve of their election to the Senate.

Hughes had been the campaign manager, and such a watch was way beyond anything he'd ever been able to afford. For White, whose family owned half of Ohio and part of Indiana, a Rolex was a trinket, a drop from a bucket brimming with money. It was the most expensive piece of jewelry that Hughes ever wore, and though he could afford better now, he couldn't afford it legally.

"Aren't you supposed to be on the links with Raleigh at two-fifteen?" he reminded White.

"The old man canceled. Too cold for him. Personally, I think he just doesn't want me to kick his ass again. Last time out, I beat him by nine strokes. We're doing drinks at the Benson instead, two-thirty."

"Good. Remember, let him bring up the Stoddard thing. Play it cool, let him court you. He doesn't need to know you want it more than he does."

"I will be an iceberg," White said. He waved at the computer projection frozen over his workstation. "You ever play DinoWarz?"

"I can't say as I have, no."

"Very stimulating mano-a-mano combat scenario. There's a full VR version that puts you right in the middle of the action. Some junior high school kid built it and put it on the net. Fun. You should try it sometime."

Hughes smiled and tried not to show the contempt he felt. White was rich, the son, grandson, and great-grandson of wealthy men. It wasn't just a silver spoon he'd been born with, but a platinum one encrusted with diamonds. If he'd wanted to, White could have blown a million dollars a year for his entire life and never depleted his share of the family fortune. He wasn't a total fool, but he was a dilettante, a dabbler; the office was for him an adult version of DinoWarz, and Hughes believed it meant about as much. White thought being a United States senator was . . . fun.

"One other thing," Hughes said. "That bombing in Louisiana."

"Oh, yeah. Terrible thing."

"Worse than terrible. The kid who did it got the formula for the explosive off the net. A supposedly top-secret military formula."

"No shit?" White leaned forward, and his face came close to the translucent holoproj of the two combatants. He waggled his fingers and the image vanished.

"I think this plays right into your hearings on Net Force. They are supposed to stop such things."

"That's true."

"You might want to mention it when the budget hits the table. I'll have Sally work up the report on the bombing. That young woman guard who was killed was in college, a new-lywed, about to graduate."

"A shame," White said. "Tell Sally to highlight that part."

"Of course."

The intercom chimed. Bertha. "Sir, your limo is here for your two-thirty."

Hughes stood. "I'll be in my office," he said. "And I'll meet you for the staff meeting at four."

"Thanks, Tom."

After the senator was gone, Hughes went down the hall to his own office. He nodded at Cheryl, his secretary.

"Anything pressing?"

"Louis Ellis called from Dayton. He's going to be in D.C. next Thursday and he wants the senator's ear for a few minutes."

"Have Bertha pencil him in for half an hour in the morn-ing." Ellis, one of White's father's drinking buddies, had con-tributed half a million to White's last reelection campaign, more or less legally via various PACs. He'd also given them that much cash under the table, a nice chunk of which had found its way into Hughes's own safety deposit box, where it joined a thick sheaf of crisp hundreds already there.

Hughes had been very careful about living beyond his means. His public face was exactly what was expected for a senator's chief of staff making a paltry ninety grand a year. But under various guises, Hughes had a fat line of electronic credit. Still, it never hurt to have some hard currency in case of emergencies.

If his plans went as expected, he'd be able to use the bills in his box to light his Cuban cigars, if he felt like it.

"Anything else?"

"Your massage therapist called. She will be at your house at seven."

Hughes nodded. Brit would give him a good massage, that was true enough. But that was only half of the service she provided.

He went into his office and closed the door behind him.

Hughes's office was a spartan affair whose only artwork was a Picasso on the wall behind his desk. He didn't particularly care for Picasso, but a picture worth that much on an office wall certainly impressed people who *did* care about the old Spanish dauber. Depending on his mood, he would give different stories when asked about the painting. Sometimes, he told them he'd bought it at a garage sale for fifty bucks just to watch their jaws drop. Other times, he said a woman had given it to him in gratitude for his lovemaking abilities. Once in a great while, he told the truth—that the painting was a gift from his boss—but that was never as much fun.

He sat behind the desk in a wooden teacher's chair. In fact, the chair had once belonged to his high school civics teacher, Charles Joseph, who had told Hughes he would never amount to anything. He kept the chair to remind him that where he was going in the not-too-distant future was going to be beyond old Joseph's—or anybody else's—wildest dreams. Senator White and his family would look like paupers compared to Hughes. Everything was going as planned.

He grinned. That was the trick, wasn't it? But he was well on the way. He was, Hughes reminded himself, the smartest man he knew. He could pull it off.

No doubt in his mind.

The com chirped.

"The Vice President is on three," Cheryl said.

"I'll take it," Hughes said. "But let's let him wait a few seconds. We don't need an uppity Vice President, do we?"

Cheryl chuckled, and Hughes felt pretty good himself.

So far, so good.

Friday, December 17th, 2:40 p.m.
Quantico, Virginia

In his office, Alex Michaels looked at the clock blinking in the corner of his default holoproj, a bucolic scene of a modern-day cattle drive blocking automobile traffic on a back road in Colorado. Michaels had worked one summer on a dude ranch while he was in college. He hated cows as a result, and the picture was another one of Jay Gridley's little jokes. The young man loved to do such things. Thought he was funny.

Michaels grinned. Jay *was* pretty funny, though Michaels preferred that somebody else be the butt of the young man's jokes.

But the clock said that it was ten minutes past the time Lieutenant Joanna Winthrop was supposed to be here for her meeting, and that didn't go with what he'd read about her in her history jacket. He touched the intercom's manual control. His secretary was a temp, filling in for Nadine, who was on vacation. Maybe she had made a mistake.

"Liza, isn't Lieutenant Winthrop on for two-thirty?"

"Yes, sir, Commander," the young woman said. She sounded rattled. "She's uh, here, sir, but, uh, she's *occupied.*"

Occupied? Michaels went out to see what was going on.

On the floor next to his secretary's desk, with a rat's nest of red, white, and blue wires in her lap, sat Joanna Winthrop. She had a pocket tool of some kind, probably a Leatherman, and was using it to twist two of the colored wires together.

He had not forgotten how attractive she was, but it still came as something of a shock to him to see her.

Winthrop was one of the most beautiful women Michaels had ever seen. She was tall, lean, had long, natural honey-blond hair pinned up, and green eyes that put expensive emeralds to shame. She wore a blue jumpsuit and black boots that would have made most women seem dumpy. On her, the drab clothes looked positively sexy.

She glanced at Michaels. "Hello, Commander," she said. She shoved the tangle of wires under the desk, stood, closed her folding pliers, and said, "Try it now."

Liza tapped at her command module's keyboard. "Hey! It works. Thank you!"

"No problem," Winthrop said. She flashed a radiant smile, perfect save for one slightly crooked tooth that gave it just enough character so it didn't look fake. She turned the grin in his direction, and Michaels could feel the warmth of it from fifteen feet away. A stunning woman, beautiful *and* smart, a lethal combination. She was single, in her mid-twenties, and much too young for him at his ancient age of forty; still, she was pleasant to look at, no question.

"Sorry I'm late, sir," Winthrop said. "Liza's keyboard input had a short, and you know how Computer Services works; they'd be two hours getting a tech up here unless it was an emergency. And in an emergency—"

"—it would take *three* hours," Michaels finished. He smiled at her. It was a standing joke in Net Force. "Well, come on in."

He gestured at the door, and waited for her to precede him into the office. He was merely being polite, he told himself. It wasn't just to get a look at her backside. Although, he had to admit, that was worth seeing. It reminded him of an old Flip Wilson joke, about the preacher's wife being tempted by a new dress she was trying on. The Devil said, "Buy it, honey, buy it!" And the preacher's wife said, "Get thee behind me,

Satan!'' And the Devil did, then he said, ''Mm. Looks good on you from *here* too . . .''

Michaels shook off the semi-erotic thoughts. Winthrop was a subordinate, more than a dozen years younger than he, and he didn't need any entanglements just at the moment. But it had been a long time since his divorce had become final, and things had not been too good at home for a lot of months before he'd moved out. He hadn't been in bed with a woman since.

There was only so much space in a man's life that work and hobbies would fill. You could only read yourself to sleep so many nights of the week.

He glanced up and saw Toni standing in the doorway of her office, leaning against the jamb, watching him. Michaels felt guilty, even though he hadn't done anything. He gave her a half smile, then went into his office. If he was going to leap off a cliff into an office romance, Toni would be his first choice, but that was a bad road to even contemplate. Toni was a coworker and a friend, and he certainly didn't want to damage either of those relationships for the sake of romance. Friends were harder to come by than lovers.

Well. At least that was what he'd heard. It had been so long since he'd had a lover, he had forgotten how to play that game. And it wasn't exactly like riding a bicycle.

He looked at Joanna Winthrop, who stood in front of the chair across from his desk, waiting for him. A drop-dead-gorgeous woman. Despite himself, he could easily imagine what her hair would look like unbound and spread over a pillow, what her face would look like staring up at his in passion. . . .

He gave himself a twitch of a grin. Fortunately, his shower came equipped with plenty of cold water. And he was probably going to be using his share of it tonight.

''Thanks for fixing the keyboard,'' he said.

''My pleasure.''

He moved behind his desk, sat, and gestured for Winthrop

to do the same. She did so. Back to business now.

"We have a little problem, Lieutenant. Colonel Howard thought you might be willing to help us out."

"Yes, sir, whatever the colonel wants. He thinks well of you, sir."

Michaels looked at her. Really? A few months back, hearing that would have been a surprise. Although after the kidnapping of the mad Russian, maybe Howard did feel a bit better about having a civilian commander. Michaels had risked his job ordering that, and Howard had done outstanding work on it. Maybe a little mutual respect had come out of the mission.

"And he thinks well of you, Lieutenant. Yours was the first name he suggested when I asked him for assistance."

"Sir, if it's all the same to you, please call me Jo, or Winthrop. This rank business isn't necessary unless we're in the field."

"Fine, Jo. Might as well call me Alex, while we're at it. We're pretty informal around here."

"Yes, sir. Uh, I mean, right, Alex. So, what's up?"

He smiled at her and waved his hand over his computer controls.

3

Colonel John Howard wore his old Gortex windbreaker, covering the S&W Model 66 .357 short-barreled revolver nestled in the Galco paddle holster just behind the point of his right hip. When he had occasion to carry while out of uniform, he preferred this kind of holster. It used a plastic paddle that slipped between the waistband and shirt, so he could put it on and remove it without having to take off his belt and thread it through the loops. It was convenient, and just about as concealable as a regular belt slide or pancake holster—

Ten yards away, a mugger with a knife leaped out of the darkness and ran at him. The assassin was no more than two seconds away.

Howard shifted his hips slightly to the left, opening a gap between his jacket and body, and swept his right hand back and under the Gortex. He grabbed the wooden grips of the revolver, automatically unsnapping the thumb-break safety snap on the holster when he closed his hand. He pulled the Smith, thrust it toward the mugger as if punching him one-

handed, and pulled the trigger. At this range, trying to line up
the sights was too slow. Instead, you could use the whole gun
silhouette to index the target.

Six feet in front of Howard the mugger stopped cold as the
91-grain Cor-Bon BeeSafe frangible bullet slammed into his
center of mass at just under 1600 feet per second.

The second shot was a quarter second behind the first.

The mugger froze, and glowing red lights pulsed on his
chest where the rounds impacted. Most people didn't realize
just how fast a running man with a knife could move. Another
half a second and the ersatz thug would have been all over
him.

Howard glanced at the computer next to the shooting box.
There was a small holoprojection of the mugger over the computer and stats under it. Elapsed time: 1.34 seconds from start
to shot. Organ hit: heart. Estimated one-shot-stop percentage:
94. The revolver didn't hold as many rounds as an H&K Tactical pistol, but it was a kind of talisman for Howard, and he
was more comfortable with it.

As he reholstered the gun, he noticed his right shoulder felt
sore. Well, no, not so much sore as . . . tired somehow. After
one draw? Seemed like he'd been tired a lot lately—

"Not bad for an old man," Sergeant Julio Fernandez said.
He was in the next shooting box at the indoor range, making
a lot of smoke and noise with his beat-up old Army-issue
Beretta 9mm.

"Reset," Howard said. He grinned.

The mugger vanished. Had it been a real attacker instead of
a holoprojic target, the frangible bullets would have each
dumped 550 foot-pounds of energy into the man and, because
the rounds were designed to fragment on impact, would have
shredded the attacker's heart into mush, *and* they wouldn't
have over-penetrated and gone on down the street to maybe
kill some little old lady out walking her dog. This was a very
important consideration in an urban scenario. Of course, frangible wasn't good for shooting through solid walls or car

doors, but the next two rounds in the cylinder were standard jacketed hollowpoints that would do that just fine. If the mugger had been in a car, Howard could have cycled past the first two rounds, or, in a hurry, just pulled the trigger twice to get to the jacketed stuff.

"Morning, gentlemen," he heard somebody say behind him. The wolf-ear headphones he wore amplified normal sounds, but cut out anything loud enough to damage his hearing. He turned.

It was his boss, Alexander Michaels.

"Commander. What brings you to the range on a Saturday morning?"

Michaels patted the taser clipped to his belt on his right hip. "Requalification. Thought I'd come down when it wasn't too busy."

Howard gave him a small smile and shook his head.

"Not a fan of the kick taser, Colonel?" Michaels asked.

"No, sir, not really. If a situation is dangerous enough to require a weapon, then it ought to be a real weapon."

"I am given to understand that the taser has a ninety-percent one-shot-stop rate, whether it penetrates clothes or not. It will defeat standard Kevlar vests, and there aren't any bodies to clean up afterward."

Howard could almost hear Fernandez grin. "Sergeant, you have a comment?"

"Well, unless the guy you shoot has anything real flammable about his person, sir. Then he might just burst into flame. At which point your non-lethal weapon turns your guy into the Human Torch. It has happened a few times."

"The sergeant is correct. However, the biggest drawback, sir, is that you only get one shot," Howard added.

"Everybody is required to carry a spare reload or two. I'm told an expert can do that in about two seconds—snap off, snap on, be ready to fire again."

"In which time somebody just average with a handgun would have shot your taser expert four or five times. Or his buddy would have—if there is more than one of him. Sir.''

Michaels grinned. ''Well, you know how it is with us desk jockeys, Sarge. The weapon is more a formality than anything. We don't get out into the field that much.''

''That's not what I hear, sir,'' Fernandez said.

Howard held his grin. Whatever Michaels said, he had faced an assassin who had snuck into HQ and he'd shot her dead using her own gun. That had earned him a bit of respect in a lot of opinions, including Howard's own.

''Besides, I have dedicated and trained men like you to do all my light fighting,'' Michaels said.

''Good thing,'' Fernandez said, but quietly enough so Michaels probably didn't catch it.

''I'll let you get back to your practice,'' Michaels said. ''Have a good day, gentlemen.'' He walked to the end of the long row of shooting boxes and began to set up for his session.

Sarge shook his head, then looked at Howard. ''Tasers, nightgowns, sticky foam, photon cannons, beanbag shooters, what are the feebs gonna come up with next? Sugar-and-spice spray? Flower-petal launchers? Seems like a lotta effort for not much gain.''

''We live in politically correct times, Sergeant. Subgunning a mob is bad PR, even if all of the people in the mob are terrorists with pockets full of hand grenades. It looks bad on the evening news.''

''Bleeding-heart liberals are gonna take all the fun out of being a soldier someday, sir.''

''I expect they will, Sergeant.''

''You know the definition of a conservative, sir?''

''I am afraid to ask.''

''A liberal who's been mugged.''

Howard grinned. ''Light up your target, Sergeant, and let's see if you can shoot as well as you talk.''

''Little side bet, Colonel?''

''I hate to take your money, but if you've got so much you can afford to lose it, you're on.''

The two men laughed.

• • •

At the end of the row of shooting boxes, Michaels heard the colonel and sergeant laughing. Probably at him and his taser. Well, not everybody was a soldier. His father had been a career Army man and that had been enough to sour Michaels on it. He knew he could kill somebody, if it was self-defense, or to protect somebody he loved. He had done so when the assassin had slipped into Net Force HQ and used Toni to ambush him in the gym's locker room. He'd shot the woman known as the Selkie after she had shot him and tried to stab Toni. It was necessary, but it was not an experience he wanted to repeat.

He set his computer for a practice run on the taser qualification scenario, checked to make sure the spare compressed gas cartridge holder was on the left side of his belt, and then pulled the taser and inspected the weapon to make certain the cartridge in it was still active. It was. He reclipped it to his belt, took a deep breath, and blew it out. "Activate," he commanded the target computer. "Two to thirty seconds, random start."

The new-model taser was wireless. He wasn't sure he quite understood exactly how it worked, but supposedly the twin needles were essentially small but highly efficient capacitors. Powered by a simple nine-volt battery, each needle was slightly thicker than a pencil lead. The pair carried high-voltage, low-amperage charges, somewhere around a hundred thousand volts, and when they both struck a target, a circuit was completed. The compressed gas propellant—nitrogen or carbon dioxide, depending on the model—would spit the needles up to fifty feet with enough force to penetrate clothing. At normal combat range, about seven or eight yards, the weapon delivered a knockdown jolt virtually every time. There was a tiny, built-in laser. When you squeezed the handle, the little red dot from the laser showed you where the needles would bracket when they hit. If you missed, the backup feature was a pair of electrodes in the handle that would allow the

taser to function as a stun gun—if the attacker got within
range. What the device looked like was a long and skinny
electric razor, or maybe one of the old *Star Trek: Deep Space
Nine* phasers.

Operation was easy enough. You pointed the taser at a target, squeezed the handle, lined the laser's dot up, and thumbed
the firing stud. If everything went right, half a second later
your attacker was jittering on the floor in electrically induced
convulsions, and any interest he might have had in harming
you was the last thing on his mind. Recovery after a couple
of minutes was virtually total, but you could do a lot in a
couple of minutes to an assassin sprawled helplessly on his
back.

Of course, such a device could be used by the bad guys too.
To counter that, all tasers were required to carry taggants in
their propellant, thousands of tiny bits of colored or clear plastic that would identify the registered buyer. There was no way
to sweep all these tags up after a taser was fired—

A mugger appeared and ran at Michaels. The mugger had
a crowbar in one hand. He raised the bar of steel as he ran—

Michaels pulled the taser from his belt, pointed it, and
squeezed the handle. The little red dot danced up and down
on the mugger's leg, but that didn't matter. Anywhere on the
body was good. He thumbed the firing stud—

A splash of yellow light flared on the mugger's leg, but he
kept coming.

Shit—!

Michaels grabbed the taser's cartridge with his left hand,
pressed the two buttons that ejected it, fumbled for the spare
cartridge, but it was too late. By the time he got the thing
reloaded, the mugger was on him. A loud buzzer blared. The
mugger froze.

Damn. He should have tried for the stun-gun backup.

The computer image to Michaels's left strobed the letters
FTS-G in bright red. Failure to Stop—Gotcha. The tiny image
of the mugger on the proj showed the reason why. The needles

were designed to spread apart, to make the circuit's arc big enough to work. At the distance he'd fired, the leg hadn't been a good target. The left needle hit the mugger's thigh square on, but the right missile had been ten inches to the right—a clean miss. He must have jerked his hand when he touched the firing stud. It didn't take much to screw up the shot.

Had this been a real mugger, Michaels would have been looking at a crushed skull—unless Toni's *silat* instruction would have let him dance the crowbar and poke the guy with the stun-gun electrodes. And he wasn't good enough at that to trust it yet.

He shook his head in disgust. He picked up a spare cartridge from the supply on the table and put it into his belt holder. He reclipped the taser to his belt. "Reset," he told the computer. "Two to thirty seconds random start."

He pointedly did not look at Howard and Fernandez. He knew they'd be smiling.

Saturday, December 18th, 8:15 a.m.
Washington, D.C.

Toni sat on the lounger her oldest brother, Junior, had given her for Christmas three years ago. He owned a furniture store in a nicer section of Queens—which wasn't saying much—and had gotten stuck with several chairs he couldn't sell and couldn't ship back, since the manufacturing company had gone out of business between the time he ordered the shipment and when it arrived. It was a comfortable chair, but kind of a putrid, mottled green color that apparently hadn't overwhelmed any of his customers. Somebody might as well get some use from it, he'd told her.

She smiled into the phone, a vox-only connection with her mother. Mama had never cottoned to the idea of picture phones. What if the phone rang before she put her face on? If her hair was messed up? If she was in the shower?

"Mama, if you're so worried about how much these calls are costing me, why don't you get an ISDN or a DL and let Aldo hook Papa's computer to it? For ten dollars a month, we could talk over the net as much as we want."

"I don't wanna be foolin' with no computer business," Mama said. "It's too complicated."

"It's not any more complicated than using the telephone. All you have to do it turn it on and tell it my number if you want to call. If I call you, you just have to touch a button when it beeps, and you get audio and video."

"It's too complicated."

Toni grinned again. Mama would never change. There was a bare-bones computer in the ground-floor brownstone apartments where Toni had grown up, a birthday gift from Toni and the boys a couple of years ago. Most American homes these days had some kind of house computer, but Mama didn't want anything to do with it. While she didn't cross herself when she walked past it, Toni had long believed that Mama looked at the thing as if it were the spawn of Satan, just waiting to ensnare her in its tendrils and drag her off to electronic Hades. Sophia Banks Fiorella was sixty-five, and had six children, five of them boys, all of them college-educated. Aldo, at thirty-one, the youngest child save for Toni, was a high-level programmer for the State of New York's judicial system, and if he couldn't convince Mama to use the computer after all the Sunday dinners trying, Toni was wasting her time.

"So, whenna you comin' home?"

"Thursday night late," Toni said. "They're giving us the 24th off, but I have to work on the 23rd."

"You need Papa to pick you up at the airport?"

"Papa is *not* supposed to be *drivin'*, Mama, he can't see that good. I thought Larry was gonna talk to him about that." Toni noticed that her Bronx accent had thickened considerably as she talked to Mama. It always did. "That" sounded an awful like like "dat," and the "-ing" endings to words lost the "g" completely.

"You know your father. He don't hear what he don't wanna hear."

"We're gonna get one of those steering-wheel lockbars for the car if he doesn't stop it."

"Tony Junior already tried that. It took Papa about two minutes to figure out how to take it off. He's not stupid."

"I didn't say he was stupid. But he *is* half blind and if he keeps driving, he is gonna kill somebody."

"Okay, so Larry or Jimmy will pick you up."

"I'm not flying, Mama, I'm taking the train and I'll catch a cab from Penn Station."

"Late at night my daughter should be inna cab? That's dangerous, a young girl by herself."

Toni laughed. She was pushing thirty and adept at self-defense, more so than any man she knew. She carried a taser with which she was qualified Expert, and had been a federal agent for years, but Mama didn't want her riding in a taxi from the train station.

"Don't worry about me. I've got my key, I'll go to the guest unit."

"Mike is coming from Baltimore with his wife and children, they'll be in the big bedroom and the kid's room."

"I'll stay in the little bedroom. Don't worry, Mama, I'll see you Christmas Eve morning, okay?"

"Okay. Look, you need to go, this call is probably costing you a fortune. I'll see you Friday. What time do you want to get up? You want to sleep late?"

Toni grinned again. It didn't matter what time she said, Mama would be at her door at six-thirty sharp, and breakfast would be ready. "About six-thirty," Toni said.

"Okay, I'll get up early. I love you, baby. You be careful."

"I will be, Mama. I love you too."

Toni put the phone down and shook her head. One of the joys of her big Catholic family was the annual holiday gathering. What with her brothers, their wives, and the nieces and nephews, there would be twenty-some people at Mama's, not even counting the uncles, aunts, and odd cousin or two who might show up for dinner. It wasn't so crowded since Papa had bought the units on either side of the old one and knocked out walls to make one large apartment, but even so, it would be bustling.

Toni was very much looking forward to it. Too bad she couldn't bring Alex with her. Mama would be so thrilled that Toni had a potential husband—and any man she looked at more than twice was, as far as Mama was concerned, a potential husband—that she wouldn't be able to sit down, she'd be so busy doing things for him.

Maybe someday.

4

Saturday, December 18th, 11:45 a.m.
Arizona Territory

Jay Gridley rode the net.

On a horse.

Until recently, he had favored a Dodge Viper in virtual reality, playing scenarios that involved superhighways and high speed. Hell of a car, the Viper, a rocket with wheels, and he liked putting the pedal to the metal and feeling the wind in his hair. But he'd gotten into a Western frame of mind a couple of weeks ago, and after doing a fair amount of research had built himself a cowboy scenario. You could use just about anything you wanted for virtual reality—VR—net travel, and it didn't have to be historically accurate; you could have cowboys and spacemen in the same scenario. But when you were a programmer at Jay's level, you had certain standards. At the very least, it had to be consistent, and above all, it had to *look* good.

In this scenario, Jay wore button-fly Levi's, real cowhide pointed-toe cowboy boots, and a plaid wool shirt, along with a red bandanna, a cream-colored Stetson hat measured in gallons, and a Colt .45 Peacemaker six-gun strapped around his waist in a period leather holster. No drugstore cowpoke clothes for him, no pearl-button shirts with fringe, or chaps or anything like that. He sat upon a hand-tooled saddle, and his horse was a pinto stallion named Buck. Well, formerly a stallion—the VR horse had been gelded, to keep him from tearing off after passing female horses. Jay had thought about a white horse or even a palomino, but figured those were maybe a bit over the top. Most of the off-the-shelf software would never have gotten into this kind of detail, but they weren't held to his standards.

Buck picked his way along a narrow switchbacked trail that wound through the foothills of a VR mountain range in the Old West. Jay kept a lookout for rattlesnakes—sidewinders, they called them out here—Indians, or desperados who might want to stick him up. There was a net nexus coming up, represented by a little town called Black Rock ahead a couple of miles, but the sun was almost straight up and it was oven-hot and bone-dry here, and he needed to stop for a drink. The rocky trail was mostly bare, with only a few lizards and some scraggly bushes that might grow to be tumbleweeds some-day—if they were lucky, and if they didn't spontaneously burst into flame first. . . .

He grinned. Damn, but he was good. A very tight little scenario, if he did say so himself.

He reined up next to a dried and dusty stream bed, dismounted, and took a swig from his water bottle, a canvas bag with a wooden plug. The canvas bag held about a gallon, and was woven loosely enough so it allowed a little liquid to seep through it, the idea being that the evaporation would cool the water, but it was still pretty warm. He took his hat off, poured a pint or so into it, and offered it to Buck. The horse noisily lapped the water from the hat.

"Not far now, boy, a few more minutes."

From around the bend came the sound of an approaching wagon. Jay dumped the water from his hat and put the Stetson back on. He loosened the Colt in its holster. You never knew what kind of scum was around. Best to be ready to shoot first and ask questions later.

It wasn't a wagon, but a one-horse buggy, drawn by a big gray mare. The horse's shoes clop-clopped on the hardpan, and the iron-bound wooden wheels clattered over small rocks. The driver was a woman, in a ground-length cotton dress that had once been dyed indigo, but sun-and-wash-faded now to a pale blue. Since she was seated, the dress was hiked up enough to reveal the tops of her high-button shoes. She also wore a blue bonnet, not quite so faded as the dress, tied under her chin. On the seat next to her was a thin stack of books.

Why, it must be the schoolmarm.

Jay relaxed, and reached up and tipped his hat as the woman approached.

"Howdy, ma'am," he said, in his best cowboy-speak.

As the buggy drew closer, he could see she was a good-lookin' woman—no, not just good-lookin', she was downright *gorgeous,* a few stray blond hairs escaping the bonnet, beautiful green eyes—

Aw, hell. It warn't no schoolmarm, it was—

Lieutenant Joanna Bimbo Winthrop.

Damn!

She pulled the buggy to a stop ten feet short of Jay and smiled. "Well, well. Jay Gridley. Fancy meeting you here." She climbed down from the buggy and stood facing him from a few feet away. Her face went blank for a second.

Jay knew what she was doing. She was in her own net program and she was re-phasing to allow his to set the joint scenario.

Her face came back to life and she looked around, seeing now what Jay was seeing.

"Well, yee-haw, little doggies," she said. She smiled.

"What are you doing here, Winthrop?"

"Perhaps this silver bullet will tell you." She held out her hand, and upon it was a shiny handgun cartridge. "Go ahead, bullet, tell him."

The cartridge was silent.

"Very funny." Jay wasn't in any mood to be insulted by the likes of Bimbo Winthrop. "And what *freeware* are *you* running?"

"Not freeware, horsie-boy. Something with a little subtlety." She waved at the high desert around them. "And a little complexity."

Oh, *really*?

In the Real World, Jay was sitting in his office chair at HQ, wearing full VR gear, connected to his workstation and the net. In RW, he finger-jived out of his Old West program to let Winthrop's vehicle become the default. In half a second, the VR blinked and reformed into Winthrop's—

He found himself on the boarding platform at a train station. Winthrop stood across from him, and a passenger train was stopped behind her. Her hair was in a bun, tucked under a wide-brimmed hat, and she wore a long, dark cloth coat over an ankle-length gray wool dress. From her clothes and the style of the train, he guessed it was late nineteenth or maybe early twentieth century. A sign on the station to his left said "Klamath Falls." It was winter, the air crisp and cold, and fresh snow was six inches deep on the ground, with higher drifts piled up outside the roofed platform. Passengers boarded the train, the women in long dresses and coats and hats, the men mostly in suits, hats, and overcoats. There were a few working-class souls mixed in among the more affluent passengers, wearing caps and jackets and workboots. A big pale guy who looked like a bodybuilder in a tan duster stopped to help an old lady lift her bag onto the train. A little girl ran by, trailed by a dog. It looked like a setter or a retriever of some kind. The smell of coal smoke hung heavy in the air, mixed with the dregs of cooling steam . . . and just a hint of unwashed body odor.

People hadn't bathed every day back when. That was a nice touch.

And looking around, he saw she had done a pretty clean job on the scenario. No gray areas, no sketchy backgrounds, plenty of detail, even to the wood grain in the fir posts supporting the platform roof.

He looked at himself and saw he wore a three-piece gray wool suit and black-leather dress shoes. A gold pocket-watch chain draped across the vest. He saw a slip of colored paper in one of the vest's pockets and removed it. A train ticket. He could read every word on it, down to the fine print. A *very* nice touch, that.

Well, okay, he had to admit it, this was a first-class piece of work.

He didn't have to admit that to *her,* however.

"All abooard!" the conductor yelled.

"Well?" she said.

"It's a little busy," he said. "I prefer mine." He overrode her program, and half a second later was back standing in the desert next to Buck, looking at her and the buggy.

"What do you want?" he asked her.

"I was looking for you. We're going to be working together, whether either one of us wants to or not. I know you don't like me, and you're not on my top-one-hundred list either. But I'm a professional, I can get around that."

"Meaning I can't?"

"No, Gridley, meaning exactly what I said. This isn't about who is the better programmer, it is about getting the assignment done. Commander Michaels wants me on the project, I'm on it. We don't have to hold hands and walk through the spring meadows, but we also don't have to get in each other's way, can we agree to that?"

Jay looked at his horse. He could see why cowboys spent so much time on the trail. Women, especially pretty women, tended to complicate things. He knew he was a better programmer. He hadn't gotten any doors opened because of *his*

looks, and he was damned sure Winthrop had. But he sighed
and nodded. "All right. We can stay out of each other's way."

"If I come up with something before you do, I'll pass it
along."

"Fat chance of that," Jay said. It was under his breath,
however.

"Excuse me?"

"Nothing. I'll do the same for you."

She said something he didn't catch.

"Pardon?"

"Nothing," she said. "I'll leave you to your scenario."

She climbed back into her buggy and snapped the reins over
the big mare's back. "Giddyap," she said. She waved as she
drove away from town.

Jay watched her go. The horse whinnied.

"Yeah, pal, my sentiments exactly," Jay said. "Come on,
we got bidness in town, Buck old boy."

Jay put his left foot into the stirrup and mounted up.

They moseyed toward town.

Saturday, December 18th, 11:45 a.m.
Chevy Chase, Maryland

Hughes had his virgil—his Virtual Global Interface Link—in
the limo, but he didn't want to use it to call Platt. Supposedly,
the telephone signal was binary-encoded and nobody could
understand him if he used the phone in the virgil, but he didn't
trust it. It was a great toy, about the size of an electric shaver,
and in addition to the phone it had in it a GPS, clock, radio,
TV, modem, credit chip, camera, scanner, and even a fax. Of
course, if he hadn't been White's chief of staff, he wouldn't
have access to such a device. He couldn't have afforded it,
and likely couldn't have gotten on the list to get one even if
he had saved up the money.

There was a pay phone just ahead, a landline, and as random as any. He directed his driver to pull over.

It was cold out, a damp wind blowing, and the sky had that dark, heavy, nacreous gleam of snow clouds about to let go. Hughes stepped into the graffiti-covered clear-plastic paneled booth and pulled the door shut. He set the phone for vox-only, no vid, slipped the one-time throwaway scrambler over the mouthpiece, tapped in the number, let it ring once, then hung up. Platt had the gear to trace the number on his end, and also a matching scrambler. Nobody was going to decode their conversation.

Thirty seconds later, the phone rang. Unless it was a very large coincidence, that would be Platt.

"Yes," Hughes said.

"Hey," Platt said. He managed to shoehorn a whole lot of southern Georgia into that one drawn-out word.

"Okay, what's the situation?"

"Well, we got us a little problem there. Seems the Lord High Ooga-Booga wants to see you face-to-face 'fore he seals the deal."

"Not possible. I sent you to be my representative."

"What I told El Presidente Sambo, but he ain't listenin', it's some kind of native thing. You know how these darkies are, it's always somethin'."

Hughes ground his teeth together. Platt was a cracker, a racist, and probably a member in good standing of the Georgia Ku Klux Klan and the Sons of the Confederate Veterans. Sending him to Guinea-Bissau, a little dirt-poor tropical country on the North Atlantic coast of west Africa shoehorned in between Guinea and Senegal, was an invitation to disaster. Platt was so white he gleamed, and ninety-nine percent of the population in Guinea-Bissau was black; worse, they spoke Portuguese or Criola, or French, plus a slew of African languages with names like Pajadinka, Gola, Bigola, and the like. As far as he knew, Platt didn't have any foreign languages. He had trouble enough making himself clear in English past that Georgia cane syrup of his, but somehow he always managed. Being six and a half feet tall with a build like Hercules probably helped—people tended to be polite to Platt even if they didn't like him. And while he was crude, he wasn't stupid. He liked to play the good old boy and let people think that was all there was to him, but he knew his way around computers, from laptops to extended mainframes, he could shoot any weapon capable of firing, and fix a computer or a gun if either of them broke.

"Anyway, what El Presidente said was, you don't come and set down for a little chat, it's nooo deal."

Damn! Hughes fumbled for his electronic calendar, punched up the month of January, and looked at it. It would be tricky. He'd have to come up with some kind of hurry-up junket not too far away, then sneak into the country. He had a couple of passports and visas he could use. It was a bitch, and it wasn't going to be cheap, but it was doable. He said, "All right. Tell President Domingos I will be there on . . . January 13th. That's a Thursday."

"Thursday, the 13th. I got it."

"And you come to Washington. I have other business for you."

"Washington." That came out as "Warsh-ing-ton." "Shoot, there's almost as many jigs there as there are here. You know what else? There ain't but four thousand telephones in this whole country. They still use drums, I reckon. You know, the natives are restless? And uppity too. I get one more buck staring at me, I'mon put the hurt on him."

"Don't kill anybody."

Platt laughed. "Me? Shoot, I ain' gone kill nobody. I'mon just knock a few ub'm off the sidewalks." He laughed again, a gravely, raucous noise. "Only thing is, they ain't *got* no sidewalks most places here. I guess I can wait to do that in Washington."

"Just come back. What about the leaks?"

"I got the next one on a timer. Set to go off bright and early Monday morning, matter of fact."

"Good. Good-bye."

Hughes uncapped the phone's mouthpiece and dropped the scrambler into his pocket. Jesus. Platt was a lunatic, probably psychotic and sociopathic, and a sharp and dangerous tool. Necessary, but just as apt to cut the hand that held it as anything. Hughes would have to be careful, and pretty soon he would have to figure out a way to make Platt . . . go away. For good.

Hughes opened the phone booth's door. A blast of cold wind hit him, raising chills on his neck. He could smell the snow coming. Better get back to the city before it turned the roads into parking lots.

He nodded at the driver as he got back into the limo. "Let's go home."

5

The invisible green-eyed demon had its claws sunk deep in Tyrone Howard's back, and it hurt like he wouldn't have believed only a couple of months ago. He felt sick to his stomach, he wanted to throw up, scream, or punch somebody—maybe do all three at once—and none of these were viable options. The students at Eisenhower Middle School were used to seeing some weird things in the dingy green halls, but a thirteen-year-old boy running amok in a jealous rage was not one of them.

The reason for Tyrone's pain stood thirty feet away, smiling up at the quarterback of the football team, one large and muscular Jefferson Benson. Belladonna Wright was a year older than Tyrone and, without a doubt, the most gorgeous young woman in D.C. On the East Coast. Maybe in the whole world. And since he had done her a favor by helping her pass her computer class, they had spent a little time together. She had more or less ditched her old boyfriend, Herbie "Bonebreaker" LeMott, who was in high school and the captain of the wrestling team. Since then, she and Tyrone had gone to the mall, had done VR, and had sat in her bedroom and kissed until he thought he was going to explode. He was absolutely, totally, triple-back-somersault-in-a-full-layout in love with Bella. And there she stood, in her microskirt and halter top and squeegee slope-plats, talking to another man. Smiling at him. At a man who could tie Tyrone into a square knot and shotput him fifty feet without breaking a sweat. All Tyrone had going for him was his brain, and while the mind might be mightier than muscle in the long run, in a face-to-face matchup, the guy with the muscle would pound you into a breaded cutlet if all you could wave at him was your *brain*.

"Uh-oh. Looks like trrrrouble in paradise," came the voice from behind him.

Tyrone wasn't looking directly at Bella. He was using his peripheral vision as he stood fiddling with the door to his locker. He didn't have to look at the speaker—it was James Joseph Hatfield, a hillbilly from West Virginia who had such bad eyes he couldn't even wear contacts, and thus went around peering through thick plastic lenses that made him look like a giant white hoot owl.

"Shut up, Jimmy-Joe."

"Hey, nopraw, rider, she's just *talkin'* to him, not fishin' for his trouser eel—"

Tyrone turned to glare atomic bombs at his best friend.

"All right, all right, be cool, fool," Jimmy-Joe said. "But think about it, bro. If she wanted a big dumb jock, she'd still be with Bonebreaker, right? I mean, he makes Benson look like a shrimp."

And Benson made Tyrone look like a *microbe*. "Yeah. Maybe."

"Go slowmo, Joe, you worry too much." Jimmy-Joe slapped Tyrone on the back.

As Tyrone watched peripherally, pretending not to, the large and muscular Jefferson Benson turned and headed down the hall, moving in that oiled-ball-bearing rolling walk of his. People moved aside to let him pass.

Bella looked up, saw Tyrone and Jimmy-Joe. She smiled and waved. "Hey, Ty!"

Tyrone's sick feeling lifted when he saw her smile at him. He felt like Atlas must have felt when Hercules took the world from him. All of sudden, life was wonderful. He could sing, he could dance, he could float like a cloud.

Bella came toward him. People stopped to watch her. Queen of the Hall, she swayed like a palm tree in a tropical breeze as she walked. His heart pounded like native drums in Tyrone's head. Man—!

She stopped in front of him. "I'm going to the mall after school, if it doesn't snow again," she said. "You going?"

"Oh, yeah," Tyrone said. "I planned to."

"Exemplary, Ty. See you at the Shop."

Bella flashed her perfect smile again, patted him on the shoulder once, then left. Tyrone watched her go, a man in a trance, unable to look away. His shoulder was hot where she'd touched him.

"Calls you Ty. Puts her *hand* on you. Slip, you are about as DFF as it gets," Jimmy-Joe said. "Data flowin' *fine*."

Tyrone grinned. Yes, yes, that was true. Life didn't get much better, did it? How could it? The most beautiful woman in the world had just arranged to meet him instead of the football thud. It was absolutely amazing, was what it was. Amazing. Wonderful—

"So, how's the upgrade goin'?"

Tyrone watched Bella round the corner and vanish from view. He savored the memory of her from behind.

"Hel-lo? Mission Control to Deep Space Vessel Tyrone, do you copy?" He made the sound of a staticky radio. "Come in, DSV Ty . . ."

Tyrone shook off the trance. Jimmy-Joe was asking about the revision to the netgame he'd built and posted, DinoWarz. "Oh, that. I haven't had much time to work on it."

"Haven't had *time*? You are feekin' me, right?"

"No feek," Tyrone said. He had been spending every spare minute he could scrounge with Bella. And when he wasn't with her, he was thinking about her. Dreaming about her.

Lusting after her . . .

"Rider, you are stalled *out*!"

"It's just a game," Tyrone said.

Jimmy-Joe stared at him as if Tyrone had just morphed into a giant roach and started doing a demented jitterbug.

"Just a game? Just a *game*? You got a testosterone short in your cerebrum, chum."

The bell for class rang, and Jimmy-Joe walked off, shaking his head. "I will see you later, slip."

Tyrone stared at his friend. He didn't understand. Games were fine, but how could a game compare to holding hands with Belladonna Wright? To kissing those warm and magical lips. To putting his hands on those warm and—

Don't follow *that* thread, Tyrone. Not here and now.

A video game? Even a VR full-flex, compare with Bella? It couldn't. No way.

He hurried toward his own first-period class. And he was going to the mall after school, dupe that to the eighth power.

Monday, December 20th, 9:05 a.m.
Quantico, Virginia

Julio Fernandez looked at the holoprojection floating in the air behind the instructor. The image was a series of mathematical equations interspersed with pictures of what appeared to be an old-fashioned paper theater ticket, a crumbly cookie, and a heavy metal safe with a big mechanical tumbler lock dial. Remedial computer imagery for dumbots.

The instructor said, "All right, who can tell me what the phrase 'security through obscurity' means?"

Fernandez stared down at the screen built into the top of his desk. *Pick somebody else,* he thought. There were fifteen people in the computer programming class, so the odds weren't that bad that the dipwit teacher would call on one of his classmates, except that the dipwit seemed, for some reason, to have it in for Fernandez. The teacher's name was Horowitz. He was maybe twenty-four, short, dumpy, wore frazzled suits, had acne, and his face always looked as if he had a painful rash on his private parts. Horowitz also looked as if he would rather be scratching that rash naked in public than suffering through this class, and Fernandez knew how that felt. If there was any other way, he wouldn't be here either. At least the man was a civilian and not—thank God—an officer.

That the classroom smelled like old sweat long gone sour didn't help.

Of course, he could have downloaded all the lectures and texts for this class and studied them at home on his own. Nobody was holding a gun to his head and making him attend. Most of the other students were new feebs—FBI Academy students—and this class was mandatory for them, though more a matter of form than anything. They were all college grads, most of 'em law school grads too, and this dinky little access course was a snoozer they could pass in their sleep.

Not so for Sergeant Julio Fernandez, whose computer literacy was right up there with his knowledge of quantum mechanics, or the mating habits of great blue whales, which was to say, very lame on his best day. He'd tried absorbing the stuff on his own, and it slid out of his mind as if his brain were made of solid Teflon. He'd hoped that listening to the teacher and having other students ask questions and offer answers would somehow help, but so far, after three sessions, it hadn't done much to advance his knowledge of the subject, which he hated, but which he *needed* to know. When it came to using his hands or his weapons, Fernandez didn't give away anything to anybody. He could set up camp in a jungle or a desert and live off the land, but when it came to anything past button-punching a computer, he was dense, and that wasn't good for a Net Force man—

"Let me see . . . Sergeant Fernandez? Security through obscurity?"

Great. Just freakin' great. "Sir, I believe it means that a certain kind of computer system's security is sort of like a . . . fortress. You know it is there, you can find it easy enough, but the doors into the place are armored or booby-trapped or rigged with so many locks you can't open 'em, even though you can walk right up to them."

"What a charming simile. You know what a simile is, Sergeant?"

Some of the feebs chuckled.

Fernandez felt himself flush under his swarthy skin. He was old enough to be this kid's father and the little bastard was jerking him around. "I know what a simile is."

"Well, as it happens, by what is no doubt a major miracle, you are essentially correct. Today's lecture will cover principles of how to accomplish various forms of security, from firewalls to encrypted passwords, from private-access tickets and their expiration dates and times, to security cookies, both fresh and . . . stale."

A few of the feebs laughed at the stale-cookie thing.

The teacher waved his hand and the holoproj vanished, and was replaced by another. This one showed a small boy sitting in front of a workstation. The kid looked to be about five years old. Probably who this class was aimed at, little kids.

Fernandez gritted his teeth. Even when he gave the *right* answer, this dipwit twisted it so he looked stupid. Horowitz must get his jollies like that, making students look bad. He certainly wasn't going to get much action otherwise, as lemon-faced and pimply as he was.

Maybe this was a mistake. Maybe Fernandez should be spending his time on the range instead of having his tail twisted by young Master Horowitz. Maybe he should just bail out and paraglide away, and spend his time doing something

he knew how to do: ground-pounding, dirt-soldiering, pick
'em up and set 'em down and count cadence while you are at
it.

For just a second, he enjoyed that thought.

No. He was gonna learn this crap if it killed him. So when
the young shavetail lieutenants started rattling off their compu-
babble on a mission, he could nod and at least vaguely know
what the hell they were talking about.

One lieutenant in particular came to mind. . . .

"So, who can tell us what happens when an electronic ticket
expires on an encrypted access site? Sergeant Fernandez?
Since you are on a metaphorical roll, would you like to give
us another of your charming little homespun similes?"

Fernandez regarded the man. He was mightily tempted just
to get up and walk out. His second choice was to get up and
teach Horowitz how to breathe again after he punched him
one good shot solidly in that soft gut. Now there was a *real*
pleasant thought—

"Come, come, Sergeant, speed is of the essence! In computer programming, in life, in *everything*. He who hesitates is
lost *and* last!"

"I believe you are mistaken in that, sir."

Horowitz regarded him as a frog might view an uppity fly.
"Oh, really? Please elucidate. Show us the error of our ways."

Fernandez said, "Sir. When I was going through my basic
training, we had an old master sergeant who was teaching us
the use of small arms. He told a story about when he'd been
a recruit, about a rivalry between two drill sergeants from different companies.

"Seems there was a military shooting match both guys had
entered, a course of fire using the then-issue M16's."

Fernandez looked at Horowitz. "That's a fully automatic
rifle, the M16. You know what a rifle is, sir?"

Horowitz frowned. Good thing Fernandez wasn't depending
on getting some kind of grade in this class—he'd never pass.

But the feebs had had some firearm training at this point, so he had their attention.

"So the first sergeant, name was Butler, he came up to the line. The timer beeped and he locked and loaded. Or at least he tried to. Nothing happened, the magazine wouldn't feed the round. So he dropped the magazine and inserted a fresh one, only cost him a few seconds. Same thing happened. Since the course of fire was limited to two magazines, he was SOL. He raised his hand, and got a DNF—that's a Did Not Finish.

"So the second sergeant was up, his name was Mahoney. He locked and loaded, fired the course. Did a respectable time, nothing to write home about, but enough to keep him in the top five, if he was lucky. Clean shooting, moderately fast and accurate.

"Meanwhile, Butler figured out what his problem was. He had inadvertently overloaded his magazines by one round each. This compressed the springs too much and they wouldn't feed the rounds. So Butler asks for a reshoot due to equipment failure. It was a slow day, and the RO—that's range officer—let him go again after everybody else was finished.

"And this time, Butler came out hot. He smoked everybody. Shot the fastest time, didn't miss anything, knocked 'em down left, right, and center like he was a machine. Butler was thirty seconds faster than Mahoney through the course. Guys who had been laughing at him before suddenly looked at him with a new respect. No doubt about it, the man could shoot.

"So Butler grins at Mahoney, gives him a mock salute, and swaggers off.

"Mahoney is packing away his weapon and gear and one of the other shooters who knows about the rivalry comes over. 'Too bad,' the guy says, 'I know you really wanted to beat him.'

"And Mahoney smiles and says, 'He won the contest, but if we'd been on opposite sides on a battlefield from each other, Butler would be history and I'd still be here. You don't get a second chance in a firefight hot zone if you're up against a guy who is any good at all. And there ain't no second-place winner in a gunfight neither.' ''

Fernandez looked at the porky young instructor. "A slow shot that hits the target is better than a fast shot that misses. Sir."

The class laughed, and it was Horowitz's turn to flush. "See me after class, Fernandez."

"My pleasure."

When the other students were gone, Fernandez stood six feet away from where Horowitz sat at his desk. The instructor said, "Sergeant, your attitude needs some adjustment. I realize this is a non-credit class for you, so you aren't required to get a pass/fail, but if you were, I am certain you would be repeating this course next term."

Fernandez stepped up to the desk, put his hands on it, and leaned toward the younger man. He was well within Horowitz's discomfort zone, invading the man's space. Horowitz leaned back as far as the chair would allow, and fear stained his face.

"Listen up, sonny. You got the social skills and wit of a water buffalo. You're so busy trying to score points and show everybody how clever you are that whatever teaching abilities you have—if any—can't get out of where you have your head shoved. I know this is like talking to three-year-olds for you, but you're supposed to be a teacher. That's your job, and you're dogging it."

"You wait just a minute!"

"Shut up," Fernandez said. He kept his voice flat and quiet. Horowitz did just that.

"I'm an easygoing guy most of the time. That's why you aren't on your knees observing the remains of your most recent meal spattered all over your shoes and the floor. I'm done here, junior. I won't be back. Lucky for both of us."

So much for his resolve to learn this shit. Oh, well. There

were other ways. There had to be. He leaned back from the desk, smiled, and turned to walk away.

Behind him, Horowitz's voice was shrill, shading right up the scale and into soprano: "What is your superior's name? I am going to report you for threatening me!"

Fernandez turned, still smiling. "My CO's name is Colonel John Howard. Give him my regards when you call. And I didn't threaten you, sonny. If I had done that, you'd be needing a fresh pair of pants. Adios."

As he left the classroom, Fernandez shook his head. His inner voice said, *Dense move, Julio, m'boy. Scaring a little pissant teacher isn't going to help you learn anything.*

Yeah, yeah. But it sure felt good, didn't it?

He was almost sure he heard his inner voice chuckle.

6

Platt strolled along the sidewalk next to the Mall in a T-shirt
and jeans, without a jacket, pretending to ignore the hard chill
and dirty, slushy snow the plows had piled up along the curb.
It wasn't really all that cold, right around freezing, but he sure
as hell felt it. Least the wind wasn't blowin', and he had his
steel-toed Kevlar boots on, so his feet weren't cold. Thing was,
at six-four and 225, he didn't have any body fat to speak of—
he couldn't pinch any on his ridged six-pack belly—so no
insulation. He worked out five times a week in a weight room
when he was where he could get to one, had a decent gym of
his own at home if he didn't feel like goin' out, and used big
elastic bands or a portable apparatus when he was on the road.
The portable thing, which was basically just some screw-
together pipes made out of titanium and spun carbon fiber,
assembled into a frame that would let you do chins and dips.
Cost a damned fortune, but it was worth it. It didn't weigh
hardly anything, and when it was disassembled it would fit
right into a regular suitcase. Between the bands and body

weight, you could keep the tone on your upper body for a couple of weeks without the iron, if you needed to. Didn't do much for the lower body, but that was what one-legged squats and stairs were for.

He didn't like Washington, not the town, not the folks who lived and worked there, not the big old marble buildings, wasn't nothin' *about* it he liked. But if you walked around in the cold without a coat, people would stare at you just like they would anywhere else—except maybe Los Angeles.

Platt grinned. He remembered the first time he'd been in L.A., twelve or so years back when he'd been a green kid just off the farm outside Marietta. He was walking down Hollywood Boulevard, a hick tourist gaping at the gold stars in the sidewalk, when he passed an old lady standing in front of the Chinese Theater. She was stark naked, smiling and waving at everybody. That didn't seem right to him, that somebody's poor ole granny was bare-assed on the street like that, so Platt whipped out his phone and called the po-lice. Told them about this nekkid woman. And the bored cop on the phone said, "Yeah. Uh-huh. Which naked woman are you calling about?"

Which naked woman. Like there was more than one, which it turned out, when he asked the cop, there was.

Jesus. According to the po-lice, somebody got naked on the street four or five times a week in Hollywood. Damn. Them folks had smogged-up brains out in La-La-land.

He looked at his watch. Just after ten. He grinned again. About now, that spring-loaded time-release file would be hitting the web hard, and it was gonna be like a ton of fresh feces whapping into a big ole industrial-grade fan. If that bomb down in Louisiana didn't get their attention, this one would sure as hell wake 'em up. Gonna pop a few strands when it landed, for damn sure.

Ahead of him, coming in his direction, were two black men. African-Americans, was that still what they called themselves? Sheeit, these brothahs in their wool suits and camel-hair overcoats had probably never been within five thousand miles of

Af-ri-ka, probably born in Mississippi or Georgia, and come to the big city for white poontang and cheap dope. Way Platt figured it, you were born in this country, you were an *American,* period, and you didn't hear white people talkin' about how they were German Americans or French Americans or English Americans. That was all bullshit, just one more way the spooks got uppity. Call themselves anything they want, they were still darkies, they couldn't hide that.

The two in suits stared at him, but they weren't right. They were too small, too civilized. Probably lawyers or political staff guys who hadn't been in a fistfight since they were pickaninnies.

Platt grinned, and he could almost hear the jigs thinkin': *Look at that crazy fool white man, running around in a T-shirt in the cold!*

Yeah, but he a big *crazy fool white man. Why don't we just cross on over the street here?*

A block or so later, he spotted the one he wanted. He was a big buck, wearing jeans and motorcycle boots, a leather jacket, and Gargoyle shades, thought he was so cool. Almost as big as Platt. And alone. Platt didn't mind a couple, but he wasn't stupid. A gang was not a good idea unless you were armed, 'cause they sure as hell would be, even though guns were all kinds of illegal in this city. All Platt had on him was a little aluminum-handled Kershaw liner-lock, blade just about three inches, and while he could snap it open as fast as a switchblade and could slice and dice somebody into bloody mush with it, a knife wasn't the smartest choice against three or four gangbangers strapped with shooters. He didn't like to carry a gun in the city unless he had a particular need for one, and he didn't want to use the knife if it was one-on-one—unless the jig pulled one.

Or unless it turned out the boy was a karate or judo guy who knew his stuff. Most of that crap was worthless, it didn't work on the street, but now and then you'd run into one of them smart enough to keep it simple, with the skill and timing

to make it work. Had to give them that, some of them could
dance real good. That would get you your ass kicked pretty
good. If that happened, he could sneak the knife out and hide
it, wait for an opening, though a guy who knew enough of
that gook fighting shit to thump you barehanded usually knew
how to deal with a blade too. Platt had a few nasty memories
about bad guesses he'd made. But this guy in the leather jacket
didn't look like no Bruce Lee, and besides, Platt just wanted
to stomp somebody a little, not kill him.

"What you starin' at, *boy*?"

The big black man stopped. "Who you callin' *boy*,
cracker?"

"I don't see nobody else around, do you? Boy?"

Leather boy took his shades off and carefully slipped them
into his pocket. He smiled.

Platt matched the smile. Oh, this was going to be fun. . . .

Monday, December 20th, 10:20 a.m.
Quantico, Virginia

Alex Michaels sat at his desk, looking over the latest computer
dump into his electronic in-box. Came in every half hour, the
new business, faster if it was flagged, and there was always
some fresh crisis that Net Force had to take care of or the
country would go to hell in a handbasket.

He on-screened the latest batch and scrolled through them:

Somebody had stolen a couple million dollars worth of In-
tel's SuperPent wetlight chips from a plant in Aloha, Oregon.
There was a name for you, Aloha. Town's founder must have
spent a pleasant time in Hawaii. The chips were small enough
so that they could all fit neatly into a shirt pocket without
causing the pocket to sag, and good luck on finding those
before they made their way to Seoul to be restamped and installed.

Next item . . .

Stanley the Scammer had opened a new VR store, once again selling porno. There was no product, past the handful of public-domain teaser j-pegs and QuickTime VRs he used to sucker his customers in to buy. He took their electronic money, promised to send them a bunch of nasty stuff, then shut the VR shop down and shifted to a new location. They had busted Stanley a couple of times, always in New York City. Stanley would rent a cheap flophouse room with a plug and phone, hook his computer up, run his scam, and usually skip before the local cops got there. While he wasn't moving across state lines himself, his victims were from all over, so it was Net Force's problem. And it was compounded by the fact that most people who got ripped off buying pornography didn't particularly want the proper authorities to know that was what they were doing, so most of the customers ate the loss and kept quiet about it. Explaining to the wife that you lost a hundred dollars trying to get a copy of the ''Darla Does Detroit'' VR was something most men wanted to avoid. The wife might get curious about all that time hubby was spending in his workshop with the door closed.

Stanley's was a classic scam, and the reason most confidence men who were any good could continue to pull off their games was that they appealed to the illegal or immoral in people, made them partners in the sting. A guy worried that he was doing something wrong was hesitant to run to the police to complain when he got cheated.

Of course, there was always *some*body who cared more about their money than their reputation, and so some sucker always reported Stanley.

The main problem was that there were dozens, scores, *hundreds* of small-time thieves like Stanley, and anytime they ripped off somebody computronically across a state line, Net Force heard about it.

Michaels shook his head and scrolled the proj:

Here was a report of a money transfer gone bad at a small

bank in South Dakota. Some enterprising cyberstealer had siphoned a couple hundred thousand into his account during a
series of fast e-shifts. The Feds' safeguards had caught it, albeit a bit late, and the money was quickly recovered, but they
still had to catch the thief, who had run in a hurry, and figure
out how he had managed to slip the federal wards even as
long as he had. It had been an inside job—the thief worked
as an auditor for the bank. It almost always was an inside job,
given how good the Federal Reserve kept track of money these
days.

What else did they have here?

"Sir," Liza broke in, over the com. "I've got Don Segal
from the CIA on the hot line. He says it's an emergency!"

Michaels smiled at his secretary's excitement. Most emergencies didn't turn out to be all that exciting. "I'll take it,"
he said.

"Hello, Don." Segal was the AD for foreign intel-
gathering, a nice guy whose wife had just given birth to their
third child, a boy.

"Alex. We've got a big problem."

"I've got to appear before White's committee tomorrow
morning," Michaels said. "Bad as that?"

"I'm serious here, Alex. Somebody just posted to the net a
list of all our sub-rosa ops in the Euro-Asian theaters."

"Jesus!"

"Yeah. Every American spy in Europe, Russia, China, Japan, Korea—*all* of them have just been outed. State is crap-
ping big octagonal bricks. A lot of the ops are in supposedly
friendly countries, our allies. That's going to cost us some
favors and a lot of mea culpas, but we've also got agents in
places where they'll get shot first and questioned later. We've
put out a total recall, but some of them aren't going to get out
before they get picked up."

"Damn," Michaels said.

"Yeah. Damn. And think about it—if he got Europe and

Asia, who's to say he didn't get the Middle East, Africa, or South America?''

Michaels couldn't even speak. ''Damn'' wouldn't begin to cover it.

''We got to find this guy, Alex.''

''Yeah.''

7

Monday, December 20th, 10:25 a.m.
Quantico, Virginia

Joanna Winthrop washed her hands, reached for the paper-towel dispenser, and looked at her reflection in the large mirror over the sink in the women's restroom.

She shook her head at her doppelgänger. All of her life people had told her how beautiful she was, men—both young and old—and more than a few women, but she still didn't see it. She had learned how to pretend to ignore the stares, but people still stopped her on the street, strangers, to tell her how attractive she was. It was flattering. It was interesting.

It got in her way.

And it was a mystery to Winthrop. She had a sister, Diane, who truly *was* beautiful, and next to whom she had always felt dowdy. Her mother at fifty was a knockout, and her smile wrinkles and gray hair only served to accent her perfect bone structure and muscle tone. True, Joanna wasn't *ugly,* but of the Winthrop women, she was a distant third insofar as looks were concerned. In her opinion.

Of course, that wasn't what most other people seemed to

think. It had been a mixed blessing all of her life. Sure, it had been fun to be invited to all the parties when she'd been a kid, to always be at the top of everybody's lists, to be popular and sought-after. She had accepted it as the norm, never questioned it—until she looked up one day and realized that most people considered her nothing more than a ... *decoration*. All she had to do was stand there, smile, and be pretty, be an ornament, and that was enough for them. It wasn't enough for her, it wasn't anything she had done—nothing she had earned, she'd been born that way. Who could take credit for that?

Boys were tongue-tied in her presence, but they lined up for the chance to be fumble-mouthed, and eventually she realized that to most of them, she wasn't a real person, but a trophy—to be pursued, captured, then displayed. Looky here, guys, look what's hanging onto *my* arm. Don't you wish she was *yours*?

She was smart, she did well in school, stacked up well against objective academic standards, but nobody seemed to care about that. Being pretty was more important than being smart to everybody. Everybody except Joanna Winthrop.

Being pretty got old. Too many people couldn't see past it—or didn't *want* to see past it.

She tossed the damp paper towel into the trash can and glanced back at the mirror again. The first boy she'd slept with, at seventeen, had been the president of the science club, not any of the dozens of jocks who had chased her. He was intelligent, soft-spoken, and handsome, in a consumptive dying-poet kind of way. A sensitive, caring, bright young man who respected her for her mind. That was what she had thought.

He'd bragged about sleeping with her to his friends the next day. So much for his sensitivity, his caring, his respect for her mind. It had broken her heart.

Most of the girls she knew were jealous of her looks, especially the pretty ones, and they were resentful and catty. Her only real friend in school had been Maudie Van Buren, who had been plain, fifty pounds overweight, and addicted to black sweatsuits and running shoes. Maudie didn't care about looks—hers, Joanna's, anybody's—and she didn't understand why Joanna was so upset about being popular. She'd love to be on anybody's list for anything, she always said.

They'd gone off to different universities, Winthrop to MIT, Van Buren to UCLA. But they kept in touch. And each year, they got together for a week at Maudie's uncle's mountain cabin outside Boulder, Colorado. During the break between their junior and senior terms, they had managed one of their best ever conversations. Maudie had gone on a diet, started working out, and in six months had dropped her excess weight, tightened up, and emerged from her sweatsuit-fat-chrysalis stage as a slender—and beautiful—butterfly.

Over bottles of silty, home-brewed beer that Maudie's uncle had stocked the fridge with before he left, the two young women had talked.

"I think I finally get it," Maudie said. "About the pretty thing."

Winthrop sipped at the cloudy brew. "Uh-huh."

"I mean, when I was a big tub, anybody who bothered to spend time with me did it because of my personality, such that it was, and it wasn't as if I had to carry a stick to clear myself a path through my admirers when I went out. Now, I get calls from guys who thought I was invisible when I was a whole helluva lot bigger than I am now. It's like I suddenly got rich and everybody wants to be my friend." She took a big slug of the beer. "I mean, the depth of a guy who is only interested in you because of your looks is about that of a postage stamp, isn't it? Kind of hard to feel a lot of trust for somebody like that. 'Oh, baby, I love you for your mind!' sounds a little hollow when he's fumbling to unsnap your bra strap."

Joanna grinned around another swig of beer. "Tell me about it, sister."

Maudie looked at her, as if seeing her for the first time.

"You've had to deal with this your whole life. How did you finally get past it?"

"Who got past it? I bump into every day I go out. You learn to live with it."

"I may start eating again," Maudie said. "Who needs the stress? Maybe it's better to be fat and sure of my friends than skinny and suspicious."

"No, I think the best thing is to find somebody who can get past your face and boobs, who doesn't care too much about either. It's okay if they think you look good, that's fine, as long as they realize that isn't all there is to you."

"You got somebody like that?"

"I got you, babe."

"I mean somebody male."

"Well, no. Not yet. But I'm ever hopeful. He must be out there somewhere."

"Better be careful. I might find him first."

Both women laughed, and drank more of the malty home brew—

Winthrop's virgil cheeped, and she pulled it from where it was clipped onto her belt. Incoming call. The caller ID showed it was Commander Michaels. It must be important if he was calling her from just down the hall.

"Yes, sir?"

"We have a situation here, Joanna. If you could come to my office, I'd appreciate it."

"Be right there," she said.

She discommed, stuck the virgil back on her belt, gave herself a final glance in the mirror, and started for the door.

Monday, December 20th, 10:45 a.m.

Michaels looked at the three leaders of his computer team, as good a group of people as he'd ever worked with. They all looked back at him with anticipation as he finished laying out the scenario.

"All right, folks, there it is. CIA is justifiably upset and they'd like us to do something about it. Forty years of work is going down the tubes, and more might follow that any second. Let's have some risk assessment and scenario building here. Jay, what do we have so far?"

"I wish I could say it was good news, Boss, but so far, zip city. I don't think we're dealing with some kid hacker. What little I've found is a little rougher than the Russian we just dealt with. The guy snuck in and out, but he didn't track a lot of mud—I haven't found his footprints yet."

"Toni? How is he getting this stuff?"

"Three possibilites," she said. "One, he's cracking his way into secret files and stealing it; two, somebody who knows it is feeding him—or three, he knows it himself."

"So he could be almost anybody," Joanna said. "Somebody outside the walls, or inside them."

"How do we find him?" Michaels asked.

They all looked morose, and Michaels knew why. If the guy hadn't left an obvious trail, and if he didn't come back and blunder into a hole and break his leg or something, finding him would be iffy at best.

"All right, skip that. How do we stop him?"

Again, Michaels already knew the answer, but he wanted to get his team cranked up to full alert.

Jay said, "We've already put out the word to all federal agencies to harden systems, change passwords, reschedule downtimes from periodic to random, all like that."

"Which will help if he is by himself outside and looking in," Toni said, "but not if he's a cleared employee."

"Or being fed by somebody who is," Joanna added.

"We set some rattle cans up on real obvious targets," Jay said. "Squeals, squeakers, telltales, like that, but if he was dumb enough to blunder into those, he probably wouldn't have gotten in in the first place."

Michaels nodded. It wasn't their fault, but they had to catch this guy before more people started dying. He had to be hard here. "Folks, this guy, whoever he is, has caused at least one death we know of, and maybe more, and is likely to cause more. He's compromised our national security, pissed off our friends and enemies alike, and way down at the bottom of the list, he's also making Net Force look bad. There are people who will use this against us, and that's a problem, but that's the least of our worries. I want to see some contingency plans, some operational scenarios that will nail this bastard and get him off the net. Use whatever Cray time you need, spend what you need to spend, call in favors, whatever. This is critical, priority one. We have other business, sure, but this sits on top of the pile, understood?"

They nodded, murmuring assent at him.

"All right. Go."

After they had left, Michaels stood staring into infinity. It never rained but it poured. And it was his job to stop the rain.

Monday, December 20th, 12:05 p.m.

Toni stretched her legs, dropping into the left *sempok* position by sliding her right foot behind and past her left, sinking until her buttocks touched the floor, then bouncing up and across to the opposite side. A good *silat* player could defend or attack from a seated pose, could leap to her feet, kick, sweep, punch, or move quickly to one side. It didn't always look pretty but it worked, and that was the point. In *silat,* the object was to get the job done, not strike attractive poses for anybody watching.

She looked up and saw Alex walk into the gym carrying his bag. She raised her eyebrows in surprise. She hadn't expected him to come in for class today, not given all the crap going on with the spy thing.

"I didn't think I'd see you here," she said.

"Me neither," he said. "But there's not much else I can do about things at lunch. Everybody I'd want to talk to will be out and I hate to interrupt somebody trying to grab a quick bite. Besides, exercise tends to clear out the cobwebs. I'll get dressed, see you in a minute."

He headed into the locker room, and Toni went back to limbering up. Poor Alex. He took all this so personally, as if everything that happened was all his fault. She fielded as much of it as she could, tried to take care of him, but she couldn't shortstop all of the crap that landed on his desk.

Of course, given her choice, she would be able to make his life a lot more relaxed away from work. He needed somebody to take care of him, to rub his back, to fix him a drink before dinner, to—

—screw his brains out?

Toni smiled. Well, yes. That too. *That* wasn't likely to happen. He was still faithful to his ex-wife, at least as far as Toni knew. It was both an admirable and a frustrating trait in him. Although she had certainly seen how he looked at Joanna Winthrop, with her drop-dead good looks and bedroom eyes, and that had made Toni's belly knot in cold fear. How could you compete with a woman who had a face that would launch a thousand ships, a body to match, and who was as bright as a thousand-watt bulb to boot? Hardly fair, her being beautiful *and* smart.

Toni blew out a sigh. She could hardly blame him if he wanted to chase the beautiful lieutenant, could she? Alex didn't feel for Toni the way Toni felt for him. She *loved* him, and even so, even so, *she* had stumbled. Of course, that one-night stand with Rusty had been a big mistake. She'd repaired it as best she could immediately after it had happened, and he was dead now, so nobody knew about it and nobody ever would. Except her. She knew. She was in love with her boss, but she had slept with another man. How could she get around that? It felt awful.

Toni threw an elbow at an imaginary opponent. Too bad she couldn't control her love life as easily as she could a physical attack. Life would be much easier. Get into a fight with a would-be partner and throw him, then he'd be yours forever.

Too bad it wasn't that easy.

Monday, December 20th, 2:05 p.m.
Bladensburg, Maryland

Alone, Hughes drove to one of his safe houses for the meeting with Platt.

There was always business that couldn't be handled long-distance, just as in Guinea-Bissau, and one needed places to conduct such business away from curious eyes.

This hideaway was a basic third-floor single-bedroom apartment deep in the bowels of one of the new monster apartment complexes just over the District line, in Maryland. The complex was part of the extended bedroom community that had come to surround the nation's capital, accreting slowly over the years at first, then suddenly metastasizing like some architectural cancer, expanding in huge pressed-wood, ticky-tacky lumps and clots in all directions. Such places were the modern equivalent of tar-paper shacks—although probably not as sturdy.

Here was one of these cheap constructions, the River View Province. Three stories high, a thousand units strong, less than six months old, it was a perfect place to hold clandestine meetings. Nobody knew their neighbors, and it was so large nobody noticed who came and went. It was between Colmar Manor and Bladensburg, just off SR 450, and if you were on the third floor in the unit Platt had rented, and if you stood in the kitchen sink and leaned out the window, you could indeed see the north fork of the Anacostia River—for what *that* was worth.

Hughes drove a rental car, a small, plain gray Dodge something or the other that looked just like a million other cars on the road. He might as well have been wearing a cloak of invisibility for all he was likely to be noticed. He wasn't likely to run into anybody he knew out here, and he wasn't going to be recognized by anybody except a political junkie, none of whom would see him and Platt together in any event.

He wended his way through the vast parking lot, got lost when he took a wrong turn at one of the stupidly named and numbered lanes—Catbird 17—then finally arrived at the assigned parking slot for his apartment. He pulled the car into the space and shut the motor off. He looked around. Cold, clear, nobody around except some big guy walking a pair of brown and black German Shepherds on long wind-up leashes. The dogs snuffled the air, looking back and forth, keenly alert and searching for wolves to bark at. How could you live with two dogs that big in one of these little places? The poor guy must spend half his day walking those monsters; otherwise they'd eat all his furniture and wear holes in the carpet. Hughes liked dogs, and though he didn't have time for one now, maybe he'd get a whole pack when he got set up. He'd have the room, and the time to fool with them.

He took the elevator to the third level, headed down the hall to the unit, opened the door with a plastic keycard, and stepped quickly inside.

Platt was already there. He stood in the kitchenette, and he had what looked like a plastic bag full of ice cubes pressed against the right side of his head. The big man had scratches and a brush burn on one cheek, and the knuckles on both hands were torn and crusted with flecks of dried blood.

"What the hell happened to you?"

Platt grinned, and moved the bag of ice away from his head. "I had me a little ar-gu-ment with one of our underprivileged black brothers. He clipped me a good one on the

side of the head. You want to ice something like that down
pretty quick, otherwise you wind up with a cauliflower ear.
I'm too pretty to let myself get to lookin' like some punch-
drunk ole boxer.''

Hughes stared. ''You were supposed to keep a low profile.
You weren't supposed to draw attention to yourself.''

''Didn't get no notice to speak of. Boy lost a couple
teeth, maybe got a broke rib or two, he'll be just fine in a
week or three. Probably didn't even go to the hospital.
Shoot, any wog dentist could put them teeth back in. I left
before the po-lice showed up, if they ever did. It was just a
little ole dance, nothin' much. He moved pretty good, we
had us a fun time.''

A man who got into fights for fun. Platt was surely crazy.

''You got somethin' for me?'' Platt said.

Hughes removed a thick manila envelope from his briefcase
and tossed it at Platt, who caught it one-handed.

''There's twenty thousand in there, all in used hundreds.''

''That ought to keep pork chops on the table for a couple
weeks,'' Platt said.

''Just be sure and get that list from the NSA satellite clerk.''

''Yeah, I'm looking forward to those codes. I'mon be able
to get HBO for free.''

Hughes shook his head.

''You see 'em runnin' around like chickens with their heads
cut off over at Langley? Bet we get ourselves a new CIA
Director real damn quick.'' Platt laughed.

''The spy list did create quite a stir,'' Hughes allowed. ''But
we've got to keep the pressure up.''

''No problem. Japanese Stock Exchange codes go out in the
mornin', and the flight information for the Hijos del Sol car-
tel's cocaine shipments gets fed to their main rivals, Hermanos
Morte, tomorrow afternoon. It'll be knee-deep in blood and
snowing the Devil's Dandruff all over Colombia before it gets

good and dark. DEA is gonna be having kittens down there trying to figure out what's what."

"What about the banks?"

"I got some stuff coming out on Wednesday. Nothin' big, just a couple of thousand East Coast ATMs going wonky, givin' out beaucoup cash to anybody who uses a smartcard. Be real interesting to see how much of it gets turned back in."

"All right. Anything else I need to know?"

"Nope. I got me an appointment with a masseuse this afternoon. She's gonna relieve my tensions *allll* over."

Hughes shook his head again. Platt didn't know it, but he'd been under surveillance for six weeks, by a very discreet—and very expensive—investigative firm hired to keep tabs on him. Since Hughes trusted the big man about as far as he could throw him one-handed, he thought it wise to make sure Platt wasn't playing any games he shouldn't be playing. No doubt Hughes would hear from his hired operatives about the street fight later. As he would hear about the "masseuse" who came to minister to Platt's needs.

The woman would be black, of course. They always were.

Platt had availed himself of outcall massage services fourteen times in the last six weeks; had sampled the wares of half-a-dozen prostitutes in Guinea-Bissau during his stay there, along with a streetwalker working the airport during his long stopover in Cairo. All had been black women, more than twenty of them. He did not mistreat any of the trulls, as far as Hughes's investigators could determine, nor was he interested in anything other than heterosexual-style relations, no whips or chains or funny clothes.

Platt's racism was apparently not wide enough to encompass females of African heritage. A wonderful dichotomy, Platt. He would beat up a black man in the morning, then fornicate with a black woman in the afternoon. Hypocrisy was such a wonderful thing. The world wouldn't be able to run without it.

"All right," Hughes said, "I'll call when I have something else for you."

"I hear you," Platt said. "See you later, alligator."

8

Tuesday, December 21st, 8:25 a.m.
Washington, D.C.

The Senate meeting room was too warm by at least five degrees, which certainly didn't help Alex Michaels feel any less sweaty. He sat on the hot seat at the table reserved for victims of the inquisition—more euphemistically known as "witnesses called to give testimony"—facing the panel of senators, whose dais was raised high enough so there was no doubt who was in charge. That had to be, in a society that equated height with superiority. Next to Michaels sat Glenn Black, one of the FBI's top legal eagles. The two of them, backed by a gallery of other witnesses and interested watchers, faced the eight senators of Robert White's Governmental Finance Oversight Subcommittee.

Net Force's budget was the only item on today's docket, and after a pretense at politeness, the charge, led by White, was in full attack.

It was going to be a long day.

Michaels hated this part of his job, sitting in front of committees whose members might—and usually did—range from idiotic to brilliant, but who almost never knew what was *really* going on about much of anything. No matter how smart, the senators were at the mercy of their staff people who supplied them with information. While some of those on various staffs were pretty sharp, they were usually limited in what they could find out. A lot of agencies were reluctant to be totally forthcoming when called for information that might whittle away at their budget for the next fiscal year. What the senators got from their people was generally on a par with reporting on the six o'clock news. Like a rock skipping across the surface of a pond, only the information that was in easy view was even touched upon, and that only briefly. The depths below were hidden and, for all practical purposes, inaccessible.

Being ignorant of the truth never stopped men like Senator White, however. And while he wasn't the dimmest bulb on the string, his wattage was hardly what you would call blinding on his best day.

"Commander Michaels, what exactly are you trying to tell this committee? That Net Force doesn't *care* if some nut makes public information about how to build bombs that kill young newlywed girls?"

"No, sir, Senator White, I did not say that." Michaels was beginning to get pissed off, and his reply was a little more clipped and sharp than it ought to be. Black leaned over, put his hand over Michaels's microphone, and whispered, "Take it easy, Alex, it's only eight-thirty. We're going to be here all day. He's just playing to C-SPAN's cameras and the audience at home."

Michaels nodded, and under his breath said, "He's a fool."

"So when did *that* become a liability for holding public office?"

Michaels grinned. Glenn was right. It was going to be a long session; no point in losing his temper. Michaels usually kept a low profile at these things, and that was considered a good idea. Let them rant. When it came to the actual vote, the sound and fury before didn't count for much. He knew that. Still . . .

White went on: "It sounds to me as though you're saying that Net Force has more important fish to fry, Commander. And I have to tell you, sir, from where I sit, your oil doesn't seem hot enough by half."

He must have a new speech writer, Michaels thought. Somebody trying to downplay his rich man image and give him a little folksy touch. Good luck, writer boy.

Michaels knew that his boss, Walt Carver, the Director of the FBI, was in the audience behind him. So far, Carver had been able to keep White at bay, using his network and ties from when he'd been in the Senate, but White was getting more aggressive all the time. At the very least, Michaels had to put on a decent performance while on the hot seat, and not embarrass himself or the Bureau.

"I'm sure I don't know as much about oil as the honorable senator from the state of Ohio does."

Michaels hadn't really planned to say that, it just kind of slipped out. There were a few chuckles. It was a small dig at White's wealth, some of which had come from petroleum shipping, a business run by his grandfather.

White frowned. Michaels held his smile in check. Maybe it wasn't smart to pull the lion's tail, especially when the lion had you in the cage with it, but it sure felt good.

"There seem to be some serious problems in your organization," White said. He shuffled through some hardcopy. "We are talking about issues of national security, about which I will not speak in public, but these are grave matters that Net Force is failing to address properly." He looked at Michaels. "What is the point in funding an agency that doesn't do its job, Commander Michaels?"

"I'm sure, Senator, that you know much more about agencies that don't do their job than I."

More laughter, but Michaels caught a warning look from Glenn, and it was easy enough to interpret: *Easy, boy. Not smart to get into a fight with the man who controls the microphone. Especially not smart to make him look bad on TV.*

Michaels sighed. He had to watch his mouth. And even if he did, it was going to be a *very* long day.

Tuesday, December 21st, 10 a.m.
Dry Gulch, Arizona

A day's ride from Black Rock was the Western town of Dry Gulch. Jay Gridley hadn't been disposed to spend that much time in the scenario, so he'd logged in on the edge of town. Black Rock had been a bust, no sign of the bad guys, so Gridley had moseyed on.

It was close to high noon, and the sun hammered the bleached road so dry that clouds of reddish-gray dust hung in the windless air after every step his faithful steed Buck took. Just before he reached the outbuildings behind the blacksmith's shop and livery, Gridley took the U.S. marshal badge from his Levi's pocket and pinned it on his shirt. The silver gleamed brightly in the hard, actinic light. He didn't want anybody catching that mirror-shine on the trail, but in town he wanted the official muscle the badge offered.

Like Black Rock, Dry Gulch looked like a place from a Western cowboy vid, circa the mid-1870's. The main street—and the *only* street—was fairly wide, situated between rows of false-front shops. Here, among others, were the dust-spackled Tullis Good Eats Cantina, Dry Gulch General Store, Mabel's Dress Shop and Tailors, Honigstock & Honigstock Attorneys-at-Law, King Mortuary and Undertakers, the Dry Gulch Bank, the La Belle Saloon, and the sheriff's office and city jail.

Jay nodded and tipped his hat at an elderly woman in a long dress crossing the street. "Howdy, ma'am."

The old lady gave him a suspicious glare and hurried on, stepping onto the boardwalk next to the storefronts. The walk was a foot higher than the street, and that made sense. It probably flooded here during the infrequent rain, and you'd want to be above all that sudden mud.

A couple of boys chased barrel hoops down the dirty road, driving the flat metal rings with short sticks, laughing. A quail offered his song in the distance, not the usual "bob-*white*" whistle, but the more urgent "baby! baby! baby!" mating call.

Jay reined Buck up in front of the sheriff's office. A gray-whiskered old man sat on a wooden chair, whittling on a big stick with a jackknife. He looked like a miner, with a leather vest over a grubby red-and-black checkered shirt, tan once-upon-a-time canvas pants, and black boots.

The saddle gave out a leathery creak as Jay put all his weight into the left stirrup and dismounted. He wrapped Buck's reins around the horizontal hitching post.

The old man spat a foul-looking brown stream at a lizard scurrying along the boardwalk looking no doubt for shade. Missed him by two feet.

"Missed 'im, damn," the old man said. He had a voice that sounded as if it had been soaked in a barrel of whiskey, then pickled in heavy brine, and then left out in the desert for thirty or forty years.

Jay nodded at the old man and started for the door. His boots clumped on the boardwalk.

"You lookin for the shurf, he ain't around," the old man said.

Jay stopped. "Where would I find him?"

"Boot Hill!" The old man cackled until the laugh turned into a wheeze, then a cough. He spat more tobacco juice, but the lizard was already well out of range. "Damn, missed 'im."

"There a deputy around?"

"Yep—planted right next to the shurf!" This brought on another round of cackling, wheezing, and coughing.

Must have been sitting here praying for a stranger so he could say that.

When he managed to get his breath back, the old man said, "The Thompson Brothers came to stick up the bank three days back. I 'spect you bein' a marshal, you know who *they* are. They kilt two tellers, the shurf, and the deppity. Shurf got one of 'em, and Old Lady Tullis blowed 'nother one off'n his horse as they were ridin' out, cut him down with that old 12-gauge coachgun she keeps behind the counter o' her cantina. Course that left three of 'em still ridin' hellbent for leather, but they didn't get no money and they ain't likely to come back to this town real soon, nosiree Bob!"

"What's your name, old-timer?"

"Folks 'round here call me Gabby."

I can't imagine why. "Well, Gabby, I'm trackin' down some shysters from back East. Bad hombres."

"Ain't been no tinhorns stop off here lately," Gabby said. "Maybe some passin' through on the stage. Wells Fargo office's down t'other end o' town." He pointed with the stick he'd been carving on. "Past the whorehouse there."

"I'm obliged, Gabby."

Jay walked back to Buck, mounted, and walked the horse toward the Wells Fargo office. He nodded again at Gabby. Of course, the old man could be a firewall. Might be the sheriff was snoozin' in his office, his feet propped up on his desk or in a cell bunk. Or maybe he was havin' a drink at the cantina or the La Belle, and Gabby had been posted there to stop any strangers lookin' to talk to the local law. Jay would check out the stagecoach office, check with the telegrapher—he saw the telegraph poles so he knew the town was wired—and if he didn't get anything there, he would circle back and bypass Gabby to be sure he was tellin' the truth.

Jay smiled. Who would have ever thought of a firewall as a tobacco-chewing, lyin' old fart who looked like a forty-niner?

Jay was almost to the Wells Fargo depot when a big, swarthy, black-haired man with a drooping handlebar mustache and a pair of holstered guns stepped out into the street in front of him. "Hold up there, pard."

There was a definite air of menace about the man, who wore a black suit over his boiled white shirt and tie, and a derby hat instead of a cowboy hat.

Jay looked at the man. The guns he wore weren't Colt .45 Peacemakers like Jay's; they looked like Smith & Wesson Schofield .44's, top-loaders with seven-inch barrels. Powerful and accurate, damn fine weapons, but slow from the holster. When it came to fast draws, size mattered. Shorter was better. . . .

Jay dismounted and led his horse to another hitching post, this one next to the whorehouse. Four horses were already there. There were three large windows on the second story of the big house, and three or four pretty women in colorful petticoats and underwear leaned out of the open windows to look down at the two men in the street. Jay tipped his hat to the women. "Afternoon, ladies," he called out.

The women tittered. One of them waved. "Come on up, Marshal!"

Jay grinned, then turned back to face the man in the derby hat. He moved away from his horse so Buck wouldn't be directly behind him. "What can I do for you, amigo?" Jay said.

"Fact is, I don't like lawmen. I think mebbe you need to turn around and head back where you came from." The big man cleared his coat back from his holstered revolvers. "It would be good for your health."

"You got a name?" Jay said.

"Name is Bartholomew Dupree. Folks call me Black Bart," the man said.

Well, of course *they do.*

Jay dropped his hand next to the butt of his Colt. "Sorry, Bart, I got business at the stage depot. Why don't you just stand aside and let me pass?"

"Can't do that, Marshal." He waggled his fingers, loosening them.

Definitely a firewall, and a tough one. So Jay was on the right track; his quarry had passed this way. And he wasn't about to give up because there was a roadblock. Lonesome Jay Gridley hadn't gotten to where he was by accident. He was the best.

"Make your play then," Jay said.

Bart went for his guns. He was fast—but Jay was faster. The .45 spoke a hair before the twin .44's, a throaty roar, belches of thick white smoke erupting around tongues of orange fire. Speckles of unburned propellant stung Jay's hand. He recocked the big single-action revolver, but it wasn't necessary. Bart dropped to one knee, guns falling from his suddenly nerveless fingers, then toppled to one side. Dust splashed from the street, joining the stink of black powder smoke.

Jay uncocked, then holstered his gun and walked over to where Bart lay on his side in the dirt. Got him right between the eyes, Jay noted with satisfaction.

Teach you to mess with Lonesome Jay. Pard.

He thought he heard music coming from the saloon behind him, a kind of echoing *wah-wah-wah* sound that was more synthesizer than upright piano. He grinned. Too many Eastwood movies when he'd been a kid.

A dark-haired man in a gray banker's suit and steel-rimmed spectacles came out of the arcade next to the house of ill repute and walked to where Jay stood looking down at the corpse. "Perhaps you might have need of my services, friend?" He tendered a business card. "Peter Honigstock, Attorney-at-Law," it said.

Jay turned so his marshal's badge was visible to the lawyer. "Nope. Just the undertaker."

"Ah," Honigstock said.

He turned back, nodded at the soiled doves in the whorehouse, then headed for the stage depot. And after that, he was gonna mosey on back to the sheriff's office and have a few words with old Gabby. The lyin' bastard.

9

Tuesday, December 21st, 3:25 p.m.
Washington, D.C.

In his study at home, John Howard leaned back in his chair,
looked away from the terrain maps of the Pacific Northwest
and glanced at his watch. He realized he was going to have
to leave for the airport to pick up Nadine's mother in about
five minutes. The idea of fighting rush hour traffic made him
feel even more tired than he already felt, which was plenty
tired enough.

He didn't know what the problem was, or why he was so
worn out lately. He couldn't get a pump working the weights,
was winded so bad after a couple miles into his usual run he
had to slow down almost to a walk. And he wasn't sleeping
real well either—dropping off early, tossing and turning all
night, then waking up tired and groggy. What it felt like was
overtraining, but he hadn't been working that hard, no more
than maintenance stuff. And there wasn't anything pressing at
work: some training exercises in the high desert in Washington
state coming up, and some winter work in the snow, in the
hills of West Virginia, in mid-January. Other than that, nothing.

Could he be getting old?

No, he was only forty-two. He knew guys ten years older who could run him into the ground; it couldn't be something that simple.

No? Some folks age faster than others, don't they, Johnny boy? Remember your twentieth high school reunion? Some of the guys you graduated with had so much gray hair and so many wrinkles they looked old enough to be your father. You'd pass them on the street, you'd never know who they were. Maybe your clock is running fast. . . .

Howard shook his head. He didn't need to be going down *that* road, thank you very much. He didn't even have any gray hair yet, and he looked better than he had at twenty, with more muscle. Maybe he just needed some vitamins.

He pushed away from the chair and stood. It wasn't going to do anybody any good sitting here thinking about being old, not when his mother-in-law would turn into a black volcano spewing hot bile if he was late fetching her. That woman had a mean streak on her, and a mouth to go with it. He'd best get moving.

Nadine was in the kitchen, working on supper, and Howard started in that direction, to tell her he was fixin' to take off. Might as well stir up Tyrone while he was at it.

The boy was in his room. But instead of being glued to the computer chair as he usually was, he was lying on the bed, hands behind his head, staring at the ceiling.

"You okay, son?"

"I'm fine."

"About time to go pick up Nanna."

Tyrone turned his head slightly. "I think I'll stay here."

"Excuse me?"

"I mean, I'll see Nanna when she gets here."

Howard stared at his son as if he had suddenly sprouted horns and a tail. Not go to pick up his grandmother? What happened to the boy who used to chant, "Nanna! Nanna! Nanna!" over and over, bouncing all over the car the entire way to the airport? Who'd practically knocked the old bat down, hugging her and dancing around like he was demented?

"She'll wonder where you are."

"She's gonna be here for a week."

It was that girl, of course. Girls turned boys into adolescent beasts struggling to crawl out of a mud pit of raging hormones. And Tyrone was officially a teenager now, becoming quiet, sullen, withdrawn, and about as communicative as a fence post.

"You can have your calls forwarded—" Howard began.

Abruptly, Tyrone sat up, then stood. "I'm going to the mall," he said.

Howard felt a stab of anger. "Wait just a second, mister. You don't *tell* me what you're doing; you *ask*!"

Tyrone came to attention, executed a crisp, snappy salute, and said, "Yes, sir, Colonel Howard, sir!"

Rage enveloped Howard. He had to restrain himself from reaching out and slapping the boy. He was tired, he didn't feel great, and he was about to spend an hour and a half going to and from the airport to pick up a woman who had never liked him and who had never been shy about telling him he wasn't good enough for her daughter. What he sure as hell *didn't* need was lip from a kid who thought his old man was a fossil who'd ridden to school on the back of a grass-eating dinosaur.

For a few seconds, Howard didn't say anything. The rage abated just a hair as he remembered he'd once been young and stupid himself, sure that his parents couldn't begin to recall through their aged fog how it had been to be young. But even so, if he'd pulled his father's chain the way Tyrone had just pulled *his* . . . ?

Howard had a temper. Once, when he'd been about six or seven, his little brother Richie had snuck up behind him while they were playing cowboys and Indians and clonked him on the head with the butt of his toy revolver, to knock him out like they did on television. It hadn't knocked him out, but it had sure pissed him off. He'd bellowed like an angry buffalo, turned around, and chased Richie across the street toward their house, fully intending to brain the little bastard when he caught him.

Their father, who'd been in the front yard trimming the azalea bushes, had heard Richie screaming and moved between him and Howard.

"What's going on here?" his father had said.

And Howard, eyes and mind blurred with killing rage, had yelled something *supremely* stupid: "Get out of my way!" and then swung his own toy gun at his father's legs to move him aside.

The next thing he remembered, he was lying on the ground, looking up into the warm summer afternoon, wondering how he had gotten there. The old man had cuffed him upside the head and straightened him out *instantly*.

Howard, who had never raised a hand to Tyrone, now knew how his father must have felt. He offered a silent apology to the old man. *Sorry, Pop.*

And Tyrone, who up until lately had been a model son, looked down at the floor and said, "Sorry, Pop," echoing Howard's thoughts.

Adolescent angst. *Think back, John. Remember how it was that nobody understood how you felt, nobody could* possibly *know how you felt.*

"All right, forget it. I'll get Nanna, you go ahead to the mall. She'll understand."

He saw the boy take it in, think about it. Loyalty to his grandmother warred with his infatuation for his girlfriend.

This time, loyalty won.

"No, I'll go with you to the airport. If I don't, Nanna will blame you." He grinned.

Howard returned the grin. *There* Tyrone was. Back, for at least a moment.

Nadine, with the instincts of a wife and mother sensing trouble, drifted into the doorway. "Hey, you two. Everything okay back here?"

Howard turned to look at his wife, still the most beautiful woman he'd ever known, more so after fifteen years of marriage. "Everything is just fine," he said.

At least for now, it was. But Tyrone was only thirteen. They had six more years of this to look forward to.

Lord, Lord.

Tuesday, December 21st, 8:15 p.m.
Washington, D.C.

Naked, Platt lay on his stomach on the bed in the little hotel on C Street, not far from the Library of Congress. A woman, who was also naked, straddled the small of his back, leaning into her hands, pushing and digging into the muscles of his neck and shoulders, the traps and delts. Her thighs and crotch felt warm against his skin.

She actually gave a pretty good massage, which was unusual for outcall girls. Most of 'em just gave a few half-assed wipes with their fingertips, maybe a little scratchy-scratch with their nails, but this girl was putting something into it. He'd give her a good tip for that. She was tall, a little thin, no tits, but a great ass. And her hands were a lot stronger than you'd guess by lookin' at her.

"Damn, honey, you hard as a rock," she said, pressing hard with her thumbs into the trigger points just under the scapulas. It hurt, but it was a good kind of hurt.

"You ain't seen the half of it, baby," he said. "Wait till I roll over."

She laughed. "Yeah, I noticed you pretty big, for a white boy." She wasn't talking about his muscles. "What line of work you in, Mr. Platt?"

"I'm an expediter," he said. "For a big import/export business. I travel a lot. Get to travel all over the world, make things happen."

"That a fact? I always wanted to go overseas. Never been out of the country. I always wanted to go to Japan."

Her hands felt damn good on his neck as she kneaded the tight muscles there. "Uh-huh," he said. "You don't want to go back to Africa? See your homeland?"

"Sheeit, what I want to do that for? There's plenty of black folks in *this* country."

He laughed. He liked her. "Maybe next time I get to Japan, I'll bring you back a souvenir."

"I'd like that. A nice red silk kimono."

Platt rolled over. She lifted a little, then settled back down over his legs when he got turned. He grinned at her. "One red silk kee-moan-oh, no problem."

"My, would you look at that?" she said. She flashed even, white teeth, bright against her chocolate skin. "What *do* we have here?" She reached down. He slid his hands around under her butt and lifted her slightly. Hel-looo, *baby*!

Tuesday, December 21st, 8:15 p.m.
Washington, D.C.

In his office, Hughes finished a synopsis of what he wanted White to say at his meeting with the vice president tomorrow before White went back to Ohio for the holidays.

There was a knock at the door. Speak of the devil.

"Bob?"

"I thought I'd find you still here," White said. He sauntered into the office and put a small package onto the desk. "Christmas present. You didn't think I'd forget, did you?"

Hughes smiled. "Now how could I think that, Bob? I wrote the reminder in your day log myself."

Both men laughed.

Hughes reached into the drawer, pulled out a Christmas-wrapped box, and handed it to White. It was hard to buy stuff for a millionaire who bought himself whatever he fancied, but Hughes always worked to find something unusual. And he knew White loved being surprised.

"Can I open it?" Just like a kid.

"Sure."

Eagerly, the senator ripped off the green and red foil and pulled the lid from the box. He removed what looked like a small leather candy dish mounted on a wooden stand from the box. Inside the leathery cup was a game infoball, an iridescent, silvery orb the size of a marble, made to be slipped into a SonySega PlayStation, a device that White had owned since the first ones had come out. He looked at Hughes and raised one eyebrow.

"That's the beta-test full-VR version of DinoWarz II," Hughes said. "Won't be generally available for a few more months."

"Really? Wow, thanks, Tom! How'd you get it?"

"I have a few contacts in the right places."

White rolled the ball in his fingers, and Hughes could see he was itching to run home and play the game. The senator looked at the container. "This a candy dish? Looks unusual."

"It's a plastic-coated bull scrotum," Hughes said.

"What? You're kidding."

"Nope. I can think of a few people you might want to offer peppermints to from it."

White laughed and shook his head. "Well, I'll be taking the family jet home in the morning. You need a ride any-where?"

"Nope. I'm hanging around here, finally be able to get some work done with you out of the way."

They laughed again.

"Guess I better open my present now," Hughes said.

He did so. Inside was a carved ivory figurine, seven or eight inches long, a woman stretched out, lying on her side, propped on one elbow. Hughes knew what it was. It was a Chinese medical doll. Once upon a time in China, women of breeding never let any man but their husbands see them unclad, sometimes not even their husbands. When they needed to see a doctor, they took the doll with them. When the doctor asked where the pain was, they showed him on the figurine, and he made his diagnosis based on that and symptoms, without ever seeing or touching his patient's body. Knowing White, Hughes figured this statuette was probably worth a fortune. The work was exquisite.

Hughes made appropriate noises. "It's beautiful, Bob. Thank you."

"Well, it isn't a bull scrotum, but it's the best I could do. It belonged to some emperor's wife or concubine, I forget which. Bertha's got the documentation on it. She'll give it to you after we get back from the holidays."

"I appreciate it, I truly do. Working with you has been so beneficial to me, I can't begin to tell you how much."

That was surely the truth.

"I couldn't have ever gotten the job without you, Tom. Merry Christmas."

"Merry Christmas," Hughes said. *And with any luck at all, the New Year will be my best ever—though it might be your worst, when the shit hits the fan. . . .*

10

Alex Michaels wanted to keep the staff meeting short so they could get back to their desks. With Christmas only a few days away, not much work was getting done as everybody geared up to go off for the holidays. The office didn't shut down, of course, there was always a skeleton staff, but anybody not stuck with that duty who wanted to take off early could do so. He looked around the conference room, at his primary players: Toni, Jay, Howard, and Joanna Winthrop. They were all senior enough, except for Joanna, and she was working out of Howard's command, so they didn't have to stick around here for Christmas.

"Okay, that pretty much covers the basics. You all know this poster business is critical, so take your flatscreens and if you get any bright ideas, log them in for the rest of us."

He already knew their plans, and no matter where they were, they'd keep grinding away at this thing. Toni was going home to the Bronx for a week's visit with her family. She'd be back next Wednesday. Jay's parents were visiting relatives in Thailand, so he was hanging around the city and would probably would spend much of the time here at HQ. Howard had relatives visiting. He'd be in town. Joanna was going to meet an old friend at a mountain cabin in Colorado. She'd be back Monday. And Michaels was going to Boise to see Susie. And Megan too.

There was a case of mixed emotions.

"Anybody got anything new?"

Jay said, "Well, I came across some interesting statistics in the new Murray Morbidity and Mortality Report. According to the MMMR, life expectancy for men in Washington, D.C., is the lowest of any metropolitan area in the country. In fact, it's lower than any rural area too, except for a couple of counties in South Dakota. Sixty-three years. Whereas if you live in Cache County, Utah, you can expect to live fifteen years longer, a ripe old seventy-eight. And you can add eight or ten years to both those numbers if you're a woman."

"I bet it *feels* a lot longer in Washington," Howard said.

"I don't know," Toni said. "Have you ever been in Utah?"

"Yeah," Jay said. "I think maybe they all get too *bored* to die."

Michaels smiled. "Fascinating. Anything that might relate to what we do in *this* agency, Jay?"

"Nope. I got through the poster's firewalls, but the trail petered out, a dead-end in a box canyon. I haven't been able to draw a bead on him since."

"Yee-haw," Joanna said quietly.

"Excuse me?" Alex asked.

"Private joke," she said. "Sorry."

"All right. That's it. If one of you catches the poster before we take off for the holiday, I'd bet big that Santa Claus will put something nice in your stocking, a Presidential Commendation at the least."

"Oh, boy," Jay said. "A new floor for my parakeet's cage."

"I didn't know you had a parakeet," Toni said.

"I don't, but for that, I'd get one."

"Somebody has to represent the agency at the L.A.W. convention in Kona on the Big Island in February," Michaels said.

"Me! Me!" Jay said. "Send me!"

"Catch us a crook and you can work on your tan."

Joanna chuckled.

"What's funny?" Jay asked.

"Nothing. I'm just imagining myself on that black sand beach I've heard about."

"Don't pack your bikini just yet," Jay said.

"No? Well, I wouldn't start buying Coppertone in bulk either, if I were you."

"I think that's got it," Michaels said. "Back to work."

As the meeting broke up, Sergeant Julio Fernandez arrived. He nodded at Michaels, and moved to talk to Colonel Howard, where the senior officer stood talking to Lieutenant Winthrop.

"Colonel. Lieutenant."

"Sarge," Howard said.

Michaels caught a quick glimmer of something on Fernandez's face when he looked at the young woman. Well. He could understand how the sergeant might appreciate Winthrop.

Back at their offices, Toni approached Alex. "Got a minute?"

"Sure."

In his office, she produced a small package, wrapped and decorated with a red bow. "Merry Christmas," she said.

"Thank you. Can I open it now?"

"Nope. Got to wait until Susie opens her gifts. You'll want this then."

"Ah, intrigue. All right, I'll wait. Here, I got you a little something." He opened his desk drawer and removed a flat box, this one wrapped in the hardcopy Sunday cartoon section of the Arlington newspaper.

She smiled at the wrapping, hefted it. "Book?"

"Go ahead and open it."

She did, carefully peeling the tape from the edges and unfolding the colorful newsprint.

"You going to save the paper, Toni?"

"Sorry. Old habit." She got to the book. "Oh, wow."

It was a 1972 first edition of Donn F. Draeger's *The Weapons and Fighting Arts of Indonesia.*

"Where did you find this? It's a classic." She flipped through the pages, again with care, looking at the black-and-white illustrations. "I've never seen an original, only the on-demand-print and CD versions."

He shrugged. "Picked it up somewhere. I thought you might like it."

Yes, he had "picked it up somewhere," all right. He'd had a bookseeker service hunting for six weeks for the thing, and it had cost him a week's salary when they'd found it. Oh, well. He didn't spend a lot of money. Outside of his living costs and Susie's child support, his only hobby was the restoration of old cars. His current project was a Plymouth Prowler. That wasn't cheap, but when he finally finished and sold the car, he'd get all he'd spent back, and then some. The book had made a dent in his bank account, but Toni deserved it. He couldn't do his job without her. And the look on her face when she saw the thing was worth a lot too. He smiled.

Toni was about to close the book when she got to the title page. "Hey, it's autographed!"

"Oh, really? Huh. How about that?" That autograph had jacked the price of the book up a few hundred dollars.

Impulsively, she hugged him.

God, she felt good, pressed against him that way. She could stay there all day. . . .

Toni pulled away and gave him a big grin. "Thanks. My gift is nothing compared to this. You shouldn't have."

He shrugged. "Hey, a big meteor could fall on me while I'm taking the trash out tomorrow and what good would money be? I really appreciate all you do around here, Toni."

There was a silence that started to get awkward. He said, "So, you're going home to see your folks?"

"Yes. There'll be a big gathering, all my brothers and sisters-in-law, and nieces and nephews, the uncles and aunts. Regular army of relatives." She paused. "I hope your visit with Susie goes okay."

"Yeah."

"Well, I'd better get back to work. Thanks again for the book, Alex."

"You're welcome."

Thursday, December 23rd, 6:45 a.m.
Quantico, Virginia

Joanna Winthrop took advantage of the take-off-work-early offer from Commander Michaels to book a deadhead seat on an early military jet leaving from Quantico and stopping off in Denver on its way to Alaska. When she mentioned it to Colonel Howard, Sarge Fernandez had offered to take her to the flight.

"I can catch a cab," she'd said.

"No problem, Loot, I'm heading out that way anyhow, got some errands to run. I'll swing by and pick you up."

It did make it easier for her. "Sure."

So now she rode in the front seat of Fernandez's personal car, a slate-gray seventeen-year-old Volvo sedan. She smiled. "Funny, I'd have figured you for a little racier ride than this."

"It gets me there. Slow and steady. And it doesn't spend much time in the shop."

"Well, I appreciate the lift."

"No problem."

They rode in silence for a few minutes, but she was aware of him giving her small peripheral glances. Well. He was a man, and she knew that look.

He said, "You mind if I ask you something personal, Lieutenant?"

Oh, Jesus, here it comes, she thought. He's going to hit on me.

She'd had plenty of practice shutting male attention down when she wanted to. Although Fernandez had a certain Latin charm about him, it wouldn't be a good idea, a relationship. Even though the ranks were more quasi- than real-military in Net Force, and there wasn't a specific prohibition *against* fraternization as in the Regular Army, there *was* a difference in their respective statuses. So she could let him down gently. "Fire away."

"Has working with computers always been easy for you?"

Hmm. That wasn't what she expected. "Excuse me?"

"I've watched you. You're good at it, that goes without saying, but you make it look easy. I was just wondering if it was. Easy, I mean."

She thought about it for a second. She didn't want to sound egotistical, but the truth? "Yeah. I guess it does come without a lot of effort for me. Always has. I had a kind of affinity for it."

He shook his head. "I can strip a heavy machine gun and put it back together in the dark in a pouring rain, but when it comes to bits and bytes, I'm a techno-dweeb."

She laughed. Men so seldom admitted to their shortcomings, it was refreshing to hear.

"I mean, I've tried to learn, but I have this block, the information just bounces off, it doesn't sink in. I tried a class recently, but I had a . . . personality conflict with the instructor. I think he just recognized that I was as dumb as dirt and would never get it."

" 'A thing can be told simply if the teller understands it properly.' "

"Excuse me?"

"George Turner, a writer I admired in college. You know how a computer works, basic theory?"

"Yeah. Well, actually . . . no."

"Okay. Let's say you're on guard duty, you're watching a door. You open it when somebody with the right password comes by, you close it if they don't have the password. You follow that?"

"Sure."

"Now you know how computers work. A door is open or it's closed. A switch is on or it is off. The answer is yes or no when somebody gets to the place you're standing guard. It happens fast, all the switching, but that's the base, and everything else links to that."

"No shit? Sorry, I mean—"

"No shit," she said.

"Damn. How come nobody ever put it that way before?"

"Because you've run into crummy teachers before. A good teacher uses terms a student can relate to, and she takes the time to learn what those terms are. When I was in college, I took a psych course. There was a story they told, about biased IQ tests for children. You know, you show a picture of a cup, and you show a saucer, a table, and a car, then you ask, what does the cup go with?"

"Yeah?"

"So in middle- and upper-class America, the kids with working brains all pick the saucer, because cups and saucers go together, right?"

"Right."

"But in the poor parts of town, cups might go with tables, because they don't have saucers. And among kids from home-less families, cup might go with car, because that's where the family lives."

"Economic bias," Fernandez said.

She nodded. He wasn't a dummy, no matter what he said. "Exactly. Same thing holds true for racial or religious or other kinds of cultural factors. So then everybody thinks these kids are stupid, and so they get a different level of teaching, when the real problem is on the other end, in the minds of the ed-

ucators. Because they didn't take into account the students'
knowledge as well as their own.''

''I get it.''

''There's nothing wrong with your mind. All you need is a
teacher who can put things in terms you already know how to
relate to. You're a soldier, find a soldier who knows computers, you can learn from him.''

''Or her,'' Fernandez said.

''Or her.'' She looked at him. ''Are you asking me to teach
you?''

''I would be ever so grateful if you would,'' he said. Kept
a straight face while saying it too.

She smiled. ''This isn't some ploy to get next to me because
you think I'm beautiful, is it, Fernandez?''

''No, ma'am. You have knowledge I don't have, and I'd
like very much to learn it. This is part of my job and I'm not
good at it. That bothers me. I don't need to be Einstein, but I
do want to understand as much of it as I need to understand.
I mean, yeah, you *are* beautiful, but what's more important
here is that you're *smart*.''

She blinked and looked at Fernandez in a new light. My
God, if he was telling the truth, he admired her for her *mind*.

''We might be able to work something out. Come see me
when the holidays are over.''

''Yes, ma'am.''

''And bag that. Call me Joanna.''

''I'll answer to just about anything, but my friends call me
Sarge or Julio.''

''Julio it is.''

She grinned again. *Ooh, wait until Maudie hears about this!*

11

"Would you care for something to drink, sir?"

Alex Michaels looked up from the in-flight magazine, from an article on the construction of the world's tallest building, the new twin towers in Sri Lanka. The new structure would be, when finished, seventy feet taller than the second tallest building—which was also in Sri Lanka.

"Coke?" he said.

"Yes, sir." The flight attendant handed him a plastic cup of ice and one of the new biodegradable plastic cans of Coke. The can would keep for ten years, as long as it wasn't opened, but once fresh air hit the inside, the plastic would start to degrade. In nine months, it would be a powdery, non-toxic residue that would completely dissolve under the first rain that hit it. Throw the can on the ground, and in a year it would be gone.

The flight attendant moved to the next row of seats. Michaels poured the soft drink into his cup, then sat and watched it fizz and foam. He was in business class, the equipment was one of the big Boeing 777's, and he sat next to the wing door on the starboard side. He liked to get that seat when he could, next to the exit door. It always seemed that there was a little more room in the exit row, although that might have been his imagination. The main thing was, if there was trouble on the plane, he wanted to be in a position to *do* something.

He'd started asking for the exit row after a flight to Los Angeles when he'd seen an elderly man who might have weighed a hundred pounds sitting next to an emergency door. Yeah, the guy might get a burst of adrenaline under stress, so he could pop that door right open if the wheels collapsed on landing or some such, but Michaels didn't want to risk his life and the lives of the other passengers on that. Maybe the old guy would get a burst blood vessel instead. Then again, maybe the old guy was like Toni's *silat* teacher, and there were hidden strengths there. Michaels knew he shouldn't be so judgmental. But still, better a fairly strong forty-year-old GS employee in front of that door than a seventy-year-old lightweight. Better odds for all concerned.

Of course, he'd rather fly first class too. A couple of times, he had gotten agency upgrades on official business, and it was more comfortable, but he could never justify the expense when it came to personal flights. The way he figured it, the back of the plane got there at the same time as the front did, all things going as planned, and to cough up several hundred dollars extra for cloth napkins and complimentary champagne seemed excessive.

There was enough time for an in-flight movie before they got to Denver, where Michaels had to switch planes for Boise. The airlines had gotten a lot better about not losing luggage, but he wasn't taking any chances. He had his single soft-side roller tucked into the overhead compartment, along with Susie's main Christmas gift, a band/vox synthesizer. Apparently she had discovered a kind of music called technometo-funk, which was all the rage among the kids. Michaels tastes ran to jazz fusion, classic rock, 40's big band, or even long-haired classical. He hadn't followed new-wave pop stuff for years. He knew he was getting old when he read the news, saw the Billboard Top Ten list, and realized he didn't recognize the names of any of the songs, or the artists who performed them. Who could take seriously a song called "Mama Moustache Mama Sister," by somebody who called himself "HeeBeeJeeBeeDeeBeeDoo?" Or "Bunk Bunk!" by "DogDurt"?

With the synthesizer, Susie could supposedly program herself into any group, then hear and see herself performing on stage with them. It seemed like an advanced toy for somebody her age, but it was what she wanted. It had been a bitch to find one too. Apparently every other kid in the country had to have one of the things. Fortunately, Toni had found one, so he could be a hero to his daughter.

Toni did that a lot, made him look good.

He looked at the screen built into the back of the seat in front of him, a screen that could be angled for viewing so that even if the person sitting in that row decided to lean back all the way, you could still see it. No. He didn't feel like watching a movie, playing video VR, or monitoring the progress of his flight via a little animation of a jet flying along over a map. It was nice just to sit with a magazine in his lap and gaze out at the cold ground below. Fortunately, the weather was clear, and the Ohio landscape below, much of it covered with snow, sparkled white in the setting sun.

It was going to be midnight, East Coast time, when he landed in Boise, assuming he made his connection and the flight went as scheduled. Ten p.m. in that part of Idaho. He had a rental car reserved at the airport, and a room booked at the Holiday Inn, not far from the house where his daughter and ex-wife lived. Where they had once all lived together. There was a spare bedroom in the big old clunky two-story house, two if you counted the sewing room, but Megan hadn't offered and he hadn't asked. The armistice between Alex and his ex was uneasy. She was a sniper, quick to shoot and too accurate for his comfort. Better to have a safe house where he could hole up and gather his forces for the battle. There was a lot to be said for a nice quiet Holiday Inn, with room service and a double lock on the door.

He wondered how many other people thought about holidays in such a fashion? As an ugly guerrilla war to be waged quick and dirty and retreated from as soon as possible? Why did unhappy families gather, if it made them so miserable? A lot of people he knew would just as soon cancel the big holidays and keep their families at a safe distance. . . .

In his case, however, the answer was easy: Susie. Whatever else, she needed to know she had a mother and father who both loved her and wanted her to be happy, even if they couldn't be happy with each other.

Certainly this wasn't something he had ever foreseen for himself when he'd been courting Megan, when they'd been young, in love, with the world by the tail, so full of themselves they could never envision failing at *any*thing, much less their marriage. Ah, the arrogance of youth, when you knew everything, and didn't care who knew you knew everything, since you were willing to tell them all about it at great length if they blinked at you.

Boy, that had been a long time ago in a galaxy far, far away. . . .

Maybe he could get some sleep. Just lean over against that cool plastic window with one of the little puffy pillows, and turn it all off.

There was an idea that had much appeal.

Thursday, December 23rd, 5:15 p.m.
Washington, D.C.

The car was small, black, and looked like an old Fiat. The driver heard the siren behind him and pulled over, next to a row of small shops that appeared to be closed. There was a shoe store with a Nike swoosh on the glass, and an electronics store with small television sets in the window. The words on the storefronts looked to be German or Austrian, maybe Croat.

The Fiat's door opened and a smallish man in a long, dark coat stepped out of the car. He had his hands up next to his shoulders, to show he was unarmed. The sun was bright, but the street seemed deserted save for him.

A pair of policemen approached the Fiat, pistols drawn. The uniforms they wore had that Middle European look, odd-shaped billed caps with checkering on the front, leather jackets over dark blue shirts and ties, and dark blue trousers with a yellow seam-stripe on the outside of the legs. One of the cops moved to stand in front of the small man in the long coat; the other cop checked out the car.

The first cop gestured with the gun and said something. The small man turned around and put his hands on top of the Fiat, and the cop patted him down. No weapons.

The second cop talked into a small com, but kept his pistol pointed in the Fiat driver's direction. Second cop listened to the com for a moment. He nodded at the first cop, and said something.

The small man leaning against the car shoved away from it, swung his elbow up, hitting the cop behind him in the face, and knocking him down. The small man ran. The second cop darted around the front of the Fiat, raised his pistol, and fired—four, five, six times. The gun belched orange fire and white smoke, and the empty shells showered the car. The brass hulls glinted in the bright sunshine like gold coins as they bounced and dropped to the sidewalk.

The small running man fell, face-down on the street. He moved his arms and legs, as if spastically trying to swim on the concrete.

The cop who had been elbowed in the nose recovered. He moved to where the small man lay on the street. He pointed his pistol at the back of the downed man's head. He fired.

The little man spasmed one more time, then went limp.

Thomas Hughes blew out a big sigh, then froze the recording's image. The two cops stood over the dead man—and there was no doubt he was dead, a bullet to the back of the head from three feet away sure as hell did that.

Man. They just *executed* that poor sucker. And all of it caught on the surveillance cam mounted on the dashboard of the police car.

Hughes leaned back in his chair and looked at the frozen holoprojection. He felt a flash of regret, but he buried it. The man was a spy, he had known there were risks. He'd had to know what might happen to him if he got caught.

Of course, he probably hadn't thought his name would be stolen from a top-secret list nobody was supposed to have access to and posted to the net so anybody who bothered to look would know who he was.

Hughes had gotten the recording from one of *his* spies—actually one working for Platt. And it was brutal to watch, a man getting murdered like that. It turned your stomach, made you queasy.

But there it was. You couldn't make an omelette without breaking a few eggs. It was necessary. What were a few spies, easily replaced, compared to the long-range goals Hughes had in mind? Not much, not really. The end in this case surely justified the means. People died every day. A handful more wouldn't make a difference in the grand scheme of things.

The new Quayle addition to the Senate office building where White had his offices was nearly empty. Not a lot of people were working at this hour on the day before Christmas Eve. Hughes assumed that the other Senate office buildings—the Russell, the Dirkson, the Hart—were also mostly deserted, save for security and cleaning personnel, with maybe a few young staff members trying to make points while everybody else was off for the holidays. Not much official work got done from early December on into the new year, but a lot of ground-work did get laid.

White had once had offices in the Hart Building, back when they'd still had that ugly modern-art sculpture of cut-out metal, Mountains and Clouds or some such, in the atrium. The staff on the upper floors had spent a lot of time sailing paper airplanes down to land on top of the sculpture. They'd had contests to see who could get the most to hit and stay.

He sighed again. The stakes were high, and the cards had to be played correctly or the game would be lost. It was a pity about this agent, and about the others who would be imprisoned or maybe killed, but there was no way around it. There was a lot of inertia to overcome to get something as big as he had in mind to move—a lot. This spy was the first, but he wouldn't be the last who had to die for Hughes's plan to go forward. It was too bad, but that was how it was. In this world, you could be a hunter or the hunted, and sheep were prey for wolves, plain and simple. It was the first law of the jungle—the strong survive at the expense of the weak.

And Thomas Hughes was a survivor.

He saved the recording into a file for White to look at later, then started to wave the computer off. He'd done enough here for the day. Time to go home, order in some takeout, and have a glass of wine and a nice hot bath. Maybe he'd lift a glass to the poor operatives who had to suffer for his scheme. Why not? It wouldn't cost him anything.

His com cheeped. It was the secret number, rerouted though something like sixteen satellite bounces so it couldn't be traced to him.

He checked the scrambler to be sure it was on, even though it was automatic on this number, and clicked on the vox-altering circuit, picking Old Lady for the latter. Whoever was on the other end would hear what sounded like a ninety-year-old woman talking.

"Hello?" he said.

There was silence for a moment.

"Who's there?" Hughes said.

"I have some information concerning certain . . . shipments."

Hughes knew who it was. A mid-level manager at the National Security Agency, a man with top secret clearance, but a man who had a secret gambling problem and was deep in the hole to his bookies. His voice was altered too. Hughes had been waiting for the man to come up with something for him. The gambler didn't know who he was speaking to. "Go on."

"It concerns some volatile . . . minerals."

"I'm still listening."

"I need fifty thousand."

Hughes could almost hear the man sweating. "How much of the . . . volatile substance are we talking about?"

"Nineteen pounds. In four packages. On the same day."

Hughes considered that in amazement for a moment. Nineteen pounds of weapons-grade plutonium was being moved at the same time? Certainly not by the same agency inside the U.S., even broken into that many sub-critical-mass chunks. The NRC and NSA would have kittens if somebody did something that stupid. But he had to check.

"This is domestic movement?"

"Of course not. Two are, two are foreign. Six pounds, seven pounds, four, and two."

"When?"

"In two days. You want the particulars or not?"

"Fifty thousand, you said."

"Yes. In cash. Nothing bigger than a hundred."

"All right. I'll have somebody meet you at the place, tonight, nine p.m. Bring the information."

Hughes broke the connection. He hadn't planned to escalate things quite this much, this fast, but when something like this fell into your lap, you grabbed it and ran with it.

He tapped his com. Platt answered right away.

"Yeah?"

"Swing by here."

Platt said, "When?"

"Now."

He would give Platt the money and send him to fetch the information. Anybody with access to some explosives, a good metal shop, and some electronics from Radio Shack could build an atomic bomb, but without the right fissionable material it was nothing more than a mildly dangerous science project. There were a lot of groups out there who would pay millions to get their hands on nineteen pounds of weapons-grade plutonium. You didn't need that much to build yourself a nice and dirty little nuclear bomb. It would make a helluva bang when you set it off.

Now he could really give Net Force something to think about.

12

Toni climbed the familiar brownstone steps, steps that she had swept clean daily when she had been studying with Guru DeBeers. Somebody else must be doing the job now, for there was no snow or ice or dirt on them. The chicken-wire glass doors were closed and locked, but Toni still carried her well-worn key. She opened the door and stepped into the building. The hall was marginally warmer than it was outside.

Guru's apartment was the third one on the left. As she reached up to knock, the old woman's gravel-and-smoke voice came from within:

"Not locked, come in."

Toni grinned. Before she even knocked, Guru knew she was there. She was sure the woman was psychic.

Inside, the place looked as she remembered it from last year, and from her childhood. The old green couch with the needlepoint doily here, the overstuffed red plush chair with its needlepoint there, the short coffee table with one leg propped on an old Stephen King novel, all were in their usual places.

Guru was in the kitchen, crushing coffee beans in the little hand-powered grinder she had brought with her sixty years ago from Jakarta. She cranked the handle slowly and the smell of the beans, shipped to her by a distant relative who still lived in the highlands of Central Java, was sharp, rich, and earthy.

The two women faced each other. Toni pressed her hands together in front of her face and moved them down in front of her heart in a *namaste* bow, and Guru returned the greeting. Then they hugged.

At eighty-something years old, Guru was still brick-shaped and solidly built, but frailer and slower than she had been. As always, her clean and carefully set white hair smelled slightly of ginger, from the shampoo she used.

"Welcome home, *Tunangannya*," Guru said.

Toni smiled. *Best Girl,* what Guru had called her almost since they'd met.

"Coffee in a minute." Guru dumped the freshly ground coffee into a brown-paper cone and set it into the stainless-steel basket over the carafe, then poured hot water from a cast-iron kettle that had been heating on the tiny four-burner stove. The smell was delightful, almost overwhelming.

Guru waited until most of the water filtered through, then added a bit more. She repeated this until the kettle was empty. She took two plain white china mugs from the doorless wooden cabinet over the stove, then poured fresh coffee into them. There was no offer of cream or sugar. You could drink it any way you wanted at Guru's—as long as it was black. Adulterating coffee was, according to her way of thinking, very nearly a sin of some kind. Guru's religious beliefs were an amalgam of Hindu, Moslem, and Christian, and difficult to follow at best.

Wordlessly, the two women moved into the living room. Guru took the chair, Toni sat on the couch. Still without speaking, they took sips of the hot coffee.

Guru made the best coffee Toni had ever tasted. In fact, it spoiled her for drinking the stuff anywhere else. If Starbucks could get its hands on Guru, they would triple their business.

"So. How is life in Washington? Has your young man yet seen the light?"

"Not yet, Grandmother."

Guru sipped her coffee and nodded. "He will. All men are slow, some slower than others."

"I wish I could be sure of that."

"Not in this life, child. But if he fails to notice you properly, he does not deserve you."

They drank more coffee. When they were almost done, Guru said, "I think it is time to tell you a story. About my people."

Toni nodded but didn't speak. Guru had taught her a lot using this method, telling her Javanese tales and legends.

"My father's father's father came from Holland on a sailing ship in 1835. He came to work as an overseer on a plantation that raised indigo and coffee and sugarcane. Back then, the country was not called Indonesia. The pale men called the islands as a whole the Dutch East Indies, or sometimes, the Spice Islands. To my people, our island was Java."

Guru held up her empty cup. Toni stood, took both cups, went to the kitchen, and refilled them. Guru kept talking.

"My great-grandfather went to work on the farm, just outside of Jakarta, which had not nearly so many people then as it does now. He was married, with his wife and two children left behind in the country of his birth, but as was often the custom with white men in a foreign country in those days, he took himself a native wife. My great-grandmother."

Toni brought Guru's coffee back to her, reseated herself on the couch, and sipped at her own brew.

"In due course, my grandfather was born, first among six brothers and two sisters. When my grandfather had eleven summers, my great-grandfather sailed back to Holland, to rejoin his wife and children there, now a wealthy man. He left his Javanese family well-provided for, not always the custom with white men. He never saw or contacted them again.

"My great-grandmother's family took her and her children in, and life went on."

Toni nodded, to keep the flow going. Guru had told many tales, but never one about her family that was so personal.

"My grandfather's mother's brother, Ba Pa—The Wise—took it upon himself to teach my grandfather, whose Dutch name was Willem, how to be a man. My grandfather grew up strong, adept, and eventually became a soldier, part of the native army." She sipped at her coffee. Then she said, "Go into my bedroom and look at the nightstand. There is a thing upon a small silk pillow there. Bring it to me."

Toni nearly choked on her coffee. In all the years she had trained and known Guru, she had never been past the closed door into her bedroom. She had conjured all kinds of fantasies as to what it must look like in there. Maybe shrunken heads dangling from the ceiling, or walls covered with Indonesian art.

It was nothing so weird. It could have been any bedroom, belonging to any old woman. There was a bed, a carved, dark wooden chest at the foot of the bed, teak or mahogany, and a tall and dark wardrobe, also of wood, with a mirror that had lost part of its silvery backing. On one wall was a painting of a nude girl standing in a pool under a waterfall. The room smelled of incense, patchouli or maybe musk.

But on the nightstand was a red pillow, and upon the pillow was a *kris* inside a wooden and brass sheath.

Toni knew what it was. She had done some reading about Indonesia, curious about the country that fostered the martial art she studied, and while she had never trained with a *kris,* she had played with plenty of knives.

She picked the weapon up. She couldn't tell from the sheath what the shape of the blade was, but the typical Javanese *kris* was a foot to a foot and a half long—this one looked to be maybe fifteen or sixteen inches—and had a wavy, undulating double-edged blade, made of layers of forged, hand-hammered steel. Thus, like the swords of Damascus or the samurai *ka-*

tana, the final knife had a grain, a pattern in the welded metal itself.

She hurried back into the living room, wanting to hear the rest of Guru's story.

Guru traded the weapon for her empty coffee cup, which Toni quickly refilled.

"My great-uncle Ba Pa had no sons, only daughters, and when it came time for my grandfather to become a man and receive his *kris,* this is the one he inherited. It had been in the family from my great-uncle's father's father's father's time."

With that, the old woman drew the knife from the wooden sheath and held it up.

It was an undulate blade, a ribbon of steel with six or seven curves on either side, narrowing from a wide base under a slightly curved and short pistol-like handle to a sharp point. The metal was black, it had a dull, matte look, and on one side there was a little loop of steel protruding under the inside of the guard, almost like a tiny tree branch. On the other side of the blade were tiny, jagged teeth-like points.

"In the days when spirits were still powerful in Java, this *kris* had much *hantu*—much magic." She waved the weapon. "It has thirteen *luk dapor,* thirteen curves, and the *pamor* is called *udan-mas*; it means 'golden rain.' Here, you see?"

Guru pointed at the pattern in the metal, which looked like little drops of rain had spattered upon dry ground.

"This *kris* was supposed to bring good fortune and money for its owner.

"Some believe a good *kris* could kill slowly an enemy simply by stabbing his shadow—or even his footprints. If an enemy approached, a good *kris* would rattle in its sheath, to warn its owner of danger. The sight of the naked blade would turn a hungry tiger in its tracks. According to my great-uncle's grandfather, this *kris* once flew from its sheath like the *garuda* and cut the wrist of a thief trying to enter his house during the dark of the moon."

Guru smiled. "Of course, some of these old stories might have become embellished with the telling."

She returned the weapon to its sheath and held it in both hands on her lap, her coffee now growing cold on the doily upon the small table next to her chair.

"My grandfather gave this to my father when he became a man, and my father gave it to my only brother when *he* became a man." She stared into space, remembering. "My brother died in the war against the Japanese before he could begin a family. Many of our young men died in that war. My father had no sons, no nephews after that war. So the *kris* came to be mine."

They sat quietly for a moment.

"I bore my husband three sons and a daughter. Two of my sons live, and I have six grandsons and a great-grandson, and two granddaughters. My sons are old men, my grandsons are teachers and lawyers and businessmen, my granddaughters are a teacher and a doctor. They are a fine family, successful, scattered all over the country, and they are all good Americans. There is no wrong in this.

"But of all my family, none have studied the arts. Well, no, I do have a grandson in Arizona who plays tae kwon do, and one of my sons does tai chi to keep his joints limber, but none of them have studied *silat*. You are my student, the holder of my lineage, and so now, this *kris* now belongs to you."

The old woman held the dagger out on the palms of her hands to Toni.

Toni knew this was no small thing for Guru, and she had no thought for refusing. She knelt in front of the old woman and took the weapon in both of her hands. "Thank you, Guru. I am honored."

The old woman smiled, tobacco stains on her teeth. "Well you should say so, child, and a credit to my teaching that you should *know* to say so. I could not have wished for a better student. You should keep this on the red silk pillow near the head of your bed when you sleep," she said, waving at the *kris.* "It may make an American lover nervous, though." She giggled.

Toni looked down at the smooth wood of the sheath. Why was Guru giving this to her now? She had a sudden chill.

"Guru, you aren't . . . I mean, your health isn't . . . ?"

The old woman laughed. "No, I'm not ready to leave just yet. But you have more need of the *hantu* than I do. I have had a full life, and you are still unmarried. A woman your age needs to think of such things. It is a magic blade, after all, *kah*?"

Toni smiled. "More coffee, Guru?"

"Just half a cup. And tell me more of this young man who has yet to recognize your spirit. Maybe together we can find a way to wake him."

13

Julio Fernandez went to early mass at St. Gerard's, in Alexandria. He sat in the back of the small church, listening to Father Alvarez drone on in a dull monotone broken only occasionally by a louder "Lord," which tended to rouse the sleepy congregation.

Fernandez was used to being up this early, of course, but usually he'd be moving, doing laps or running the obstacle course or otherwise keeping his blood circulating. Sitting on the hard wooden pew in a too-warm and stuffy building listening to the old priest who could preach this sermon in his sleep—and might well be doing just that—was not a good way to stay alert.

Still, if he hadn't come to mass, he might have thought about lying to his mother, and he did not want to actually do that. He was on duty and couldn't fly back for Christmas with the relatives. Well, that wasn't strictly true. He could have gotten leave because he had seniority, but there were other men with families locally who needed the time more than he did, so he had volunteered—but he didn't have to tell Mama that. He would call her later today, she would be expecting that. There would be aunts and uncles and at least half of Fernandez's six brothers and two sisters would be there in La Puente at Mama's with their broods, probably bitching about the El Niño rains forecast to pound southern California. It wasn't as if Mama was going to be rattling around in her house alone; still, she wanted to hear from her children who couldn't get there, and the first question she would ask him after how was he doing would be had he gone to mass this morning? Mama suspected that her third son was more lapsed than good Catholic, and she was right in that suspicion, but at least he could tell her he had in fact been to early mass. He could tell her how Father Alvarez, who had once been a parish priest where Mama went to church some forty years ago, looked. Old, Mama, he would say, the man must be at least five or six hundred years old. I kept expecting somebody from the Cairo museum to come in and grab him, to take him back to King Tut's pyramid where he belongs.

Mama would laugh at this, tell him how awful he was, but it would make her happy that he went to mass, at least on Christmas, and it wasn't too much for a son to do for his mother, was it? One time a year?

So he'd get a few points for this—assuming he didn't doze off on the pew, sleep all day, and completely miss calling home. . . .

Saturday, December 25th, 7 a.m.
Boise, Idaho

Alexander Michaels rang the doorbell of the house that had once been his. It was a big, wooden, two-story home built in the early 1900's, at the top of a slight rise, with a high front porch at the top of ten broad steps. When the house had been built, it had been just outside what was then the city limits. Boise had engulfed the neighborhood long ago, but the houses along the street were still much as they had been a hundred years past. Outside of a new paint job that matched the old pale blue, and a couple of repaired steps and slats in the porch floor, the house looked the same as he remembered it. The same glider he'd installed when they'd bought the place hung on rusty chains at the south end of the porch, looking out over a somewhat cold rhododendron bush that would blossom a hard pink come the first warm weather. He'd spent some wonderful hours in that squeaky old wooden swing, looking out over that rhoddy bush, listening to the wind play in the big Doug fir trees that shaded the lot.

He heard his daughter's footsteps and her yelling as she raced for the door. "Daddy's here! Daddy's here!"

Susie flung open the door and jumped. With her present under one arm he had to make the catch one-handed, but she helped by wrapping her arms and legs around him and hugging him tight. She wore a pair of red-flannel pajamas and butter-yellow fuzzy slippers. "Daddy!"

"Hey, squirt. How are you?"

"Great! Great! Come in, we've all been waiting on you to open presents!"

Michaels stepped into the house, and what Susie had said registered.

We've *all* been waiting for you? Did she mean herself, Megan, and the dog Scout?

Susie slithered down and took off running down the hall for the living room. And sure enough, little Scout, the poodle who thought he was a wolf, came sliding around the corner from the kitchen, scrabbling on the hardwood floor, trying vainly for traction, to greet Michaels. The dog barked once, saw who it was, and wagged his tail so hard Michaels thought he might fall down. Michaels squatted and put the presents down as Scout ran and jumped into his arms.

Two for two, he thought.

As he stood, the little dog licking his face, Megan stepped into the hall from the living room.

Tall and leggy, with long brown hair worn in a ponytail, she was still one of the most beautiful women he had ever known. She wore a black T-shirt and blue jeans, her feet bare. She also looked nervous. "Hello, Alex."

"Hello, Megan."

"Come on in. Susie is about to pop."

He put the dog down, picked up the presents he had brought, and followed his ex-wife into the living room. *Oh, well. Two out of three . . .*

They had put up a large tree, an eight-footer, easy to do in a place with such high ceilings. The tree glistened with lights and fake snow and ornaments and tinsel. There was a fire in the wood stove, burning brightly behind the thick glass. Susie was on her knees under the tree, amidst a pile of wrapped gifts, grinning.

And standing by the old plush blue couch was a stranger, a big man with a full beard. He wore jeans and a blue work-shirt and cowboy boots. He looked to be about thirty, a good ten years younger than Alex, and at least five years younger than Megan.

Megan walked over to the bearded man. She slipped her hand under his arm, smiled at him, then turned back to look at Michaels and said, "Byron, this is Alex Michaels, Susie's father. Alex, this is my friend Byron Baumgardner. He's a teacher at Susie's school."

The big man grinned, showing nice, white teeth, and ambled over to take Michaels's hand. "Glad to meet you, Alex. I've heard a lot about you."

Michaels felt his belly twist into a frozen knot. So. This was Byron. He forced a smile as he stuck his hand out. "Byron."

The two men shook hands. Michaels shot a glance at Megan. She had looked nervous, and now he knew why. Here was a nice surprise on Christmas. Meet the new boyfriend. Your replacement.

"Can I open my presents now, can I?"

"Sure, honey," Megan said.

Michaels smiled at Susie as Byron moved over to stand next to Megan. The bearded man put his arm around Megan.

Michaels felt sick. He wished the ground would open up and swallow him. He wanted to be anywhere on the planet instead of here. Anywhere, for any reason.

Saturday, December 25th, 11 a.m.
Bethesda, Maryland

On his back on the bench, Platt squared himself under the weight, put his hands on the bar in a false grip, and took a couple of deep breaths. Counting the bar, 440 pounds lay heavy in the bench-press cradle. He nodded at the spotters on both sides. "Ready," he said.

The two gym rats, both hard-core steroid boys bigger than he was, moved in a hair and put their hands under the end of the bar, not touching it, but ready, just in case.

Platt gathered himself to lift the weight off the rack. Took another deep breath, and shoved, let part of the air out as he cleared the stand and began to lower the Olympic bar toward his chest.

The first rep went up pretty easy.

"One," the gym rats said in unison. Like he couldn't fuckin' count.

Second rep was a little harder, but he got it to lockout.

"Two!"

The third rep was hard. He had to blow it up, arching his back, to get it locked.

"Three!"

He knew his limits. "I'm done, take it," Platt said.

The two bodybuilders caught the ends and helped him re-rack the barbell. Platt blew out a big exhalation and sat up.

The guy on the left, who had a shaved head and a purple sweatband above his eyes, said, "Lemme try a few."

Platt nodded and switched places with Baldy. As he squared up on the bench press, Platt glanced around the inside of the place.

They had a pretty decent setup here at the new Gold's Gym. Lotta free weights, a bunch of piston machines, some bikes, rowers, elliptical walkers, and stair climbers. They even had one of the new peg machines in one corner. Mirrors on all the walls. It was Christmas, but there were twenty people in here working the iron. Gym rats, most of them, serious bodybuilders or weightlifters, most of them on the juice. You didn't miss a workout because it was a holiday. You'd never get anything done that way.

You could always tell somebody who was stackin' serious 'roids. They had that crepe-skinned, veiny look, the whites of their eyes got yellowy, they were usually balding, and a lot of 'em had acne on their back and shoulders. In the locker room with their clothes off coming out of the shower, some of 'em had bitch-tits and little bitty balls and peckers too. But they were strong, as Baldy on the bench here showed Platt. He did ten reps with four-forty and racked the bar by himself, then sat up, grinning. "Okay, I'm warmed up. Lou?"

The other gym rat traded places with Baldy, then Baldy and Platt spotted him while he did his benches. He only made eight reps, and Baldy called him a pussy.

"Want to do another set?" Baldy asked Platt.

"No, thanks. I got to go do chins and dips. I can come back and spot if you need it."

"Cool. Later, dude."

Platt headed for the chinning rack. Strong, both of the bodybuilders, stronger than he was. Then again, he didn't take anything but vitamins and a few aminos and supplements, and he didn't have to worry about his liver rotting or getting brain cancer or shit like that. Or 'roid rage. Blowing up and killin' somebody who cut him off in traffic. Fightin' for fun was one thing, losin' control was something else. And these guys were so strong they tore muscles and ripped tendons right off the bone sometimes. He'd seen a guy benching six-fifty once rip a pec. The muscle rolled up his chest like a window shade, and the guy was looking at major surgery and a lot of down time. Stupid. Wasn't any point to all this stuff if you weren't healthy enough to enjoy it.

His sweats were already soaked, but Platt figured he could do a couple sets of chins and dips, no weight, alternating, to finish off his pump. Half an hour in the sauna and hot tub, a shower, and he was done.

He wondered if that bento place over on Wisconsin was open today, A couple plates full of grilled chicken skewers and rice with hot and sweet sauce would sure taste good about now. He'd go check it out.

Saturday, December 25th, noon
Sugar Loaf Mountain, Boulder, Colorado

The big fire roaring away pushed the cabin's chill into the room's corners. The place smelled of cedar and woodsmoke and pine. Wonderful.

"Merry Christmas," Joanna Winthrop said. She raised her champagne glass and tapped it against the glass Maudie held.

"Same to you," Maudie said. They drank.

"Mmm. This is great," Winthrop said.

"It ought to be. It cost eighty bucks a bottle."

"Jesus, you spent that kind of money on *champagne*?"

"Not me. It was a gift from an admirer. I think he wanted to lick it off my naked body."

"Why didn't you let him?"

"Because we went to a movie and he made a disparaging remark about one of the actresses who was a few pounds over-weight."

"Ah. Fat jokes, the squash of death."

"Unless you're fat—then it's okay." Maudie sipped at the champagne again. "I'll send him a nice thank-you e-mail for this."

"I'm sure he'll appreciate it."

They giggled.

"So, tell me more about this Sergeant What's-his-name. Anything serious in the offing?"

"Too early to tell. So far, all we've talked about is computers, about which he knows zip. But he seems like a sweet man. And he admires me for my mind."

"Uh-huh."

"Well, either he does, or he's very, very clever about taking the long way around to get my pants off."

"Hah. Men will cross a desert in July on their hands and knees over broken glass if they think they'll get laid when they get to the other side."

"True. But I have a good feeling about this one. How many men have you met who will admit they don't know something about everything?"

"So far? Let me see . . . oh, if you total them all up, about, roughly, approximately . . . none."

"So I'm one up on you."

"Oh, girl. You got a picture? How about a com number?"

"Oh, no, you don't. You should be able to find one in California."

"You'd think so, wouldn't you? I'm thinking about putting an ad in the personal sections of the local alternative weekly paper. 'Fat, ugly woman, smart, looking for man who can appreciate me for my mind.' It would be interesting to see who answers."

"I'm sure that would work." She lifted her glass. "Cheers."

"Uh-huh."

They drank. They laughed some more.

There were worse ways to spend Christmas.

14

Saturday, December 25th, 2:15 p.m.
Ambush Flats, Arizona

Jay Gridley was getting a little tired of the Western scenario and he considered switching it. He hated to do that in a VR session, though, jump genres. After this time, he'd use a different program.

At the moment, he was in the small Western town of Ambush Flats, walking up toward the telegraph office. A Christmas wreath hung in the window.

"Mornin' Marshal," the telegraph clerk said. The man wore a card dealer's green eyeshade, a boiled shirt, and a thin, dark tie. "Happy Christmas. Shame you got to be travelin' on such a day."

"And you workin'," Jay said. "Any messages for Marshal Gridley come through here?"

"Nossir, I don't believe they have." The man made a show of checking the stack of yellow paper next to his key. "Nope, don't see none."

"Uh-huh. And any messages a marshal ought to know about pass through your ears or fingers?"

"Nossir. I'm a law-abidin' citizen, Marshal. I don't truck with such things."

It wasn't that Jay didn't believe him—but he'd learned the hard way that truth was a valuable and sometimes rare commodity on the net. And Jay needed to know if that was what he was dealing with here.

There were several ways he could do this. He could pull his gun and order the telegrapher to lie down on his belly. He could point out the window, and when the man looked, clonk him on the back of the head and knock him cold. Or he could use subterfuge, which was his preferred method. "Well, I appreciate it, friend. Thanks. Adios."

Jay left the telegraph office and moseyed around to the back of the building. There was a wooden barrel of trash next to the door. He pulled a strike-anywhere lucifer from his shirt pocket, scratched it on the barrel's metal hoop, and tossed the flaring match into the trash. Paper caught, flamed, and in a few seconds, there was a hot little fire blazing away in the barrel. Jay looked around and spotted some weeds growing from under the building. He pulled a handful of the greenery and tossed it into the flame. Thick white smoke poured out as the green plants began to burn.

Jay walked around to the front of the building, found a shady spot under an overhang, and leaned against a porch post. He didn't have long to wait.

"Fire!" somebody yelled. A bell started to ring. Folks came a'runnin' too.

The telegrapher sprinted through the front door of the office, away from the sudden smoke pouring in from the back, and looped around the building to see what was what.

Jay sauntered back into the building and began to go through the stack of telegrams. Nothing to see.

There was a locked wooden drawer next to the telegrams out in plain sight, and he used his Barlow jackknife to slip the simple lock so he could get at the hidden documents in the drawer.

He grinned. Breaking into an encrypted e-mail sorter using a brute-force generator didn't sound nearly as colorful as rifling the telegrapher's desk in his marshal persona. It wasn't as much fun either.

There was a lot of junk in the drawer. Some shady money exchanges, illicit love letters, porno, the usual stuff people tried to hide. Technically speaking, what he was doing wasn't altogether legal, but he wasn't going to use it in court, he was just looking for information. If he hurried, he would be gone before the telegrapher got back, and nobody would ever know he'd been snooping in private affairs.

Looked like a waste of time again—hello? What was *this*?

Jay read the message, growing more alarmed as he went. Somebody had sent particulars on the routes for four shipments of plutonium—that didn't translate into this scenario as dynamite either—to a group calling itself the Sons of Patrick Henry! Jay had heard of them. They were a militia group that danced on the edge of treason and had a membership that made Attila the Hun look like a flaming red Communist.

And the stuff was moving today. Holy shit!

Clutching the message tightly, Jay ran.

Saturday, December 25th, 12:25 p.m.
Boise, Idaho

With the racket blaring from Susie's new musical toy, having a conversation was difficult. Not that Michaels felt much like talking anyhow. Megan was making it perfectly clear by the way she kept touching, leaning, or rubbing against Byron exactly what she wanted her ex-husband to know. At first, the jealousy had been so powerful it had made him feel heartsick and nauseous. Now he was beginning to get pissed off. Megan had a cruel streak he had always known about. He'd loved her in spite of it, but it wasn't pretty to be on the receiving end of it. She could have asked her bearded boy toy to stay home and let Michaels have this time with his daughter, but she wanted to show Susie's father exactly where he stood with her mother—which was outside her house, peering in through a locked window.

He was supposed to stay for lunch, and if he hadn't thought it would upset Susie, he would have already bailed and gone back to his hotel.

At a point when Megan had gone to check on the turkey she was cooking, and Byron had gone to get some more wood for the fire, Michaels remembered the little present Toni had given him. It was in his coat pocket. He walked to where he'd hung his coat, fished the little gift out, and opened it.

When he saw what it was, he laughed.

"What's funny, Dadster?" Susie yelled over the blasting noise she thought was music.

He tucked the present into his shirt pocket. "Nothing, swee-tie, I just remembered something."

Toni had gotten him a pair of electronic earplugs. According to the instructions, they would allow the wearer to hear normal sounds, but would damp any high-decibel noises that might damage a wearer's hearing. Funny woman, his assistant.

His virgil cheeped.

He frowned. He had forwarded all incoming calls to his vox mail. The only messages he should be getting were Priority One coms, and if that was what this was, it was bad news. He checked the caller ID. Jay Gridley.

"What's up, Jay?"

"Chief, we got a major problem here. Somebody just tried to hijack four shipments of plutonium. We headed off three attempts, but at one in France there were a lot of dead bodies after the smoke cleared, and at one in Arizona we were too late, they got away with it. Colonel Howard is on the way with a strike team, we got National Guard and state police and local cops crawling all over the place down there, and about half a bomb's worth of plutonium on the loose.''

"That's awful, but why is this *our* problem? Shouldn't it be CIA for the foreign and regular FBI for the domestic?''

"Well, it's ours because the message giving the yahoo militia who did it the times and places came out of a Net Force workstation, Chief. Right here in HQ.''

"Oh, shit!''

"Yes, sir. You might want to think about going to Arizona or coming back here or something.''

Michaels looked up and saw Megan frowning at him from the hall.

"I'll call you back.''

"What?'' Megan said.

"Something has come up,'' he said. "I'm going to have to miss lunch. Sorry.''

"Big surprise,'' she said. Her voice was bitter. "Got to go save the goddamned world all by yourself again, don't you?''

"Listen, Megan—''

"They can't get along without you for one day? It's Christmas!''

With bad timing, Byron chose that moment to step into the room with an armload of split oak and alder for the fire. "What's going on?''

"Alex isn't staying for lunch.'' She said it loudly.

Susie came out of her music trance. "What? You're leaving? You just *got* here!''

"Daddy's work is more important than staying to visit, honey,'' Megan said. "You know that. He's a very important man.''

Michaels glared at Megan. Then he looked at his daughter. "I'm sorry, baby, but it's an emergency.''

"It's okay. I understand.''

But she didn't understand, he could see that. And Megan wasn't going to make it any easier. "I'll get back as soon as I can to visit you again,'' Michaels said.

"About the time Hell freezes over,'' Megan said.

Michaels gritted his teeth. "In the hall," he said to Megan.

"Excuse me?"

"I'd like a word with you in the hall, please."

Megan stared daggers at him. Michaels went to hug his daughter and kiss her good-bye. "You learn how to work this thing, and when I come back you can show me all the songs you know."

"Exemplary, Dadster. I love you."

"I love you too, little bit. You take care of your mother."

In the hall, Megan stood with her arms crossed, so tight she was almost humming with tension. Byron was right behind her.

"You come all the way out here, drop off a present, and leave. That's just great, Alex. You're a terrific father." Her sarcasm was so acid you could etch glass with it.

And it hurt, just as she knew it would. She knew how to find the cracks in his armor. She always had. And the needle she used to stab him was loaded with poison, just as it had been during the last year of their marriage, and during the divorce. When she got pissed off, she stopped playing fair. He said, his voice tight, "I'm doing the best I can."

"Your best is crappy. If you loved your daughter, you'd do better."

"So you told me a couple of thousand times already. Must be nice to be perfect in every way. How do you stand being around us mere mortals?"

"Hey, take it easy there," Byron said. "No point in getting nasty."

Michaels looked at the big bearded man as if he had just turned into a giant upright toad. "Excuse me? She can tell me I'm a lousy father and that I don't love my daughter, but I can't fight back? Why don't you go get some more firewood, Byron? This is a private conversation."

Megan flared at that. "Anything you can say to me, you can say in front of Byron."

"Really?" Michaels's temper was smoldering now. He was

about to flame on, and if he did, he would say something he would regret. He tried to hold onto as much calm as he could. "Listen, you don't want me here, you and Byron have been doing everything short of tearing each other's clothes off, and I suspect some of that was for my benefit. Fine, you made your point."

"It doesn't matter how I feel about you, Alex. It's how your daughter feels."

"I'm not going to let you beat me over the head with that anymore! I love my daughter and she knows it. If *you* really loved her, you wouldn't be turning her against me at every opportunity. You can really be a bitch when you want, you know?"

That got her attention. It was the first time he'd ever said something that direct about her, and her eyes went wide in surprise.

It got Byron's attention too.

"That's it, pal," he said. "You're outta here!" He reached out and grabbed Michaels's arm with both hands.

Boy, was *that* the wrong thing to do.

Michaels reacted without thinking. He swung his elbow at Byron's head, keeping it in tight, as if he were holding a marble in the crook of his arm, just like Toni had taught him. Bone met bone with a solid *thwack!* and Byron fell as if his legs had suddenly vanished.

Son of a bitch. It worked!

Megan dropped to her knees and grabbed at the fallen man. "Byron! Byron! Are you okay?"

Susie's music boomed from the other room where she played, thankfully oblivious to all this.

Byron blinked, tried to sit up. "What happened? Did I slip on something? Why am I on the floor—?"

He'd live, he was just stunned.

Megan looked up from the fallen man at Michaels. She said, "We're getting married! And Byron wants to adopt Susie!" Her voice practically dripped venom.

Michaels felt his soul freeze, then begin to shrivel. There it was, in black and white, no mistaking it. He had loved this woman beyond measure, and she was doing everything she could to hurt him. How could he have been so blind?

When he could find a breath, he spoke, and his voice was cold. "Congratulations. I'll send you a toaster. But he will adopt Susie over my dead body. I'll spend every penny I have and every penny I can borrow on private detectives and lawyers. And if Byron here spends a night under this roof *before* you get married, you'll find yourself in a custody battle like you wouldn't believe! You want to play rough? Fine."

With that, he turned and stalked out.

In the cold air, snow clouds gathered and threatened. Perfect. Just perfect!

Well. You wanted an excuse to leave, didn't you? Better be more careful what you wish for next time, Alex. You might get that one too.

Damn! He couldn't believe what he had just done. How he had lost control.

Damn!

Compared to what he'd just felt, terrorists stealing nuclear material didn't seem so bad.

15

Michaels rode in the second helicopter of his trip, heading for the hijacking site on Interstate 10, about forty miles west of Phoenix. A small military jet had been waiting for him when the first copter dropped him at the airport in Boise. It had been a straight flight, and fast.

The Arizona sky was clear and sunny, and he could see what the pilot had told him was the Bighorn Mountains ahead of the copter.

John Howard had flown out in one of Net Force's chartered 747's with his strike team, and was setting up a command post at a truck stop just outside Tonopah, Arizona.

The chopper pilot brought his craft in for a landing not far from a pair of helicopters already on the ground. Big Hueys, they looked like. In addition to the copters, the ground was a beehive of activity—cars, trucks, troops, flashing lights.

Practically speaking, it would have made more sense for Michaels to have gone back to HQ; once you got to be the commander of a group like Net Force, you were supposed to be a desk jockey—they paid you for your managing abilities, not to go play in the field. But the idea of sitting in his office parked in front of the computer station and com gear waiting to hear what was going on did not appeal to Alex. He needed to be out doing something after that whole scene in Boise.

Dust and sand kicked up as the copter settled. He saw John Howard in his field uniform, holding on to his cap as the wind blasted him.

Michaels exited the craft and walked to where Howard stood.

"Commander."

"Colonel. How is it going?"

"This way, sir."

Howard led him toward what looked like a Texaco truck stop. Along with a dozen big commercial rigs, clearly local, there were a few smaller Net Force trucks and cars, brought by the cargo version of the 747 that the strike force used. There were a couple of large igloo tents erected behind the main truck stop building, and big power lines snaking into the tents from six rumbling gasoline-powered electrical generators parked near the larger of the tents.

A chilly wind blew across the dry land, but inside the mobile tactical unit—a fiberglass-framed tent the size of a small house—the air was warm. A dozen techs worked on various electronics, mostly computers and com-gear. Several other soldiers in the strike team checked weapons or assembled field equipment. Julio Fernandez looked up, saw Michaels, and saluted.

Howard stopped in front of a big flatscreen on a stand. He picked up a remote and clicked it. A turning-globe map appeared on the screen.

"Here's what happened, as best we can tell," Howard said. "Somebody sent the routing information for four shipments of plutonium scheduled to move today to a paramilitary group that calls itself the Sons of Patrick Henry. Here are the sites."

Red dots pulsed on the map. France, Germany, Florida, and Arizona.

"We got word of the leak from Gridley at HQ at about the time the attacks began. All four went off simultaneously. We got word to the convoys ASAP. The Florida and German convoys took alternate routes and encountered no problems.

"The French attack had already begun, as had the one here. We alerted French authorities, and they got there in time to stop the assault. Eight of the attackers were killed, four wounded seriously, several seemed to have escaped. The driver of the French truck and four of the guards were killed, three more were wounded. Some civilians got caught in the cross fire, all locals.

"We called the Army transport group here too late. By the time the National Guard and state boys and girls showed up, it was all over. The Army lost two drivers, eight more men, and two women. Looks as if the wounded soldiers were executed after they were downed, assault rifle or pistol rounds to their heads. The terrorists took their dead or wounded with them, but there was enough blood without bodies on the road and surrounding territory to know the Army's shooters connected with at least a few of them.

"They left behind a couple of antitank mines to slow pursuit. The state patrol lost two cruisers and three officers. And five civilian cars also got blasted. Six civilians are dead and three more in the hospital probably won't make it. Everything the state and local police can put on the ground or in the air is out looking for the terrorists."

"Jesus."

"Yes, sir. The shipment was en-route from Fort Davy Crockett, Texas, to Long Beach, California, where it was to be taken via ocean vessel to a location that the Army does not wish to reveal to us. Seven pounds of WG plutonium."

"Where do we stand?"

"We know who did it. We know where they are."

"Have you told the local authorities?"

"No, sir. We've sent them off in other directions. It gives them something to do. And if they should get too close, they'll be warned off." He fiddled with the remote. The screen image shifted to an overhead view of a group of small buildings surrounded by a fence. The image zeroed in, growing larger in distinct frames, until details as fine as cars and even a couple of people could be seen.

"This is the nearest bolt-hole the Sons maintain. It's just north of the Gila Bend Indian Reservation, not that far from here. These people apparently own property all over the country, and they've got branches all over the world. We've got the place footprinted with one K1 Albatross spysat, and we've requested that the military shift another one into the same orbit. Which they are doing."

"How good is the sat coverage?"

"Not perfect. Any bird high enough to be in geosynch orbit has to be at least 22,300 miles—36,000 kilometers—and IR or optical resolution to six feet at that height is iffy, especially in a hot desert, so spysats that can see guys running around on the ground have to be a lot lower, which means they are whipping past any given point at speed, so they can't sit and watch one spot. We'll see 'em, but it'll be a fast look. Computers'll fill that in."

"This is where you think they took the plutonium?"

A yellow box blinked on and outlined one of the structures. "There's a tracker built into the outer shell of the radioactive transport box. NRC and NSA don't allow anybody to ship this stuff via FedEx. This is where they took it, sir. GPS puts it in the southwest corner of this building, right there. Since it's Army gear, there's no fudge-factor on the satellite bounce, so we can pinpoint the GPS unit to within plus or minus five feet. It's in there. I doubt they took it out of the box to play with."

"Where is the Army?"

"They're massing their teams thirty miles south of the bolt-hole, on the old Luke Air Force target range. So far, they are holding off, but Military Intelligence is having a fire hose of a pissing match with the FBI over who gets to shoot whom, so everybody is waiting for the spray to settle back in D.C. before anybody moves.''

Michaels waved that off. Nothing they could do out here about weenie-waving uplevels. Somebody would figure out what to do soon enough. Then they'd see who got to step up to the plate.

''What are our options, the tactical considerations, if we get the nod?''

Howard flashed a tiny grin, teeth bright against his chocolate skin.

''Fast and dirty. We can give the Air Force a call, and they can drop a big smart rock that'll squash the Sons flat before they ever know it's coming. Army's got a few of those they'd be happy to use too. End of immediate problem. Of course, that could spread plutonium dust all over the surrounding countryside, which might upset the locals. The evening news would have a field day when they found out, and they likely would notice if the local goats started giving glow-in-the-dark milk.

''Unless they have another chunk of this stuff already, they aren't going to build a fission bomb. Even if they *do* have enough for a critical mass, it isn't like they can just pop open the container and drop it into their bomb like a flashlight battery. It'll take some fine-tuning, and whatever happens, they aren't going to *have* that much time.''

''You don't see any possibility of negotiation here?''

''No, sir. We're talking everything from treason, to multiple murder, to a dozen other local, state, and federal felonies. They give up, they are all history, and they know it. Their manifesto is 'Give me liberty or give me death.' They aren't going to give up, and we can't dick around long enough to let them think about things they might do with that heavy metal they borrowed.''

''I see.''

''It is possible they could have rigged the container with

conventional explosives so if anybody comes after them, it would give us the same scenario as the Air Force attack. Our staff psychologist doesn't think this is likely. They are paranoid enough, but this is a big prize, and they won't be in a hurry to lose it. So he says.

"Our first pass with the locals indicate that the attack wasn't set up very well. They didn't notice anybody poking around until yesterday. This engagement does not appear to have been the result of a long-term, well-laid plan. This is consistent with Gridley's finding that the transmission of the intelligence was less than day and a half ago. They mounted this operation in a hurry, on the fly, and they were lucky to get away with one out of four tries."

"And you don't think they've booby-trapped the container."

"No, sir, I don't. This feels like a come-as-you-are party and they had to hit the ground running. They haven't had time to think about it much.

"I see an infantry-style assault in the dark as our best bet. Since these guys are gun nuts, they've probably got spookeyes and motion detectors, but we can get close enough to knock those out and be on top of them before they have time to figure out what's happening. PEE for the spookeyes, jammers for the motion sensors."

"PEE?"

"They're new, sir. Photosensitive Epilepsy Emitters. Brainwave flashers. They cause seizures or nausea in a lot of people who see them. And at night, they are bright enough to blind a guy using starlight spookeyes anyhow. So the guards watching the dark are either having fits, puking, or bumping into the furniture.

"Jammers shut down the transmitters on wireless sensors. Unless they've got hardwired sensors, they won't know where we're coming from until it's too late. And even hardwired, knowing we're coming and being able to do anything about it is not the same thing. My troops'll be in SIPEsuits. The Sons' surplus AK-47's, M16's, and handgun fire won't get through the armor.''

"What if they have heavier weapons? Rockets, AP, like that?''

"We've got half-a-dozen jump troops who can use parasails well enough to hit a spot the size of a dinner plate from six thousand feet at night, using their spookeyes. I can put them inside to sap the fence before we hit it from outside. I've got green hats, black hats, SEALs, the best of the best on this team. These camo clowns won't know what hit 'em no matter what they're shooting.''

Michaels nodded. "So if uplevels gives us the job, you'll be ready to go when?''

"We're ready right now. Optimal time would be 0230 hours. Most of the terrorists will be asleep. I've run a dozen computer scenarios, and our numbers average about eighty-seven-percent success. Realistic range is from seventy-five to ninety-four percent.''

"You want this one, Colonel?''

Again the smile, larger this time. "Yes, sir. You bet.''

"I'll call the director and see what the situation is.''

Howard watched as Michaels moved off to a quieter part of the tent to use his virgil to call the FBI's director. The colonel looked around at his men and women, confident they could do the job. They were all volunteers, nobody had to be here, and he would lead them into Hell to pull the Devil's tail, secure in the knowledge they would follow without batting an eyelash.

Did he want this operation? Sheeit, he couldn't imagine anything he could want more just at the moment. He could be home, sitting on the couch, digesting Christmas ham and listening to his mother-in-law give him a hard time. Storming a nest of terrorists who'd swiped a chunk of radioactive bomb material was easy duty compared to that. . . .

"Sir, we got the second bird coming on-line, about to step on the location," Fernandez said.

"Copy, Sergeant. Let's see it. Put it on the holoproj so we get a three-dee view."

"As the colonel orders," Fernandez said. "Hey, Jeter! Three-dee!"

Howard moved toward a folding aluminum display table where the holographic projector had been focused. After a few seconds, the image appeared. It started out as a black-and-white. Then the computer furnished false colors so that it looked almost like a model.

"Give it to me from a hundred feet up and three hundred feet out," Howard said to the tech.

"Sir," Jeter said.

The image shifted viewpoints. The computer filled in the details based on images in its memory, but it was probably a pretty accurate representation of the place. A two-story ranch house sat in the middle of the compound, which was surrounded by a chain-link fence, probably ten feet high. There was also what looked like a wooden barn, plus a pole shed that was just a roof and half-a-dozen upright supports, and a smaller storage building behind the house. Four trucks, two cars, and a single-engine high-wing airplane were parked in front of the main house. There were two guards on the gate, and either the spysat's optics or the computer had decided they were both short-haired men in baseball caps, with rifles or carbines slung over their shoulders and holstered side arms. A third guard with a large dog patrolled the fence in the back. A fourth figure, a woman in a dress, stood in front of what appeared to be chickens, tossing feed to the birds. Optics weren't so good that they could see chicken feed from however many thousands of miles up in space, but they were good enough to guess that the woman had long black hair and fair skin. Amazing.

"We have any idea how many are in there, Julio?"

Fernandez drifted over and shook his head. "No, sir. Most

we've seen at a time's half a dozen—four men and two women. No children, thank God. They could have fifteen or twenty in there, given the number of vehicles. IR doesn't work real well through a roof. My guess is, they don't know we know where they are.'' He glanced at his watch.

"Got an appointment, Sergeant?"

"I was supposed to call my mother after I got out of mass. I didn't get around to it."

"Use one of the landlines and call her, Julio. I don't want your mama mad at me because I made you work on Christmas."

Fernandez grinned. "Sir. Thank you."

Howard watched his best soldier—and probably his best friend in the world—amble toward the phone bank.

Michaels came back, clipping the virgil onto his belt, next to his taser.

Howard raised his eyebrows.

"It's ours, Colonel."

Howard grinned, real big.

Michaels shook his head and sighed. "I already had occasion today to remember the old saying 'Be careful what you wish for, you might get it.' Colonel. You just got what you wanted. Merry Christmas. I hope it doesn't blow up in our faces."

16

Saturday, December 25th, 9 p.m.
Bladensburg, Maryland

Hughes had just walked into the safe house apartment and noticed that Platt wasn't there yet when his virgil buzzed. He looked at the ID. Senator White. He felt a stab of worry, even though he knew there was no way White could know where he was and what he was doing there.

"Hello, Bob. Merry Christmas."

"Tom. What's all this I've been hearing about some kind of nuclear material getting stolen?"

"Nothing that concerns us directly. Well, except that the word I hear is that this was another one of those deliberate leaks into the aethernet."

"Jesus Lord."

"Oh, worse than that. My sources tell me the leak came from Net Force Headquarters, right smack dab in the middle of the FBI compound itself."

"I'll have Michaels's head on a platter if that's true! And Walt Carver's ass for desert!"

Now there *was an image.*

"It'll keep until after the holidays, Bob. The terrorists fell down, only one of the attacks was even partially successful, and I am given to understand that that one is about to be rectified by our military and other federal agencies. No great harm was done. Enjoy the season. We can nail all this down when you get back to town, before the session gets rolling. I'm keeping tabs on things from this end. Don't worry."

"All right, if you say so."

Platt swaggered in, circled his hand to his forehead, lips, and heart, and added a couple of circles, then held it out to Hughes in a bastardized salaam. Hughes waved him off.

"Give my love to June and the girls and the grandkids," Hughes said to White.

"I will. Merry Christmas, Tom."

After he switched off the virgil, Platt laughed. "So, our little game ruffled your boss's feathers, hey?"

"Don't worry about him. I've got it covered."

Platt walked to the refrigerator, opened it, and took out a plastic bottle of apple juice. He opened the bottle and drank half the juice in three big swallows. "Seems like such a waste, though. Telling the Sons of Whoever about all the shipments, then telling the feds on 'em."

"Right. I was really going to give those fruitcakes the material to build a working atomic bomb. If they put the thing together, assuming they could, what do you think would be the target city?"

"Couldn't happen to a nicer town," Platt said. "Full of stuck-up assholes who think they're better than the rest of the country." He burped. Took another swig of juice. Said, "Ahh, that's good stuff."

Hughes shook his head. Platt was definitely a loose cannon. Sooner or later, he was going to shoot the wrong way or blow himself and everything around him into bloody pieces. "You need a sense of history," Hughes said. "Washington is our nation's capital. I don't want to destroy it."

"It's just about money, huh?"

"No, it's also about power. But that doesn't mean I have to be a homicidal maniac to get what I want."

"What about the guys guarding the u-rain-e-yum? You don't feel like they're dead because of you? Was your fruit-cakes that hosed 'em."

"I didn't pull any triggers. I didn't tell anybody else to either. If I give you a bread knife and you cut somebody's throat instead of using it to slice bread, that's your fault, not mine."

"Unless you knew I wasn't gonna use it for bread when you sold it to me. And this wasn't exactly no bread knife, was it? More like a headsman's hatchet."

"I didn't ask the Sons, they didn't tell."

"Oh, yeah. The information we fed 'em was for study purposes only."

"No, it was to get things rolling in the direction I wanted them to roll in."

Hughes didn't really think he could explain it to Platt, but for a moment he felt the need to try. "Do you know anything about how the Japanese traditionally made their samurai swords?"

"I have a sheath knife with a Damascus blade," Platt said. "It's kind of like how they make them in Damascus. The Japs fold and sandwich the steel over and over and hammer it out, then temper the edge harder than the blade."

"Right. But do you know how a master swordsmith would get started? How he would actually light the fire for his forge?"

"I dunno, a Zippo?"

Hughes ignored the wisecrack. "The smith would hammer on a piece of iron bar until it began to glow red. Then he'd put the iron into a bed of cypress shavings soaked in sulfur."

"No shit? That must have taken a while, to get the iron that hot just by whacking it with a hammer."

"Exactly. Making the finest swords the world has ever seen is not like ordering a Whopper and fries at the local BK. It takes skill, precision, patience. Which is what we need too. Our goal here is not to blow things up. Let's not forget that.''

''I hear you.''

''Good. I think it's time the subversive group responsible for all these problems on the net steps up to claim credit. Let's show them the manifesto.''

Platt grinned. ''Hot damn. I've been waitin' to do this.''

''Don't embellish it, Platt. Just like I wrote it.''

''Nopraw, hoss. It's bad enough without me fiddlin' with it. The wogs and sand nigrahs are gonna *love* this!''

A loose cannon with a short fuse. If Hughes didn't deactivate him soon, Platt was going to screw the whole thing up. A couple more weeks, a month, they'd be over the hump, and Platt was going to have a fatal accident. Maybe just . . . disappear.

Saturday, December 25th, 9:35 p.m
In the air over southern New Jersey

Toni sat on the left side of the commuter jet, staring into the dark over the ocean in the distance. She couldn't see the water, but she could see where the lights on the land ended, as if sliced off by a knife.

She smiled to herself when she had that thought. There had been some problem when she wanted to take the *kris* onto the plane. They didn't have any trouble with her taser—most of the airlines would allow federal law-enforcement officers to carry tasers or even guns on their planes—but long and wavy-bladed daggers were apparently something else altogether.

No way was Toni going to check the *kris*. Whatever its monetary value, it was irreplaceable, and according to Murphy's Law, if one item got lost in the baggage roulette on this flight, it would be the *kris*.

Airline officials weren't going to allow her to carry the knife, despite the illogic of that versus a taser or a gun. Toni didn't tell them that she could kill somebody with her hands almost as easily as she could do so with a knife. That probably wouldn't have been helpful. In the end, after she threatened to call the FBI and have the plane held on the ground for security reasons, the officials relented. She could take the knife, if she let the flight crew have charge of it until they landed. That was good enough. The *kris* would be in the plane with her, and it was doubtful they could lose it with the doors closed.

The copilot said he'd watch the cardboard box very carefully.

Jay Gridley's call had come as a surprise, but it wasn't such a great loss that she had to leave the annual gathering a little early. She'd gotten a chance to see her family and Guru DeBeers, they'd all exchanged presents, and had eaten a huge Italian Christmas dinner. Mama and Poppa had gone to evening mass with as many of the relatives as they could bully into going with them. The fun part of of the gathering was mostly done, and the inevitable too-close-together friction would be warming up about now. She loved her family, but after a couple of days cooped up in the apartments with them, things could get a little contentious. She'd left them trying to convince her father he shouldn't be getting behind the wheel of his car anymore, and she knew that was a war the family was going to lose.

It surprised her too that Alex had cut short his visit home to fly from Boise to Arizona. He wasn't a field operative, and she worried about him. John Howard wouldn't let Alex do anything dangerous—she hoped—but it still gave her butterflies thinking about Alex being on-site for a hot op. He should be back at HQ, and the strike team should be doing its job without him.

When she'd called him, he'd told her she didn't need to go into HQ herself, but she'd cut that short. If this was important

enough for him to be there, it was important enough for her
to get back to work too.

She leaned back in the seat and stared through the window.
The jet was half-empty. Not a lot of people traveling on
Christmas Day.

Saturday, December 25th, 11:15 p.m.
Sugar Loaf Mountain, Boulder, Colorado

Sitting in the propane-heated spa inset into the redwood deck
behind the cabin, Joanna and Maudie watched the snow fall
into the hot water and melt. The deck had three eight-foot-
high walls of cedar slats and wicker screen surrounding it, to
keep occupants hidden from the neighbors' view, with the
cabin as the fourth wall, but there was no roof. The spa itself
was big enough to seat six people in comfort, maybe eight if
they were on real good personal terms. Upon the steaming
water and the two women in it, fresh snow fell, fat, heavy
flakes, adding to that already piled up eight or ten inches deep
on the deck, pristine save where it had been footprinted by the
naked women going to and from the tub.

Winthrop took another sip from the second bottle of champagne they'd bought, splurging their own money for the good
vintage after they'd polished off Maudie's admirer's gift.

Maudie raised her glass and watched a few snowflakes hit
the wine. She said, "Problem with this is that you get spoiled
real quick. After the expensive stuff, the cheap champagne
tastes like something you'd clean your oven with."

Winthrop waved her own glass. "Hear, hear." She reached
across the big oval-shaped fiberglass tub with her foot and
snagged the floating thermometer. She dragged it to her, lifted
it, and looked at it.

"Hundred and six," she said. "And the air temperature is
what? Twenty, twenty-five?"

"Sounds about right."

Winthrop shook her head, and the melting snow fell from her hair into the water with a tiny *slush!* sound.

"I wonder what the poor folks are doing," Maudie said. "You know, it might not get any better than this. Friends, Moet & Chandon, hot water, and snow."

"Amen, sister. Well, except for maybe a couple of hunky young studs."

"Wouldn't do much good in this," Maudie said. She dragged her free hand through the water. "You never heard of the Boiled Noodle Effect?"

They both laughed.

From inside the cabin, a com chirped, a one-two . . . three rhythm.

"That's mine," Winthrop said. "Damn."

"Don't answer it. Anybody asks when you get back to work, tell them we were in a digital dead zone. Mountains and all."

She considered it for a moment. "Nah. I better. Could be my family."

Maudie shrugged, waved at the French doors. "Go and sin no more."

Winthrop stepped out of the water, and felt an almost immediate chill despite the red glow of her skin as she padded through the snow to where a pair of thick beach towels hung on a rack next to the doors, under the roof's overhang enough so they didn't get rained or snowed on.

"Damn, girl, if I was into women, you'd be my first choice," Maudie said. "You got a *great* butt. Speaking strictly as somebody who knows how much work it takes to get one to look like that, of course."

Winthrop grinned. "Beauty is only skin deep," she said as she wrapped the towel around her. It was cool, but not too cold.

"Yeah, but a great butt is a joy forever!"

Inside the cabin the fire crackled in the big stone fireplace.

Winthrop walked over a patch of cold wood floor, onto the Oriental rug, and picked up her com.

The caller ID showed the name "Lonesome Jay Gridley." She grinned in spite of herself. "Hello?"

"Lieutenant. I take it you haven't been watching the network news lately?"

"Nope. I've been enjoying champagne and a hot tub lately."

"I thought not, or you'd have called. A few things you need to know."

She listened as he filled her in on the situation with the terrorists attacks on nuclear transports. When he was done, she said, "Christ. I'll catch the next plane I can get back to HQ."

"That isn't necessary, I believe we can get along without you for a couple more days. Enjoy your hot tub."

"What aren't you telling me, Gridley? I hear something else hiding there. What is it?"

"Not much. That leak I mentioned that seemed to come from inside Net Force?"

"Yes?"

"It came from your station."

"What?"

"Yes, ma'am, no doubt about it. You weren't here when it went out, of course, and we all know you had nothing to do with it, but I'm sure glad it didn't come from *my* station. Byebye. Talk to you later."

He discommed.

Winthrop stared at her com as if it were a rat come to life in her hand.

Oh, *man*! This *sucked*!

17

Howard looked around. His strike team troops were loaded in three transport vehicles, and they were parked in a dusty stretch of desert with a slightly overcast sky. Without their headlights, it would be very dark out here. The troop vehicles were highly modified Toyota Land Cruisers—mostly just the engines, frames, and wheels left from the originals—and they all wore flat-black carbon-fiber stealth shells. Close-range radar was cheap, a rig swiped from any big powerboat or sailboat would be sufficient for a ranch house, and since they had the cruisers, they might as well use them.

The trick was not so much to be completely invisible, but rather to be hard to see and identify—until you were right on top of whoever was looking at you. Even the new stealth gear wasn't a hundred percent efficient on a land vehicle, but it would give a radar operator an odd blip that might be mistaken for ground clutter or maybe even a herd of deer or something. Probably the stealth shells wouldn't even be necessary; so far, there hadn't been any radar signature emitted from the ranch, so maybe the terrorists hadn't had time to get a unit, or if they had, to set it up. But you tried to cover all the bases as best you could, just in case.

Each of the vehicles held six troopers, suited, locked, and loaded. The assault suits were modified from Regular Army SIPEs, slimmed down a bit since field operations were usually in and out, and the LOL—live-off-the-land—systems weren't necessary. The tactical suits should be enough to turn away what the average terrorist had to shoot at them. The shirt-vests and pants were cloned-spidersilk hardweave, with overlapping body pockets lined with ceramic plates. Boots and helmets were Kevlar, with titanium inserts in the helmets.

The slimback CPUs were armored and shockproofed, and the tactical CPUs did everything from encrypting long-range radio and short-range LOSIR units, to downloading and uploading sat-links and giving motion-sensitive heads-up displays. Except for the LOSIR headsets—line-of-sight-infrared tactical coms—the strike team would keep radio silence until after they had secured the objective. And since LOSIR signals were encrypted, even if the terrorists had a full-range scanner, they wouldn't get anything but gibberish. Besides, by the time the strike team was close enough for the terrorists to scan and hear LOSIR, it would be too late even if they *could* understand the voxtrans.

Weapons of choice were H&K 9mm subguns, and H&K tactical pistols. They had considered using the 5.65mm OICW, with the 20mm grenade launcher. The bullpup-stocked weapon had an outstanding bracketing/tracking target laser, and it could drop an explosive round into a trench where you couldn't even see an enemy, but Howard didn't completely trust it. Too many bells and whistles with the cameras and computers, and besides, they didn't want *any*thing blowing up on this operation, not even a little bit. Bad enough that the SIPEsuit radios went out every time a thunderstorm passed within a parsec, or that the tactical comps sometimes got confused and had to be reset on the fly.

Howard himself carried a much more unofficial weapon, a 1928 Thompson .45-caliber submachine gun that had belonged to his grandfather. The vintage gun wore a loaded fifty-round drum and had the gangster front grip and sight-through-the-top bolt-slot. He almost never carried the beast, since it weighed about fifteen pounds and was a bear to haul around, but somehow it had felt like the right thing to do on this operation. Normally, he'd be using a .30-caliber assault rifle, or a 7.62, but like the S&W revolver strapped to his right hip, the tommygun was a good-luck piece—an old, but still *functional,* good-luck piece.

His antique revolver and Chicago typewriter notwithstanding, whoever these camo clowns were, they didn't have the state-of-the-art combat gear that Net Force had.

Howard would be going in his Humvee, which also wore a radar-slipping shell. He glanced over at his ride and saw Fernandez grinning back at him from the driver's seat, camo paint darkening his face below the SIPEsuit's helmet.

In war, sooner or later, this was what it came down to: troops going in against troops. The Air Force could drop tons of bombs or smart missiles, the Navy could shell or hard-rain rocket a target from fifty miles offshore, but in the end, it was the infantry that had to go in, to take and hold the ground.

Next to Howard, Commander Michaels said, "I would say I'd like to go with you, Colonel, but that wouldn't be true. I'm a lousy soldier. I'd trip over something and get in somebody's way."

Howard grinned. "Yes, sir, and that is why you pay us the big bucks. I expect that Assistant Commander Fiorella would have my family jewels if I allowed you to go along anyhow."

Michaels smiled.

Howard looked at his watch. "The transport plane will be entering the drop zone in thirty-three minutes. It's running whisper-props, but even so, out here, sound carries. It won't slow down and even if the terrorists do hear it, they'll be listening for a change in the engine sound, which they won't hear. If we work it right, our assault teams should be flashing puke-and-dizzy lights hot and hard to distract the guards as our four sappers float into the compound on their parawings. I've got a man standing by who will simultaneously cut the power line to the ranch. They've got backup power next to the storage shed, a little gas or diesel generator, but it won't kick on automatically, somebody will have to go out there and start it. Time that happens, he'll have company waiting for him.

"We've had a series of spysats providing continual footprints of the area, so we pretty much know where every terrorist is. We'll have continual coverage through the expected duration of the attack, and a little longer too, just in case things don't go quite as planned. There are three guards posted, two at the front, one at the rear, and if it goes as planned, they will be taken out by the time the two vehicles reach the fence. The main gate is to the front, but there are two smaller gates to the rear, at the north and south corners. Alpha Team will hit the main building with flashbangs, while Beta Team covers the rear of the house, the barn, and the storage shed. Delta Team will patrol outside what's left of the fence in case anybody slips past us. With any luck at all, we'll have them rounded up before they can get their pants on.

"Of course, it's said that no battle plan survives first contact with the enemy, so we'll just have to go and see."

Michaels nodded.

Howard glanced at his watch again. "All right, people, this is it. Let's roll!"

"Good luck, Colonel. Give 'em hell."

"Thank you, sir. We will."

Howard hurried to the Humvee. They had gotten an exact distance from the compound to this location from the footprinting satellite. They'd be running on spookeyes without lights, but the terrain was mostly flat with a little scrub, and they had a route mapped, so they should be able to calculate their speed and distance and nail it to the second.

"Drive, Sergeant. And switch off the brake lights. I don't want the yahoos to see us flashing red because you stopped for a lizard in our path."

"Already done, sir. I've been down this road before."

Fernandez slid his helmet visor down and clicked his spook-eyes on, then cranked the engine and moved out. Howard picked his computerized helmet up from the floor by his feet and slipped it on, put the visor down, and lit his own night-vision scope. He buckled his three-point seat belt into place, snapping the black steel latch shut with a hard *clack*!

The landscape seemed to light up in that eerie, washed-out green that the starlight amplifiers traded for the seemingly opaque darkness. Then the suit's computer kicked in, adding false colors to give a more realistic image, and it was almost like driving in a somewhat dim and hazy afternoon.

"You don't think this pointy-nose plastic stuff is really going to hide us from radar, do you?" Fernandez said. "Seems like a shame to ruin a perfectly good truck by hanging all this crap on it."

Howard said, "I don't think the boys in the ranch had time to set up a full-scale HQ. They only had a day and some to plan the attack. I'd be surprised if they had a mobile field unit roll into this location with radar or doppler."

"Would you look at that," Fernandez said. "Bugs Bunny!"

A jackrabbit angled across their path, then cut sharply back and stopped as the Humvee rolled past. It sat there watching as the cruisers also zipped past, turning its head to track them. Howard looked over his shoulder at the small creature.

I wonder what a rabbit thinks when he sees four black vehicles with pointy-nose plastic crap hanging all over them rumble past his burrow at two in the morning.

"There's something you don't see every day," Fernandez said.

"Excuse me?"

"Probably what the rabbit was thinking."

Howard smiled. They'd been serving together for a long time. Must be a little telepathic spillage.

He was pumped, but even so, there was this . . . weary feeling, as if he could stretch out and take a long nap, could sleep for a week, and still not wake up feeling refreshed. What was this all about, this lethargy? It was worrisome. Well. He'd have to deal with it later. He had business to take care of just now. Serious business.

Alex Michaels walked back to the AWD car they'd given him, a little Subaru Outback. The strike team was out of sight in the darkness, heading for a rendezvous with the bad guys ten miles away. He should have stayed at the tent HQ back at the Texaco truck stop in Tonopah, but even if he wasn't a front-line soldier, he had wanted to come at least this far. By the time he got back to the tent, Howard's attack would be in full swing, maybe even over. All things going well.

He started the car, then headed back to the dirt road a mile or so away that would take him to the highway a couple miles past that.

This was a risky business, the assault. If it went sour, it would probably be bad enough so he'd be looking for a new job.

He laughed to himself. It seemed like every time he turned around, his job was at risk. But that went with the territory. Steve Day, the first Commander of Net Force, had never mentioned that part to him. Maybe if he hadn't been killed by that Russian computer genius's assassins, he would have eventually gotten around to telling Michaels about it. . . .

It was really dark out here, the only source of illumination his headlights, and he bounced along for what seemed like a lot longer than a mile, the little car rocking pretty hard over some of the dips and holes in the ground. He reached the dirt road.

Finally.

For just a moment, he wasn't sure about which way to turn.

Then he remembered he had followed Howard's Humvee off the road into the desert by making a right; therefore, he should turn left to head back in the direction of the highway. He hadn't been tracking on the odometer, but it seemed like that had been a couple-three miles.

Alex paused, then made up his mind. There was no danger, he knew, not to himself nor to Colonel Howard's strike team. The terrorist camp was several miles away—at least four or five—so he could head this way for a couple of miles. If he didn't hit the highway by then, he'd turn around or check his virgil . . . something he was reluctant to do. That would be admitting defeat. He had always hated to ask for directions, a legacy from his father, and even looking at a map was considered unmanly in his family. The Michaels didn't get lost, according to the old man.

He turned left and picked up a little speed now that he was on a road of sorts.

A large bug splashed against the windshield in front of his face, leaving a blob of greenish goo. The body fluids of that one joined those of several other low-flying moths, mosquitoes, beetles, and whatevers. Apparently the insects didn't hibernate for the winter here. He wasn't driving that fast, and you'd think they could see him coming for a long way off, but they kept splattering against the front of the car. He turned the wipers on, smeared the bug goo around, added the washer fluid to the mix, and managed to clear a patch of glass he could see through.

The road dipped into a gully, then came up, and he rolled over several half-buried rocks in the dirt, jolting him hard enough so his head nearly hit the ceiling.

He didn't remember that part of the drive coming in. None of it looked familiar. Dark as it was, he couldn't see anything but what was in the cone of his headlights, but surely he should have reached the highway by now.

Had he somehow taken a wrong turn?

He looked at his odometer. The highway couldn't have been

more than three or four miles from the dirt road. He must have come that far, he'd been driving for at least twenty or thirty minutes. It was 2:20 a.m. Howard would be hitting the terrorists in five minutes.

Maybe it was time to check the GPS.

Well, not yet. Give it another mile. If he didn't see the highway by then, he'd turn around and backtrack.

Michaels shook his head. Brother. Wouldn't that be a story for the folks at HQ? You heard about how Commander Michaels got lost in the desert?

I don't think *so, Alex, m'boy.*

There was a hillock ahead that curved to the left. As he rounded the curve, the dirt was loose, and the car fishtailed and slipped traction, so he slowed to a crawl. To his left, there was a little stand of scrub trees, stunted pines or some such, none of which looked to be more than ten or twelve feet tall. That was practically a forest out here.

A man stepped out of the scrub growth. He wore chocolate-chip desert camouflage pants and a jacket, and held a short assault weapon in his hands, pointed at Michaels's car. He waved the weapon, his meaning clear: Pull over.

An AK-47?

For a moment, just a moment, Michaels thought it must be one of Howard's troops, but then he knew the man was all wrong. Wrong clothes, wrong gun, wrong place.

Fear spasmed in Michaels' belly as he realized who this must be:

It was one of the terrorists—!

Oh, shit! What had he done?

Better still—what was he going to do now?

18

Howard looked at his watch. A gift from his wife on his thirty-fifth birthday, it was a Bulova Field Grade Marine Star, with a black face and a dial light, an analog quartz whose battery was recharged by the smallest body motion. It wasn't the most expensive watch made, not by a long shot, but she had saved for a year to buy it. It kept dead-on time, and right now the sweep second hand was moving toward 0225 hours. Thirty seconds left . . .

It was time.

"Ready to rock, Sergeant?"

"Just call me Elvis."

The four vehicles were rolling, slowed somewhat to time their arrival. The compound was just ahead, a smear of hard yellow flaring in the spookeyes' optical field from the security light mounted high on the wall of the barn. Which illumination should be going out just . . . about . . . now . . .

The compound went dark.

"Better make sure your filters are up, Colonel, the light show is about to begin."

"I've been down this road before, Sergeant."

Both men smiled.

Time slowed for Alex Michaels as the gunman walked toward his car. It seemed as if he had days, weeks, *months* to decide what to do. The problem seemed to be that he couldn't move. Well, he could, but the speed of his movement bogged down to match the gunman's walk. Just to lift his hand from the steering wheel seemed to take forever.

In what couldn't have been more than a couple of seconds, Alex sorted through all the possibilities he could think of. He could try to talk his way out of it. He could stomp the gas pedal and haul ass, ducking low so that when the guy opened up on him he might not get hit. He could pull his taser and hope to get the needles into the man in camo gear before he was hosed with jacketed death. He could shit or go blind.

So many possibilities. How to choose?

The gunman got to within a foot or two of the door, and motioned with the assault rifle's muzzle for Michaels to roll his window down.

Choose, Alex. Choose!

The PEE lights strobed like an electrical storm gone insane. The polarizing filters in the suit's helmet visor blocked the effect—plus they were behind the lights, and thus got only a partial hit anyhow.

"Gate dead ahead!" Fernandez yelled. "Looks like our sappers have taken it down along with the guards. Might as well have rolled out a red carpet for us."

"Don't count those chickens just yet."

The Humvee rolled through the gate, and one of the sappers waved at it as it went past.

"Alpha has landed," came a voice over Howard's LOSIR. "We're in the door."

"Beta's got the back door," came another voice.

"Delta's on patrol," came a third.

Fernandez slewed the Humvee to a stop by the shed where the chickens were kept, not far from the barn. Howard bailed out, the Thompson held ready, and Fernandez was next to him in two seconds.

"You didn't lock the keys in the car, did you?"

"Negative."

"Good, I hate it when you do that."

Truth of it was, Howard himself should have stayed outside the fence in command mode and directed traffic from there. He didn't really have a function here, except as backup for Alpha, which they ought not to need—

"We're in, got static, stand by—"

Howard heard gunfire, both over his helmet phones and in real time. It came from inside the main house.

"Two terries down, two down! Alpha intact!" Alpha's team leader called. "Target just down the hall, stand by." There came the sound of more gunfire from inside.

"So far, so good—" Howard began.

He felt the impacts of the bullets before he heard the shots, and the incoming rounds hit hard enough to jolt him. *Thump, thump, thump,* three of them, all on the left side, but the armor held—

Damn! Howard turned, saw a man and a woman in the doorway to the barn, illuminated by the bright yellow-orange of their muzzle flashes as they fired bursts from fully automatic rifles at him and Fernandez. Now and then, a tracer left a glowing red trail in the darkness. Bad idea—tracers worked both ways—

Another bullet hit Howard on the torso. It felt like being whacked with a hammer.

Shit—!

Michaels took a deep breath, then pressed the button to lower the window with his left hand while he carefully pulled the taser from his belt with his right hand.

The terrorist stepped right up to the car.

"Excuse me, officer," Michaels said. "What's the problem?"

Michaels already had his left hand on the door's latch. He took another deep breath, then stared off in the distance and saw a series of dim light flashes. That would be the attack on the compound.

"What the hell is *that*?" Michaels said, still looking into the distance.

The gunman must have caught a glint of light peripherally. He glanced away from Michaels to get a better look—

Michaels yanked the latch up, threw his weight against the door, and slammed it into the surprised gunman. It wasn't enough to knock him down, but it did rock him off balance.

"God damn—!" the man began. He flailed with the weapon and his empty hand, trying to catch his footing, but slid a little in the loose dirt on the road. He recovered a hair, enough so he could swing the assault rifle around—

Michaels pulled the door shut. A little too hard—the door's latch handle came off in in his hand—but he didn't have time to worry about that. He thrust his taser through the open window, pressed the laser aiming stud, saw the red dot on the center of the man's chest, and fired the weapon. It seemed to take eons—

The man jerked, juttered toward the car as the capacitor needles fed him however many thousand volts they held. The assault rifle nosed skyward and went off five or six times in one long noise—*blaaaat!*—flashing red-orange and making less noise than it seemed it should. The gunman spun to his left and corkscrewed, hit the dirt, and continued to spasm, the gun still gripped tightly in one hand but no longer firing—

Michaels couldn't open the door, since the handle had broken off in his hand, but he grabbed the window frame and hauled himself headfirst out of the car, did a sloppy dive and forward roll, and came up next to the downed man. He bent and jerked the AK-47 away from the gunman, then took two steps back and pointed the weapon at the man.

If this sucker tried anything, he was going to blast his sorry ass to kingdom come!

The tasered gunman didn't seem too interested in doing much of anything just at the moment.

Michaels exhaled out his held breath. Damn—

Howard looked at the man and woman who had opened up on him and Fernandez. Oddly enough, what he found himself thinking was: *Tracers. Huh. Probably one every fifth or tenth round. What had they been doing out in the barn? Why hadn't somebody picked up their heat sigs?*

Next to him, Julio turned and leveled his H&K subgun at the shooters.

Howard swung his own heavy weapon around—

"Shit!" Julio said. He dropped to one knee, his return fire chewing up the ground five meters in front of him. "I'm hit," he said. His voice was calm, as if he was talking about what he was going to have for breakfast.

One of the shooters must have armor-piercing rounds—

But they weren't using concealment or cover, just standing there hosing, so Howard V-stepped hard to his left, brought the Thompson up to a quick-kill point, and triggered a five-round burst at the man. *Braap!* Orange tongues lanced from the tommygun, and the Cutts compensator on the end of the barrel took part of the flaming orange and spewed it upward, forming a fiery letter "L" in the darkness that helped keep the recoil down and the barrel from climbing too much.

Without waiting to see the effect on the man, he shifted his index to the woman. *Braap!*

The shooters collapsed, and the man beat the woman to the ground by maybe a half second.

Howard spun three-sixty, looking for more attackers. Clear. His heads-up showed him a strike-team suit signature as one of the sappers moved in toward the two downed terrorists. The sapper waved an "I-got-'em" at the colonel, who turned away.

"Julio?"

"I'm okay, John," he said. "Took it just above the knee, to the inside. I don't think it hit the bone. Of course, I could be wrong."

"We have the objective," Alpha's team leader said over the LOSIR. "Eight terries down, Alpha Team secure, no casualties."

Howard blew out a big breath. Thank God. He said, "Copy, Alpha, good work. Doc, Julio took one in the leg. We're at the southwest corner of the chicken coop, get over here PDQ."

He couldn't see them, but the term LOSIR was not strictly accurate—there was always a little bleed, enough to keep coms working when somebody ducked behind a tree or wandered off center.

Doc, the medic, rode with Delta. "On the way, sir. Let me drop my passengers. Forty-five seconds. Go! Out, out!"

Thirty seconds later, Delta Team's vehicle, empty except for the driver, Doc, plowed right through a section of fence, slapped it flat, and skidded to a stop ten feet away. Doc bailed and ran to where Julio sat, both hands pressed against the hole in his armor.

Doc flicked his helmet spotlight on and used a suitcutter to open a big flap in the leg of the wounded sergeant's armor. He sliced away the pants leg to reveal the hole in the flesh. He bent the leg up and looked at the exit wound.

"Looks like twenty-caliber high-velocity hardball," Doc said. "Through-and-through, missed the bone, no expansion. Neat little hole about the size of a drinking straw, bullet hot enough to cauterize the wound. We'll have to clean out fibers. Otherwise, I don't see any problem."

Doc grinned, leaned away from the leg, and looked at Fernandez. "Jesus, some people will do anything to get a few days off."

Fernandez said, "You do what you have to do to get a break."

Howard nodded, relieved. "Let's hear it, people," he said into the LOSIR.

The reports came in.

"A walk in the park, sir," Alpha's team leader said. "We make it six terries KIA, in the house, two wounded but still alive, two undamaged and in restraints. Objective is patent, no leaks, b.g. radiation levels normal. Send Doc on in when he gets a minute."

"Nobody came out this way," Delta's team leader said.

"Three terry guards down, one KIA, two slightly damaged," the head of the sapper team said. "They didn't lay a glove on our guys."

"Hell, we've been watching *paint* dry back here," Beta's team leader said. "We coulda stayed home and seen it on TV for all we had to do. We won't even have to clean our weapons." He sounded disgusted.

The sapper who had gone to check out the shooters in the barn came out carrying a big bunched sheet of heavy material, black on one side and silvered on the other. "Found this in the barn, Colonel," he said.

Howard looked at the sensor shroud and nodded. That was why nobody picked up a heat sig on the terrorists who'd been hiding in the barn. They'd been shielded. He'd thought about radar, but not about heat-sink camo. A mistake on his part, but fortunately not a fatal one.

Howard blew out a sigh. They had the stolen nuclear material and Julio was going to be okay. It could have been a lot worse.

Time to call Michaels.

"Commander?"

"Colonel. Everything okay?"

"Yes, sir. Objective achieved, terrorists neutralized, we have one minor injury on our side. Sergeant Fernandez picked up a little scratch."

Sitting on the ground with his leg bandaged and an amp of

dorph injected to kill his pain, Fernandez said, "Bet you wouldn't call it that if it was *your* leg."

Howard grinned.

"Outstanding, Colonel! Congratulations. Please pass it on to your team."

"Thank you, sir, I will. We'll see you at field HQ soon as we get things cleaned up here."

"I'm on my way there now," Michaels said.

Howard frowned. "Sir? You aren't there yet?"

"I, uh, took a little ride in the country," Michaels said. "I picked up a . . . hitchhiker you might find it interesting to talk to when you get back."

"Sir?"

"Never mind, Colonel, I'll explain it when I see you. You got us out of a nasty spot and I appreciate it. I'll make sure the whole country appreciates it."

"Sir. Discom."

After he signed off, Howard considered his relationship with Commander Alexander Michaels. The man wasn't bad, for a civilian. Not bad at all.

"Can we hurry this up and go home, sir?" Fernandez said. "I have an early tango lesson I don't want to miss."

Howard laughed.

19

Tyrone Howard thought he might just go nova, might just shatter into a million billion pieces.

He sat on Bella's bed, his arms around her, and they kissed. Everything he knew about kissing she had taught him in the last couple of months, and he thought he was starting to get the hang of it. Her back felt hot under his hands, even through her shirt, and there wasn't a strap across her smooth skin. . . .

She broke the kiss and let out a big sigh. "You have to leave now, Tyrone. I'm supposed to go to my aunt's house and we have to lift in like ten minutes. I have to change clothes."

"Uh-huh," he said. He leaned in and kissed her again. That went on for another minute or two. She leaned back.

"Really, Tyrone. I have to go."

"Uh-huh." He kissed her some more. It wasn't as if she was trying real hard to get away, given as how she had her hands on the back of his head pulling him closer.

Finally, she pulled away again and said, "I'll see you at the mall tomorrow, you duplicate?"

"Uh-huh. I doop that." He reached for her, but this time she put one hand on his chest and held him off. "Come on, Ty."

"Okay." He blew out a breath. "Okay. But it's hard to leave."

"I bet it is," she said, smiling. "Here, let me make it easier for you." She took his hand in both hers, kissed it on the palm, then pressed it against her left breast.

His mouth fell open, his brain went into vapor lock, he forgot how to breathe. His bug eyes must make him look like a giant frog.

It was the most exciting moment of his life.

She moved his hand away from her warmth and gave it back to him. She grinned real big and stood. "Shoo. Go." She waved at him with both hands in a sweeping motion.

He stood, knowing what a zombie must feel like. He would jump off the top of a tall building if she wanted.

Explode. He was going to just . . . blow up and splatter all over the room. It would make a big, gooey mess. How could he not? He couldn't *stand* it!

Monday, December 27th, 2:00 p.m.
Quantico, Virginia

Julio Fernandez was in what passed for the infirmary at HQ. It wasn't much, just a few beds in a small ward, and he was the only patient. He lay on the bed flipping through the commercial entcom channels on the TV, looking for something that would keep his attention. He didn't need to be here. Doc had swabbed out the little hole in his leg and patched it with synskin, then given him a tetanus shot and told him to avoid heavy squats or marathon running for a few days. But Net Force policy was that certain injuries required compulsory treatment, which in the case of gunshot wounds meant at least a twenty-four-hour medical observation period. It had to do with liability and insurance and crap like that. He wasn't going to sue anybody. He knew that, the colonel knew it, but a lot of people sued a lot of other people these days—there were more lawyers in D.C. than there were roaches—so they'd stuck him in bed, started an IV with antibiotics, and given him the television remote. They'd also given him one of those short, open-up-the-back hospital gowns.

He looked at the time sig on the TV screen. He'd come back from the raid and been examined at noon. So he was stuck here until noon tomorrow. Boredom and cafeteria food loomed and threatened. Jesus.

A nurse came in, and with her was the colonel. He grinned real big.

"Very funny, sir. Wait until the next time you get shot."

"Not my policy, Sergeant Fernandez. I don't make the rules, I just do what they tell me."

The colonel sat on the foot of the bed and glanced up at the tube. "Anything good on?"

"Best things are reruns of *I Love Lucy* and trash sports. I just saw the middleweight North American sumo winner—he goes maybe one-eighty, two-hundred—beat the heavyweight— a fat guy pushing seven hundred pounds. Big guy came roaring in, the little guy stepped aside and tripped him. Fatso fell out of the ring, shook the camera he hit so hard."

"David and Goliath," Howard said. "There is a precedent."

"David cheated, he used a sling."

"Goliath had a sword."

"Yeah, and only a fool brings a knife to a gunfight."

"How's the leg?"

"Fine. I could take you on the obstacle course right now."

"Uh-huh. I'd almost rather be doing that than going home."

"Your mother-in-law still there?"

"Until next Sunday."

"Serves you right. Sir."

"I stopped by the office on the way over here. Seems there was a complaint about you from one of the civilian instructors in the feeb unit. Did you know that you were 'vicious, brutal, perhaps even psychotic'? A man unfit for Net Force service, and a man who was very likely a threat to public safety?"

"Yes, sir, I believe that pretty much sums me up."

"What did you do to this Horowitz, Sarge?"

"I leaned on his desk and told him he should think less about posturing and more about doing his job."

"Lord, Sergeant, how do you expect to get away with such behavior? What kind of savage are you?"

"An unrepentant one, sir."

"Well, I will send word to Mr. Horowitz that I have taken his counsel and disciplined you appropriately." Howard reached over and took the TV remote, pointed it over his shoulder at the wall-mounted set, and clicked the power off. "No television for the next hour, Sergeant."

"I thought the idea was *punishment,* sir."

Both men grinned.

By the time she got back to HQ, Joanna Winthrop knew the party was over. The terrorists had been taken down, the stolen plutonium recovered, and the only thing she had to do now was figure out who had gotten into her workstation and used it to give the Sons of Whoever the information about the shipments.

But somebody had told her that Julio Fernandez had been shot and was in the infirmary and so, instead, she bought a small vase of flowers and went to see him.

He was the only patient in the infirmary. Since a lot of the Net Force staff had opted for the long holiday, including, apparently, the medical staff, the place had an echoey feel to it.

"Sergeant Fernandez."

"Lieutenant Winthrop."

"I heard you got shot."

"A scratch. I'm stuck here overnight, SOP, but I could go out dancing if they'd let me."

She put the vase on the table next to the bed. "You're just lying here, doing nothing? No books, no entcom?"

"The colonel was here, you just missed him. He turned the set off. I'm being punished."

She raised her eyebrows. "For being shot?"

He chuckled. "No, even Howard's not that hard-assed."

He told her about his computer class.

It was a funny story. When he was done, she laughed. "Tough CO, isn't he?"

"Yeah. I really wanted to see how the middleweight wrestler was going to do against the light heavyweight."

They both laughed.

"So, how are you doing?" Julio asked. "I heard about the workstation business."

"Oh, don't worry about that. I'll figure it out."

"Any suspects?"

"At the top of my list? Jay Gridley. He doesn't like me. He thinks I slept my way into this job."

"Seriously?"

"That he thinks I used my feminine wiles? Or that he planted the leak in my station? Yes to the former, no to the latter. We aren't buddies, but I respect his abilities. Though if you tell him I said so, I'll deny it."

"Deny what?"

"He might keep stuff from me, but I don't think he's nasty—or stupid—enough to try to implicate me in a federal crime. After this assignment, I'm back with our unit, so I'm no threat to his position. And he has to know I'm going to figure out who did it. Just a matter of time."

There was a moment of quiet when neither of them spoke.

"So how was it?" she asked. "The sortie?"

"By the numbers," he said. "The bad guys weren't in our league. They were outsmarted, outmaneuvered, and outgunned. Only mistake we made was mine. I'd been awake, I wouldn't be spending the night here with my leg propped up and a draft on my butt. One of the yabbos hiding in a sensor nest had a few rounds of AP in her weapon. Fortunately, she was either rattled or a lousy shot. She cooked off most of a thirty-round stick and only nicked me one time. Guy with her was a better shooter, but he was using hardball and tracer, his ammo couldn't pierce the suits.''

"Too bad I missed it," she said.

"You've been on a few field ops."

"Nothing lately. The colonel thinks I'm more useful in front of a computer. Last time I was in the field, I was in the HQ tent thirty miles away from the action."

"He's right," Fernandez said. "Grunts like me are a dime a dozen, but a computer genius is harder to replace."

She smiled. "I need to get back to work. Anything I can do for you?"

She saw him hesitate a second, and wondered if there would be an off-color remark. If he was looking for an opening, this was a good one.

He shook his head. "No, ma'am, but thank you for asking. I'll catch up on my sleep. See you when I get out." He flashed her a nice smile.

She resisted a sudden urge to lean over and kiss him. She was really beginning to like this guy.

"Later, Julio. We'll talk about computers when we get all this straightened out"

"I'd like that. Thanks for stopping by." Another hesitation, then: "Jo."

Jay Gridley had given up on the cowboy scenario because it felt too slow. True, speed in a scenario didn't translate to RT—real time—but if you were poking along on a horse when you felt like racing on a big Harley motorcycle, it made a subjective difference.

So now Jay turned to one of his favorite action heroes,

borrowing from one of the early classic James Bond movies, *Thunderball*.

Over the landscape he flew, zipping through the air with the famous Bell Rocket Belt on his back.

Of course, in RW, the Bell device was not a belt at all, but a large and very heavy backpack. And it didn't have much of an operational range in RW either. Jay had done some research when designing his scenario. The original rocket belt was essentially nothing more than a pair of fuel tanks, some handlebars, a throttle, and a couple of rocket nozzles. How it worked was, hydrogen peroxide sprayed into a fine mesh, producing a very hot and hard steam that spewed from the rocket nozzles with a few hundred pounds of thrust. It was loud, dangerous, and you only had twenty-some seconds of lift, maybe thirty with the right fuel mixture and tuned nozzles, and that was it. You could lean in the direction you wanted to go, and later some maneuvering jets were added, but if you were a hundred feet up in the air when the gas ran out, you were going to fall and smash into the ground real hard.

A later version, the Tyler Belt, was a bit more efficient and gave a little more flight time, but the hops were still short and quick. A small jet-engine model that was theoretically capable of giving the wearer half an hour in the air had eventually been designed, but the U.S. military had claimed exclusive use of the new engine for its Cruise missiles.

So the personal backpack craft of science fiction just kind of fizzled out. The existing rocket belts wound up in museums or television commercials or movies, but that was it.

Jay's version of the rocket belt had a secret—but theoretically possible—fuel and a miniature jet engine that gave him an hour in the air and an automatic safety reserve to allow him to land when the fuel ran low. He could have given it infinite power in VR, of course, but that took some of the fun out of it. Realistic limits were better for the scenarios he created. Any fool could do fantasy; it took some skill to keep it believable.

Anyway, while it wasn't as fast as a jet or even his pedal-to-the-metal Viper, it was a real rush to fly along with the wind blowing in your face and ruffling your hair, to be able to leap tall buildings wearing the technological equivalent of seven league boots.

The way Jay figured it, if you couldn't have fun, why bother?

Right at the moment, Jay was zooming over the new sixteen-lane South China Causeway, from just outside Xianggang, Hong Kong, heading north to Jiulong, on the mainland, looking for Wong Electronics trucks. These were easy to spot from the air, given that they had bright orange roofs, each of which was numbered. In RW, without a VR scenario enabled, the "trucks" were actually packets of binary information gathered and collated at nodes and squirted across the net. RW was just too boring.

Wong Electronics made some minor pieces of hardware, but they specialized in transmission software, readers and mailers, and certain kinds of security programs. Whoever had snuck into Winthrop's computer had erected a couple of firewalls and dug two deadfalls on his or her way out to cover his or her ass, and from the size and shape, even without the snipped-off ID codes, Jay knew the walls 'n' falls were top-of-the-line Wongware.

If he could locate, then sneak a ride on a Wong truck and get into their database, maybe he could find out who had bought the firewalls and deadfalls. It would be a brute-force cruncher of a project, but he had access to the power. Maybe the breaker had gotten sloppy and left a trail he could follow.

Ah. There was one of the orange-roof trucks now, a couple hundred feet below and half a mile ahead. He'd just drop on down and stow away. Breaking a lock on one of the trucks' doors would be easier than taking his shoes off for a player of Jay's ability.

He throttled back on the belt's thrust and started to lose altitude. He would very much like to find out who had used

Winthrop's computer before she did. It would be a loss of face she would hate, he'd be shiny as a new wetlight chip, and he would *love* it: *Oh, that? I ran the guy down, didn't I mention it? Piece of cake, I'm surprised you didn't do it yourself by now. No, no need to thank me, Lieutenant, I was just doing my job. . . .*

Jay reached the rear of the truck, shucked off the jet pack, and got out his lock picks. It took him forty-five seconds to get the door open. He closed it quietly behind him.

That's Gridley. *Jay* Gridley . . .

From a thousand feet above Jay Gridley, Platt watched, holding slow and level the little helicopter he'd found himself flying in when he'd dialed into Gridley's scenario. Kind of neat, the rocket thing the guy wore, and the backgrounds were all sharp and laid in thick too. The little half-breed gook had some skill.

Of course, Platt had a little skill himself. Plus he had access to all kinds of secret crap that a U.S. senator could put his hands on. Anything that White could touch, Hughes could touch, and whatever Hughes had, Platt could play with. There were real advantages to knowing top-secret codes. Platt could rascal stuff from the folks who built Net Force's computers, folks who had done the original hardware and programming, and who knew where all the back doors were hidden.

You hired a guy to build you a castle, he was gonna know where the secret compartments were, 'cause he *put* them there.

Platt watched the Net Force operative settle toward the orange roof of the Wong Electronics truck on the freeway below. The man dropped his jet pack, opened the truck's door, and climbed inside.

This was gonna be as much fun as goin' upside somebody's head. This little gook with his jet pack didn't have a clue who he was dealin' with. Not a fuckin' clue. He was gonna get his ass kicked, and Platt was gonna love doin' it too.

He let the helicopter sink a little.

When he was over the truck and maybe sixty feet up, he opened the copter's window and leaned out, a twenty-five-pound barbell weight in one hand. He extended the weight, lined up, and let it drop.

The steel plate fell, hitting the cab. The driver swerved into the car in the lane next to him. He slammed on his brakes and skidded to a halt. Nobody got hurt, but it ought to rattle little Jay pretty good.

Platt hit the copter's throttled, rose, and veered away. By the time Jay-Jay got his shit together, Platt would be long gone.

We havin' fun now, ain't we?

20

Friday, December 31st, 4 p.m.
Quantico, Virginia

It was Jay Gridley who was the bearer of the bad news.

Alexander Michaels was feeling pretty good that there hadn't been any more top-secret leaks into the net for the entire workweek. He was about to go home and enjoy a quiet beer or two on New Year's Eve. He planned to be asleep by the time midnight rolled around, and with it the year 2011 and whatever joys and griefs it would bring. But as he was getting ready to leave his office to beat the traffic, Jay came in with a couple of sheets of hardcopy in his hand.

"I think you ought to take a look at this, Boss."

"It can't wait until Monday?"

"I don't think so."

"Why don't I like the tone of that?"

Jay tendered the hardcopy. Michaels looked at it. He started to read it aloud:

"Overlord Beasts of America:

"Know you Beasts that your days are numbered. Know you Oppressors of the Disenfranchised People, that the Number of the Beast is 666, and that the Number fast approaches. We, the Representatives of the People, we, The Frihedsakse, will bring Low You Despoilers of Earth, You Masters of Tyranny.''

Michaels looked up from the hardcopy at Jay. ''Fried socks? Freed sex?''

''Close enough. Our universal translator says it's Danish. Means 'axis of liberty.' ''

''Danish? I never *heard* of any Danish terrorists! Denmark is a peaceful, civilized country where you can let your old grandma go for walks alone at night without worrying she'll get mugged.''

''Sure. She won't get mugged, but she might slip and freeze and maybe turn into a granny-sicle,'' Jay said.

Michaels shook his head and continued reading:

''For Your Wicked Ways are Manifest and Myriad, and we Shall Reveal your Sickness to All. All Shall Know You for your Evil, and the Weapons of your Sinful Ways Shall be used Against You, for the Power of Knowledge is the Light that All Demons Fear and the Power of Knowledge is given to the People.''

''Brother,'' Michaels said. He looked at Jay again. ''So why didn't you add this one to the pile of other whackaloos claiming responsibility for the leaks?''

''Read on, McDuff.''

''You cannot Hide from the Light of Justice, nor can You Run from the People's Retribution, nor will Fortresses save You, for you are Hated by the People.''

''A kind of loose interpretation of Machiavelli, that part,'' Jay said.

''Against You the People will throw All that is needed to Defeat you. The End is Near. Prepare for your Doom.''

It was signed ''The *Frihedsakse*.''

Michaels looked at Jay yet again.

''Next page,'' Jay prompted.

On the next page was a list of numbers.

"As nearly as we can tell, those are the original posting times and dates for all the major leaks we've been running down. There are a couple there we missed. We went back and strained a lot of stuff posted then, using the Super Cray Colander. We found a posting of the master list for last month's new American Express customer names and numbers. The other posting we found reveals the codes for all the computer-controlled railroad safety lights and switches on the main commuter line between Washington and Baltimore. A bright hacker could use those to pile half-a-dozen trains up into big heaps of smoking scrap before somebody figured out what was going on. We called American Express and Amtrak."

"Jesus."

"Unlikely anybody would know those specifics unless they posted them in the first place, Boss."

Michaels looked at the number. The last one in the sequence read:

12/31/10–1159.59

"That's tonight? December 31st, one second before midnight?"

"Yes, sir. If these are the guys, they are going to leak something just as the New Year arrives. Be my guess it won't be a recipe for mulled wine."

"Shit."

"I hear that, Boss."

"Any way to trace this?"

"Sure. We already did. Posted on a public BBS from a pay phone in Grand Central Terminal, New York City, at 3:15 p.m. today. Rush hour, New Year's Eve. No sig, no ID, no residual DNA from the modem jack on the phone, no fingerprints. A six-phone bank next to a coffee shop. Phones are in a dead zone, no security cams watching 'em. Records show thirty-seven calls were made at those six phones between 5 p.m. and 5:20 p.m. Good luck trying to find whoever sent it."

"Better tell your shift they won't be partying tonight."

"Already done," Jay said. "We're scanning all the major

nets we can, we've turned all of our search engines on, have squealbots roaming, and we've informed all of the big commercial services to grab anything coming in from 11:55 p.m. to 12:05 a.m. I expect we're going to get real sick of reading 'Happy New Year!' but if he posts anything on a major board or node, we should get it pretty quick.''

Michaels said, "Good work, Jay. I guess I'll be in my office.''

"Happy New Year, Boss.''

"Yeah. Right.''

PART TWO

Secrets Made Manifest

21

Platt sat in the kitchen of his house, the house that had belonged to his mother before she died, his laptop computer on
the wooden table next to the fridge. He took another big ole
slug of the Southern Comfort and Coke over ice, and giggled.
Four minutes it had taken the Net Force pukes to snag his
posting. He'd have thought they coulda done it in less, given
they knew exactly when it was coming and all, but okay, cut
'em a little slack, they did have a lot of territory to cover.
He'd stuck a squealer on the note and dropped it into a public
chat room on the World OnLine commercial service, the WOL
room marked "Gay Texans."

Steers 'n' Queers, he called that room, after an old joke his
uncle had once told him about Texas. He liked to check in
there once in a while and do a little VR vampire stuff on the
fags, leading them on and all before he blasted them. He had
a great little piggyback virus, a Trojan horse he could embed
in an e-mail. That was a hot piece of software, infecting e-
mail, since you supposedly couldn't do that. The queers'd

open the mail, read a few lines of the hot sex stuff he put in, then *bap!* the virus would infect their computer. Unless they had the latest immune system software installed, it would eat their drive in about two days.

Served 'em right for being fags.

He took another snort of the blended liquor and Coke, and laughed again. He was remembering little Jay Gridley hopping out of that VR truck, trying to figure out why the sucker had slewed to a stop in the middle of the freeway. Time he got it, it was too late. Haw!

Platt was on the wireless modem, had beamed a signal to a rebroadcaster, and then into a little throwaway stupecomp he'd set up in a rented room in San Diego, California. The stupe-comp was set up for e-mail only, and rigged so it logged onto WOL and then sent the message and squeal at exactly 11:59: 59 Eastern Standard Time. When the squeal went off, it sent the signal back to the stupecomp, which routed it back through the rebroadcaster and to his laptop, to let him know. Then the stupecomp wiped its hard drive and RAM disk clean, then fried the modem's memory real good—a complete wipe that *nobody* was going to undo—and shut itself off. Probably they'd have a team of feds kicking in the room's door in an hour or two, but that was okay. It'd give 'em something to do, but finding the computer in San Diego wasn't gonna do them no good, no good at all. They couldn't get anything off it that was gonna point them at him, three thousand miles away in Georgia laughing his ass off.

He lifted his glass, rattled the ice cubes, and held it up in a toast. "Yo, Net Force. Happy Fucking New Year!"

He drained the rest of the dark brown and slightly fizzy liquid in two big swallows, put the glass down on the table, then shut the laptop off. The info in the squirt wasn't much, a list of all the patients treated for STDs—sexually transmitted diseases—reported to the Atlanta CDC MedNet for the last six months. By law, certain things had to be reported to the states, and eventually some of these things wound up at the

Centers for Disease Control. There were a few eyebrow-raisin' names on the list, politicians, actors and actresses, some high-profile big-money types, and even some visiting big shots, including a couple of sand nigrah princes. No real tactical value, the list, but it would be embarrassing as all hell trying to explain to your wife just how come you was treated for the clap. Mainly it was something to rattle Net Force's cage, to show that the little manifesto Hughes had cooked up was legit. A throwaway, that was all.

Outside, the sounds of firecrackers and gunshots still echoed through the cold Georgia night.

"Oh, yeah, yeah—we havin' fun now, ain't we, boys?"

Saturday, January 1st, 2011, 1 a.m.
Washington, D.C.

Hughes sat in bed, reading a recent biography of the Norwegian Vidkun Quisling. Quisling, a career army office whose name later came to be synonymous with "traitor," had in the late 1930's, formed a national socialist party in his country, the Nasjonal Samling. The party hadn't done much, had never had any real power, but then the Germans had started a war and, in due course, had invaded Norway. Quisling tried to form his own government, which the Germans knocked down pretty quick, but since he was a home-grown national socialist who had once met with Hitler, the Nazis saw him as one of their own. Quisling became a collaborator who was ultimately deemed responsible for sending hundreds of Jews to the death camps, along with trying to convert the schools and churches into pro-German organizations.

One of the first things the Norwegians had done after their liberation was to round up and arrest scores of known collaborators. These were quickly tried, then quickly executed.

Quisling had been at the top of their list.

The biographer was convinced that Quisling's policies had cost Germany the war. Had he not tried so hard to "Nazify" the country, the writer was convinced there would not have developed much of a Norwegian resistance movement. The Norwegians were from good Viking stock, not the least bit cowardly, as evidenced by the famous tale of their king and the Jewish symbol—when told that Jews must wear the Star of David sign in public to show who they were, supposedly King Haakon VII took up the symbol himself and urged all his people to do the same. That could be apocryphal, of course, but truth should never stand in the way of a good story. The Norwegians were also smart enough to figure out which way the winds of war were blowing. If things hadn't been bad at home, they would have hunkered down and allowed the storm to blow itself out. But Quisling's policies pissed them off.

The resistance movement was never more than a small thorn in the Nazis' side, but it did cause a fair amount of industrial sabotage. Foremost among the attacks was a major strike against the heavy-water production facilities in Rjukan. The writer postulated that if the Germans had been able to speed up their atomic experiments, they would have likely developed a working atomic bomb before the United States did, and that such a weapon would have turned the tide of war in their favor. A few of those in the noses of V2 rockets launched from ships off the U.S. mainland at American cities would have done the trick.

If you accepted the theory, that was a reasonable assumption. A mile-wide smoking crater in the middle of New York or Washington, D.C., would have given the Americans something to think about, all right.

Too bad for them, the Germans ran out of time. It was left for America to build fission bombs that finished off the Japanese; atomics hadn't even been needed to beat the Germans.

Hughes thought this Quisling-cost-the-war theory was something of a stretch, but the writer nonetheless echoed a valid point from all the vaults of history: For want of a nail, a war *could* be lost. One man, in the right place, at the right time, could alter the course of the entire world. There was a popular sci-fi plot device that frequently used this idea. What would happen if a time traveler went back and throttled Hitler as a boy? Or some Christian zealot time-traveled and rescued Jesus from the cross? Or a fumble-footed paleontologist went back and accidentally killed the first protohuman ancestor from whom mankind would evolve?

A butterfly flapping its wings in Kansas today contributes to the tornado in Florida tomorrow. All things are interconnected, so the theory went.

Hughes grinned. He dog-eared the corner of the page and closed the biography. He turned off the light, settled down into his orthopedic biofoam pillow, and stared into the darkness.

Quisling had probably not been aware that he was a contributor to history. Certainly he hadn't wanted to be remembered as a traitor. But men who were less than adept did not control their own destinies, much less how they personally would be viewed years later. History, after all, was written by the victors.

History . . .

Hughes had always been fond of the story about the French physician Joseph-Ignace Guillotin. Elected to the French National Assembly a few years before the Revolution, and being a man of medicine and of a kindly nature, *Le Docteur* Guillotin's major political ambition seemed to be a wish to make criminal executions less painful. He had witnessed a few botched beheadings, wherein a headsman had gotten sweaty-palmed, or had arrived drunk, and had had to hack several times at a screaming victim's neck before managing to lop off the offending head. Such a thing was barbaric for civilized people like the French. The Scots, the English, *mon Dieu!* even the ignoble *Poles* possessed bladed mechanical devices they used for executions—although these were mostly for nobles, to be spared the embarrassment of an inept headsman. So the doctor helped pass a law requiring that legal execution be performed by a machine that would not miss, to be more humane to the condemned, rich and poor alike.

Le Docteur hardly wanted to be remembered by history as the man primarily responsible for the head-cleaving device at first called *La Louisette*. He certainly had *not* wanted to see the killing machine, which he had no hand in inventing, tagged *la guillotine,* the name that eventually stuck.

What a wonderful legacy for one's relatives. A family name with which to inspire gasps and revulsion, how lovely that must have been. And how ironic, given *Le Docteur*'s good intentions.

But men like Quisling and Guillotin had been small of vision, and not gifted with Hughes's intelligence. In a few days, he would be going to Guinea-Bissau, to sit with the head of that small country's government, to strike a deal that would someday be viewed by history as one of the most daring and clever schemes of all time. If history was written by the victors, then surely he would write his own.

He did not for a moment doubt it.

Saturday, January 1st, 2011, 7 a.m.
Washington, D.C.

In her kitchen, waiting for the coffee maker to finish brewing, Toni held the sheathed *kris* in both hands. Traditionally, *silat* players would not want a "used" *kris*. If you didn't know who had owned it or what he had used it for, you might be inheriting some bad *hantu*; you might find yourself connected to dead people by an evil blade, soaked in blood and karma. But since this was Guru's family blade, it was certainly reputable.

Maybe it did have enough magic to help her with Alex. She had been sleeping with it in its wooden sheath on her night-stand, blade carefully pointed away from her head. She was willing to take any help she could get. . . .

Even if she was peeved with him just now. It hadn't taken long for the story to get back to her about his little adventure in the desert during that raid on the terrorists. Naturally, *he* hadn't told her, but it hadn't taken long for him to figure out she knew either. He was supposed to be the Commander of Net Force, not a foot soldier! How dare he risk himself like that?

Toni grinned as the coffee maker chose that instant to gurgle and belch the last of the coffee into the pot, a kind of brewed raspberry noise, almost as if making fun of her.

She put the *kris* onto the counter, laying it softly on a clean dish towel, and grabbed her cup from the cabinet. Oh, well. Life was never boring.

Saturday, January 1st, 2011, 7 a.m.
Oro, California

Joanna Winthrop stood in the warm spring sunshine, waiting for the train to arrive. She wore a long, yellow patterned dress, a bonnet, and held a small tube-shaped brown leather travel satchel. The year was 1916. She was at the Oro Station, in northern California, and the surrounding fir and alder had sprouted new greenery to herald Persephone's return from the Underworld.

Joanna had been impressed with that legend as a girl, how the Lord of the Underworld had kidnapped the beautiful Per-sephone, and how her mother, Demeter, Goddess of the Corn, had been so wracked with grief that she turned her back on mankind, causing a cruel winter in which no crops could grow.

Joanna had always felt a certain sympathy with women who had gotten into dire straits because of their beauty.

According to the mythology, after a year of this cold misery, Zeus finally intervened, sending Hermes to ask the Lord of the Underworld to allow Persephone her freedom. The Lord of the Underworld was not happy about this request, for he did, in his own brutish way, love the woman he had kidnapped to be his wife. But one risked the wrath of Zeus with great care, if one dared risk it at all, so by Zeus's request, Persephone was released. Demeter was so overjoyed that the flowers blossomed and the grasses grew, and spring came. Alas, her daughter had eaten seeds of the pomegranate during her stay in the Underworld—there's always a catch in these things— so Persephone was required to return to the Underground for a portion of each year. And each time, Demeter's grief at losing her daughter caused winter to fall upon the Earth. . . .

It was a wonderful and imaginative story to explain the seasons. Although you'd think Demeter would have wanted to cut the apron strings after a few thousand years. God-time must be different.

Too bad she didn't have Zeus to help her find the hacker who had used her computer station. She could use the help. The guy had left a trail, but it was faint, and rigged with booby traps all along the way. She was beginning to get really pissed off. When she found this guy and turned him over to the feebs, she was hoping to get at least one clean kick at his testicles before they hauled him away. Having your supposedly secure computer station used for sabotage was, at the very least, embarrassing.

It was one thing to be thought beautiful when it got in your way. It was another thing entirely to be thought inept at what you did for a living.

The incoming train's whistle blew twice, steam-powered hoots that echoed into the station. There were only a few passengers waiting in her scenario, none of them paying any attention to her. She liked this time; it allowed her to wear clothes that could utterly conceal her shape and most of her features. People had been polite to each other in 1916, and the pace of life, just before America entered the Great War for Civilization, had been more stately than brisk.

The locomotive arrived, pulling a passenger train of some sixteen cars, blasting clouds of steam, its great wheels squealing and squeaking to a halt at the platform.

Well. It didn't matter how many traps this bodoh left in his wake, she *was* going to track him down. . . .

22

Monday, January 3rd, 8:02 a.m.
Quantico, Virginia

Alex Michaels leaned back in his chair and wished he was somewhere else. Just about anyplace would do, instead of sitting here listening to one of Senator White's staffers drone on at him over the phone.

"You understand our problem, don't you, Commander?"

Oh, yeah, he understood, all right. He made a sympathetic noise he didn't mean: "Um."

Congress was still out for the holidays, but the staff people got a lot of work done when the bosses weren't around. Probably more than when they *were* here, getting in the way. The truth of it was, Washington was run by staff. Without them, most congressmen and senators would not have a *clue* as to what was really going on. How some of the most influential people in the country ever got elected amazed Michaels. Some of these bozos probably had to be led to the bathroom and shown how to work a zipper.

"So I can pencil you in for the committee meeting?"

Michaels thought about it for a second. What if he said no?

That would be fun. They'd have to subpoena him. Would Net Force security keep out a federal marshal looking to serve papers if he asked them to? Probably, but Michaels would have to leave the building sooner or later. And the good senator would make mounds of political hay out his refusal to take the hot seat voluntarily. Did the Commander of Net Force have something to hide? An honest man doesn't fear a few questions, does he?

"I'd be happy to talk to the senator's committee."

"Thank you, sir. Eight a.m. on Monday the 10th. I'll e-mail you to confirm."

"This isn't going to be another of those week-long deals, is it, Ron?"

"No, sir. The senator is going on a junket—uh, a *fact-finding* mission—to Ethiopia on the 12th, so we'll wrap by Tuesday."

So, at worst, he'd be on the hot seat for a day or two, assuming nobody else was slotted. And it was unlikely that he'd be the only sacrificial lamb—White's committees always had plenty of victims they wanted to skewer. What an idiot.

After he hung up, Michaels leaned forward in his chair, feeling tired. He'd like nothing better than to take the day off, go for a nice long ride on his bike, to enjoy the cold, crisp morning while working up a little sweat. Or, as long as he was wishing, why not a week in Tahiti? Lie on the beach, soak up whatever rays the sunblock would let past, drink coconut and tropical fruit and rum. Listen to the waves break. Boy, did *that* sound good.

He grinned at himself. There was a pile of work on his desk that he couldn't get done if he worked twenty-four-hour days for a month. The deeper that pile got, the more he felt like dragging his heels. Did everybody feel that way? Or was it a contrary streak in him, just like wanting to spend money the most when you were dead broke?

Well. You knew the job was dangerous when you took it, right?

Right.

Monday, January 3rd, 11:15 a.m.
Quantico, Virginia

John Howard sat on Doc Kyle's couch in the base clinic, watching the older man flip through the hardcopy print out.

Kyle shook his head. "I don't know what to tell you, John. X-rays, EEG, EKG, sonograms, MRI, MEG, everything is normal. You have the blood pressure of a man half your age, your reflexes are great, there's nothing growing in any dark corners that shouldn't be there. Your don't have AIDS, hepatitis, prostate cancer, or herpes. Your cholesterol is low, your liver enzymes are good, hormones are normal—all your bloodwork is all dead-center normal, except for what might be a little bit of a white cell shift to the left, a few segs, that might be indication of a virus. Might also be lab error, it's that close. You're as healthy a specimen as I've seen all month."

"So why am I so tired all the time?"

Kyle, a full bird colonel, was sixty, and a career military man. Howard had been his patient for years. Kyle grinned. "Well, now, none of us is getting any younger. A man your age needs to realize he's not going to be able to run basic with the recruits forever."

"A man my age? Jesus, *I'm* not a man my age!"

Kyle laughed. "Come on, once you hit forty you have to expect to slow down a little. Sure, you can hold the Reaper at bay with diet and exercise, cheat him pretty good, but the time when you could wine, women, and song it up all night long, then grab a full pack and hump it all the next day are behind you. What you did for a light workout as a shavetail is overtraining for a colonel old enough to be that boy's father."

"You're saying I should slow down."

"Not 'should.' You *will* slow down, that's the nature of the beast. You're in better shape than most twenty-year-olds I see in here, no question. But the fact is, a twenty-year-old in peak condition is going have better legs, faster recovery, and more energy than a forty-year-old in peak condition. I'm not saying you should park your butt in the rocking chair, smack your gums, and wait for senility, but you need to recognize the reality. If you hit the gym four times a week, better cut that to two. If you jog ten miles a day, drop it to five. Warm up more, stretch before and after you sweat hard, give yourself more recovery time. You don't have the reserves you once had, simple as that. You can maintain a vintage aircraft pretty good, but sooner or later the metal fatigues, no matter how many times you rebuild the engine and the hydraulics.''

Howard stared at him. It wasn't as if the doc was giving him a death sentence—

Well, yes, it *was*. That was *exactly* what he was doing. He was reminding him that the grave was still out there—and it was closer than it used to be.

Just what I needed to hear. Howard blew out a sigh. ''All right. Thanks, Doc.''

''Don't take it so hard, kid. You might have a couple more good years left. You want me to write you a prescription for some prunes and Geritol?''

Outside, the January sky was clear and cold. Howard walked toward his office, thinking about what Kyle had said. So, okay, he'd ease up a little on his workouts, see if that helped. If Doc was right, then he'd feel better.

Of course, he'd also feel worse, knowing that there wasn't something simple that could be fixed. Nobody had come up with a cure for getting older yet. And this was the first time he'd realized that it was going to happen to him too. Somehow, he'd always felt as if he'd live to be ninety, and except for a few wrinkles he'd look and feel the same then as he had at twenty or thirty.

Maybe there was something to be said for dying in battle while your brain was still sharp and your eyes unclouded by time. At least it was quick. Maybe it was better to be burned-out ashes than cold, ancient dust.

Monday, January 3rd, 11:15 a.m.
Washington, D.C.

Tyrone's life was over.

He stood inside CardioSports, between the wrist-heart-monitor display and a display case of stopwatches, staring through the front window into the mall. From where he stood, with the rack of ski jackets behind him, he'd be hard to see from the tables at the food court, just across the mall's main walkway, but he could easily see Bella where she sat at one of the tables.

Where she sat, with somebody.

Where Belladonna Wright sat with Jefferson Benson, facing him across the little round white table, holding his hands with her hands, smiling at him.

Smiling at him.

Oh, *God*!

He felt sick, as if he was gonna throw up, as if somebody had punched him in the solar plexus hard enough so he couldn't breathe. And he felt a cold and hot blend of sad, aching misery entwined with mindless, killing rage. He wanted to scream, to run to where Bella sat, to smash Jefferson Benson's face in with his fists, to kick him enough times to break every bone in his body. He wanted to do that, and then spit on him.

But what Tyrone did not want to do was look Belladonna Wright straight in her lying face. Not at that moment.

He was on afternoon shift at school, like she was, and so he'd asked her if she was going to the mall. They could meet, grab lunch, head for classes?

No, she'd said. *Not today.* She had to run some errands, she'd said, so she wasn't going to the mall. She'd see him later at school.

Fine. That was nopraw.

And yet, there she was. Sitting there with Benson, holding his fucking hands, smiling at him.

Tyrone stood there, pretending to examine the heart monitors, unable to look away. It was like when you saw somebody do something really stupid on a vid, something so stupid it embarrassed you just to be watching it, and you wanted to look away, but you couldn't, you watched it anyhow. He didn't want to be here. He didn't want to know that Bella had lied to him. He didn't want to see her holding hands with Benson. But he couldn't move, couldn't turn his head away. He had to watch. Even though it felt as if there was something alive in his stomach, something with teeth and claws trying to dig its way out of him.

He never would have known if he hadn't come to the sport store looking for a birthday present for his father. It had never occurred to him that Bella would be at the mall. She'd said she wasn't going, and it had never crossed his mind to believe otherwise. Truly had never occurred to him.

She'd *lied* to him.

As he watched, Bella stood, and so did Benson. They moved around the table, closer to each other. Benson bent over.

Tyrone wanted to scream, to pound himself on the sides of the head.

The worst thing he could imagine happened. Benson kissed her.

No, there was something even worse than that—she kissed Benson back. Tyrone saw their mouths working and knew it was a tongue kiss. Benson put one hand behind her, put it right on her butt. Pulled her closer.

Bella let his hand stay there.

It lasted forever. A million years.

Finally, they finished. Benson turned and went one way, Bella the other.

Tyrone stood frozen, a worn-out statue of old bronze, unable to even blink. It was like the time on the parachute ride in Florida, that big free-fall drop. His belly fluttered, came all the way up to his throat. He was paralyzed on the outside, even though his guts roiled like a nest of beheaded snakes.

What should he do? Should he go out and confront her? Tell her he was just passing by? See what she said? Would she lie to him again?

Did he want to know that?

Oh, man, oh, man! He wanted to die. Right here, right now. Just go up in a blast of fire and smoke and be dead and gone and not have to know this, not have to think about it, not have to *deal* with it.

Bella had betrayed him. That was it, that was it, there was no way around it. She could have explained being in the mall, maybe even explained meeting Benson by accident and having lunch, but no way could she explain the last part. The kiss. The hand on her ass.

Right now, he hated Jefferson Benson so much that he would have killed him if he could have figured out a way to do it and get away with it. Maybe even if he couldn't get away with it. But Benson wasn't the real problem. Tyrone knew that. Bella was the problem. What really hurt was that Bella had let him kiss her. That Bella had wanted him to kiss her. That she had *enjoyed* it.

She wanted somebody else. Instead of Tyrone.

That was the thing that made Tyrone sickest.

What was he going to do?

How could he live with this?

At that moment, he couldn't see any way. No way at all.

23

Julio Fernandez stood in the cold at the start of the obstacle course, next to the chinning station. The morning trainees had come and gone, and the afternoon group didn't come on until after lunch. Some civilian feebs ran the course at noon now and then, along with senior troops trying to stay in shape, but right at the moment he was the only one at the chin racks.

He spent five minutes warming up, rolling his shoulders and stretching his neck. If he didn't do that he would probably strain his traps, and walking around with a sore neck for the next week didn't appeal to him, especially given his already gimpy status.

There were four sets of three bars there—hardwood dowels, each two and a half feet long, an inch and a half in diameter, mounted in six-by-six pressure-treated lumber posts. Each of the crosspieces was set at a different height. The lowest was about six and a half feet off the sawdust, the middle one was a foot higher, the highest a foot above the middle one. Usually he could easily jump up and catch the highest of the bars, but his leg bothered him a little more than he'd let on. Until the muscle got a little less sore, he wasn't going to be dunking any basketballs. Or springing up to catch the top chin bar. But he could grab the middle one easily enough. He did so, palms forward, using a full grip about eight inches wider than his shoulders. It didn't really matter how tall the bar was because when he did chins he pulled his legs up into an L-sit to work his belly muscles anyway. Kind of like a gymnast, although he wouldn't get many points for form. He didn't point his toes enough.

He curled his hips up, pointed his legs—he could even feel *that* in his wounded leg—then chinned himself, going up at a medium speed, coming back down at the same speed, to a full hang. Anything else didn't work the lats enough.

One.

He repeated the move, then did it again, getting into the rhythm.

. . . two . . . three . . . four . . .

Doing it in an L-sit made it harder, but that was the point. He wasn't trying to see how many he could do, cheating to a half-hang and then pumping it back up. The idea was to make the muscles work.

. . . five . . . six . . . seven . . . eight . . .

Some guys used a false grip, with their thumbs hooked over the bar for more lift, instead of under and around the fingers. And some guys used wrist straps, on the theory that their forearm muscles and hands would get tired before they wore their lats out, and chinning was primarily a lat exercise.

. . . nine . . . ten . . . eleven . . .

Fernandez figured that there wasn't much point to his back being so strong that his hands couldn't keep up. It wouldn't do you much good to have lats like Superman if you didn't have the grip strength to use them.

. . . twelve . . .

He let himself down, lowered his legs, released the bar. He

was warmed up pretty good now. He shook his hands and arms out, flexed and extended his fingers, rolled his shoulders a couple of times, then turned his hands around so the palms faced him, and caught the bar in an underhand pull-up grip, this time spaced about shoulder-width. That was the only difference between chins and pull-ups, whether your palms faced away or toward you.

One . . . two . . . three . . . four . . .

The biceps started to burn first, but the forearms were right there too.

. . . five . . . six . . . seven . . . eight . . .

It was getting tough now. He blew out a hard breath, sucked in a deep lungful of air, gutted it out.

. . . nine . . .

Come on, Julio, you can make it!

. . . ten . . .

He dropped, hung on to the bar for a second, then let go.

"I didn't think you were going to make that last one," a woman said from behind him.

He turned. Joanna Winthrop.

He grinned. "Me neither. Course, if I'd known you were watching, I'd have managed a couple more. I wouldn't want you to think I was a wimp."

She wore running shoes and sweats, dark blue pants, and a matching hooded shirt with the Net Force logo on the front. "I doubt I would think that. Twelve chins and ten pull-ups? On a good day, I might do six of either. Not both."

"Well, I don't want you to feel bad, so how about I just skip the one-handed sets?"

She laughed. "Thank you. I appreciate it."

"So, what brings you out here?"

"Too much time at the desk. Every so often, I have to get away and clear my head."

"I hear that."

"How's the leg?"

"You want the macho answer? Or the truth?"

"Oh, both, please."

"Well, the macho answer is, 'Ah, no problem. Little old bullet wound like that can't slow a *real* man down. Hell, I hurt myself worse putting on my socks. I was just about to go run the course. After which I'm probably gonna jog around the compound a couple times, then go find a pickup rugby game somewhere.' "

"I see. And the truth?"

"That sucker is sore, stiff, and if I tried to run the course, I'd get maybe halfway to the first hurdle, cursing like a sailor, before I collapsed and fell down hollering in pain."

She laughed again. He liked that, making her laugh. She relaxed when she did it; she lost some of that tightness in her face that made her look just a little too cool to approach.

She said, "You're going to give macho men a bad name, Julio, admitting something like that."

"I'm trusting you to keep it a secret," he said, his face held as grave as he could manage. "If they found out, I'd be labeled a sissy, and drummed right out of the Manly Men Society."

"My lips are sealed."

They smiled at each other. "So, you gonna do the course?"

"That was the idea."

"How about I hobble along and watch?"

"I can live with that."

She started a series of leg stretches, and he moved over to lean against the chin supports. He watched.

Monday, January 3rd, 12:15 p.m.
Quantico, Virginia

Alex was running a little late, and Toni was already dressed and warmed up, practicing *sempok* and *depok* postures, dropping to sit, then springing back to her feet, when he made it to the gym.

"Sorry," he called, headed for the dressing room. "I got hung up on a call."

"It's all right."

He was back out in a minute, dressed in a black T-shirt, black cotton drawstring pants, and a white headband. He also wore wrestling shoes. They didn't like you to work out on the mats with shoes that might leave marks.

She bowed him in and set him to practicing his *djuru*. He only knew the first one, but it was obvious he had been practicing away from class. Another month or two and he'd be ready to start the second *djuru*. Pretty quick. She'd been four months before Guru had given her *Djuru* Two.

After about fifteen minutes, she called a stop. He'd worked up a pretty good sweat, his shirt was damp and the headband was soaked. She walked to where her jacket was folded next to the wall, bent, and pulled the *kris* in its sheath from under the cloth.

She walked back to Alex and showed him the weapon. "Look at this."

He raised his eyebrows. "Is this Indonesian?"

"Yes. It's called a *kris*. K-r-i-s. Sometimes spelled with an E after the K, sometimes with a double S. My Guru presented it to me when I went home for Christmas. It belonged to her great-grandfather. It's been in her family for more than two hundred years." She handed it to him.

He pulled it from the wooden sheath and looked at the blade. "Wow. How'd they get that color and texture?"

"The shape is called *dapor*. This one is a *kris luk,* the wavy-blade pattern. The waves are always an odd number. There are also straight *kris*. The blade is made by welding and hammering various kinds of iron or steel together, then forging them into one piece. It's etched, they use lemon or lime juice and arsenic on the blade to darken and bring out the patterns in the steel. The surface pattern is called *pamor*. There is a lot of meaning attached to what kind of *dapor* and *pamor* a blade has, and who crafted it and how.''

"Security didn't say anything when you brought this in?"

"I told them it was a paperweight. Feel the edge."

"Not very sharp," he said, testing it with his thumb.

"That's because it is primarily a thrusting weapon. One doesn't use a *kris* for household chores, only against an enemy or a wild animal. It's pretty much a ceremonial weapon, although it can certainly be used to kill in the hands of somebody who knows what he or she is doing. It was the traditional execution weapon for a long time."

He hefted the weapon. "Interesting. Is it valuable?"

"Moneywise, probably worth several thousand dollars. But the real value is in the thing itself.

"The *kris* are considered little temples by many Indonesians. The makers are called *Empu,* and depending on how one produces the *kris* and the wishes of the client, certain . . . magics are included in the forging. Many of the traditional *kris* are designed to be lucky, in war, or love, or business."

"Which is this one?"

She shrugged. "I'm not sure yet. The magic apparently changes a little with each new owner." *Lucky in love,* she hoped.

"You aren't going to stick me with it, are you?"

She smiled. "And piss off Security? No, I thought we'd start with the wooden knife for practice. But I wanted you to see it."

He put the dagger back into its sheath and handed it to her. "Thank you for showing it to me."

She took the *kris,* went back to her jacket, and rewrapped the weapon.

Back in front of Alex, she said, "Okay, let's work a little on applications from the *djuru.* Throw a punch, right here." She touched the tip of her nose.

He stepped in and shot a weak straight right at her nose. She double-blocked it without any effort. "That's not a punch! And let me see the other hand bracing the right. It's not that much slower, and remember, this hand"—she raised her right fist—"never goes into battle without this one." She put her left hand on her right forearm. "Just like the *djuru*."

"Can I ask a question?"

"Sure."

"Why?"

"Because *silat* is based on structural principles and not raw power. You have to have base, angle, and leverage, but you must use proper technique to get them. See, you are bigger and stronger than I am, and if you punch really hard, I might not be able to deflect it using pure muscle. But if I brace my block thus, and my hips are corked properly, I have a mechanical advantage. Remember, this stuff was created with the idea that if you needed it, your attacker was going to be bigger, stronger, faster, probably armed, and there might be four of five of him. They might also be as skilled as you. You might be able to muscle a guy your size or smaller, but you can't outmuscle three or four who are bigger and stronger."

"And faster," he said. His voice was dry. "And as skilled."

She laughed. "Yes. But speed and power and even skill are not nearly as important as timing. Ask me what the most important thing is about comedy."

"Huh?"

"Go on, ask me."

"Okay, what is the most important thing about—"

"Timing!" she said, cutting in.

He smiled. "Got it."

"You will, you will. Practice makes perfect. Now, again. Punch."

He stepped in, and threw another right, harder this time, and braced with his left hand.

She blocked it and demonstrated the counter. ''Good,'' she said. ''Again.''

This was going well. Maybe the *kris* was lucky in love. Wouldn't that be nice?

24

Jay Gridley walked into the small storefront tobacco shop to the jingle of a spring-mounted warning bell on the door frame. The bell tinkled again as the door closed behind him with a solid *chunk!* The smoke shop was not far from Government House, on one of the danker streets facing Back Bay. The time was late 1890's, and the British Raj was still in full sway; Bombay was, of course, Indian, but the English flag draped heavily over the city, as it did the entire country.

Rule Brittania.

Inside, the shop was dark and hazy with fragrant blue smoke. The man behind the counter was also dark, a native, dressed in a white shirt and summer suit, and the smell of his blended pipe tobacco hung sweet and heavy in the still air. He took another puff from his heavy, curved briar, and added that smoke to the already abundant cloud.

A month-old copy of the *London Times* lay upon the counter next to a large glass jar full of cheap cigars, a small wooden box of strike-anywhere matches, and a metal tray of cedar lighting sticks.

Jay himself wore a white linen suit and a tan planter's hat. He nodded at the shopkeeper. "You have other newspapers?" He waved at the *Times*.

"Yes, sir, we have them in the back, next to the humidor," the man said, in that singsong lilt of a native Indian who'd learned English only as an adult. He exhaled smoke with the words.

Jay touched his hat brim and moved to the shelves to the left of the counter, next to the closed glass door that led into the humidor room where the good tobacco and cigars were kept.

He glanced at the papers. There was *The Strand,* the *New York Times,* and something from Hong Kong in Chinese. Not what he was looking for—ah, there it was. *The Delhi Ledger,* a small publication put out in English that sold mostly to expatriate Brits homesick for King and country. Or was it Queen and country? Sure, must be Victoria, it being the Victorian age and all. He ought to know his English history better, he supposed.

He thumbed through the cheap newsprint and smudged the ink, getting it on his fingers. Well, at least that was a nice touch.

Ah, there it was. The reference he had been trying to run down. The article was ostensibly about Danes come to visit India, but there in the fluffy travel piece was the name he wanted: The *Frihedsakse.*

Once upon a time, Jay would have thought it was odd to find a bit of information about Denmark in an Indian infonet, but not anymore. Information was like dust; it blew around in the wind and wound up in places you'd never think it would. The logical place to start hunting for information on a Danish terrorist organization would be in Denmark, or at least in the Scandinavian countries, and certainly he had combed through those nets with the best search engines and squeekbots Net Force had, but he'd come up empty. So he'd widened his search, and this was the first real hit he'd had. Time was passing—it had been a week without any real leads—and while it had been quiet, there was no guarantee it would stay that way.

He took the paper to the front, paid for it, and went out into the Indian afternoon. It was overcast. What time of year was it? Monsoon season? He was getting slack in his old age. There was a time when such a detail would never have gotten past his scenario research, even if he'd been in a hurry. Oh, well. Things changed. While it was still important to look good, getting the job done counted for more.

Tuesday, January 11th, 10:15 a.m.
Blacktown, New South Wales, Australia

Jay had switched from his tropical linens into an Abercrombie & Fitch khaki outfit, shorts and a short-sleeved shirt, complete with stout walking shoes and a pinned-up Australian bush hat. His next stop was a small library in Blacktown, just north and west of Sydney. It was the middle of summer, and warm, and the library was not air-conditioned, even though he'd picked a contemporary time to run his scenario.

Not a bad transition for a couple minutes' work.

"Can I help you, sir?" the librarian asked. Jay loved Australian accents. He used them for secondary characters all the time.

"Yes, ma'am, I'm looking for this periodical." He put a slip of paper onto the woman's desk. She put on her reading glasses and looked at it.

"Oh, right. In the magazine section, go past the record kiosk, on your left, about halfway down the rack."

"Thank you, ma'am."

"You're American, right?"

"Yes, ma'am."

"Nice to make your acquaintance then."

Jay smiled, tipped his hat, then headed for the magazine racks. This was perhaps a little more time-consuming than a non-VR search, but if he couldn't have fun, why bother?

Tuesday, January 11th, 10:30 a.m.
Rangoon, Burma

Jay found a mention of *Frihedsakse* in a backline infonet connected to a major shipping company. Not much, just an unconfirmed rumor, connected to the sinking of an oil tanker. Well. Great avalanches from little snowballs sometimes grew. He gathered the information in and moved on.

Tuesday, January 11th, 10:40 a.m.
Johannesburg, South Africa

In a police station in Boksburg, a man arrested for stealing a car had been searched. There had been nothing in the arrestee's wallet save a business card, upon the back of which was the handwritten word *Frihedsakse*. Next to the word was an old-style internet-provider ID number. The IP probably wasn't active, but that didn't matter. If it had ever been active, there were ways to trace it.

A quick check of the dates on the information showed that it had been in the police system for five months. A pix of the card had a day and time stamp on it as verification of the item's log into the evidence locker at the central storage vault in Johannesburg.

Jay collected the card. He grinned. These terrorists didn't know who they were messing with. He was Jay Gridley, the man who had run the mad Russian programmer to ground. These balrogs didn't have a prayer.

Tuesday, January 11th, 10:50 a.m.
Kobe, Japan

At a beef ranch in Kobe, somebody had broken in and stolen, of all things, a case of beer, which was to be fed to the cattle. Investigating policemen had no clues, save one: Scrawled on the wall next to ten cases of beer that had been left behind was the word *Frihedsakse* in kanji.

Jay made note of that.

So it went, a tiny bit here, an even smaller bit there. This was sometimes the way of computer sievework. You strained slowly, but very fine. If you did it right, you might come up with a bunch of pieces so small that none of them would mean anything but, puzzled together, you might have something. Jay was gathering his ducks. When he had enough of them, he would put them into a row. And when he had enough ducks in a neat row, he would get some answers. And then?

Well, we'll just see, won't we? I got your fried sex right here, pal. . . .

Tuesday, January 11th, 11:15 a.m.
Miami Beach, Florida

Platt strolled along one of the touristy streets near the canal, enjoying the seventy-degree weather. Around him, people walked, dressed in all the bright colors of the rainbow, plus a bunch of colors not found anywhere naturally. Old, young, white, black, domestic, foreign, Miami Beach was always cookin', there was always action. It might be snowin' like a sonofabitch up north, in Washington or New York City, and still be practically summer down here in the land of sin.

Life was sure grand when you could just pick up and go to where you could walk around in a T-shirt and shorts in the middle of the winter.

Platt ambled along, not going anywhere in particular, just strolling, soaking up a few minutes of the warm sunshine before he had to go back into his room and plug into the net.

He watched a black girl in a tank top and short shorts stride by, and smiled at her big and tight backside after she passed. Fine-lookin' woman.

A tall man in a purple crushed-velvet jumpsuit passed on in-line skates, laughing. He was throwing quarters every which way, and had a passel of children chasing him, scooping up the change.

Platt passed two window-shopping old ladies, all in lime green and hot pink, baggy Bermuda shorts and halters, both of them burned leathery and the color of dark toast, but with silicone implants that were the only things not sagging on them. The old broads must be in their seventies or eighties, and their faces were pulled so tight by plastic surgery that their fake boobs probably bobbed up and down when they smiled.

If there were some kind of big disaster that destroyed a lot of civilization's records, then maybe a thousand years from now, when some scientist got to digging up old coffins or shit, he might scratch his head and wonder when he opened them: Why were there so many caskets with these two little plastic sacks of Dow Jell-O in there with all the bones?

Fake boobs didn't do it for Platt. Didn't matter how big they were if they weren't real. Hell, if he wanted to handle stuff like that, he'd just go on down to the hardware store and buy himself a couple of tubes of bathtub caulk. Go on home, squirt a couple of big blobs into bowls and let them dry, squeeze that. Sheeit . . .

Platt grinned again. He was just stalling, so he wouldn't have to go back to work. He sighed. Might as well get to it.

He didn't have any illusions about how good he was on the net. He was better than some, but not as sharp as the real experts. In VR, some of the Net Force players would dance circles around him in a head-to-head match. Thing was, tricky and pretty sharp beat real sharp every time. And the Net Force pukes were fooling themselves, so that helped a bunch.

Back after he'd first left home and gone on the road for a while, Platt had met an old grifter name of James Treemore Vaughn. Jimmy Tee, they called him. He was probably pushing seventy, had white hair, and looked just like your kindly old gramps. Kinda guy you'd trust with your wife, your kid, your money. Only Jimmy Tee was a con man, working the small cons by the time Platt had met him, though in his prime he had done a lot of second- and third-man parts in big stings. Earned big, spent big, didn't have a pot to piss in. But he knew more about people than a trainload full of psychiatrists, hookers, and bartenders put together. He could rope a mark, sting him, and send him on his way thinking Jimmy Tee had done him a big favor.

They'd sat in a bar in Kansas City once, Big Bill Barlow's place, Jimmy Tee having a weakness for good blended whisky, and the old man had taught Platt a major lesson.

"Thing is, boyo, if you work it right, a mark will do most of the work for you. Yeah, you can set him up, hammer him good with the pitch, pull a fast close, and take off with the score, but if the mark knows he's been had, sooner or later he'll scream. A good con gets you the money. A great con gets you the money—and the mark doesn't know he's been had."

Platt was fascinated. "Yeah?" He waved at the bartender, who came over to fill up Jimmy Tee's glass.

"Oh, yeah. See, there's a lot of people out there who are faster, smarter, stronger, and meaner than you. You face off with them, you get the crap kicked out you. A big guy comes at you, you don't try to block him balls against balls, you just redirect him a hair. Nudge him in a direction, and get out of his way. The trick is to make him think that's the way he wanted to go in the first place. You can do that, you can write your own ticket."

In the warm sunshine, Platt smiled again. Old Jimmy Tee

had been dead and gone what? Five, six years? But his lesson had stuck.

The Net Force guys were looking for terrorists because that was what they were most afraid of. So, zap, Platt and Hughes gave them some terrorists. And the trick was to hide little clues here and there, hide 'em well enough so when the Net Force dogs went sniffin', they had trouble finding those little rabbits in their hidey-holes. If you were lookin' for somethin' you just knew was there and you couldn't find it, well, that made you look just that much harder.

This whole bullshit Danish thing was Hughes's idea, but it was pretty smart. Platt had started planting stuff about the Fried Socks thing five or six months ago, so some of the clues were absolute boilerplate when it came to real time. Net Force could poke and prod at the information and no matter how they scanned it, it would come up real—well, at least real in that the thing had been sitting in somebody's memory archives since months before the manifesto showed up.

Some of the clues were yet to be put into place, but when they got there, they'd be backdated to seem as if they had been there for months or years. By the time the Net Force pukes got to those, they'd have checked the earlier stuff and found it to be more or less legit. So they would convince themselves that the later stuff was okay by the time they found it. They wouldn't bother to check, or if they did they'd do a half-assed job, since that was what they wanted to believe.

If it looks like a rabbit, smells like a rabbit, and hops like a rabbit, well, hell, it's a rabbit, ain't it?

You give a guy a sack of coins and he dips into it and pulls out eight or ten at random and they all assay out as pure 24-carat gold, he is gonna believe that all of the suckers in the bag are real. He'll figure no way anybody could tell which ones he'd pick, it's pure chance, so he's covered.

Guy like that would completely forget all the sleight of hand he'd ever seen, forget that there were magicians who could fan a deck and let him pick a card—any card—and the trickster would know what it was before the mark ever touched it.

The hand doesn't have to be quicker than the eye—if the eye doesn't know where to look.

The trick, Jimmy Tee had said, was not to embellish it too much. Just give the guy a direction and get out of his way. The smarter the guy was, the quicker he would fool himself. If you did it right.

Net Force was hot on the trail of a Danish terrorist group. Platt knew this because some very expensive and practically undetectable squeal programs had told him that the feds hunting for the terrorists had finally started to find his planted clues. Clues that were hidden enough so they had to work at finding them, and clues that were mysterious enough to keep 'em guessin'.

They didn't trust anything too easy. Most people figured if it didn't cost anything, it wasn't *worth* anything. But if they had to slog through a swamp, swatting at mosquitoes, then what they found hiding in the hollow of the third dead cypress on the left, well, hell, that was why they'd come, right?

Wrong. But that was the trick.

When the hounds caught the quarry's scent, when they knew for sure they were on the right track, then he could let them see the rabbit. When it took off running, they'd follow it. They'd never catch it, because it wasn't real. It was a phantom, a spook, a ghost.

And boy, it was gonna be fun to watch them chase that sucker.

But of course, the thing he had to do was make sure the hounds still wanted to chase the critter. So this afternoon, he was going to give 'em a new reason. A real good reason, this time . . .

25

Tyrone Howard pretty much wanted to die.

He lay on his bed, staring through the ceiling, unable to move for the weight of what Bella had dropped on him. He had replayed the conversation a hundred times in his head, and every time, it came out the same. There wasn't any wiggle room, no way to put a good face on it. She'd dropped him, blap, just like that.

He'd seen her at school, she'd acted just fine, and although he'd told himself he wasn't, he was *not* going to say anything, in the end it had spewed from him in a hot blast, as if he'd been punched in the belly and the punch had knocked his words out with his wind.

"So, meet anybody *interesting* at the *mall* lately?"

Give her credit, she wasn't stupid and she didn't try to pretend she didn't know what he was talking about. Right there in the hall, outside his last-period class, she let him have it, full spray, nozzle tight:

"Maybe I did. What business is it of yours?"

Wham! Another punch to the gut. "What business is it of *mine*. Jesus, Bella, I thought we were—you and I—I mean, we were—"

"What? *Married?* Well, *attenzione* Ty-ree-o-nee, we are not. I like you, you're sharp, but I have other friends, you copy? I see them when and where I want. You praw that?"

He was too stunned to think about his response. Maybe if he'd thought about it, if he'd had time to consider it, what she said, he'd have said something else, but he didn't have the time. He said, "Yeah, I do have a problem with it."

She'd glared at him as if he'd slapped her. "Oh? Really? My game, my rules, that's how it is. You want to play, you play my way."

Then he really put his butt into it. He said, "No. I don't think so."

That *really* burned her. He thought she was going to spit on him for a second. Then she said, "Well, then, tell you what, slip, you just lose my com number, okay? I don't have time to be holding your hand and showing you what's what, little boy."

And then she turned and left. His world went gray. He couldn't hear the students around him, couldn't see anything, couldn't feel anything—except a twist in his stomach. His gut was knotted as if he'd just jumped off the top of a very tall building and was in free fall. With the ground coming up fast . . .

On his bed, he replayed it again, searching for a small crack, a word that could have a double meaning that he had somehow missed, a magic word that, once he grasped it, would turn the whole conversation on its head and make it mean something altogether different. But he couldn't find it, that magic word. It just wasn't there.

"Son? You okay?"

Tyrone looked at the doorway. His father stood there.

"Your mother is worried about you. Is there something going on we can help with?"

His knee-jerk response was to wave his father off. *No, nothing, I'm fine, just tired, nopraw.* But he was too sick at heart to even lie about it.

"Bella and I broke up," he said.

His father came into the room. He leaned against the wall next to Tyrone's computer. "Not your idea, I take it?"

"No. Not my idea."

"You want to talk about it?"

"No. Not really." But then, as they had with Bella, the words somehow just came tumbling out. He told his father all about it, about seeing her in the mall, about her kissing that jockjerk, about seeing her in the hall. It just flowed from him like some kind of sour, bitter fluid.

John Howard listened to his son, felt his anguish and pain, and ached for him. If he could stand between his child and the world and stop anything from ever hurting him, he would do it, but he knew it didn't work that way. Some lessons you had to learn on your own. Some pain had to be endured. If you were to be tempered so that your edge would stay sharp, you had to go through the fire, be annealed, quenched, and heated again. But it hurt to watch your child suffer. More than anything else he could imagine.

Finally, the boy ran down. His grief was intense, all-consuming, it filled his world. He couldn't see any way around it.

There was nothing Howard could say that was going to heal this wound. A broken heart accepted no medicine except time. That the first case of puppy love squashed would some day be nothing more than a small scar in the grand cosmic scheme of things was not what Tyrone wanted to hear. *You will survive this and get over it* was the truth, but it would not provide much comfort right at this moment. Still, it was all he had to offer.

Howard sighed. "When I was sixteen, I was in love," he said. "A girl in my school, Lizbeth Toland, same class. We were tight, went everywhere together. I gave her my junior class ring. We called it 'hangin' out' back then. We talked about going to college together, getting married, having children. It was pretty serious.''

Tyrone stared at him.

"It's kind of hard for you to imagine me with anybody except Mom, isn't it?''

Tyrone nodded. "Yeah.'' Then he must have realized that might not sound too good, because he said, "Well, no, I mean, well, I—I never really thought about it.''

"That's okay. For the longest time, I believed my parents must have found me on a doorstep or under a cabbage leaf—the idea of them having sex together was beyond my comprehension.''

Tyrone shook his head, and Howard could almost read his thoughts: Gramma and Grampa? Having sex? *There* was a puker pix.

"Summer after my junior year, I went to ROTC camp. Lizbeth and I wrote each other every day—snailmail mostly. And we talked on the phone when I could get to one. She said she missed me, couldn't wait for me to get back, and I felt the same way.

"Then I got a call from my best friend. Rusty Stephens. He'd been at a bar one night sneaking in to drink beer with a couple of buddies. They'd seen Lizbeth there, with somebody he didn't know, partying pretty good.''

"That's terrible,'' Tyrone said.

Howard nodded, knowing his son knew just how he had felt when he'd heard it.

"Yeah, I thought so. I called her, asked her about it. She had a perfectly reasonable explanation. She'd been in the bar, sure enough, but the guy she was with was her cousin, come to visit with his folks, and her mother had told her to take him out. So it was family, it didn't mean anything, they didn't do anything, it was her cousin.''

Howard shook his head. "I believed her. How could I not?

We loved each other, we trusted each other. And I wanted to hear there was a reason other than what I was most afraid of, so I was happy.''

"So what happened?"

"The summer went on. Rusty called again. He'd seen Lizbeth out again, dancing, drinking. Different guy, different place. He took it upon himself to follow them when they left. They drove up to Lover's Point, parked in the guy's car, fogged up the windows in the middle of July.''

"Oh, man," Tyrone said.

"Right sentiment, but I used harsher language when I heard. I was pretty torn up about it. I called Lizbeth and asked her about it. She denied it. Said whoever told me they'd seen her was a liar.

"So here's the situation. Either my girl was stepping out on me, or my best friend was a liar.''

Tyrone shook his head. "What did you do?"

"I checked it out. I called a couple of the guys Rusty said had seen Lizbeth. They confirmed his story, at least part of it.''

"That's terminal," Tyrone said.

"Yeah. But it gets worse."

His son raised his eyebrows in question. "How could it get worse?"

"I called Rusty. Told him to go see Lizbeth and to get my ring back. If she was going to lie to me, we were through.''

"Did he do it?"

"In a manner of speaking. He went to see her, told her what I'd said. She refused to give him the ring, but they talked for a long time. She said some . . . unkind things about me.''

Tyrone blinked at him.

"Called me a 'stupid shithead,' Rusty said."

"Jesus."

"So, I thanked Rusty for his efforts and said I'd take care of it. I bought a train ticket and waited for a long weekend in August when we didn't have much going on at camp. Went home. I got there on a Friday night late, caught a cab to Lizbeth's house. When I got there, I saw Rusty's beat-up old Chevrolet parked out front. *He must have come by to try and talk to her again,* I figured. Maybe even to get my ring back. *Good old Rusty.*

"I got out of the cab, walked over toward Lizbeth's front door, then I heard a noise coming from the Chevy—and I stopped and looked into the car. I saw Rusty and Lizbeth wrapped around each other in the front seat, both of them half undressed."

"Fuck," Tyrone said.

Howard considered saying something about his son's language, but this wasn't the time. In the grand cosmic scheme of things, a bad word didn't mean much. "It didn't get that far," Howard said. "I thought I was going to die, right there, on the spot. I didn't know whether to pull good old Rusty out and beat the crap out of him, or to turn and take off before they noticed me."

"What happened?"

"I stood there for what felt like a couple of million years, watching them kiss and fondle each other. It didn't seem real, like it was a bad dream. Then all of a sudden I got cold, really cold, as if I had turned to ice. August and it was probably still eighty-five degrees outside, hot, muggy, and I was cold. I reached out and tapped on the driver's-side window. They both jumped a couple of feet. When they turned and looked right at me, I smiled and waved good-bye. Then I left. The cab was gone, and I started to walk home.

"Rusty caught up with me a half a block or so away, on foot.

"He said, 'John! I can explain!'

"And I looked at him and said, 'No, you can't.' I was as cool as a barrel full of liquid oxygen. On the one hand, I wanted to smash his face in, but on the other, I was somehow . . . removed from it all. Like it was some kind of dream or vision, that I wasn't really even there. I said, 'You aren't my friend anymore Rusty. I don't want to talk to you, ever again.' ''

"Jesus, Dad."

"Yep. Lost my girl and my best friend at the same time. I didn't know then this kind of thing happens all the time, so often it's a cliche, and I don't guess it would have mattered if I had known. They were both lying scum and they deserved each other. I could have punched Rusty's teeth in, but I figured, like my momma used to say, karma will get them. People who do crap like this will get theirs someday. I didn't want to have anything else to do with them, even to the point of not bloodying my knuckles on Rusty's lying face.

"So I understand how you feel about all this, Tyrone, and all I can say is, you'll get over it eventually. It's terrible now, but someday, it won't seem so bad."

"Yeah? You still remember what happened to you pretty good."

"I didn't say you'd *forget* it. And it'll never go away completely, but it won't hurt as much as time goes by. Eventually there'll be a little scar that only aches a little if you poke hard enough at it. I know this doesn't help much, but that's the truth."

There was silence. Howard waited, to see if they were done, if he should leave or if the boy wanted to talk more. Finally, Tyrone said, "So, what happened to them? Rusty and Lizbeth. Did karma get them? They get run over by a bus or like that?"

Howard grinned. "Not exactly. They got married right after graduation. Went to college. He's now a medical doctor, she's an English professor, they have three kids, and according to my relatives back home who keep me up to date about such things, they have a wonderful marriage."

"So much for cosmic revenge."

"Thing with karma is, it might take a couple of lifetimes to catch up with you," Howard said.

"Oh, good."

"What's done is done, Ty. You can't take back what you

saw and heard, and if you could arrange to drop a piano on Bella and her new friend, it really wouldn't make you feel any better. Revenge hardly ever brings peace with it. Besides, if Lizbeth and I hadn't split, I'd never have met and married your mother. I figure I came out way ahead on the deal. No comparison." He smiled.

He got a small smile back from his son.

"You gonna eat supper?"

"I don't think so. I'm really not hungry."

"Okay. I'll cover it with Mom."

"Thanks, Dad. And, uh, Dad? Thanks for telling me the story."

"You're welcome, son."

26

The garage sure felt empty.

Michaels stood in the doorway to his garage, looking at the larger of his two big metal tool caddies. His most recent project car, the Plymouth Prowler, was gone, sold within a couple of days after he'd gotten it running right. He'd cleaned it up, and had taken it out only a few times, top up—it had been too cold and wet to drive the little convertible the way it was meant to be enjoyed—before his phone had rung with a potential buyer. That was how most of these things were done among the people he knew who restored old cars. Somebody told a friend, who told somebody else that this guy had a project car that was close to being finished, and if you were interested, you didn't want to wait for an ad on the net, because by then it would be too late.

Michaels smiled and walked back into the house. Might as well see what he had for supper.

In the kitchen, he dug around in the freezer and came up with a choice of Gardenburgers or teriyaki chicken sandwiches. He shrugged. The Gardenburger was going to get freezer-burned if he didn't eat it pretty soon, but hell with it, he wanted the chicken. He tore the plastic bag to vent, and stuck the sandwich into the microwave to thaw.

So, that was how it had gone. The phone had rung one evening, and a man with a lot of money who knew somebody who knew somebody asked about the Prowler.

Michaels figured out what the car had cost him, what the parts had added to that, and how much labor it had taken him to rebuild the engine and the transmission and linkage and bodywork. He added thirty percent to that, and named a figure.

The potential buyer agreed with the number so fast that Alex realized he could have asked for more. Then again, he didn't restore old cars to make a living—although it was nice to know that if he ever decided to chuck Net Force he probably could survive that way. All you needed was a garage and some tools, and he already had those. . . .

The microwave began its repetitive cheep, and as he reached for it, the phone also called him.

"Hello?"

"Uh, yeah, hello? I'm looking for Alex Michaels. The guy who does car stuff?"

Well, think of the Devil. "You found him."

"Oh, hey. My name is Greg Scates, I got your name from Todd Jackson."

Todd Jackson was the man who had bought the Prowler. "How are you, Mr. Scates? What can I do for you?"

"Well, uh, I've got an old car Todd thinks you might be interested in."

"What kind of car?"

"It's a Mazda MX-5, a 1995."

Michaels's eyebrows went up. MX-5 was better known in the U.S. as the Miata. A little drop-top two-seater, a lot smaller than the Prowler. He wasn't a big fan of Japanese hardware— he liked the big Detroit iron—but a Miata? He'd always thought those were on a par with the little MG Midgets. Fun.

And in '95 they still had the flip-out headlights too. Barn doors, they called them.

"So, tell me a little about the car."

"I have to be honest with you, Mr. Michaels, I don't know a lot about it. It belonged to my father, who passed away in November. He bought the car new after I'd left home. He drove it for a few months, but he didn't really have the reflexes for it—my mother was afraid he was gonna kill himself in it—so after a while, he put it in storage."

Interesting. "What kind of shape is it in?"

"I can't really say. Dad pulled the tires off it and put the car up on jacks in his garage—my folks live down in Fredericksburg—he drained all the fluids out of it, coated everything with Armor-All and some kind of grease, then put a cover over it. The tires are in plastic bags in the garage. As far as I know, it's been sitting like that for about sixteen years."

Michaels felt a surge of interest. You heard about these things, low-or-no-mileage cars stored in somebody's barn for future sale. He'd never happened across one himself, but it was a common fantasy among car people—a rare model in near-mint condition, inherited by some relative who didn't have a clue what it was worth and who'd sell it for pocket change.

He moved to the kitchen computer terminal, next to the pantry, and called up the Classic Book. Even though the car was only sixteen and technically not a classic, it would be in there. Given the average half-life of cars since the eighties, sixteen was fairly old.

Mazda, Mazda, ah, there it was. . . .

"So, what do you figure the car is worth, Mr. Scates?"

"Greg, please. I don't know. But Todd says if you're interested, you'll offer me a fair price."

Michaels looked at the computer readout. Hmm. Classic Book said the little two-seater convertible wasn't cheap if it was a '95 in good condition. And one that had been on jacks, assuming it was in better shape for being stored, would be worth even more. Still, he could swing it, given what he'd made on the Prowler. He'd have to see it first, of course.

"I'm interested, Greg. I'd like to take a look at it. But I'm not going to be able to get to Fredericksburg until Saturday. Can you sit on it that long?"

"No problem. It's been in the garage for years, it can wait a couple of more days."

Michaels nodded at the unseen speaker. "Good."

He got directions and a time, then hung up.

Well, well. Interesting how things worked out. With any luck at all, he'd have a new project car pretty soon. Sure would help that empty garage. And having a goal outside of work was always good.

Time for the teriyaki . . .

Thursday, January 13th, 9 a.m.
Bissau, Guinea-Bissau

Hughes rode in a bullet-proof Cadillac limo from his hotel toward the new Presidential Palace, and the ride was not particularly impressive. Even though the former President, Joao Bernardo Vieira, and his African Party for the Independence of Guinea-Bissau and Cape Verde, had dragged the locals kicking and screaming into the modern era, it was still a third-world country. Actually more like a fourth- or fifth-world country. Half-dressed natives worked and shopped in outdoor market stalls that dotted the streets among office buildings. There were open sewers just off the main roads, and a lot more dirt roads than paved ones. Finding a working public telephone was a rarity.

Agriculture and fishing were the main economic activities—ninety percent of the million and a half souls here worked on farms or boats, or processed the crops or fish that came from the land and sea. The primary exports were cashews, peanuts, and palm kernels, and they imported four times more goods than they shipped out—which wasn't saying much. The main local non-agricultural products were soft drinks and beer. National debt was high, exploration of minerals was minimal, and Guinea-Bissau was quite simply among the poorest countries on the planet. Most people here ate rice, and not much of it, and considered themselves lucky to have that. If they lived to be fifty, they were well ahead of the game. Less than forty percent of the population was literate, most of those men. Education was not wasted on women here—maybe one in four could read more than her own name.

There were no railroads, only a couple thousand miles of badly paved roads, one airport big enough for international flights to land at, and it was cheaper to use local pesos for toilet paper than it was to *buy* toilet paper. You didn't offer a left hand to greet people here. . . .

Given a choice, almost nobody civilized would choose to live in Guinea-Bissau. Unless they were at the top of the food chain. The very top.

At least it was the dry season. During the monsoons, you didn't walk, you waded.

Hughes leaned back in the car seat and stared at the multicolored swatches of pitiful humanity walking or standing along the street, staring at the passing limo. He was on his way to meet President Fernandes Domingos, a not-particularly-bright man who had somehow lucked into the job. Fortunately, Domingos *was* bright enough to know a good deal when he heard it. The Presidente had been out of the country, had spent much time in Johannesburg and London and Paris, and had developed a taste for things nearly impossible to enjoy in his own country without a lot more money than he could currently steal. These things included fine wines, finer women, and expensive evenings at the casinos in Monaco.

If things went as planned, Hughes would make Domingos richer than he had ever dreamed of being, and able to indulge his tastes in more pleasant circumstances than the dirty streets of Guinea. Domingos in turn would make it possible for Hughes to—for all practical purposes—eventually *own* the entire country.

Even a third-world pit such as this one currently was had an inestimable value—or it would, in the right hands. Political asylum alone was worth a fortune, not to mention what was hiding under the ground. Yes, Guinea-Bissau definitely had potential, in the right hands.

In *his* hands.

"The Compound is just ahead, sir," the driver said. He was large, white, and had a clipped, posh-English accent. On the seat next to him lay a submachine gun, and Hughes knew that under his chauffeur's coat the driver also carried a large-caliber pistol, and from what else he knew, the man had the ability to use both weapons expertly. He was an ex-British military operative of some kind, hired to make sure the President's special guests got where they were supposed to get in one piece. There wasn't much chance of being assassinated by locals, but the neighboring countries, such as Senegal and Guinea, were always wrangling with Guinea-Bissau or each other, sending ratty armies across ill-defined borders to loot and rape, and there was some small possibility of terrorism from saboteurs.

Since he was not officially supposed to *be* here, it would hardly do to have too high a profile—like a shoot-out with some half-baked crazed spy. Fortunately, the U.S. ambassador in this backwater owed Hughes several large favors, and if the man wasn't exactly in Hughes's pocket, he was *circumspect* in the extreme. You didn't get to be a full ambassador without learning which way the wind blew, then setting your sails accordingly.

Hughes turned his attention to the palace compound. The main building was big, ostentatious, three stories tall, and made of some slightly pink native stone, with glazed blue tiles on the roof. The architectural style looked to be a bad blend of Mediterranean and Spanish-style villas. The compound was maybe ten acres and a dozen buildings, and surrounded by a fifteen-foot-high matching stone wall topped with what looked like broken glass.

Hughes shook his head. This kind of spending fit a pattern he'd seen all over the world. The less wealth a country had, the larger the extravagances the top dogs lavished upon themselves. The rich got richer and the poor got poorer. What a surprise.

The limo arrived in front of a big electrically operated metal gate in the pink stone wall. A pair of guards with assault rifles outside the gate drifted over and bent to look inside the limo. The Brit nodded at them, and it was obvious they knew him, but he offered his ID anyway. The guards checked the ID, then waved at a third armed guard inside the gate at a small kiosk. The gate swung outward to admit the limo.

The driveway was circuitous, and wound around several sharp-angled turns bounded by ponds or dirt mounds covered with grass. Platt had explained that to Hughes. If you managed to get a car full of explosives through the gate, you weren't going to be able to build up enough speed to ram the palace hard enough to put your vehicle inside before you set it off.

The President was largely beloved—but apparently not universally so.

Eventually, the limo arrived at the entrance to the main building.

Standing in front of a set of tall, carved wooden doors was President Fernandes Domingos, along with a pair of bodyguards and a large-busted but otherwise willowy blond woman in a white blouse, a short black skirt, and three-inch heels. Very attractive, the woman. Domingos's mistress, perhaps?

Hughes alighted from the limo as the driver held the door. He smiled at Domingos, who flashed a set of perfect teeth in return.

"Ah, Thomas! How *good* to see you again!" Domingos spoke good English with an accent from South Africa, the country to which he had been sent for his university education. A university at which, apparently, Domingos had majored in sex, gambling, and drinking.

The two men shook hands. The President was short and heavyset, with a webwork of spidery veins across his nose and cheeks, visible despite his dark complexion. The broken vessels were probably due to incipient alcoholism. At fifty, he had a dissipated look, an aging rake who needed a magic picture in the attic, but unfortunately didn't have one. His namesake ancestors had been Portuguese, and somewhere along the way they had obviously taken a dip or two into the native pools, for he was darker than most Europeans, and what was left of his thinning, dyed-black hair was very curly. But Domingos's features were otherwise not Negroid, despite Platt's racist slurs.

"Mr. President. I am honored."

Domingos waved that away. "No, no, none of that, we are friends! Please, come into my humble home. And I would like you to meet Miss Monique Louis, who has just recently returned from Paris. I am sure you two will get along famously!"

Hughes eyed the blonde, who smiled lazily at him, a hint of come-hither in her expression. *"Bonjour,"* she said. "So nice to make your acquaintance."

Ah . . .

Unless he was terribly mistaken, the good President had apparently provided him with a . . . *companion*. Well. She was attractive enough. And Domingos certainly had enough practice in such matters to have selected an expert trull. Why not? Negotiations could sometimes be arduous, and Hughes might as well relax after they were done—but only afterward.

The tall doors were carved in bas-relief, images of native people, proud faces and young bodies, most of them nude, a kind of gallery of tribal Africa. Platt must have loved that when he'd seen it. Hughes could almost see the cracker shaking his head in disgust. Except for the naked black women, of course.

The doors swung silently open, each operated by a black man dressed entirely in white—shoes, pants, shirt, coat. Monique moved over, took Hughes's arm in hers, and smiled at him, and they followed the President into the palace. The bodyguards swung into position behind them.

This, Hughes decided, should be interesting.

27

At Mac's, one of the last old-style hard-core gyms in Manhattan, Platt grunted through a set of heavy squats. Wasn't no ferns or New Age music playing here, no chrome and red leatherette magnomachines or yuppie VR slantwalkers, just racks and racks of iron—dumbbells, barbells—and benches and racks and a concrete floor with a few rubber pads on it. Mirrors on the walls and good lighting, the place had those, but that was it. You didn't come here to get a nice glow, you came here to sweat—and to know pain.

He was in the safety rack, so the weight wasn't gonna fall and crush his ass, but that didn't help his thighs. They burned as though he was standing hip-deep in molten lava. Four hundred pounds on the bar across his shoulders, and after the first set, each rep was a war. He hated squats, hated 'em, and after a couple of heavy sets, he could barely move. He'd puked more than a few times after squats, in such pain he couldn't even stand up without help, but that was how it went. You wanted to be strong, you had to move big weight, that was

the name of that tune. Those little pansies who did leg exten-
sions with fifty pounds and thought they were working out
made Platt want to laugh. You didn't see those guys here. Mac
would laugh their asses right out of the building.

Excuse me, sir, but where are the cardiowalkers?

Why, just go out the front door and a couple of miles that
way, hoss. Look for a spa full of sissies, you'll fit right in.

Down Platt went, legs cooking in their own juices. Below
horizontal, butt almost on his heels.

Up he came, vibrating, shaking, quivering, fire flowing
through his veins and arteries, burning his muscles, hot right
to the bone.

Man!

Three more, and he was able—barely, finally!—to rack the
weight. He grabbed a towel, wiped the sweat off his face and
neck, and moved to the water fountain. Around him, the clang
of steel echoed as men grunted and strained against the big
plates. There were a couple of women here, bodybuilders on
the juice, so they looked like men. That kind of woman didn't
appeal to him at all. He liked to see a woman in shape, but
not a male shape caused by mojo steroids that did everything
but grow a *dick* on her.

Well. Enough of this. Time to shower and head for the place
in Queens where he had his throwaway computer set up. The
feds were about to get another surprise, courtesy of the Fried
Sex gang. A big surprise this time.

Platt laughed aloud. He didn't see how life could get much
better than this.

Friday, January 14th, 8:00 a.m.
Ambarcik, Siberia

Jay Gridley leaned into the fierce wind coming off the East
Siberian Sea, a wind so strong and cold that it would blast an

unprotected man to death in a matter of seconds. Enough wind so that the rocks along the shore were bare of snow, despite more than ten feet of it having fallen in the last two months. The snow had been blown away like so much dry talcum powder. The locals here liked to joke about how cold it got. There were people in Alaska or Canada who bragged about throwing a pot of boiling water into the air and watching it freeze on the way down. In Siberia, they liked to say, the water would freeze while still in the pot. Sometimes while the pot was still on the fire, *da*?

It was an unlikely place to be hunting for clues to a Danish terrorist organization, maybe more so than any other, but there was a blowhole in the ice up ahead where seals came up to breathe, and one of those "seals" was the packet of information he wanted to find. Jay was armored against the cold—electrically heated underwear, including socks, hat, and gloves—with four layers of material over that—polyprop, silk, wool, and fur—a face mask, and heavy boots. Even so, he felt the cold prying at the mask he wore, digging at the smallest seams in his clothing. This was as close a VR scenario as he could build to what the locals actually faced, and he wondered how they could stand it. The houses here were all heavily insulated, with triple doors and windows, dead spaces in the insulated walls, and even so, you could store your food in an unheated back room and it would keep all winter long.

Brrr.

A Klaxon began screaming at him, loud and insistent. What the hell was that? Where was the sound coming from? He turned, put his back to the wind, and saw a tower in the distance.

Jay did the mental shift and realized that the Klaxon was his real-time override, back at his workstation. Oops. Something bad—the override's threshold was dialed up high enough so only something really nasty would set it off. A fire in the building, a major system failure, the pizza delivery truck had a flat. . . .

Better check this out quick.

Jay logged himself out of VR.

Toni was in the middle of a stack of electronic correspondence when her workstation crashed. One second she was dealing with a memo from Supply telling her that Net Force had exceeded its normal monthly quota of phone and virgil batteries, the next second the screen went blank.

Crap. Just what she needed, a computer failure—

The screen relit then, only out for a second or two, but the memo from Supply was gone, and in its place was a picture of a man's hand. All of the fingers were curled down and held in place by the thumb—except for the middle finger, which stood straight up. The image rotated slowly on its axis, and there was no mistaking the ancient obscene gesture.

She heard her secretary laugh. "What?" Toni yelled.

"My computer is giving me the finger," her secretary yelled back.

Toni had a sudden sinking feeling that this image was not confined to just two stations.

It didn't take long for her to learn she was right.

Good Lord. Somebody had hacked into the Net Force computer system and given the organization the bird.

This was bad.

Toni met Jay Gridley as they both headed for the conference room. Joanna Winthrop beat them there by half a second. Alex was already there. He didn't even wait for them to sit down before he started in.

"All right, what the hell happened?"

"Frihedsakse," Jay and Joanna said simultaneously. They glared at each other, then both tried to talk at once.

"I found the—"

"They came in by—"

"One at a time," Toni cut in, before Alex could say it. "Jay?"

"They got in through a subsystem in FBI Personnel. It's a dedicated Direct Line used for submitting resumés and job applications. In theory, it's not supposed to be cross-linked with secure systems without gate passwords for every upload or download, but in practice a lot of times, somebody opens the link to supervisors looking for new employees, and they leave it open so they don't have to spend five minutes every time they need to relink to send a file. Somebody got in on that line and into our mainframe."

Toni could see that Joanna was eager to talk. "Lieutenant?"

"Our circulating antivirals caught the program almost immediately. There was no damage to hardware or software. The rotating hand image was already on file, and it looks as if the hack was designed to get in, open that visual, and post it to our system as an EWS—Emergency Warning System—override. As far as I—I mean, as far as Jay and I can tell—nobody lost any data, and the virus didn't do anything else."

"We're running full diagnostics," Jay added, "but I can guarantee they won't find any more infection. This is nothing, a simple encapsulated program, the kind of thing a kid hacker would do just to show he could. They gave us the finger. Big deal. No harm, no foul."

Alex shook his head. "You're wrong, Jay. This is a major hit."

Jay frowned, but Toni saw from her face that Joanna understood.

Toni said, "Net Force is supposed to be the guardian for the nation's computer systems. If this group can get into our supposedly secure setup, how does that make us look? What kind of confidence is this going to inspire in our clients, when it comes to protecting *their* systems?''

"But it doesn't *matter* that they got in," Jay said. "They couldn't *do* anything! Our automatics nailed the program within a couple of seconds. It opened a picture we already had in our files. All the picture did was just sit there and shine. It couldn't have done anything else no matter what. We were back on-line before most people even noticed it. It was a glitch, no damage, zip city.''

"We're not talking programs here," Alex said. "We're talking politics. It doesn't *matter* that the terrorists didn't do any damage, what matters is that *they got in*. Even if you and I know better, people who don't understand computers are going to be afraid. Sure, they'll say, the Net Force bleebs say no big deal, but so, if it's no big deal, how come they didn't keep them out in the first place?''

Jay shook his head. "But—but—''

"Toni, see what you can do for damage control," Alex said to her. To Jay and Joanna, he said, "Try and backwalk this, see if you can get us any leads. I have a feeling this is going to get real ugly on us if we don't short-circuit it pretty quick. Go.''

After Jay and Joanna were gone, Toni sat alone with Alex.

"You okay?" she asked.

"Yes, of course, I'm fine. It's just all this." He waved one hand to encompass Net Force and all its problems

But he wasn't fine, she could see that. He had been tighter than a violin's E-string since he'd come back after Christmas. At first she'd thought it was because of his little adventure in the desert that he didn't want to talk to her about. But that wasn't the kind of thing to bother him, at least not as much as he seemed to be bothered. He'd come out a winner, captured a bad guy, no loss of face there. If anything, he came off kind of heroic. Men admired that kind of thing in other men.

She hadn't asked about his visit with his daughter and ex-wife, he hadn't volunteered, and Toni suspected that maybe the visit hadn't gone well. Even divorced, that woman seemed to run Alex's life long-distance, and Toni hated her for it. And the woman had to be stupid; otherwise how could she have ever let Alex get away from her?

But it wasn't Toni's place to ask, not given their strictly professional relationship. All she could do was offer opportunities for him to talk. If he didn't want to do that, she couldn't make him.

"Okay," she said. "You know where to find me. I'll see if I can bury this where nobody will stumble across it."

She stood, started to leave.

"Toni?"

"Mm?"

"I'm going to look at a new car tomorrow—assuming the sky doesn't fall before then. Well, it's an old car, one I'm considering buying, assuming this whole place hasn't totally gone to hell by then. Car's a little Miata, it's in a garage in Fredericksburg, that's on I-95 a few miles south of here."

"Uh-huh?"

"Well, given how much you know about cars and all, I was, uh, wondering, that is, I mean . . . would you like to go along and help me check it out?"

Toni was stunned. Where had *that* come from?! Out of nowhere, that's where! Her brain stalled, as if somebody had slapped it silly. For a moment, she couldn't think, couldn't talk, couldn't even breathe. Then her little warning voice kicked in, and what it said was:

Oh, baby! He's asking you out! *Slow, go slow, don't scare him off!*

She managed a breath. "Yeah, I'd like that. A Miata, huh? One of my brothers had one of those once."

"Yeah," he said quickly, "I remember you told me that, so, uh, your advice would really be helpful. You know."

She wanted to grin, but she held her face to polite interest. He was like a fourteen-year-old kid asking a girl out on his first date—she could see it in his expression, hear it in his voice. He was *nervous*. Afraid she would turn him down.

As if *that* was remotely possible.

It made him all the more adorable, that he was rattled.

"I, uh, want to get an early start," he said, "so why don't I pick you up about seven?"

"Seven would be good."

"Uh, where do you, uh, live? I've never been to your place."

She gave him her address and directions, still full of wonder about this.

Don't go jumping to conclusions, girl. He just asked you to go look at an old car, not for a weekend in Paris.

Shut up, she told her inner voice.

"Probably you should wear some some old clothes," he said. "It might get a little greasy poking around in an old garage. I'm going to take some tools and stuff. I might be able to get the thing running. If you don't mind hanging around while I try."

"No problem," she said.

For a long moment—a couple of millennia anyhow—she stood there staring at him, feeling so bubbly she wanted to jump up and down and scream. Finally she pulled herself away. "Okay," she said. "I'll go work on the hack."

Once she was out of the conference room, her back to Alex, she could not stop the grin. Yes! Yes!

When he'd been thirteen, Alex Michaels had ridden the Tyler Texas Tornado—at the time, the world's largest roller coaster. He'd never forgotten that weightless, pit-of-the-stomach rush as the car fell over the first drop and gravity let go of him. If it hadn't been for the safety bar, he would have floated right out of the ride.

He felt like that now, as if he had just gone over the first drop of the TTT. His stomach was fluttery, his heart was thumping along at least twice its normal speed, his mouth was dry, and he was breathing fast.

Jesus H. Christ. What did you just do? Did you just ask Toni Fiorella, your assistant, out on a date?

No, no, not a date! Just to go check out the car. She knows about cars—remember when she came to the house and saw the Prowler? She knew all about motors and hydraulics and like that! She had a house full of brothers who were into cars!

Uh-huh. Sure. Who do you think you're fooling here, pal? I was there, I remember you looking at her butt while you were on the phone talking to your daughter. And I remember silat class, too, buddy. When you and she are all entwined in one of those grappling moves. How she feels pressed against you, just before she throws your stupid butt on the ground.

He knew. He knew this was not a smart thing to be doing. Toni worked for him, and yeah, he'd gotten vibes from her that she didn't exactly find him hideous or anything, but this was dangerous territory. Toni was bright, adept, good-looking, and, oh, yes, it would be a lot of fun to get closer than they did in *silat*. There was nothing wrong with his imagination— he just hadn't let it play much since he and Megan had split up. But that last visit to the old house, that whole scene with Megan and her new boyfriend, that had pretty much put the final nail in the coffin, hadn't it? The marriage was dead, they weren't going to get back together, and when he'd calmed down later and thought about it, he realized he didn't *want* to get back together with a woman who could do to him what she had done. Megan had a nasty streak, and while it didn't come out that often, it was very mean-spirited when it did. He didn't want to be with somebody who could go postal on him at any time. That was no way to live, sleeping with one eye open.

He'd been behaving like a monk for a long time. He'd put all of himself into his work or his car, he'd run or biked thousands of miles to wear himself out, and it wasn't like it was a sin to take pleasure in the company of an attractive woman.

It didn't have to go any farther than that. He didn't have to risk losing Toni as a friend and coworker by pushing it into romance. He could keep his hands to himself, his pants zipped, and keep it platonic.

Right. Was that why you asked her to take a little drive down to Fredericksburg? To be Mr. Platonic?

Shut up, he told himself. *Nothing has happened, nothing is going to happen. We're friends, that's all.*

His inner voice laughed at him all the way back to his office.

28

When Toni Fiorella walked past her, Joanna Winthrop looked at the woman and was sure her suspicions were dead on target:

Miss Toni had the hots for their boss.

It wasn't that hard to see, given how Fiorella blossomed like a hothouse orchid time-lapse vid every time she was around Alex Michaels. He didn't seem to notice, no surprise. Men were usually stupid that way—among all the other ways. Still, he was a nice enough guy, and the truth was Winthrop had entertained a couple of fantasies in that direction herself. Well, at least before she'd started finding reasons to drop by and see Julio Fernandez. Michaels was okay, but Julio? Julio was a jewel.

In fact, she could probably break some time away from work tomorrow to get together with him and do a little computer stuff. He still wanted to learn, and she was getting more and more comfortable hanging around with him. The guy didn't seem to have any ego, at least as far as women were concerned, and he just kept surprising her with what he said and how he said it.

She grinned to herself. Yeah, let Toni pine after the boss. They were probably better suited for each other. Winthrop was finding that lately she had developed a real hankering for . . . Hispanic food.

Friday, January 14th, 5:45 a.m.
High Desert, Eastern Oregon

It was still dark outside the one-man funnel tent, dark and cold too, but at least the snow had started falling again.

John Howard wasn't exactly toasty in his mummy sleeping bag, but he was warm enough, and the face shield had kept his nose from freezing off. He didn't want to peel himself out of the bag and get up, but he had to go pee and there was no getting around that. It wouldn't be light for a while yet, but he didn't have to go looking for a place—he was all by himself. Like his grandfather used to say, he was so far out, the sun came up between here and town. . . .

He'd planned to do a winter survival weekend in Washington state after the scheduled joint Net Force/military exercises in the Pacific Northwest, but there was some kind of problem with the biochemical depot at Umatilla. Apparently one of the destabilized nerve-gas rockets had sprung a leak. It wasn't much of a leak, on the order of a microscopic spray, and it was contained and not dangerous, but the Army had been running around trying to put a media lid on it, and of course, had failed utterly to do so. As a result, the civilians nearest the depot were terrified that a cloud of poison was about to roll into town and kill every man, woman, child, and dog, and folks were being sent to visit relatives way out of town, so Net Force and the Army had canceled their exercise. The

Army figured that it wouldn't look good to have a bunch of guys in combat gear running around and going *hut-hut-hut!* all crisp and active. That would sure as hell scare folks, none of whom would believe for a second that this was just a drill and pure coincidence. Even so, Howard hadn't wanted to skip his own personal survival trip, so he'd decided to drop down into Oregon instead. The differences in the terrain between eastern Oregon and eastern Washington on either side of the Columbia weren't all that major.

Howard slid out of the sleeping bag, already dressed in long underwear, pants, socks, and a heavy wool shirt. He removed the spare socks he'd stuffed into his boots to keep the scorpions and spiders out—even though it was winter, this was a good habit to get into. He pulled the boots on after he looked for hitchhikers anyway—damn, they were chilly!—grabbed a jacket and hat, and scooted out of the tent.

The early morning sky was perfectly clear, with stars glittering in hard, sharp, fiery points. You could see the Milky Way out here, and all kinds of constellations that you'd never spot in the city. And the colors of the stars, reds, blues, yellows. Truly a beautiful sky.

He stood, ambled a few yards off along the path he'd packed down before he'd turned in the night before, and wrote his name in a snowbank piled up against what looked like a frozen and pretty-sad-about-it creosote bush.

Back inside, he lit his hurricane candle, and set up his single-burner propane stove. The mouth of the funnel tent was just tall enough to sit upright in. The tent was made of double-walled rip-stop Gortex, which kept the snow out, but still allowed most of the moisture inside to escape, so you didn't wake up with your own condensed water vapor raining on you. In the old days, he'd have gathered firewood and started a small outdoor fire to boil water for coffee and rehydration of his food, but the current land-use philosophy was for "no impact" campsites. No cutting down trees or clearing brush, no trenching your tent for runoff, no open fires, and only a minimal latrine—and even that had to be covered and tamped before you broke camp.

He grinned as he started a snowmelt pot of water heating. He'd been on a couple of outings where the ''no impact'' rule had been so strictly adhered to they'd had to bag and seal their own solid waste and pack it out. *That* had been worth a few laughs: *Here, Sarge, I saved you some Tootsie Rolls for dessert. Yeah? Well, that's funny, 'cause I got some chocolate pudding right here for you too, Corporal. . . .*

It was amazing what soldiers would joke about.

It was about twelve degrees outside right now, and the ground was hard as a rock and frozen to boot, so digging wasn't going any deeper than the snow, but he had biodegradable toilet paper pads that would disappear the first time they got wet, and by spring any signs of scat would be long gone. It wasn't likely anybody was going to be out here playing in the snow before springtime. . . .

He had a little hike ahead of him today, just ten miles. But on snowshoes and with a backpack it would work him some. He had a GPS if he got lost, though he'd try to locate his next campsite the old-fashioned way, with a compass and landmarks. It wasn't as easy as the GPS, of course, where all you had to do was punch a couple of buttons and it would tell you exactly where you were and how to get to where you wanted to go. But batteries could go dead, satellites could fall, and a compass was reliable if you knew how to allow for magnetic north and all. If you lost your compass, there were the stars, including the sun. And if it was cloudy, there was dead reckoning, though that was a little more iffy.

Truth was, he hadn't been lost in a long time. He had a good sense of direction.

At six a.m., he pulled his virgil and keyed his morning check-in code. He could also find his way out using the virgil, and could go to vox to call for help if he needed it. If something happened and he couldn't call out, Net Force or other rescuers could also find him via the little device, which had a

homer with a dedicated battery in it. It wasn't as if he were
Lewis and Clark, a million miles away from civilization. Still,
it was cold and he was all by himself out here in the middle
of the high desert, with fresh snow piled a foot and a half
deep. If anything happened to him, help wouldn't get to him
right away.

There was a real risk to being here. Which was, of course,
the point. The way a man found out what he was made of was
when he tested himself against real danger. VR only went so
far, no matter how real it felt. You always knew you weren't
gonna die in VR. But in real life, sometimes things went to
hell, and you had to survive on your wits and your skills. This
little three-day trip was not that big a deal. He'd lived off the
land on his own for a couple of weeks, in terrain ranging from
desert to jungle. There was a great sense of accomplishment
in knowing that if you survived a plane crash in the middle
of nowhere, you could probably survive long enough for help
to arrive. Assuming anybody wanted to find you . . .

How did you come to climb that big old mountain, fella?

Well, sir, it was in my way. . . .

The water started to boil, and Howard dug in his pack for
the freeze-dried coffee crystals.

Somewhere, he'd heard about an order of Zen monks or
some-such, who lived high up the slopes of an Oriental mountain. They had a little cafe there, and when climbers would
stop in, they would sell them coffee. There were two prices:
a two-dollar cup of coffee—and a two-*hundred*-dollar cup of
coffee. When asked the difference, the monks would smile and
say, "A hundred and ninety-eight dollars." The brew, the water, the cups, all were exactly the same, but there were always
those who were willing to spring for the more expensive cup.
They swore it tasted better.

He could understand that. What he was about to drink
wasn't in the same class as freshly roasted and freshly ground
premium beans strained through a gold filter and served in
fine china by a well-practiced and attentive waiter, but the first

cup of coffee on a survival camp out was always better than the best restaurant stuff. Always.

Friday, January 14th, 11 p.m.
Bissau, Guinea-Bissau

Hughes rolled over in the king-sized orthopedic bed and watched as Monique waded through the ankle-deep white carpet toward the bathroom. It was a nice view, her naked backside, and he enjoyed it until she slipped into the bathroom and closed the door quietly behind her. He grinned. She was no more a natural blonde than her boobs were real, but neither of these things detracted from her expertise as a lover. After three sessions with her—last night, a quickie at noon, and tonight— he was completely spent, tired, and more relaxed than he had been in years. This was one of the perks of wealth, a well-practiced mistress, and he toyed with the idea of hiring Monique full-time. He could afford her now, and soon would be able to afford thousands like her.

But—perhaps not. It might be better to avoid any more entanglements until his major goal was achieved. Even an entanglement as much fun as Monique.

He glanced at his watch. Just after eleven o'clock. What would that make it in D.C.? Was it four hours ahead here? Five?

It didn't matter. Platt was back there, merrily adding gasoline to various fires, setting up the project's end-stage. Hughes hadn't called the cracker while he'd been here, but that wasn't necessary at this stage of the game.

Negotiations had gone well with Domingos, even better than he'd expected. The main reason the man hadn't closed the deal with Platt had been a simple matter of money—Domingos wanted more. Hughes had anticipated all along that the

President would up the ante, and had been surprised when he hadn't done so earlier, so this was not an unforeseen bump in the road. It had merely come later than expected. For the sake of appearances, Hughes had dickered, pretended to be insulted, and had offered a stiff resistance to any change in the basic agreement. After sufficient time for Domingos to convince himself that he was the equal of a platoon of Arabic horse traders, Hughes had allowed himself to be worn down and persuaded. Another thirty mil was thrown into the pot, bringing the payout to the President to an even hundred million dollars U.S. Or, if he preferred, he could have it in French francs, Japanese yen, or British pounds. Or dinars, rupiahs, rubles, or Guinea-Bissau's own pesos.

Dollars would be fine, the President had allowed.

Hughes grinned again as the bathroom door swung open and Monique walked through the thick carpet toward him. The view was even better from the front, he decided, what with her dyed-blond pubic thatch shaved into that little heart shape. Even the breast implants had been hung by an expert medico, for they looked—and felt—quite real.

Spent as he thought he was, he felt a bit of a stirring in his groin.

"Ah, you are awake, I see."

"Not all of me."

"Oh, but I am certain I can remedy that, *oui*?"

He chuckled. If anybody could raise his hopes, certainly Monique could.

"Let's see, shall we?" he said.

29

"You want to stop for some coffee or something?" Alex asked. He waved at a service station off to their right.

"No, I'm fine," Toni said. "I had my two cups already."

The day was chilly, but clear, and traffic was light. The inside of the van was a hair too warm.

He smiled at her, a little awkwardly, she thought.

"Yeah, me too," he said.

Toni had the impression that he wished he hadn't done this—invited her to go along with him to look at the Miata. They were in the company car designated for his use, a politically correct electric/hydrogen-powered minivan. And as everybody who'd ever driven one knew, as gutless a piece of machinery as you could find. It had all the get-up-and-go of a turtle with a broken leg. Top speed was sixty-five—and that was downhill, with a tailwind and a god who took pity on you, and it took a long time to get to that fast. Range of the van was about two hundred miles—if you added both propulsion systems together. Then you had to pull over, plug in, or get a new bottle of hydrogen. Alex was allowed a certain number of personal miles every month, though he seldom used them. Easy to understand why. The joke around the agency was that if you had a roller skate, you could sit on that, push with your hands, and get where you wanted to go faster than the minivan—and your butt would hurt less when you arrived.

Alex had a fair-sized tool chest in the back of the van, along with a car battery, several cans of oil, and more cans of brake and transmission fluid.

"You talk to Jay this morning?" she said.

"I checked his vox around six, heard his update."

Toni had also checked the coded message, but to keep the conversation going she pretended she hadn't. "Anything new?"

"No. Nothing good *or* bad. We haven't run the terrorists down, though we've got all kinds of little clues. No new rascals on any systems—at least none we've found. I'm waiting for it, though. These guys are going to drop a big brick on us, I can feel it coming."

He looked at her. "I also feel a little guilty about taking the day off."

"Nothing you could do at the office."

"I know, but even so—"

A big double-cab pickup truck whipped by in the speed lane. It had to be going eighty-five or ninety. The wind of the truck's passage rocked the minivan.

"Where are the cops when you need one?" Toni said.

That got a little smile from him.

She said, "I've buried the system break-in as best I can, but we probably need to talk about what happens if it becomes known outside the house. Just in case."

He glanced at her, then back at the freeway. "Oh, I'd bet my next paycheck against a stale doughnut that Senator White'll know about it by Monday—if he doesn't know already."

"You thought about what you'll say if he calls you on it?"

"Sure. The truth. It's easier to remember." He smiled again. "I'll throw all of Jay's rationalizations at him, but that won't matter. He would like to get rid of us and pretend we never existed. Any excuse will do."

"We could sacrifice a goat," she said, half-joking. "Somebody high enough up to take the fall."

Now he looked harder at her. "You have somebody in mind?"

All right, if they were going to go down that road. She took a deep breath and started to speak. "Well, yeah, I was thinking maybe I—"

"No," he cut in. "Don't touch that control. I don't want to hear it. Nobody is falling on her sword here, certainly not you!"

The vehemence of his response surprised her. She was at a loss.

"There are always going to be idiots like White," he said. "We'll always have one wolf or another chasing our sled and howling for blood. We'll deal with them, but we won't throw any of our people off, understood?"

"Okay."

He smiled a little, to take the sting out of it. "Besides, if something happened to you, I wouldn't be able to find the door to get into HQ."

Okay, that was a compliment. You can follow that one up. Go—

She heard a siren, looked into the outside rearview mirror, and saw a police car coming up fast. The siren dopplered louder as the car drew closer. The driver sure had his foot in the fuel injector; he was flying.

Alex drifted from the slow lane over onto the wide shoulder and slowed.

The flashing light strobed Alex's face as a Virginia state trooper's unit blew past them.

"He's going after that truck," Alex said. "How about that. There is some justice in the world."

She nodded. She was in a car with Alex going somewhere other than Net Force business. Maybe there was justice.

Or maybe Guru's *kris* had some magic left in its black and convoluted steel. She grinned.

"Something funny?"

"No, just a pleasant thought," she said.

Saturday, January 15, 7:45 a.m.
Quantico, Virginia

Joanna wasn't scheduled to work this morning, but she was on her way into HQ anyway. She still hadn't run down the SOB who had used her station to post that fruitcake militia thing, though she had figured out it was done by remote and not in person—big surprise there. This latest incursion with the finger image pissed her off even more, even though it hadn't come through her in particular. It was a slap in the face, a direct challenge to Net Force that she took personally. She was going into the net for some serious webwalking to find these creeps.

Or, at least that was her intention. As she was heading in, she saw Julio Fernandez in his sweats, limping back from the direction of the obstacle course.

Well. She hadn't been able to connect with him for the last couple of days, they'd played message tag, and now there he was, in the flesh. It wouldn't hurt to say hello. Maybe she could kill two birds with one stone.

He saw her, smiled, and nodded. "Lieutenant."

"Sergeant. You on duty?"

"No, ma'am. I just finished hobbling through my morning constitutional and was gonna hit the showers before I headed home."

"I'm going to be doing some work on the web," she said. She waved at the HQ building. "You want to come along, sit in? I can show you some of the more interesting aspects of VR."

"I'd like that. I still ought to hit the showers first. I'm a little ripe."

She sniffed. "You don't stink too bad. I think I can stand being in the same room with you. Come on."

"Yes, ma'am."

They both grinned.

Truth was, she didn't mind a man who smelled like a man instead of a fruity aftershave or deodorant. Nothing wrong with a little clean sweat. It was probably all the pheromones that appealed to her. . . .

Saturday, January 15, 9:00 a.m.
Washington, D.C.

The thing was, Tyrone realized, you could only lie in bed staring at the ceiling for so long before it got boring. Real boring.

He had gone over what he'd said, what she'd said, every detail of what had happened between him and Bella a thousand times. Nothing was going to change. It was like a big rock—no matter how many times you poked at it with your finger, it was still going to *stay* a rock.

He sighed, rolled out of bed, and headed for the bathroom. He did the control finger-jive in front of the vidwall's sensor, and the default channel, the newscom, flicked on. Dad had programmed the house com unit to default to the news channel, the idea being that it wouldn't hurt any of them to watch the news now and then. Tyrone had been meaning to reprogram the thing—lock-chips were a joke if you knew *any-*

thing—but he hadn't gotten around to changing it yet.

The multimedia local news blared and flared. They were doing the traffic. First, real-time traffic, streets and highways, then virtual traffic, which parts of the net were clear, which parts were clogged, which subservers were down or wounded.

He made it into the bathroom, listening to the news with half his attention while he peed.

Dad was gone, off on his survival thing. Mom had a breakfast with her women friends—the Goddesses, they called each other—and wouldn't be back before eleven, at least. So he had the house to himself. Lying in bed wasn't going to solve anything, so he might as well *do* something.

The temptation was to log into the net and catch up on his computer work. He'd been slack to the point of droop on that during the last few months, all wrapped up in Bella, Bella, Bella. Now that he thought about it, that was pretty much all he'd done. When he wasn't with her, he had been dreaming about her, thinking about her, or talking about her.

In a flash of clarity, Tyrone realized how boring *he* must have been to be around lately. It was Bella this or Bella that, or Bella the other, and his friends—such as they were—must have elected him King of the Dull and Stupids on the first ballot. Particularly he owed Jimmy-Joe a big sorry-sorry. He remembered saying to him, "It's just a game," about the computer stuff, and the look of horror on his friend's face when he'd said that.

Man, was that a data no-flow, slip. Stupid squared to the tenth power.

But—okay, okay. That was then, this was now.

Somehow, though, the idea of sitting down and going VR just didn't lube his tube. He needed to do *some*thing, but it wasn't the computer.

So, what? What else was there?

He grinned at himself. Pretty sorry when the only two things in your life were computers and a lying girlfriend, and you didn't even have *her* anymore.

He could go to the mall. No, overwrite *that* option, Bella lived at the damned mall. He could go for a walk, 'cept his neighborhood was about as interesting as a bag of kitty litter. He could surf the entcom channels for a vid. . . .

No, no, he needed to *do* something, not just sit back and suck up data, whether it was VR, vids, or whatever. But what to do on a chilly, sunny day?

"And now for local events," the vox from the newscom droned. "Students from the Kennedy High School marching band are having a car wash to raise money for new uniforms. This will be at the Lincoln Mall Vidplex from noon to four, Saturday."

Oh, yeah, a car wash, that was exciting, helloooo slipper!

The drone continued. "The Foggy Bottom Children's Library welcomes writer Wendy Heroumin for a reading of her latest book, *The Purple Penguin.*"

Hey, hey, a children's book! Whoa, tachycardia city!

"And the Sixth Annual Boomerang Tournament begins in Lonesdale Park at eight a.m. Saturday and runs through Sunday at five p.m."

Tyrone was finishing his hands when he heard this last announcement. A boomerang tourney? What was a boomerang tourney? Those aborigine things? The sticks?

Well, hey, slip, you got zip on your drive—why don't you go and find out?

He grinned. All right. Yeah. He could do that. The new park was only a dozen blocks away, so he wouldn't even have to take pubtrans. He could just Nike on over there and check it out. One thing for sure, he wasn't going to run into Bella there. Or likely anybody else he knew either.

Why not? He'd never even seen a boomerang, except in VR, and that only as background scenario. Why not?

A short guy built like a brick was in the middle of the soccer field. He reared back with a dayglow orange boomerang in his right hand, concave side forward, one end up, and threw the thing so hard his hand went forward and touched the ground.

The boomerang did this kind of eccentric egg-rolling end-over-end flight, swooped about fifty meters straight ahead, then started to curve to the left. It kept going up, twisted so it was flat-side-down, twirled and twirled and circled back around the guy, maybe ten meters high, went behind him, headed out in front of him again, a full circle, then did a little jog up and spun toward him. The spinning orange delta-shape came right at the guy, who held his hands about a dozen centimeters apart in front of himself, palms facing each other. When the stick was just about to hit him in the chest, he slapped his hands together and trapped it.

The guy never moved his feet, he didn't have to, it came right back to him.

This was so flowing fine!

I got to have one of these!

Tyrone had been watching for about an hour. This was fantastic, there were ems and fems out there doing things he couldn't believe. They were making the things swoop and twirl, making them dive and circle, keeping two or three in the air at one time, running and catching them, laughing, tumbling, it was great.

His favorite demo had been—according to the woman narrating on the portable PA system—the war boomerang. Unlike the sport models, this one was not designed to return. The man who threw the thing was tall and thin. He wound up, putting everything he had into the throw, judging by what Tyrone could tell, and the stick, which was almost straight, and about twice as big as the sport models, flew like an arrow, straight ahead, maybe a meter and a half above the ground, it flew, and flew, and flew, just . . . kept going, on and on.

Man!

When it finally dropped, Tyrone couldn't believe how far it had flown. Two hundred and twenty meters, easy. It was like it had a jet motor in it.

There was a break in the action. Tyrone headed for the little tables they'd set up for sales. There were maybe twenty different models on the tables, various angles, sizes, colors. He couldn't begin to figure out what they all meant.

"New at this, mate?" the man behind the table said. He had an accent so thick you could lean against it. Australian.

"Yeah," Tyrone said. "But I want to learn."

"Right. How much you lookin' to spend then?"

Tyrone pulled his credit card out of his pocket and called up his balance. He'd floated a lot of shine on Bella, but he had about fifty in his account.

He told the seller the amount. What else did he have to shine it on?

"Hey, for that, you can get just about anything on the table. Though you might want to start with a sturdy model until you get the hang of it." The Aussie picked up a light-brown boomerang with one of the blade tips painted white. He handed it to Tyrone.

"You hold it by the white tip, if you're right-handed, yeah, like that, just like making a fist, thumb on the outside, there you go. When you throw, it's straight ahead, you put a little wrist into it. You need to allow for wind direction and all, but we toss in a little how-to chiplet, tells you everything you need to know to get started."

Tyrone examined the boomerang. It was wood, plywood, and while it was flat on the bottom except for a scalloped outer edge under the paint, the top edges were angled. The leading inside edge was blunt, and the leading outside edge had been sharpened so that it sloped from the full thickness to a thinner margin. The part you held onto was cut to mirror the leading edge—thick on the outside, thin on the inside. Tyrone guessed that the thing was almost half a meter long, maybe a centimeter thick in the center. Probably about a forty-five- or fifty-degree angle. He turned it over. Laser-cut into the center of the flat side was a tiny image of a black man holding a boomerang in one hand, ready to throw, and the words "Gundawarra Boomerangs—Kangaroo—Crafted in Wedderburn, Victoria, Australia.''

"Until you learn to throw it right, it's gonna hit the ground pretty hard a few times. The plywood models tend to hold up longer than the solid wood ones. And they're cheaper than NoChip. This one'll run about twenty dollars U.S.''

Tyrone hefted the stick. He realized he hadn't thought about Bella but once since he'd gotten here, and then only briefly.

"Comes with a membership in the International Boomerang Association. We've got a great web site.''

Tyrone grinned. "I'll take it.''

30

Saturday, January 15th, 11:55 a.m.
Eastern Oregon

Howard found a sunny spot to break for lunch. The relatively level patch of snowy ground was partially sheltered from the weather by some Douglas fir trees and stunted shrubs on the east side, though the growth had collected its share of solid precipitation. A couple of the smaller trees were so heavy with snow, they leaned over precariously, branches drooping.

It was warming up under the clear skies, though it was still not what you'd call warm, probably a degree or two above freezing. Big clots of partially melted snow fell from the trees to splatter on the shallow snow below, landing with wet plops.

Howard chose his cook spot away from overhanging branches. He tamped the snow down with his snowshoes into a ragged circle next to a big flat-topped rock. He used his virgil to beep in, showing he was still alive, then shrugged out of his pack, pulled the snowshoes off, and set his stove up on the rock. He dumped a couple of handfuls of snow into his cook pot, then began melting the snow to reconstitute some freeze-dried chicken and vegetables, kind of like a pot pie without the crust.

He walked around the site as he waited for the water to heat up, stomping a more solid path in the relatively shallow snow. He looked for signs of small animals, and checked for any tokens that humans had passed this way recently. He found nothing to indicate man or animal had visited here, and certainly there were no other tracks in or out but his own.

On his own, far away from home. He liked the feeling, being master of all he could see.

He rolled his shoulders, stretched his neck, and did a couple of squats and toe touches to loosen his legs. It had been two hours since his last break, and two hours of snowshoeing took a lot out of you. No matter how old you were . . .

The metal cup of water began to bubble. He circled back toward his stove, passing beneath the trees. He glanced up and saw a blob of melting snow slip from a high branch and fall, coming right at him.

''Oh, no, you don't!'' he said, laughing and dodging to the side. The big chunk missed him by a good two feet, but he stumbled and put one hand out to catch himself on the tree. That was a mistake, because his weight was enough to shake the tree a hair, and that brought a *big* cascade of ready-to-fall snow. He laughed again, spun around the tree and away, pleased with himself at avoiding most of the icy bath.

He didn't stay pleased.

The tree that lost its snow load popped upright like a bent spring released. It hit the tree next to it, hard.

The second tree snapped in half ten feet off the ground. Like a man breaking a pencil—*pop!*

The snow was not that deep, but it was too deep to run in.

He barely had time to get his arms up over his head before the tree fell on him.

Saturday, January 15th, 3:05 p.m.
Fredericksburg, Virginia

From under the Miata's hood, Alex said, "Okay, try it again."

Behind the wheel, Toni said, "Okay," and turned the key in the steering wheel ignition. The motor coughed, deeper than it had before.

"Give it a little gas, pump the pedal!"

She did. After a second, the engine caught and began a throaty rumble.

"Yes!" she and Alex said at the same time.

They were alone in the garage. Greg Scates, the car's former owner, had come and gone. Alex had taken a quick look at the Miata, then as soon as he'd seen the odometer, had said to her, "Jesus, it's only got nine hundred miles on it!"

He'd made the man an offer right then. Greg had been surprised at how much the offer was. Way more than he'd expected.

Alex had transferred the agreed-upon sum from his credit card to Greg's account and waved bye-bye as the man left.

Now Alex closed the hood, wiped his hands on a red rag, and grinned at Toni.

They'd been working on the car for several hours. They had found the tires, which were in remarkable shape inside plastic bags, and pumped them full of air using a little compressor that ran off the van's electrical system. They'd put the wheels back on the car. They had added gasoline, oil, water, transmission and brake fluid, and other lubricants, replaced the battery, and tinkered with the fuel injector. Alex had done something with the plugs and wiring, cleaned preservative off various components, fiddled with this seal and that one, and now, finally, the tiny car purred.

He had, Alex had told her, every intention of driving the thing home, even though the license tag was years out of date. "Be worth the ticket if we get caught," he said.

He cleaned the grease from his hands, walked around to the

open driver's door, and looked down at her. "It'll need a new top," he said. "And a set of new belts, plug wires, some other minor stuff. Paint is in pretty good shape, but I'm not that fond of arrest-me red. Maybe a nice teal," he said.

She grinned back up at him. She'd gotten a little dirt under her fingernails too, helping him put the wheels back on the car and passing him tools. He had been like a little boy, all excited, pointing out stuff to her. "Look at this. Look at that!" He'd gotten completely lost in the work, and in the doing of it had also lost years of responsibility. It pleased her to see him this way. So relaxed. Having so much fun.

"So, let's take her out for a little spin," he said.

She started to get out of the car.

"No, go ahead, you drive. You can use a manual shift, can't you?"

"Sure."

He finished wiping his hands, circled around the back to the passenger side, and got into the car. The garage door was already open, and the bright afternoon beckoned. Toni put the transmission into reverse and carefully backed out onto the driveway to the street, turned the wheel, and started to shift into first.

"Wait a second," he said. He twisted in the seat, caught the rear window zipper, and pulled it across behind her. He pressed the thin plastic rear window down behind the stabilizer bar, reached across in front of her, and undid the roof latch on her side, then the one on his side. With one hand he accordioned the top, folding the heavy black material down and behind them.

"*Voila!*" he said. "Convertible! It's not too cold for you, is it?"

"Nope," she said.

"All right then. Let's see how she rides."

Toni eased the clutch out—it was a bit stiff and it squeaked—and the Miata scooted forward. The short-throw stick made shifting up the gears fast and easy, and pretty soon they were rolling along a four-lane highway at sixty. It was a responsive beast, the steering tight, and cornering was a delight. She took a thirty-mile-per-hour curve at fifty, no problem.

"It's quieter than I thought it would be," she said. "And not as windy."

He said, "Push it up to about seventy and watch."

Traffic was light, so Toni goosed it a little.

At seventy, the wind seemed to slacken, as did the noise. She said as much to Alex.

"Yep, it's quieter at seventy than at fifty-five. That was part of the aerodynamic design. Isn't this great?" He grinned at the road in front of them.

A few miles up the highway, Toni pulled into a supermarket parking lot.

"Something wrong?" he asked.

"Nope. Your turn. You've been itching to take the wheel since we hit the street."

He grinned again. Boy, she liked seeing that. He jumped out of the car and hurried around to the driver's side as she moved over into the passenger seat.

Behind the wheel, he checked his outside mirror first, then the inside one. Then he looked across at the outside mirror on the passenger side. "That one's a little off," he said.

She reached out to adjust the mirror.

"Hey, I can get it," he said. "One of the joys of a car this small. Watch." He leaned over, reached across her chest, and grabbed the mirror. "See? Can't do that in the snail van."

Stretched out across her, one hand out of the car on the mirror, he glanced up at her face from a few inches away.

She could smell him, his sweat, his aftershave, and there he was, the back of his arm almost touching her breast, his mouth close enough to kiss.

Without thinking anymore, she did just that. Leaned a hair forward, put her lips on his, and kissed him.

Are you out of your mind, *Toni?*

The sudden jolt of panic shot through her like an electrical charge. Oh, no! What had she done?

She pulled back to break the kiss.

Alex brought his hand away from the mirror, put it behind her head, and held her there. He worked his lips, opened his mouth, and found her tongue with his.

There must be a God, Toni thought.

Saturday, January 15th, 12:15 p.m.
Eastern Oregon

No two ways about it, Howard was trapped.

He had been lucky, in that the waist-thick fir had enough branches on it to break the main trunk's descent enough so it hadn't smashed him to a pulp. But the tree's bole had come to rest on the back of his left calf, and had pinned him to the ground face-down. He managed to clear away a few small branches on his back and thighs so he was able to struggle to a sitting position, his butt against the trunk. His left leg was pinned, his right leg free, but stuck more or less straight out in front of him.

Not the most comfortable position he'd ever been in. There was no pain in the caught leg. Was that good? Or bad?

He could still wiggle his left foot, feel his toes inside the insulated boot, so that was comforting. Might not even be broken, the tibia or fibula, but that didn't matter.

What mattered was that his virgil was safely locked to a nice D-ring on his pack, over there by his cook stove. It was only about ten feet away, but given the present circumstances it might as well be ten million miles. He wasn't going anywhere.

He had tried to lift the trunk, then to shove it off using his free leg, but that was not going to happen. He had about fifty feet of tree on him, and even positioned a lot better than he was, probably couldn't have moved it with his muscle power alone. Where it rested on his calf, the tree was about as thick as a telephone pole.

This was not a good situation.

He was in the middle of nowhere, staked to the snowy ground like a bug to a display board, his electronics out of reach. He was dressed for the weather, but come sundown it was going to get very cold, and sleeping face-down in the snow with the air temperature below zero was not generally a good idea.

Of course, if he went more than twenty-four hours without beeping in they'd call, and if he didn't answer they'd come and find the virgil and him with it, but by then he might already be a Howard-sicle. And they wouldn't come looking before noon tomorrow.

No, all in all he would have to say this was definitely not good.

He took a deep breath, blew it out, and watched the breath-fog hang in the air. It wasn't *that* warm. In fact, it seemed twenty degrees colder than it had when he'd got here a few minutes ago.

"Okay, John," he said. "Let's take stock here. What have you got in the way of good news?"

He had a lighter in his jacket shell. There were a lot of dead needles among the green, and a whole lot of branches, albeit somewhat cold and damp, but he was pretty sure he could make a fire. So he wouldn't freeze if he did it right. He might even be able to burn through the trunk. Break the weight enough to be able to shift the tree off his leg.

Or start a small forest fire in which he got cooked real good.

Hmm. Put that one on the backup list.

What else?

Well, he had his sheath knife. He reached back on his right hip, found the handle—there was a comfort—and pulled the knife from its scabbard.

The knife was a Cold Steel Tanto, so called for the angled, Japanese-sword-style point, and was eleven inches long, five of that the cutting edge. It was a full-tang, the blade was three-eighths-of-an-inch thick across the backstrap, and it wore an artificial rubber handle, crosshatched for a good grip, and was butted and guarded with brass fittings. A fine weapon, able to kill a man with one thrust from somebody who knew what he was doing, but it had not been designed for chopping away a tree bigger around than his thigh. Still, it was what he had, and he knew if he could twist himself around long enough, he could eventually cut through the wood. It might take a long time, but it wasn't as if he was going anywhere. . . .

He felt better, knowing he had at least two options.

Well, okay, three—he could always cut his leg off from the knee down, right?

He smiled to himself.

"Okay, any other possibilities here, John? Maybe cut your jacket into strips, make a lariat, and try to lasso your pack? It's only about ten feet, you could probably manage it, and then you'd have your virgil back."

Yeah, and wouldn't that look great. Old Man Howard lets a tree fall on his stupid sorry ass, and has to call for help. Too bad he froze to death without a jacket before somebody could break a copter loose to go and get him. . . .

Maybe not. Put that one right before setting the tree on fire.

He looked down at his pinned leg. Hold on a second. There was yet another option, the LAIC Maneuver.

LAIC—Look At It Crooked.

If you couldn't solve a problem going in through the front door, what about the back door? When you had an enemy too strong to attack head-on, flanking him would sometimes work.

Howard looked at his leg and grinned. The limb had pretty much squished the snow out of its way under the weight of the tree. He'd bet it was close to or on the ground below, but even frozen dirt wasn't as hard as wood, was it? Especially with that nice warm leg lying on it, thawing it out and all.

All he had to do was dig a hole under his shin, come in from the side, hollow enough out so the leg would drop. When the calf got below ground level, the tree would be resting on the edges of the hole, and all he'd have to do would be to pull the leg out, right?

Look at it crooked.

It made sense. It made a lot more sense than trying to play Paul Bunyan with a knife, or cooking himself into Howard the damned fool crispy critter, didn't it?

He laughed. "Dig, baby, dig. You do this right, nobody will ever have to know it happened."

He shifted his position a bit, and cleared away the snow down to the dirt next to his trapped leg. No blood. That was good.

The topsoil was mostly sand, and the rocky clay under it *was* frozen, but it took less than an hour to excavate himself. In the end, his bigger worry was that the pot he'd set to heating to make his lunch would burn up, the water having boiled away, but he managed to get to it and throw it into the snow to cool before that happened.

The ankle wasn't even sprained, the snow under the leg having cushioned things enough so his pants weren't even torn. His foot was sore, but not so much he couldn't walk on it, and Howard felt immensely pleased with himself as he ate his delayed lunch.

Okay, so he was older. He could could learn to fight smarter, not harder. Growing old might be hell, but hey, it still beat the only other option, didn't it?

Ah, John, you are quite the philosopher, aren't you?

That's me.

There was nothing like a victory to give you a sense of control. It might be an illusion, but it sure felt good in the moment. Yes, sir, it did.

31

Somebody honked their car horn and laughed as they drove past, but Alex didn't care. The passion he'd thought frozen when he split from Megan was not dead, not even wounded. God, Toni felt so good. Her lips were warm, soft, her hands on his back pulled him closer, her breasts against his chest—

His virgil cheeped, and the incoming tone was the classical music sting he'd programmed from *Les Preludes* that indicated a Priority One call.

Damn!

He broke the kiss and leaned back. Fumbled with his virgil.

"Wow," Toni said. She was flushed and breathing heavy.

"Yeah. Hold that thought, okay?"

He tapped the speaker button on the virgil. "Michaels."

"Commander, Jay Gridley. Sorry to bother you, Boss, but, well, the shit has just hit the fan."

"What?"

"The Fried Sex guys just crashed the U.S. Internet Bank System. I hope you got some money in your pocket, 'cause you ain't gonna be cashing your federal check today.''

"Fuck!"

"Yes, sir, Boss, that is the key and operative word around here. The bank guys are foaming at the mouth, and the ripple effect is jamming through the net like a cattle stampede. Everybody and his kid sister have thrown up firewalls and lockouts, and the whole NorAm Net is one big crappy mess.''

"Damage control?"

"We're throwing water on it, but we're talking mega forest fire, Boss. It's hot and ugly and getting hotter and uglier every minute. We're gonna have to take some major systems off-line and shut down a bunch of the FedWeb.''

"Do what you can, get everybody we have on it. We'll be— *I'm* on my way," Michaels said. "Discom.''

Michaels looked at Toni. "I'm sorry," he said.

She shook her head. "I hope you're talking about the call.''

"Yeah, I am. But—this—" He waved one hand back and forth between them. "This is probably . . . not very smart.''

"I know.''

"I'm your boss. This sort of thing brings up all kinds of problems.''

"What sort of thing?''

He stared at her. "Jesus, Toni, you know what I'm talking about. Office romance. Supervisors sleeping with people they supervise.''

She grinned, as big as he'd ever seen her grin. "Oh, boy,'' she said.

"What?''

"You want to sleep with me?''

"Yes, of course. But given the circumstances—''

"I'll quit," she said.

"Excuse me?''

"If you sleep with me, I'll resign.''

"Toni—''

"No, I'm serious. If it would be a problem for you as my supervisor, then we can fix that. I love working for you, Alex, but I can always find another job. Right now, a personal relationship with you is more important than a business relationship.''

He blinked at her, stunned by her words. ''You would quit your job to have sex with me?''

''In a New York second.''

''Why? I'm not that wonderful.''

''You underestimate yourself. I'm serious about this.''

He shook his head. ''Jesus. Look, we have to get back to HQ and take care of this disaster, okay? Can we talk about this later?''

''Whenever you want. You want to go back and get the van?''

''No, leave it. I'll get somebody to pick up it.''

He started the Miata's engine.

Holy shit. It never rained but it poured.

Saturday, January 15th, 3:25 p.m.
Hana, Maui, Hawaii

Winthrop was on the net in Joined-VR, showing Julio some of the ins and out of the webweave. She had allowed him to conjure a program, and what he had come up with was a beach on Maui, near Hana. They were in personal persona, dressed in skimpy swimsuits, walking barefoot on a black sand beach. They listened to the breakers curl, to the seagulls cawing. A gentle breeze played over them, the sea where it lapped into the volcanic sand was warm, and the sun caressed their bare skin.

''So, what do you think?'' Julio asked

''Not bad, for a beat-up old trooper. Why did you choose this in particular?''

''I went here once, for real. I have some good memories of

it. Besides, I wanted to see what you looked like in a bathing suit.''

"I bet you say that to all the girls."

"Sure I do. But my intentions are honorable—I could have made it a nude beach, you know."

She laughed.

As they rounded a big rock and the shoreline curved inward, Winthrop noticed something odd. The water seemed to be . . . receding, ebbing away and growing shallower as she watched. It moved out so quickly that fish were left flopping on the bottom. A big eel wiggled frantically, trying to catch the subsiding sea.

"That's a nice effect," she said. "What's it for?"

He shook his head. "I don't have a clue. I'm not doing it."

The water continued to ebb, and Winthrop looked farther out to sea.

"Uh-oh," she said.

"What?"

"I just realized what's happening. See there?"

Julio squinted into the sunshine. "Looks like a big wave."

"Yeah, it's a big wave, all right, and it's going to get a lot bigger as it gets closer. It's a *tsunami*."

"A tidal wave?"

"That's a misnomer. It doesn't have anything to do with tides. They're usually caused by earthquakes or volcanic activity. Sometimes by a big meteor hitting the ocean—or somebody playing with big nukes can make one."

"So why all of a sudden is there a *tsunami* in my scenario?"

"Got me, but it looks like trouble in paradise. Something big is happening on the net. I hate to cut the lesson short, but we need to jack out of this scenario see what RW scans show."

"Yes, ma'am. You're the expert."

"Stand by—"

Saturday, January 15th, 3:30 p.m.
Quantico, Virginia

Fernandez came back to himself in the computer room, sitting next to Joanna. She was waving her hands at her computer station, calling up a rapid blur of images and words and numbers from the holoproj in front of her. And she was cursing like a sailor while she did it.

"God dammit! How the hell can this be happening?"

She waved her hands again, then tapped furiously at the keyboard on the desk.

Fernandez kept quiet, knowing this was not the time to fill her ears with foolish questions.

Whatever was going on, though, it didn't look good.

"No, no, no, you bastard! Don't route there, you'll crash the—dammit, dammit! Stop!"

Jay Gridley came running into the room, and excited as he was, he must already know what was going on.

"Winthrop, you see what the hell is happening?"

"I got it. Jesus Christ!"

Gridley slid into a chair in front of another workstation. "Man, oh, man! The kickouts at FedOne just blew."

"We need to scramble some programmers, Jay—"

"Already did it. Boss is on the way in, so is everybody else who can warm a seat."

"You call Fiorella?"

He spared her a glance from the flashing holoproj in front of him. "Didn't need to. I bounced her virgil's location. It's within a couple of feet of the boss's. She's with him." He waggled his eyebrows. "Isn't *that* interesting?"

"Old news," Joanna said. "You need to pay more attention to RW around you, Gridley."

"Screw you, Winthrop."

"In your dreams, monkey fingers."

"In my nightmares, you mean."

Fernandez felt like a fifth wheel. He didn't know what was

going on, and he wasn't gonna ask, but whatever it was, it was bad.

"The blast doors on FedTwo just slammed shut," Joanna said.

"See 'em," Gridley said. "Maybe we can reroute the—ah, piss! FedThree just rolled over too. We got a major infection here!"

"A virus?" Fernandez said.

"Not a virus, a goddamned *plague*," Gridley said. "Somebody got past the best antivirals we have and threw a replicant bomb. The bugs are reproducing and going through the federal financial systems like water through a fire hose. The only way we're gonna stop it is to shut down everything it's contaminated and flush it one system at a time."

"Crap," Joanna said. "Crap, crap, crap!" She leaned back, watching the screen flash stuff that was meaningless to Fernandez.

"Well, I'll say one thing," Fernandez said, "you sure know how to show a boy a good time."

"Hold up, hold up," Joanna said. "I got something."

"You can stop it?" Julio said.

"No, I can't. But I think I can find where it came from. Jeez, I can't believe the guy is that dumb. Jay?"

"I see it, I see it! I've got a lock! How'd you do that, Winthrop?"

"I found a ghost on my station from when he broke in here. There wasn't anywhere to go with it, it petered out, but just in case, I set up a scan-and-match."

"What does that mean?" Fernandez asked, despite his resolution not to ask stupid questions.

"It means that even if our perp bounces his signal, we can backwalk it—if we hurry, and if the sig is a match."

"Good work, Winthrop!" Gridley said. "You ready to run him down?"

"I'd like to kick his ass personally, but much as I hate to

say it, you're better at this part than I am, Gridley. Go get him."

Gridley smiled. "You know, you're not so bad after all— for a white girl. I'm gone."

When Toni and Alex arrived, there was a lot of commotion in the computer center. Jay, Joanna, and half the regular programmers were there, stations lit and working. Julio Fernandez stood next to the doorway watching.

"Julio," Toni said. "How is it going?"

"I'm not the guy to ask. I'm catching about one word in twenty. It's nasty, this thing. Gridley calls it a replicant bomb."

"Oh, shit," Toni and Alex said together.

"But Jo and Gridley apparently got a lock on the bomb thrower. Gridley is running him down somehow. I didn't understand most of that part."

"Thanks, Sergeant," Toni said.

"No problem, Commander."

Alex moved to where Joanna sat, and as Toni started to head for her office to assess damage reports, Fernandez's smile stopped her. "Something funny I'm missing?" she asked. "I could use a good laugh."

"No, ma'am, nothing funny."

"Why the grin?"

"Oh, I was just, you know, musing."

"About what?"

"You and the commander."

Toni felt herself color. "Me and the commander?"

"Yes, ma'am."

Oh, God, does it show? We haven't even done anything yet!

"What about us, Sergeant?"

"Nothing, ma'am. Just lucky how you both get here so quick."

"You're a poor liar, Julio."

"Yes, ma'am. Probably I need more practice."

"I need to go," she said.

She hurried down the hall. He knew. How? How could he know? That little slip of the tongue, when Alex said "we," instead of "I"? That couldn't be; he hadn't even been talking to Fernandez, he'd been talking to *Jay*.

Well. Worry about that later. Right now, they had a crisis to weather.

One thing at a time, girl, one thing at a time . . .

32

Platt was feeling damn good about his latest caper on the net. It was amazing what you could do when you had a bunch of secret codes and passwords, courtesy of somebody who had access to a U.S. senator. Like screw up a major segment of the entire United States electronic banking system, *blap!* just like that. Those poor feebs were running around like a bunch of chickens with their heads cut off, going bugfuck crazy trying to keep the money systems from crashing. Wasn't gonna stop it, though, not without shutting down a bunch of it, and that was the point. Because part of what was going down was a big ole safe that kept the net cowboys from robbing the bank. Once that was out of the way, things were gonna get real interestin'. . . .

He was in the bathroom when he heard the alarm go off. At first, he thought it was the smoke detector, but after a second, he realized it was coming from his computer, on the kitchen table.

"What the hell—?!"

He jumped up and ran into the kitchen.

Sure enough, the little speaker on the portable was wailing away.

For a second, Platt just stood there, staring at the beeping computer. It wasn't supposed to happen, but unless there was some kind of software malfunction, somebody had somehow accessed his primary input signal. The only way they could have possibly done that was to have caught it at the satellite *before* the bounce, and only way *that* was possible was to have been waiting for the signal, and to know what to look for when it got there.

Couldn't be. He hadn't left any clues that big.

He moved, fast. Tapped in the confirmation code. Maybe it was just a software error, a glitch that tripped the audible—

Aw, *shit*! It wasn't an error!

They had traced his signal. And if they knew where he was, they'd pretty damn quick figure out *who* he was, and they'd be on their way to have a little talk with him.

Platt shut the computer off. He had to get out of here, now!

How the hell could this have happened? What did the damned Net Force boys know that he didn't? Some kind of new technology? Crap!

Worry about it later, hoss. Right now, you get your ass in gear and lay tread, or you're gonna be speculating about it in a federal cell somewhere!

Saturday, January 15th, 9:15 p.m.
Bissau, Guinea-Bissau

Hughes smiled at Domingos across the table and raised his wine glass in salute. They were alone in the formal dining hall, Hughes and the President, working their way through the third course of a seven-course meal. The room would comfortably seat a hundred, and there was a hollow feel to it with just the pair of them at the end of a large oval table, one of half-a-dozen other tables just like theirs.

Fish was up next, some local catch, and so they'd switched to white wine, an Australian Pinot Gris, vintage 2003, that was as good as any Hughes had ever tasted. Domingos was proud of his cellar and his cook, and rightfully so.

Hughes made complimentary noises.

"You are too kind," the President said, but he was obviously pleased.

They sipped their wine, watching the waiters clear away their plates and reset for the next course.

"So, everything goes well, does it not?" the President said.

Hughes glanced at his watch. "Even as we speak, Excellency, my agents are finalizing matters. In a few days, we can make the transfers. I anticipate no problems, none at all."

"Excellent!" Domingos raised his glass. "To the future!"

"I will certainly drink to that."

Hughes smiled as he sipped the wine. Right about now, his agent Platt would be feeling an unexpected heat. He was useful, Platt was, but not the only operative that Hughes employed. And while Hughes was certain that the trick he'd played on the Southerner wouldn't result in his capture by the authorities—Platt was too canny to be caught that easily— certainly the cracker would sit up and take notice. He surely didn't want Platt in custody where he might spill everything he knew about this deal. But he did want the redneck off balance, a little edgy, and looking to his employer for some reassurance.

If a man thinks you're reaching a hand out to help him climb from a pit, he might not notice the knife in your other hand.

Platt was expendable—more than expendable, he *had* to go—and his usefulness was nearly at an end . . . but not quite yet.

The fish arrived, a single platter with what looked like a

twenty-pound sea bass, cooked whole, upon the serving tray. The smell was wonderful.

"It's the French roasted hazelnut butter that does that," Domingos said. "You can understand why I'll be taking Bertil with me to Paris when I go, yes?"

Hughes smiled. Taking a chef to Paris might be gilding the lily, but if that was what he wanted, Domingos would certainly be able to afford it. . . .

Saturday, January 15th, 4:30 p.m.
Washington, D.C.

After he'd bought the boomerang, Tyrone had spent a couple of hours at the park playing with it. It was a little trickier than it looked, but it had taken him only a few minutes to get the thing working well enough so he didn't have to run and chase it. Well, not too far anyhow. A couple of times, it had come back close enough so he had been able to catch it without taking more than a step or two.

He'd never been real big on physical stuff, but he could definitely get into this.

By the time his arm was tired and he was ready to go home, he had figured out a lot of stuff about how you stood relative to the wind, and how to figure out which way the wind was blowing. He'd watched other throwers pick up bits of dry grass or dirt and then drop them, watching to see which way they drifted. He also had a fair idea of how much wrist action a basic throw needed. This was really fun stuff.

His phone cheeped. Tyrone pulled it from his belt clip. "Hello?"

"Hey, son. How are you doing?"

"Dad? I thought you were out in the middle of snowland or somewhere."

"I am. Only guy around for fifty miles."

"You okay? You don't usually call during these things."

"Yeah, I'm fine."

There was a pause, and Tyrone sensed his father wanted to say something else, so he stayed quiet.

"Actually, I had a little excitement today. You have to promise not to tell your mother, okay?"

Uh-oh. What did that mean? "Sure, Dad. What's flowin'?"

"A tree fell on me."

"A tree? Are you all right?"

"Yeah, yeah, I'm fine. Thing snapped under the weight of a lot of snow. I was lucky, but it got me to thinking, maybe I should give you call. How are you doing?"

"Geez, Dad, a tree falls on you and you're worried about me?"

"It's what fathers do, Ty."

"Well, I'm flowing fine. I just got a boomerang."

"Really? War or sport?"

Tyrone felt his eyebrows rise. "You know about boomerangs?"

"A little. They're hunting devices or weapons, depending on the kind. I wouldn't want to be clonked on the head with one, even one of the birding models."

"Birding?"

"The sport models, that's what they were used for. If you hit something with it, it doesn't come back, but an expert can knock a bird out of the air forty or fifty yards away at a right angle to where he's standing. We played with them some in military camp when I was a kid. Been years since I've seen mine. I think it's in the attic at Grampa's."

Amazing. His father seemed to know something about everything. And he *had* a boomerang. Amazing.

"Well, I got one, a sport model. There's this tournament not far from our house, I checked it out, and I got one."

"Great. You can brush me up on how to use it when I get home. I'm out of practice."

"Yeah, that would be DFF."

"It's been good talking to you, son. I'm going to give your mother a call and say hi. And Ty? Let's keep the falling-tree thing between us."

"Right. Take care, Dad. Thanks for calling."

When he discommed, Tyrone smiled. His father had called *him* before he had called Mom. He'd shared a secret with him, something in confidence. And his father had played with a boomerang as a kid.

Man. Would wonders never cease?

Saturday, January 15th, 6:30 p.m.
Quantico, Virginia

Michaels was in his office, worrying about twelve different things, when one of those things came in.

"Alex?"

"Toni. What's up?"

"FBI and the Georgia state boys ran down the address outside Marietta. An old house, belongs to a family named Platt. Father hasn't been around for thirty years, mother died, left the place to her son."

She put a thin sheaf of hardcopy on his desk, including a photo. "That's him, the son."

Michaels looked at the image. The kid in the picture was big and muscular, in a white T-shirt and jeans, but he also looked about sixteen. "Kind of young, isn't he?"

"Only image we could find. It's about fifteen or sixteen years old. This guy Platt would be in his early thirties now. We can age the image, and we're straining him through the Cray Colander now. Neighbors say he lives at the house, but he's gone a lot."

"Seems to be something of a stretch, doesn't it?" he said.

"From Danish terrorists to a Georgia cracker?"

"Okay if I sit?"

"Jesus, you don't have to ask. Sit, sit!"

She did, and gave him a small smile.

He felt an erotic heat start to smolder low in his belly. Or thereabouts.

"I've been thinking about that," she said. "It seems kind of odd that nobody ever heard of this *Frihedsakse* before all this started."

"What do you mean? Jay has dug up all kinds of references to the group predating the manifesto they sent, going back years."

"Well, not exactly. I had Jay recheck. What we can absolutely confirm are bits here and there as old as six months. Before that, the etiology of the information is, as Jay puts it, 'somewhat ambiguous.'"

Michaels leaned back in his chair and considered that for a few seconds. "Why would that be, I wonder."

"There's the jackpot question."

"What do you think?"

She shook her head. "I don't know for sure. But just for the sake of argument, let's say these Danish terrorists didn't exist until six months ago. Why would they bother to plant information that said they were a lot older? What would be the point? I mean, so they're only six months old, what difference would that make to anybody? Are they looking for prestige? Some kind of validation? They want to be the Elks or the Masons of terrorists?"

Michaels nodded. "Good point. Why *would* they bother?"

"Maybe they didn't," she said. "Maybe it was somebody else."

Came the dawn into his head, a few bright streaks painting the dark sky of his mind. "Oh, man. Yeah, I can see that. Maybe there isn't any such group as *Frihedsakse*. Maybe it's somebody who wants us looking for a terrorist group that doesn't exist. They leave just enough clues for us to think we're finding something, to stay interested, when in fact we're spinning our wheels and not getting anywhere. Maybe it's not terrorists at all.''

''It's just a theory,'' she said.

He shook his head, suddenly angry at himself. ''But we should have checked this out before. We didn't look for another target because we had this big fat turkey plopped right down in front of us. It was too easy.''

Toni said, ''The thing is, if it's not terrorists, who is it? And what do they want? Somehow, I have a lot of trouble believing some lowbrow high-school-dropout jock from a little town in Georgia has the wherewithal to pull all this off.''

Michaels said, ''Let's put *Frihedsakse* on the back burner. Check on what systems were hit, and who might benefit from them being damaged or down.''

She stood. ''I'll go talk to Jay and Joanna.''

''Good.''

She started to leave. He couldn't let her get to the door without saying something else. ''Toni?''

She turned. ''Yes?''

''About that . . . thing in the Miata . . .''

''Do you want to forget it ever happened, Alex? Because I can't forget it, but I can pretend nothing happened, if that's what you want—''

''No,'' he said. ''I don't want to forget it. If we survive this, I think we should lie down—I mean, we should *sit* down—and discuss it.''

Jeezus, man! That was lame, Michaels. Lame, lamer, lamest. I cannot believe *you said that. You are a moron!*

Toni's smile, however, told him she had not only caught the Freudian slip, but wasn't in the least offended by it.

Bad idea, Michaels, a really bad idea. You don't crap in your nest. You never sleep with the enlisted women, his father had told him. It's always a mistake.

But looking at Toni, it didn't seem like such a mistake. She was bright, beautiful, and physically adept enough so she could kick his ass if she felt like it. For some reason, those things taken together had a powerful appeal. And she had kissed him first, hadn't she?

Yeah, right, she seduced you, and if you don't sleep with her, she'll stomp your butt? Uh-huh. Who are we trying to fool here, pal? Nobody is buying that one.

Michaels watched Toni disappear from view. He shook himself and blew out a big sigh. Worry about that later. Right now, he had bigger problems on his plate.

His com beeped. "Yeah?"

"Your ex-wife is on three," his secretary said.

Michaels laughed. Of course she was.

"Take a message," he said.

33

"There they are," Winthrop said.

"Rats," Jay said. "You had to pick rats?"

"You'd rather cute little puppies or kittens? Something about you I ought to know, Gridley?"

Jay shook his head and raised the twelve-gauge pump shotgun to his shoulder. The gun was a Mossberg with an extended magazine tube that held ten rounds. There was a flashlight and a laser mounted on the barrel. An elastic band on the gun's stock held another ten shells.

Next to him in the poorly lit alley, Winthrop raised her own weapon, a South African Streetsweeper, also a twelve-gauge, but with a big circular drum underneath that held a whole box of shells. She also had a flashlight and a laser sight mounted on the weapon.

The brown rats, the size of cocker spaniels and with mouths full of long, yellow teeth, milled around in the dead-end alley for a few seconds before they realized they couldn't get out that way. The big rodents looked around for a means of escape, and the only path out was blocked by Winthrop and Gridley.

No real problem in guessing which way they would go.

"Here they come!" Jay shouted.

The rats, at least twenty of them, came toward them like a furry tide.

Winthrop fired first, getting off two shots before Jay pulled the trigger on his weapon.

Big rats turned into bloody red clumps of twisting fur as the #4 buckshot tore into them. Five, eight, twelve of the charging animals fell. The rest kept coming.

"To your left!" Winthrop shouted. She swung her gun over and cooked off a couple more rounds. She blasted one of the rats, hitting it so hard she rolled it like a soccer ball.

Jay tracked the two rats trying to flank him on the left, fired, hit one, pumped the gun, fired, missed—

Winthrop caught the one he'd missed, then fired twice more—*whump! whump!*—and rolled two more.

Jay lined up on the last one he saw moving, put the little red dot from the laser square on the thing's head, shot it—

He blew out a sigh. Blasting plague-carrying rats was certainly more exciting than chasing down viral code strings in RW voxax or fingertap mode. In reality, the rats were circular sub routines with escape and evasion codings, eating up storage space in the Federal Reserve's KC Division. The city had been evacuated—the computer had been taken off-line—so that exterminators could come in and clear out the infestation. Mostly that didn't go over too well, but that was how it had to be.

And this wasn't that bad. A couple of the banking systems had been hit so hard they'd had to be shut down completely. *Nobody* had liked that.

Winthrop reloaded her shotgun from a pouch full of ammo she carried around her waist. And Jay had to admit, his earlier disapproval of the lieutenant notwithstanding, she looked pretty exciting standing there, shoving rounds into that big honking shotgun, smelling of gunpowder and all. There was something sexy about an attractive woman with an automatic weapon in her hands.

Probably a month's work for a shrink trying to sort out *that* symbolism, Jay figured. It was a good thing he wasn't into shrinks. He'd be broke all the time.

Winthrop touched her headset. "We've cleared the alley behind the bank," she said. "We're moving into the one next to the Thai restaurant on the south side."

Jay grinned. "You throw that in in my honor?"

"You look like you ought to know your way around a Thai restaurant."

"Of course. You like peanut sauce? Maybe I'll make us some nice rat *satay*."

"You probably would. Come on."

"As you command, mistress," Jay said. "You should have worn leather, you know. To go with the gun."

As they walked across the street toward the Thai place, she said, "Oh, by the way, nice job on running down that Platt guy."

"Shucks, ma'am, 'twarn't nothin'."

"Wrong persona, Gridley."

"Ah, I stand corrected. This is present-day, so how about, 'Nopraw, fem.'"

"Better."

"I'd never have found him if you hadn't snagged his spook. Kinda hard to believe he slipped up like that."

"Even the smartest guys get stupid sometimes," she said. "I'll take lucky over good if it gets me there."

"Amen. I hope the feebs can catch the sucker."

"Rat city, just ahead."

"Lock and load, ma'am. You want right side or left this time?"

"Left. That gun of yours throws the empties in my face on the right."

"It's always something, ain't it? But it's FS, Winthrop, FS."

She smiled.

FS stood for "Frankenstein Scenario," shorthand for the concept "If you create it, then you take care of it." Any problems in your scenario were your responsibility.

"Fine, you can build the next one," she said.

"I will. You like snakes?"

"I used to collect them when I was a little girl," she said. "Catch them with a long forked stick, put them into denim bags, and sell them to pet stores. Great things, snakes."

Shoot, Jay thought. *Too bad.* Well. There must be some icky thing she didn't like. Given how much of the federal banking system was infected, they were going to be mopping things up for a while. Surely he could figure out what made her squirm before they were done. . . .

Sunday, January 16th, 1:15 a.m.
Atlanta, Georgia

Platt knew that Hughes wouldn't like being woken up early, and it must be six or seven in spookland over there, but he wanted to be sure to catch him when he wasn't busy. Platt wasn't supposed to be calling Hughes at all unless it was an emergency, and given as how he had gotten away clean, maybe it wasn't an emergency anymore, at least not technically, but to hell with it, he was gonna call anyhow.

He hated losing the house Momma had left him, but that was done. He wasn't going home again.

He used one of the one-time scramblers and a pay phone in the lobby of the Stonewall Jackson Memorial Motel on the outskirts of College Park, just off I-285. Hughes had his virgil rigged up to rascal his call with the military-grade scrambler built into it, so nobody would trace nothin'. He needed to get this done and move out—Atlanta was a big town, but way too close to Marietta. He wanted to be a thousand miles away from both come sunrise, and he'd have to hurry to pull that off. He had a chartered plane waiting at the airport, and once he was in the air, he'd feel a lot better.

"What?" Hughes said.

Yep, he'd woke him up, all right.

"Howdy, Boss. We got a little situation here you need to know about."

"Hold on a second."

Hughes put him on hold, and Platt grinned. Six in the morning, Hughes would be in bed, and if he was puttin' Platt on hold, then he wasn't in the bed alone. Somebody was being sent to the john, Platt would bet.

"All right. What?"

"Sorry if I interrupted anything," Platt said, not the least bit sorry.

"Don't worry about that. What's the problem?"

"The feds ain't as stupid as they look. They backwalked a signal to my momma's house."

"What? How could that happen?"

"Damn if I know. Maybe they got some new techno-toy I haven't heard about. Don't matter as much how as they did it. I had to hightail it out pretty quick."

"But you got away without any real trouble?"

"Well, yes and no. They didn't see me, I was long gone time they showed up, I expect, but that place was under my own name. I'm gonna have to do a little ID switching."

"Is that a problem?"

"Not so you would notice. I got a half-dozen new me's lined up if I need 'em."

"How about the other thing?"

"Oh, the *other* thing. That went smooth as oil on a baby's

butt. Our bank boy from the place in—where was it? Minnesota? I-oway? whatever—should be able to do the deed like he's supposed to. I expect to hear from him by about noon tomorrow. Well, today now.''

"Good, good. You need anything?"

"I'm gonna have to hit one of the caches," Platt said. "I'm a little short on cash.''

"Fine, whatever you need. Listen, if there are any problems with your IDs, let me know, I'll work something out so you can get out of the country.''

Platt grinned. "Why, thank you, Boss, I surely do appreciate that. Nice to know there's somebody you can count on in today's dog-eat-dog world. I'll call you back soon as bank boy does his thing.''

"Right. Later then.''

Platt pushed the disconnect button down, pulled the scrambler from the mouthpiece, and dropped it into his pocket. He'd toss it into a lake somewhere later. Hmm. Hughes hadn't seemed as upset as he'd expected by the feds sniffing Platt out. He was a cool one, all right. Maybe too cool. Truth was, Platt trusted him about as far as he could pitch the man one-handed, and while he was strong, that wasn't all that far.

Once bank boy had done his thing, Hughes was going to be eyeball-deep in money, at least for a little while, and maybe he wouldn't need an attack dog as much as he had before. Or maybe he thought he might get rid of the old one and buy himself a new dog.

You had to pay attention at times like this, Platt had learned. People always looked out for their own interests, first, last, and in between. Pretty soon now, Hughes and Platt would have interests going their separate ways. Things could get dangerous when that happened. And Momma Platt didn't raise no fools.

Platt headed for his room. He had a couple of things he wanted to pick up there before he headed for the airport.

Sunday, January 16th, 1:45 a.m.
Quantico, Virginia

Commander Michaels called them into the conference room for a quick meeting. Winthrop looked around. Aside from herself, there was Michaels, Fiorella, Gridley, and in the hall just outside, Julio, who had hung around even though there wasn't anything he could do on-line. He smiled at her as she moved into the conference room, and she felt her spirits lift a little. She was tired—they were all tired—they'd been in VR for what seemed like months, repairing damaged systems. Sure, they'd had help from federal programmers, but this had been a major infection, and it was mud-slogging work, a lot of slow, hard steps. It took a lot out of you, but it was getting done. Most of the damage could be fixed over the next day or two. The biggest problem would come from the systems being down and the money that cost in lost time and transactions all over.

And that whole thing with the *Frihedsakse* was there too. Or wasn't there, if you looked at it hard enough. They'd been baited. Gridley was royally pissed off about that, since he'd been the one on point, but it could have happened to her just as easily. There was just enough sizzle there so you thought you could smell the steak, even though you couldn't quite see it. It was a good con, and it would have been a long time before they caught it if Fiorella hadn't pointed out the possibilities. She might not be the best programmer, but she had a sharp overview, something a lot of the techno-types didn't have.

"—Federal banking systems are still at risk, but all security programs are being updated and changed, so the old passwords won't get the guy back in again," Michaels said.

"He got those," Gridley said. "What's to say he won't get the new ones?"

That mirrored Winthrop's own thought pretty well.

"The bank programmers are using the new tag system. If somebody breaks in, we'll know where the leak got sprung."

Gridley nodded. "Yeah, that'll work for a while, but in the long run, some sharp cowboy will figure out a way around that."

"In the long run, Jay, we're all dead," Michaels said.

That brought some tired smiles forth.

"All right, what's the situation on this guy Platt? Joanna?"

She looked down at her flatscreen and called up the report. "The Cray Colander has sifted everything it could on him.

"Platt dropped out of high school in his junior year. Got into some local trouble as a juvenile—car theft, assault, underage drinking, shoplifting, petty stuff. No time in reform schools or jails.

"Our boy disappeared for the next four years. He was arrested in Phoenix, Arizona, when he was twenty, some kind of con game went bad, he punched out the victim. He got released on bail, then skipped.

"Next time we see him is when he was busted for assault and battery in New Orleans, age twenty-four. He apparently attacked a man on the street for no good reason, beat him senseless. Nobody noticed the old warrant for the thing in Phoenix. He posted bail, and never showed for the trial.

"In 2006, Platt was arrested on a drunk and disorderly charge in Trenton, New Jersey. He walked into a bar and started a fight. Four men wound up in the hospital. Through some glitch in the miracle of modern communications, the bail jumpings in Phoenix and in New Orleans did not appear on his record, and he posted bond a third time—"

"Let me speculate," Michaels said. "He left town."

"Good guess," Winthrop said.

"The last thing we have on him is an arrest in Miami Beach three years ago. Another assault charge. He attacked two men at a hot dog stand, again for no apparent reason. When the police arrived, he was taken into custody, but as they were transferring him from the car to the jail, he escaped. Both the arresting officers were injured, requiring hospitalization."

Winthrop looked up from the flatscreen. "That's it. All we have on Mr. Platt. He has no credit records, no property except for the house outside Marietta, no driver's license, no work history. He's never paid Social Security, filed a tax return, or applied for a passport. At least not under the name Platt. Another of the free-rangers who don't leave electronic tracks or paper trails."

"A thug," Fiorella said. "Hardly seems like the mastermind behind computer break-ins."

"Is there anything that ties his crimes together?" Michaels asked.

Winthrop nodded. "Victim profiles. Two things jump out. All ten of the people he assaulted, including the two cops in Miami, were African-Americans. Their average weight was over two hundred and ten pounds. The guy he thumped in New Orleans was a linebacker for the Saints—he went almost three hundred pounds."

"Wheew," Gridley said. "The guy is a racist. He beats up on black men."

"*Big* black men," Fiorella said. "No indication of martial-arts training?"

"None," Winthrop said.

"Well, isn't this lovely?" Gridley said. "We got an arm-breaker turned computer wizard, who somehow managed to snare all kinds of secret passwords and entry routines, then used them to break into the most sophisticated systems in the country. And he's smart enough to put a big fat red herring in our way so he's got us running around looking for Danish terrorists. I'm with Toni. This doesn't scan."

Michaels nodded, and rubbed at his eyes. "All right. So

Platt has help. If we find him, we'll ask him to tell us who that is. What are we doing to find him?''

Gridley said, "We're electronically crunching all car rentals, airports, and bus and train stations in a hundred-mile radius of the house, looking for single males who did business there in the last twenty-four hours. FBI has the picture and description and is checking hotels, motels, and rooming houses in the area.''

"Which includes all of Atlanta," Fiorella said. "Good luck."

"He's probably not so stupid as to keep using the Platt name, but maybe his face will ring a bell somewhere," Gridley said.

"Of course, he could be in Polar Bear, Canada, by now," Winthrop said.

"Okay, everybody take a break," Michaels said. "Go home, get some sleep, get back here early as you can tomorrow. And Jay—that doesn't mean sacking out on the couch in your office for two hours. If you aren't rested, you become part of the problem and not the solution."

"Copy, Boss."

"Thanks, people. You've all done good work."

Michaels got to his feet. The meeting was over.

In the hall, Julio leaned against a wall, favoring his bad leg. "Going back into the trenches?" he asked Joanna.

"Nope. Boss says go home and get some sleep."

"Sounds like a good idea."

"Yeah, it does, but I'm too wound up to relax. I'll probably be up until dawn." She looked at him, gave him the faintest of grins. "You know anything I can do to relax, Julio?"

He grinned back at her. "Yes, ma'am, I believe I can offer some exercises you might try. They always put me to sleep pretty quick."

"All right. Come on then. You can show me at my place."

He straightened up, stood at attention, then gave her a snappy, crisp salute. "Yes, ma'am. Anything the lieutenant says."

"Anything? Big talk for a beat-up old sergeant."

"I have hidden talents."

"We'll see about that."

They headed down the hall.

34

Platt's clean phone beeped, the little European police siren *hee-haw, hee-haw* tone he'd set up that meant the bank guy was calling.

"Yeah?"

"It's done," the bank guy said. Peterson was his name. Jamal Peterson. And it wasn't Iowa or Minnesota, he was from South Dakota. Platt knew that, but he liked to pretend he was dumber than he actually was around Hughes. Never know but how that might give him an advantage someday.

Old Jamal had scammed a couple hundred thou at the place he'd worked at up in the Dakota territory, which was why he was working for Platt and Hughes. The feds had got that money back, but it was peanuts. That wasn't the point. The point was, when it came to pulling a money rascal, Peterson was the man.

"Any trouble?"

"No. I had two hours after you let me in. I laid mines, pulled up drawbridges, and bollixed trackers during all the commotion. I got it from more than five hundred large government and corporate accounts, no chunk big enough to raise eyebrows from any one of them. By the time they notice and get panicky, the transfers will have run through the filters. Even if they get past Grand Cayman and both Swiss accounts—which they won't—they'll never get by Denpasar Trust in Bali until somebody comes up with a real big bribe. By then, the e-trans'll be long gone, if our principal collects as he is supposed to."

"How much did you get?" Platt asked.

There was a second's pause. "One hundred and eighty million, just as we agreed."

Platt shook his head and grinned unseen at Old Jamal. The son of a bitch was lying, sure as he was born. The deal was, Hughes needed a hundred and forty, and Peterson was to get twenty, which left twenty for Platt. But he'd bet his twenty against a bent nickel that the bank boy had bled himself a little extra. Or maybe a lot extra. Which was stupid. How much did a man need?

Thing was, Peterson wasn't a real criminal. He didn't have the right mind-set. He didn't know the real problems that came from stealing large money.

Because when you tapped a big score, it wasn't the police dogs you had to worry about—it was the wolves.

"All right," Platt said. "Go where I told you to go. I'll be in touch tomorrow."

Platt broke the connection. Poor bank boy. He was hooked and cooked, any way you looked at it.

As Platt made a call to make certain Peterson had been at least partially straight with him, he thought about bank boy's unhappy future.

Back when he'd been running with Jimmy Tee, the old man had told him a story about a robbery in his home town. Seems a guard who'd been working at a bank for twenty years—everybody loved and trusted the guy—grabbed the manager one morning early when he came in, tied him up, and walked off with four million and change in unmarked twenties and fifties. Got away clean. Or so it seemed.

Thing was, the guy didn't know how to keep a low profile. The cops found him three months later, dead as an old white dog turd. Somebody had snuck into his new house in Cancun and slit his throat.

There was no sign of the stolen money.

A pro, Jimmy Tee said, would have set up an identity months, or even years ahead of time. Given himself a background, met his neighbors, had a good reason to show up there one day to stay permanently. Like he'd taken early retirement from some kind of job nobody local was ever likely to wonder about. To make sure nobody else would accidentally show up one Sunday at the local bar to ask embarrassing questions like, "Hey, you remember old Mayor Brooks? Or that time when the City Council guy got caught with that hooker? You know who I'm talking about, don't you? What was his name?"

You didn't need some thread like that to unravel, so you had to think about stuff like that in advance.

And there had to be a way to launder all that cash too. You couldn't just whip out a few hundred thousand in fifties to buy a house, and even getting a car for cash was hinky. You sure couldn't stick it into a bank, not all in one chunk. Hell, anything over ten grand got reported to the IRS. They didn't care where you got your money, as long as you paid taxes on it.

There were a lot of ways to do it, clean your money, but most of them involved things that honest people never thought about.

You needed the cover, see? The cops, if they caught you, they were just gonna toss your butt in jail, but as soon as you hit the road with four million in your pocket, the bounty hunters would be right behind you. The wolves. And the bounty they'd collect if they caught you was everything you had, up to and probably including your life. If they got you, they'd put a gun in your ear and you'd give it up. And if they didn't feel like killing you, but just walked away, there wasn't a damn thing you could do about it. Who you gonna complain to about being ripped off? The cops? Excuse me, officer, but this bad man stole the money I took from the bank. Uh-huh. Right.

No, what you did with a big score was, you took your money and you set up some kind of small business, or you lived the middle-class life of a retiree, drove a car a couple of years old, lived in a nice middle-class house. You didn't send Christmas cards to your ex-wife. You didn't go to your mother's funeral. You didn't call your nephew to congratulate him on getting into college. You cut your ties with your past clean and you never looked back.

If you wanted to take a flier on the tables or the ponies, or roll around in a waterbed with a lady of the evening, you did these things quietly. You didn't go off to Las Vegas or the Gulf Coast or Atlantic City and start betting stacks of hundreds on the dice or wheels. You didn't rent the suite at the Trump or the Hard Rock Hotel and parade showgirls in and out, buying Moet & Chandon by the case either, because the cops weren't stupid and neither were the wolves. If you stuck your head up too high, somebody was gonna spot it, and come running to lop it off.

Old Jamal didn't have the brains to know this. Oh, yeah, he could slip into an on-line bank and back out again with a couple hundred million dollars in his pocket slick as a greasy snake on a marble floor, but old Jamal didn't have any street smarts.

So, even if Platt didn't give the guy up to the cops—which he fully intended to do—somebody would catch up to old Jamal pretty quick. And the dimbulb didn't *have* anybody to give up to save his sorry ass when the cops dragged him in. The man he knew as Platt was somebody else now. He didn't even know who he and Platt were working for, only that it was supposed to be some rich corporate fat cat.

So the bank would get a few million of its swiped money back pretty quick once they collected Peterson. Hughes would do whatever he was gonna do over in Booga-land with his one-forty. And Platt?

That was simple. Platt was gonna buy a hard-core gym in Kona, on the big island of Hawaii, a place he'd had his eye on for a couple of years. The gym was ten thousand square feet, had all kinds of gear—free weights, machines, the whole nine yards. It got world-class bodybuilders coming through now and then, there were fitness models who dropped by during photo shoots, and enough tourists so it was practically a license to steal. The place was well-managed, so Platt wouldn't have to do anything. He would rent a little house or a condo, work out when he wanted, maybe do a little personal training, and take things easy. The climate was perfect, you didn't need to own a heater or an air conditioner, and he'd be hanging out with the kind of people he liked: fit, healthy, strong folks. The place was his for a million-two, and that would leave *plenty* of running-around and fuck-you money. A man didn't need more than that. Business didn't do too well, you had plenty you could drop into it a few hundred or thousand at a time to even things out. Take a long time to burn up eighteen million and change that way . . .

Sure, Hughes had big plans, he was gonna be master of the world, but what was the point? You could only sleep in one bed at a time, only drive one car at a time, only eat so much a day. Playing power games didn't appeal to Platt at all. He could raise a little hell now and then, kick some ass, but that was personal, in-your-face stuff. Deciding somebody's future from halfway around the world? Forget it.

A few more weeks and he'd be out there in the warm sunshine, smiling at the tanned tourists and being a respectable businessman. It couldn't get much better than that.

So old Jamal wasn't lying, the transfer had been made. Time to get the heat down on the boy. He had already recorded the message giving Jamal up. All he had to do was dial a number and hang up, and the remote would give the feds a ring and deliver a big-time bank robber on a platter.

Adios, Jamal.

And now, one more call:

"Yes?"

"It's a done deal, hoss."

He could almost hear Hughes grin from ten thousand miles away. "Good. Everything else okay?"

"No problems at all. Keep the light on, I'm gonna see you real soon."

Breaking the connection, Platt fired up his portable computer and sent one brief signal winging its way into the aethernet. He'd learned Jimmy Tee's lesson well and had prepared for success. But he'd also prepared for failure. He didn't trust Net Force, he didn't trust the jig president of that backwater country, and he especially didn't trust good ol' Mr. Hughes. So he'd set up a fail-safe or two as insurance—'cause you never knew when a little insurance just might come in handy.

Sunday, January 16th, 7:00 a.m.
Quantico, Virginia

Naked, Fernandez rolled over in bed and marveled at his good fortune.

Naked next to him, Joanna blinked sleepily. "What time is it?"

"Around seven. Ask me if I care."

He lifted the covers and looked at her.

"What are you doing?" she asked.

"Looking at you. I know it bothers you to hear it, but you are beautiful."

"It doesn't always bother me. It depends on who says it and when." She smiled at him. "You're a little too scarred up to be called beautiful, but I'm not complaining."

He reached out, touched her face. "You know, nobody even comes in a close second to last night."

"I bet you say that to all the girls."

"No. Just you, Jo."

She sat up, the covers falling away to reveal her breasts. She reached out and hugged him. "Thank you. You can say that all you want too. And I can't remember ever having a better time with my clothes off either."

"I told you I had hidden talents."

"You want to shower?"

"No, ma'am, what I want to do is lie here in this bed with you until they come and haul us away to the nursing home. But I stink pretty good, so probably a shower is a good idea."

"Go start it. Holler when you want me to come in."

"I'll holler now then."

"No, first you warm it up. What's the point in having a lover if he won't heat the shower up for you?"

"I hadn't thought of it that way," he said. He slid out from under the covers and started for the bathroom.

"Julio?"

He stopped. "Yeah?"

"Turn around for me, would you?"

He grinned and did a three-sixty, hands held out. "Like so?"

"Yes. Okay, you'll do. Start the shower, please."

"Yes, ma'am. On the double."

35

Jay Gridley was still tired, having managed only an hour or so of sleep, but he felt good, the tiredness notwithstanding. Contrary to what the boss had said, he had camped out on his office couch, then gotten up and hit the nets early. Platt was the key to this whole thing, and while he had vanished, not leaving any real trail under that name, he might not be as smart as he thought he was. Few people ever were as smart as they thought they were, and Platt had made one giant mistake, no matter what—he had dared face off with Net Force.

There are some basic mistakes you want to avoid. You don't piss into the wind, you don't eat at a place called ''Mom's,'' and you don't pull your program on Lonesome Jay Gridley. Bad idea.

Marietta, Georgia

The inside of the telegraph office smelled of must and pipe tobacco. A cast-iron potbellied coal stove and steel chimney in the center of the room glowed with warmth that kept the hardest of the chill off, but the place was still cool. Behind a counter sat a small man puffing on a corncob pipe. The man wore a long wool coat and gold wire-rimmed spectacles.

"Good mornin', suh. Can I hep you?"

Jay smiled and tipped his hat at the telegraph operator. "Mornin', suh."

Gridley wore the dress uniform of a Confederate captain, a soft gray wool unlike the butternut colors most of the enlisted men wore. A lot of officers had their own designs cut and sewed by their personal tailors, there being little real uniformity in officers' uniforms in the Confederacy. This early in the war, in 1862, the South was not only still in it, they had won major battles against the North. First Manassas—the Battle of Bull Run—had been a rout. The South had kicked some major Yankee ass. Things had already started downhill for the Rebs after Perryville, but right now most folks here felt pretty good about their chances of winning the War Between the States.

Jay said, "Well, suh, I am Captain Jay Gridley, detached from General Lee's staff, and you could do a great service for your state and the Confederacy. We are seeking a Yankee spy, a Southerner who goes by the name of Platt. We do believe he might have been sending coded messages by wire to his Northern masters from this area."

"Well, I do declare!" the telegrapher said. "Can it be?"

"Yes, suh. Of course, we don't think he'd be so foolish as to do these treasonous acts under his own name, but perhaps he was. Could you check your records for us, suh?"

"I would be more than happy to, suh."

Polite folks, the Southerners.

After a minute of thumbing through a stack of yellow paper,

the telegrapher shook his head. "Captain, I'm afraid I cannot find any messages sent or received under the name of Platt."

"This is not unexpected, suh. However, let me describe the traitor for you, and show you a drawing we have of him. He might have used another name."

Jay laid out the general description of Platt, then proffered a pen-and-ink sketch he withdrew from inside his coat.

The telegrapher frowned at the drawing. "I am sorry to report that I do not recognize this man, from word or from representation. However, if you will wait a moment . . . ?"

The telegrapher got up and walked to the back window, a barred affair with the glass portion closed against the chill. He raised the window and yelled out, "Buford! Put down that broom and git yourself in here!"

A moment later a tall and gangly boy of thirteen or so, dressed in gray wool trousers held up by leather suspenders, a homespun gray shirt, and scuffed brown boots, appeared. "Yessuh?"

"This is Captain Gridley, from General Lee's staff. He has something to ask you." To Jay, the telegrapher said, "Buford sometimes watches the office when I take supper. He's got a fair hand with the key for such a young age, although he'll be enlisting as soon as he turns fourteen."

Jay wanted to shake his head. They did that, went off to war as young teenagers.

A lot of them never came back. Stupid thing, war. Stupid.

Jay repeated the description and showed the boy the drawing.

"Why, yessuh, Captain, suh. I do recall him. A large fellow, although he did not go under the name Platt, suh. I recollect that he called himself Rogers." He glanced at the telegrapher, then back at Jay. "I believe he was in just yesterday, suh."

Jay caught a glimpse of something in the boy's face, though he wasn't sure what it meant. He said, "And did this Mr. Rogers send or receive a message?"

The boy hesitated. "I—I think so, suh. I'm not exactly sure. Last evening was passing busy, suh."

The telegrapher, meanwhile, thumbed through the stack of telegrams for yesterday. "I don't see one to or from Rogers here, boy. You did keep a copy, didn't you?"

The boy licked his lips, which seemed to have gone very dry all of a sudden. "I—I don't remember, suh. I must have done, if he sent or got a wire."

"I cannot find one here."

Jay stared at the boy. "Buford, you love your country, don't you?"

"Suh, yes, suh!"

"Then y'all better come clean. Something was unusual about this telegraphic event, wasn't it?"

The boy looked as if he was about to cry. His face clouded over, and tears welled.

"S-S-Suh. Mr. Rogers, he sent a message and—and he give me a nickel for the copy. He took it with him. Am I goin' to jail?"

"What? How could you do that, Buford? That's strictly against regularity!"

Jay held up one hand, asking for the telegrapher to keep silent. "I'm not worried about the nickel or what you did, son. You can square that if you can answer one question for me. Do you remember who Mr. Rogers sent the wiregram to? The name? Or the station?"

"Y-Yes, suh, I remember the station."

Jay grinned. *Hah!* Now *I Gotcha, Platt!*

Sunday, January 16th, 8:05 a.m.
Quantico, Virginia

Jay thundered into Michaels's office, waving a hardcopy print out and yelling "Boss! I got him, I got him!"

"Slow down, Jay. You got who?"

"Platt. Who he's working for! You're not gonna believe this!" He shoved the paper at Michaels, who took it.

"See, the thing is, the guy was smart enough not to use his own name, but not smart enough to change his appearance. I did a scan of all new phone service in Georgia—temporary lines, mobile units, new installations—crossed them with Platt's ID. I figured once he gave up the Platt name and ran, he'd want new com gear under a new name. I threw out female names and corporation names, then checked all the logs at phone stores and service companies in the state. It took a while, but I got it narrowed down to a few, and when I started running those, I came up with a security cam shot of him buying a new mobile!"

Michaels listened with half his attention. There were several numbers on the list Jay had handed him. Circled in red was a number and written in red next to it was a name:

Thomas Hughes.

It sounded familiar, but Michaels couldn't place it. He knew the name. Where did he know it from?

"So then I got the new number and ran a trace on the calls—"

"Jay," Michaels broke in. "Cut to the finish line. Who is this Hughes you have circled?"

Jay smiled and straightened himself up to his full height. "He's chief of staff for a United States senator."

Michaels made the connection. Of course. "White? This guy is Robert *White's* COS?"

"Yes, sir. And isn't it funny that our thug computer guy is calling Hughes? What could the two of them possibly have in common, do you suppose?"

"Jesus," Michaels said.

Sunday, January 16th, 8:55 a.m.
Quantico, Virginia

Toni met Alex and Jay in the conference room. She was on her fourth cup of coffee, but she wasn't fully awake yet. She hadn't slept that well, and the worry that had kept her awake wasn't about the job. She had relived that long passionate kiss in the Miata at least a hundred times. He wanted her, there was no question about that. The question was, was he going to let himself go with his feelings? Or was he going to suck it up and go stoic on her?

"Toni, what have we got?"

"Having a word with Hughes right now is going to be difficult. He's gone on a trip out of town with the senator."

"To Africa?" Michaels asked. "Ethiopia?"

She looked at him. "How do you know that?"

"From his staff guy when he called to schedule me for a committee meeting."

She shook her head. "Yes, well, we've had somebody there check, and while the senator is making the rounds and giving speeches, Hughes isn't with him. We know he got that far, he talked to the press on the flight over and shortly after landing, but nobody has seen him since."

Jay said, "Well, we have his private number here, don't we? Doesn't matter exactly where on the Dark Continent he is. If he's got a virgil, he can't be out of signal range."

Alex said, "The thing is, Jay, we don't really want to talk to him on the virgil. This is the kind of thing you need to do personally."

"You think he might run if he knows we're on to him?"

"Right now, given what we suspect, we're talking about an end to his career and fifteen years in a federal penitentiary—if Platt is working at his direction. He might decide that retreat is the better part of valor. And if he is somewhere in Africa, extradition might be iffy.

"And we have to consider the idea that maybe White is implicated."

"Wishful thinking," Toni said.

"Probably, but you never know. We might get lucky." Alex smiled.

"What I don't understand is what he would have to gain from this," Toni said. "Yeah, he gives his boss a platform to stand on, makes Net Force his whipping boy, but that seems a small payoff for such a big crime."

"I think I have the answer for that," Joanna said from the doorway.

They all turned to look at her.

She waved her flatscreen. "I just got back from the federal money hounds. While we all were running around stamping out little fires on the bank incursion yesterday, somebody snuck in and siphoned off almost two hundred million dollars."

"Now there's a coincidence," Jay said.

"Damn!" Alex said. "Of course! It was misdirection! We thought somebody wanted to take the system down! It wasn't about terrorism at all, it was about money!"

"That lets White out," Alex said. "He's probably got more money than that in his personal checking account."

Joanna continued. "The hounds have traced part of the funds through a Caribbean bank and two Swiss numbered accounts, but they are stonewalled at some Indonesian trust company."

"Part of the funds?" Alex asked

"A hundred and sixty million," Joanna said. "Forty went somewhere else."

Toni said, "That would be a pretty good reason to break into a few computers to raise hell."

"It gets better," Joanna said. She looked at her flatscreen. "Seems an anonymous tip to the FBI has just resulted in the arrest of one Jamal S. Peterson, a former bank employee wanted for a similar kind of sting in South Dakota last month.

They recovered the money from that, a couple hundred thousand, but Peterson was not apprehended at the time. The tip claimed that Peterson was responsible for this theft too.''

''And he's been picked up?''

''About fifteen minutes ago. I just got off the phone with the special agent in Charge. Peterson had a forged passport, a one-way ticket to Rio, and a new account in Switzerland with forty million dollars in it, transferred in last night.''

''So that's all the money,'' Jay said.

''Not exactly. The hundred and sixty very large went into a bank in Bali, but there's a good chance the money has already left the building. The institution in question has a history of such transactions.''

''So Hughes, if he's responsible, has probably already gotten his hands on more money than you and I and everybody in our department will make for the rest of our lives,'' Alex said.

''That would be a fairly safe bet,'' Joanna said.

Alex sighed. ''Damn.''

''I hate to add more rain on the parade,'' Toni said, ''but with that kind of money, there are probably a dozen poor African nations who'd be happy to grant Hughes political asylum. Maybe not the Ethiopians, but some of the third-world presidents would jump at the chance to sell out. For a tenth of that much.''

Alex said, ''And that might be his plan. He might already be sitting in his new villa in Sierre Leone, sipping some banana-and-rum drink and laughing his head off at us.''

''And it gets worse, Boss. We've been backwalking the various penetrations as best we can, and casting about for any side trails, and we think we've uncovered a problem.''

Michaels looked at him. ''Why am I not surprised? What is it?''

''The way it looks to us, Platt has set it up so that he has to log in to various systems at certain times. If he doesn't, and

if he doesn't send the right messages, we think he has several
more surprises set to be unleashed on us."

"Dead-man switches," Alex said.

Jay nodded. "That's how it looks. We're tracking them as
best we can. Given enough time, we'll get them all, but if
anything happens to Platt before we do . . ."

Alex glanced over at Joanna, then back at Jay. "Stay on
it," he said, "and let me know as soon as you've got them
all."

"Right, Boss."

"First thing the rest of us have to do is find out where
Hughes is. Then we'll worry about how much immunity he
thinks he's got."

Alex looked thoughtful. "Toni, see if you can get hold of
Colonel Howard at home, would you?"

Joanna said, "He's not at home. He's doing a survival
course in Oregon."

Everybody turned and looked at Joanna. She said, "Uh,
that's what I heard."

Jay grinned at Joanna, and Toni wondered why.

"Ah," Jay said. "You get that from a certain NCO we all
know and love?"

Joanna blushed, her pale complexion flushed a deep pink.

"Of course, some of us apparently know him and love him
more than others," Jay said. Butter wouldn't melt in his
mouth.

"Go, people, find me a bank thief," Alex said, saving
Joanna more embarrassment. "Oh, and good work on what
we've done so far. You four are the best, don't let anybody
ever tell you different."

"Yeah, but—who gets the trip to Hawaii?" Jay said.

"Go, Jay. We aren't done yet. And while you're looking,
get me everything you can on Hughes. Let's find out what
we're dealing with here."

36

John Howard was nearly a mile into the morning's trek when his virgil cheeped at him.

Uh-oh. Nobody was supposed to call unless it was an emergency. He unclipped the device from his belt—he'd learned *that* lesson, thank you very much—and looked at the ID flashing on the screen.

Assistant Commander of Net Force Toni Fiorella.

He pressed the connect button. "Howard," he said.

"Colonel, I'm afraid you're going to have to cut your survival trip short. We've got a situation here, and Alex—Commander Michaels—wants you back at HQ to put your teams on standby alert."

"Copy that."

"Find a flat spot, sir, and a copter will be there to pick up as soon as possible."

"Affirmative, AC. What's up, can you say?"

"We may be doing an extraction, Colonel, though it's a little early to tell. If we can locate the quarry, it's likely you won't need to pack your cold-weather clothes.''

"Copy. I'm looking for a landing site now."

"Drop by when you get back, Colonel, and we'll fill you in. Discom.''

"Discom."

After the link was sundered, Howard began looking for a place for the copter to land. They'd home in on his virgil, and if a bird lifted from the nearest local military base, his ride should be there within the hour.

Giving up his survival trip for a real assignment was not in the least bit distressing to him. War games and camping trips were only the maps, not the territory.

Sunday, January 16th, 2:15 p.m.
Bissau, Guinea-Bissau

The web covered the world, even a backwater like this one, and it was but the work of a few minutes with a portable flatscreen to uplink via shielded modem pipe to a passing telecom sat. Another minute, a coded password, and 160 million electronic dollars flew from Bali to Bissau, into the government-owned Banco Primero de Bissau, where it was now as safe from the U.S. authorities' grasp as was the surface of Saturn.

In his room, seated cross-legged on his bed, Hughes took a deep breath and let it slowly escape. He smiled. It hadn't even been that difficult to do, to steal more money than most people could ever hope to see in their lifetimes. To most people, 160 million dollars was a fantasy—the only chance they'd ever have at such a sum was winning the lottery. For him, the money was but an intermediate step. A tool, nothing more. He was home free. He had the money, and they didn't have any idea who had taken it. He could go back to the States with

White, wrap up a few loose ends, make a few calls, and he was on his way. Even if all of this somehow blew up in his face, he still would have forty million, after he paid El Presidente. Not a bad little nest egg. That was including, of course, the twenty million Platt was supposed to get—but wouldn't need where he was going.

So easy. Amazing.

The room's phone rang.

"Yes?"

It was the President's secretary. "Good afternoon, Mr. Hughes. President Domingos sends his regards and wonders if it might be convenient for you to join him for a drink in the Blue Room in perhaps half an hour?"

"That would be fine," Hughes said. "Half an hour."

Hughes smiled again. His Excellency wasn't wasting any time.

Time for a shower and fresh clothes before he went.

Sunday, January 16th, 10 a.m.
Quantico, Virginia

"Guinea-Bissau?" Alex said. "I hope you don't think any less of me for not knowing, but where the hell is that?"

"West Africa," Toni said, "between Senegal and Guinea."

"Oh, *that* helps."

They were in his office, alone, and she had just presented him with the intelligence on Thomas Hughes's whereabouts.

Toni said, "On the North Atlantic coast. Trust me, it's there."

"Okay, so how do we know Hughes is there?"

"I have a contact at the CIA who checked it out for me. They actually have an operative in the country, and she filed a report."

"Why would the CIA have an op there? I don't even see any of the Company's maps in here. How important a place can it be if they didn't bother to map it?"

Toni shrugged. "Who knows why the spooks do anything?"

He glanced at the material. "Doesn't look like a real hot vacation spot either. Why is he there?"

"The spooks aren't being real forthcoming. My source says there is some kind of deal cooking between the country's President and Hughes, but that's all they know. Or more likely, all they are willing to say."

Alex leaned back in his chair and fiddled with a light pen. There came a knock at the door. Joanna stood there.

"Good news, I hope?" Alex said.

"Well, good that we found out the bad news," she said.

"Swell. Go ahead."

"The federal hounds paid the entry fee—that's a bribe to you and me—to bank officials in Bali and got into the account where the money was."

Alex blew out a sigh. "Was. I take it that word is key here?"

"Correct. The account was emptied less than an hour ago. Went to something called the Banco Primero de Bissau. That's in—"

"Guinea-Bissau," Alex finished.

"I'm impressed, sir. I'd never heard of the place before."

"Commanders see all and know all, Jo," he said. He gave her a rueful smile. "So, our white-collar thief and his stolen millions are in a country with whom we probably don't have an extradition treaty, no crooks from here ever having figured out how to flee there before now, right? Or if we do have a treaty, whatever deal Hughes and the local head honcho are cooking up will no doubt stall any such proceedings we might attempt? Anybody want to jump in here and reassure me how wrong I am?"

Both Joanna and Toni shook their heads.

Alex stood, put the light pen down, and paced back and forth behind his desk. After a few seconds he said, "All right. Is there any point in me calling State and telling them we want this guy back here?"

Toni shook her head again. "If Hughes thinks he is going to be arrested as soon as he steps off a plane, probably not. State can't make him come home if he's got the country's President in his pocket."

Toni continued. "Of course, he is the COS for a United States senator. He can likely throw some heavy artillery at us. Political types will owe him favors. Maybe he comes back and White steps up to bat for him."

"Maybe," Alex said. "But national-class politicos don't get to the top of the heap without knowing which bugs to step on and which ones to step around. This isn't a political gaffe, it's grand theft. Not an ant, but a stink beetle. Hughes will play hell trying to blame this on the opposition party trying to make him look bad. I'd bet White will drop Hughes like he's a lit bomb."

"All of which means what, Commander?" Joanna asked.

"I think it means if we want him, we are going to have to go and get him," Alex said.

"Hold up a second," Toni said. "He doesn't know we know he's the thief. White is due to return to the country next week. Wouldn't Hughes just come back with the senator? I mean, maybe not, but he's got a seat on White's charter. Why wouldn't he return? As far as he is concerned, he's gotten away with it. That would make things a lot easier. We wait until he lands right at Dulles and collect him, no fuss."

Alex looked at her and smiled. "You're right. Of course. He *doesn't* know we are looking at him. And now that the theft is a done deal, I would suspect there won't be any more attacks on the net by his pet thug. No emergency. We can wait a few days. That would keep me from having to explain to the Director why I invaded a third-world country and kidnapped somebody. Brilliant, Toni."

Toni smiled. Any time she could get that kind of response from him, she was happy.

"Of course, it might be a good idea if the CIA gave us a little help keeping an eye on this character, just in case he decides to go elsewhere."

"They'd be happy to," Toni said. "They lost people when that spy list hit the web. They want this guy. I'd guess if we don't get him pretty soon, he might have a fatal accident."

"That would be bad," Alex said. "We need him alive at least until Jay and Joanna have tracked down and defused his little time bombs."

"I know," she said. "I mentioned that we want him alive."

Sunday, January 16th, 10 a.m.
Chicago, Illinois

Platt had booked a commercial flight from O'Hare to Heathrow, where he'd switch airlines for the hop to North Africa, before transferring to a local crop-duster flight to Oogaboogah. Starting out on a nice big M11, then going to a DC-9, and finally a DeHavilland prop plane. Since he was flying tourist class all the way, the seats weren't gonna be that comfortable, but pretty soon he wouldn't have to be fooling with this crap anymore, and he could fly first class if he felt like it.

The plane didn't leave until the afternoon, though, and he had more than six hours to kill. He thought about checking into a room and getting a few hours sleep, but he could sleep on planes, if he could get them to give him two or three pillows, and he didn't want to take any chance he'd miss his flight, so he decided to wait at the airport. He could dick around, pick up copies of this month's *Flex, Muscular Development,* and *MuscleMag,* eat a good lunch, all like that. He only had the one carry-on bag, and he could rent a locker for that. What the hell.

Since he was so early, he wasn't in any hurry to check in. He got some breakfast, hit the magazine racks, went to the john, then found a place to sit and read near where his gate was.

He spotted the two feds when they came in. They were looking for somebody, and he didn't think that much about it, other than the usual wolf-aware-of-the-hunter kind of thing. But then he saw them see him, saw them recognize him, then pretend it wasn't him they were interested in.

Oh, *shit*!

The two feds walked off, moving quick, ignoring him, but it was too late. He was sure. They had come here looking for him, specifically for him. They were early, checking the place out for spots to set up, and they hadn't expected him to be here yet.

How had they tracked him? If they came to this international gate, then they must know he was booked on a flight with this carrier. If they knew *that*, they knew what name he was traveling under, his main passport, and all. And there was only one way they could possibly know that, because he had told only one person.

Hughes. And Hughes had given him up.

Just like Platt had given up Peterson.

Shit. He had underestimated Hughes. He should have been more alert. The bastard.

He put the magazine down. He had to get the hell out of here. The two feds would be calling for backup, and the airport was going to be a stoppered bottle in a few minutes, if it wasn't already.

Maybe the feds didn't know he'd spotted them. That might buy him a couple of minutes. But he couldn't chance trying to leave by the front door. There could already be local cops heading that way.

He stood and walked toward the exit that led to the gates. It was the fastest way out of the building.

There was a keypad lock by the door, but nobody was look-

ing right at him, so he figured he could put his shoulder against
the door and pop it, but when he looked, damned if the door
didn't open *inward*. Wasn't gonna shove that one open. Crap!

He looked around. A couple of women were opening up a
computer station at one of the nearby gates. He headed that
way.

"Ma'am? I'm sorry to bother you, but I just saw somebody
go into that door over there." He pointed.

The airline clerks looked at him. One was tall and bottle-
blond, the other was short and kind of plump, with red hair
probably out of a bottle too. "Sir?"

"That door that says no entrance, right over there? Well, it
was partway open, and some kid, I dunno, about eight or nine?
she just went in and closed the door behind her."

"I'll check it, Marcie," the redhead said.

"It's right over here," Platt said, smiling.

Once she'd punched in the number and opened the door,
Platt considered his options. Grab her and haul her ass inside,
close the door, clonk her on the head, and haul ass? Or just
remember the number, wait until she got done looking for the
kid who didn't exist, then sneak in himself?

If he'd had more time, he'd have gone with the second
choice. Less fuss. But even as they stood there, FBI and local
cops could be tossing a net over the building. Seconds might
count.

He stepped in behind the woman, wrapped his arm around
her throat, and squeezed her carotids shut. She struggled and
tried to scream, but that came out like a gargle. Thirty seconds
later she was out cold, the blood shut off from her brain. If
he held on and squeezed a little tighter, she'd croak, but he
wasn't that desperate yet. It wouldn't do any good besides;
they already knew who he was. No point in adding murder to
whatever they had. Once she was out, he tore off her blouse,
ripped it into strips, tied her hands and feet, stuffed a piece in
her mouth and used her scarf to hold it in place, then picked
her up and put her over his shoulder. He went down the ramp,

laid her on the floor at the end, around the turn where nobody could see her, then opened the emergency exit and went down the ladder to the concrete. She was coming to as he left. She'd be okay.

Noisy as hell out here.

They were unloading a jet two gates over, and Platt hurried in that direction. A guy on one of those motorized conveyer trucks passed him. Platt waved him down.

"What's up?" the guy said, yelling because he was wearing headphones.

Platt smiled. Grabbed the guy, then gave him one in the gut and one upside the head, knocking the guy senseless. Platt grabbed his earphones and hopped on the conveyer truck. He put it in gear and took off.

Probably there'd be roadblocks leading to the airport pretty quick.

Think, Platt, think!

All right. He had an emergency passport and about twenty thousand dollars of Hughes's money—a thousand in cash, and the rest in a cash-card account—plus he had a hundred grand of his own fuck-you money stashed in another cash-card account under a name nobody knew.

What he needed was a ride, and he needed it from somewhere close.

Ahead was a section of the airport where the express package and cargo service planes were parked.

He grinned as the idea hit him.

"Good morning, sir," the manager of the freight office said. "How can I help you?" He was a kid of maybe twenty-four, twenty-five, wearing a white shirt and a blue tie.

Platt smiled. "Well, sir, I have me a little problem. My name is Herbert George Wells, I've got this big ole shipment of farm machinery sitting on a loading dock in London, England, and no way to git it home." He put a lot more grits in his accent than usual. Stupider he sounded, the better.

"That's what we're here for, sir."

"Thing is, the original airline I hired? Well, they crapped
out on me, blew an engine or something, and in order to get
my tax break, I needed to have spent the money for the plane
by December 31st of last year."

The manager raised an eyebrow.

"See, it saves me about ten thousand dollars if I can show
I paid the money about three weeks ago, you understand what
I'm sayin' here?"

"I think so."

"I'd like to hire one of your planes to fly over there and
pick up my machinery—nothin' illegal here, sir, I got proper
papers on everything—but if I don't use my first charter, I'm
gonna lose ten thousand dollars. On the other hand, I really
need those parts, it's costin' me bidness every day they're
sittin' in England and not in Mobile—that's where I need to
get it, you see, Mobile, Alabama."

"It does appear to be a problem, sir."

"Well, yes. And since there's nothing illegal about my stuff
over there, let's just say, just, you know, for instance, if you
had taken this order from me, oh, say, around Christmastime,
how much of a problem would that be?"

The manager looked around. Then he looked at Platt. What
he thought he saw was a big, musclebound mechanic with his
butt in a crack. "Well, sir, if I had taken the order and somehow forgotten to enter it into the computer, that would be my
mistake. I could, ah, *correct* that when I filled out the paper-
work, pre-date it so it matched the actual date I took the order."

Platt smiled, one man of the world to another. "Well, sir,
if you was to do that, I would be mighty grateful, mighty
grateful. And Mr. Franklin and a baseball team of his twin
brothers would also be mighty pleased." Platt reached into his
shirt pocket, looked around, then removed ten hundred-dollar
bills, folded in the middle. He put the bills on the desk and
slid them toward the kid.

The kid covered the bills with his hand, opened his desk drawer, raked the money off the desk, then shut the drawer. He smiled at Platt. "All right then, Mr. Wells, what kind of equipment did you have in mind?"

Platt grinned. He had his ride, and any feds looking for him wouldn't find it—since it had been booked two weeks earlier and under another name.

Once he got to England, getting a flight to Africa would be easy.

Then he and Mr. Thomas Hughes would have some words. Yes, sir, they surely would. . . .

37

Michaels ate takeout Chinese food at his desk, using throw-away chopsticks to fish the stuff directly from the containers, not even bothering with the paper plate that came in the lunch bag. He'd ordered hot and spicy chicken with noodles, and sweet and sour tofu, but it all seemed kind of bland, and he ate for fuel, not taste. He had other things on his mind.

Toni came into his office. He looked up. Her face, while not grim, was certainly serious. "More good news?" he asked.

"Maybe we can't wait on White's chartered jet to deliver Mr. Thomas Hughes to us after all."

Michaels put the food box down. "Never rains but it pours. What?"

"It seems that about an hour ago, FBI field agents who went to Chicago's O'Hare airport to set up a surveillance on the gate where Platt was supposed to catch a plane to England goofed up."

"Goofed up. There's a nice phrase. What does 'goofed up' mean? And how did they know where he would be?"

"Once we knew who we were looking for, we found a couple of hidden accounts that Hughes had set up, small stuff, less than twenty or thirty thousand in each. Hughes tried to hide his connection to them, but not very hard. Platt used money from one of the accounts to book his ticket—and under a phony name."

"How do you know it was Platt?"

"Who else would be tapping into a slush account to buy a plane ticket overseas right now? We tipped off the field guys. The agents got there several hours ahead of the scheduled departure time, but Platt was already there. He spotted them."

"And he got away, didn't he?"

"The field agents aren't willing to concede that yet. But he did escape from the terminal building by assaulting a ticket agent and a freight handler. Stole a freight truck and disappeared. The FBI is looking, but it's a big airport."

"Yeah, that might be called a goof-up. Best-and-worst-case scenarios?"

Toni leaned against the wall. "Best case, they find him hiding behind a shipment of lawn furniture five minutes from now and take him into custody, whereupon he spills his guts and gives the federal prosecutors enough useful data to overload and sink an aircraft carrier. Hughes comes home, we grab him, he gets fifty years, and dies in jail when he's a hundred."

Michaels smiled at her. "I like that one."

"Worst-case scenario, Platt gets away, calls—or manages to *get* to—Africa, where he informs Hughes the game is over and we're on to him. Hughes hunkers down behind his money and lives happily ever after in the guest room at the Presidential Palace, then dies at a hundred from eating too much caviar."

"I don't much like that story. Why is it I think it is more likely?"

"They could still catch him."

Michaels shook his head. "Somehow, my faith in the FBI's field ops is not as strong as it once was." He paused, staring at the congealing noodles and tofu. "Where is Colonel Howard?"

"In the air, on an Air Force jet. He should be here within the next couple of hours. What are we going to do?"

"Right now, if Platt wants to pick up a phone and call Hughes, can we stop him?"

"Jay says we can. If the virgil number Platt called before is the only one Hughes is using, we can jam it so it won't accept incoming calls. But there are other phones in Bissau, some of which probably even work. We can't block them all."

"Did you lay out what's going on for the colonel?"

"Not yet."

"Call him, tell him. Tell him to lay out his incursion scenarios. Find out what our chances are of going in and grabbing Hughes."

"Are we ready to take that road yet, Alex?"

"This guy terrorized the country, caused people to die, nearly gave a big chunk of a nuclear bomb to a bunch of nuts, and stole a shitload of money. I want to see him behind bars. If we do it right, we're in and out before anybody figures out what's going on, and Mr. Thomas Hughes belongs to us. I'm ready."

"I'll call the colonel."

The intercom buzzed. "Yes?"

"Sir, your wife's lawyer is on the phone."

Great. "Get his number. Then have my lawyer call him."

Toni looked at him.

"It's a long story. I'll tell you about it when we get caught up."

Sunday, January 16th, 5 p.m.
Bissau, Guinea-Bissau

Hughes stood on the terraced balcony outside his room, looking over the pink buildings of the compound at the sur-

rounding grounds. It wasn't so bad here, when you had this
kind of accommodation. You could build yourself a decent
house in this country for twenty thousand dollars, a mansion
for less than a hundred thousand. And he had forty million.
He'd manage.

He leaned against the balcony railing, watching a shirtless
native gardener with a hoe dig weeds from a flower bed. You
could hire a guy like that for twenty bucks a month.

Yes. He'd do all right here.

The deal with Domingos had gone as smoothly as it could
have gone. A hundred million dollars had gone into El Presidente's private Swiss account, and the mineral rights for the
country of Guinea-Bissau now belonged almost entirely to
Thomas Hughes. *All* the mineral rights were his, for the next
ninety-nine years. The oil, bauxite, and phosphates alone were
potentially worth billions—at least that was what Hughes's
geologists and petroleum engineers had told him. Not to mention any gold, silver, copper, or whatever else might lay under
the completely unexploited ground here. The problem was, the
country had never had enough money in the till to do any
serious digging, and not enough trust from the big international corporations for them to take the risks. You didn't want
to spend a couple hundred million dollars to set up an operation in a place like this if you were worried about the locals
putting your managers to the spear and taking over.

But with Hughes owning the rights, it would be different.
He was an educated American, somebody that the big oil and
mine companies could deal with. He had plenty of experience
in high-level negotiations, courtesy of his work for White.
He'd tell his potential partners he had resigned to come here
and make his fortune. Hell, even if they knew he'd ripped off
the banks, it wouldn't matter. If a man thought you were going
to make him *billions* on a business deal, he'd likely be willing
to overlook a few shady things in your past. There were folks
wanted for crimes in the States who had gone on to lucrative
careers in other countries. Who was that movie director who

had run off to France or somewhere and stayed there because the locals admired his work and refused to extradite him?

Money was money. And in the billion-dollar range, ethics got real rubbery.

Hughes had scanned fully legal electronic copies of the freshly signed hardcopy agreements already stored where there was no chance of them getting lost.

He also had half-a-dozen major corporations falling all over themselves ready to drop planeloads of money on him for exploration leases.

Of course, Domingos would get a piece of that too, to go along with the "advance" he'd just collected. But when you were talking about billions, there was enough to go around. Besides, Domingos would probably have a heart attack or a stroke in the not-too-distant future, given his excesses. And if not naturally, something could be . . . arranged.

If ever a man had been in the driver's seat and in control of the bus, it was Thomas Hughes. Things were almost perfect.

When Platt showed up, he'd be getting a little surprise too. Domingos would be happy to furnish a well-trained shooter who would just as soon blast Platt as look at him. And even if Domingos hadn't been eager to help, as poor as most of the people in this country were, you could hire a small army of locals who'd be willing to put a knife into somebody—and for less than the cost of dinner for two in a good Washington restaurant.

Platt was going to become past tense within hours of his arrival. He was expecting to come and collect twenty million dollars, then vanish.

He was half right anyway.

Hughes straightened, and turned to head back into his room. Monique would be arriving soon for a little afternoon delight.

It was good to be the king, but being the man behind the king was almost as good—and certainly it was a lot safer.

Sunday, January 16th, 3 p.m.
In the air over the North Atlantic Ocean

Platt had the 767 to himself, save for the flight crew. Wasn't any stewardess to offer him drinks or membership in the Mile High Club, but he could stretch out in a nice hammock somebody had rigged in the empty cargo bay, and that was a plus. He was on his way to Merrie Olde England, and practically home free. Even if the feds happened across the kid in the freight office and questioned him, the kid had a thousand bucks he'd lose if he gave Platt up, plus some explaining as to why he had forged a date on a rental agreement.

Platt had hit a cash machine just outside the office, so he had money left, plenty enough to catch a flight to Senegal, rent a car, and buy himself a few toys. He didn't want to be landing at the Bissau airport—no, not hardly. That would get back to the Presidente pretty quick, and from the Presidente's lips into Hughes's ear, and that wouldn't do at all. Hughes expected him to be in the federal pokey by now; Platt wanted his appearance to be a real surprise.

Course, it might be tricky sneaking into the guarded compound, but even jigs couldn't see in the dark. Platt had learned how to move in the woods when he'd been a kid, and some African forest couldn't be much worse than the swamps back home. Once he was over the wall, the rest of it would be a walk.

It would be real tempting to break Hughes into itty-bitty pieces once he got to him, but all he really wanted was his twenty million. Well, okay, maybe a little extra for his aggravation and all, that would be fair. If Hughes didn't want to pay him, why, then he'd have to convince him, but that was the last resort. Push came to shove, he could kill the bastard and walk, but that wouldn't be good, he'd be broke and the law looking for him. Any way you looked at it, laying low in

Hawaii running his own gym was a lot better than being on the run.

Yep, that was how he planned it. Get some gear, sneak across the border, have a little chat with Mr. Hughes, finish this whole biz in the green. Course, he might have to find himself a can of shoe polish to blend in with the locals.

That was funny. Him, disguising himself as a darky.

He smiled. The more he thought about that, the better it got. Wouldn't that let the air out of Hughes's tires, he looked up and saw a giant spook who looked just like Platt coming in through the window?

Platt laughed aloud. Oh, yeah, it would.

Sunday, January 16th, 3:35 p.m.
In the air over Virginia

Still flying home on the Air Force transport, Howard opened a shielded com with Julio Fernandez at Net Force HQ.

"I can't go off and leave you alone even for a couple of days, can I, Sergeant?"

"No, sir, Colonel. Cat's away, the mice'll have a field day."

"Let's hear it on all this African stuff, Julio. Is this serious?"

"Far as I can tell, yes, sir. About time too. It's been pretty dull around here lately."

"Talk to me."

The sergeant rattled off a bunch of background about the country, the language, the people, the geography. A minute into it, Howard said, "Look, just upload all that into my mailbox and I'll scan it later. Let's get down to the nitty-gritty. What are we going to run into if we drop in unannounced on the Republic of Guinea-Bissau?"

"Sir. The country is defended by something called the People's Revolutionary Armed Force, called the FARP locally. They have a small Army, about nine boats worth of Navy, and an Air Force consisting of a few prop planes and surplus helicopters—if you don't count the President's unarmed Learjet. They've got a paramilitary militia, and while they supposedly have maybe a couple hundred thousand able-bodied men who could be drafted, the standing army is a twentieth of that, poorly armed and uneducated. Probably half of them could figure out how to tie their shoes—if they *had* shoes."

"I see. What else?"

"They got zip railroads, under three thousand kilometers of paved road in the entire country, and thirty-five airports, two of which have enough runway to allow anything bigger than a crop duster to land. We'd have to put our transport down in Senegal, to the north, and go in either via copter, or overland—or maybe with an airdrop and parachutes.

"There are fewer than four thousand telephones in the country, maybe three for every thousand persons, and half those don't work."

"The phones don't work, Sergeant? Or the people."

"Both, sir. Average income is a couple hundred dollar per *year*."

"I see."

"They've got three FM radio stations, four AM stations— they like rock and country and western, and a lot of trash talk. There are two TV stations, one of which doesn't sign on until dark. That's because there are maybe as many TVs as there are telephones. And probably half that many personal computers total, of which maybe a third have web access."

"Sounds like a place to do my next survival trip."

"If we cruise in over 'em anymore than a hundred feet up, we'll be safe, 'cause none of the locals can throw their spears that high. Me and a company of our second-teamers could parachute in after dark one night and be running the country by morning, without breaking a sweat."

"Lack of confidence has never been one of your failings, Julio."

"No, sir."

"You sound awfully happy for a man stuck on a dull base recovering from a shot-up leg. I recognize that tone. Who is she?"

"I'm sure I don't have any idea what the colonel is talking about."

"You'll go to Hell for lying like that, Sergeant."

"Yes, sir, and I'll have your landing site secured when you arrive."

Howard laughed. "All right. I'm going to scan in the stuff you're sending and run scenarios on my S&T system. I should be landing in"—he glanced at his watch—"about half an hour. Meet me there."

"Yes, sir."

"Pack your tropical-weights, Sergeant, and kiss your girl-friend good-bye."

"Not a problem, sir." He laughed.

"Something funny I missed?"

"Oh, no, sir. I just remembered an old joke."

"In thirty minutes, Julio."

"Sir."

38

Monday, January 17th, 11 a.m.
Quantico, Virginia

Michaels said, "All right, I think that's it. Questions?"

He looked around the conference room at the others: Howard, Fernandez, Winthrop, Gridley, and Toni.

Toni said, "Have we cleared this with the Director?"

"Currently the Director is in a don't-ask-don't-tell frame of mind," Michaels said. "If we deliver Hughes, he won't much care what we had to do to get him. And certain members of the Senate who might ordinarily scream to high heaven will be, I expect, very quiet about this particular detention." He grinned. "We also have some off-the-record help from the CIA. About as much as we want. Anything else?"

Nobody spoke.

"Good. You all have your assignments. Better go and get started."

The others left. Toni stayed behind.

"This is not a good idea, Alex."

"You heard the colonel, it should work."

"You know I'm not talking about the operation, I'm talking about *you* going along."

"Rank has its privileges, Toni. I was a good field op, once upon a time. I need to get out once in a while. The administration and politics of this job grind you down."

"It's dangerous."

"Crossing the street is dangerous."

He saw she was really concerned about him, and he didn't want to be flip, so he said, "What would make you feel better about this?"

"You *not* going."

"Aside from that?"

She looked him straight in the eyes. "If I went with you."

He started to shake his head. "I need somebody here to run things—"

"For three or four days? Bring in Chavez from nights, shift Preston over from Operations. They can handle things for that long."

"I don't know—"

"Oh, it's fine for you to go play in the field but not me?"

"It's against regulations for both of us to be on the same plane," he tried. He knew it was lame when he said it.

"You're going to quote *regulations* at me? You're going to toss the rule book out the window, go along on a mission you'd *never* get approved if the Director knew about it, and then talk to me about both of us flying on the same plane?!"

Ooh, she was mad. It was a side of her he'd never seen. And of course, she was perfectly justified in feeling that way, and he knew it.

"Okay," he said, holding up his hands in surrender. "Okay, you're right. You can go."

"I can?"

And in those two words, he heard what she must have sounded like as a little girl. In her concern, anger, and her sudden astonishment, she was in that moment drop-dead gorgeous, calling to him like a Siren. He wanted to hug her, kiss her—and he wanted to fall on the couch with her. Not a good idea, and certainly not a good idea here in the office, but that was how he felt.

Something was going to have to be done about this. *He* was going to have to do something.

"You're right. We'll work something out. That way, we'll both be looking for new jobs if this goes sour."

"I can live with that."

"Good. Now go take care of those other details we need handled, okay?"

"Right," she said. She smiled at him, stood there for what seemed a long time, then very softly, so softly he wasn't sure he had heard it, said, "I love you."

And then she was gone, and he was standing there with his mouth open, caught totally flat-footed and stunned.

Monday, January 17th, 6 p.m.
Bissau, Guinea-Bissau

Hughes sipped at his drink, a good brandy in a monogrammed crystal snifter, and frowned up at the President's chauffeur/ bodyguard.

"You're sure?"

"Sorry, sir, but he wasn't on the plane. I would have recognized him. I did drive him around when he was here before. He's rather difficult to miss."

"Yes. Well, thank you anyway."

The chauffeur departed, and Hughes reached for the Cuban cigar in the ashtray on the table next to the overstuffed chair in which he sat. The cigar had gone out. He carefully relit it, using one of the wooden matches from the carved ivory box.

"This is a concern for you?" Domingos said. He puffed on his own fine cigar and blew out fragrant smoke.

"Not really," Hughes said. "Platt will show up sooner or

later. If not today's flight, then tomorrow's or the next day's.
I have his money, and the arrangement was for him to collect
it in person.''

"Giles will take care of him whenever he arrives," Domingos said. "Not to worry."

Hughes swirled the brandy, lifted the snifter to his lips, and
sipped it. "I'm not worried at all, Mr. President."

"Please, you must call me Freddie. We are going to have
a long and very pleasant association together, no?"

"But of course. Freddie."

Monday, January 17th, 7 p.m.
Tanaf, Senegal

Platt had driven his rented Land Rover to Sédhiou, where he'd
taken the dinky ferry across the sluggish and brown Casam-
ance River, then south to Tanaf. From there, if he stayed on
the road, he was only about five miles away from Senegal's
southern border with Guinea-Bissau. If he stayed on the road,
it would take him through Olo Province south across the Can-
jambari River by way of Mansõa, and into Bissau from the
northeast. That was if he stayed on the road. Thing with a
Land Rover was, you didn't have to stay on the road if you
didn't feel like it. And most of the roads around here were
dirt tracks anyhow. He didn't particularly trust the guy who'd
rented him the Rover, but the guy was white, and he'd said
there were more ways to cross the border unseen than you
could shake a stick at, and that was probably true.

It wasn't that far, as the crow flew, from where he was to
Bissau, maybe fifty miles, but if the crow had to walk it on
these crappy paths it was not only longer, it was a lot slower
than the bird could fly with one wing busted. Platt would probably get there while it was still dark, assuming he didn't get

pulled over by some native Army patrol out for blood. He was prepared for that, having bought himself a K-bar sheath knife, a Browning 9mm semiautomatic pistol, a vintage AK-47, and enough ammunition for both guns to take out a small-town high school football stadium. Plus he had picked up two WWII surplus hand grenades—German potato mashers, the dealer told him, old, but guaranteed to work.

If he ran into some local soldiers who wanted to give him grief, he'd see if could mash *them* like potatoes. Nobody in this dark land was gonna stop him getting where he wanted to go, not without being real sorry if they tried.

And after he had gotten far enough out in the boonies, he had pulled over and taken time to apply a couple of coats of the darkest tanning foam he could find. He wasn't exactly black, but he was a kind of nutty brown, and with a baseball cap on to hide his hair, he didn't look much like a white man at any distance more than a few yards.

Platt found a cow path or something a couple of miles away from the border, leading through a grassy field and a couple of plowed areas, then into some woods. He stayed on the compass until he came to a fence that stretched off into the woods in both directions.

Must be the border, he figured.

The fence that protected the border was three whole strands of rusted barbed wire tacked to wooden posts that were mostly rotted away.

Damned savages couldn't do any better than that? Jesus. No wonder they never amounted to nothin' over here. This fence wouldn't keep the livestock in back home.

He hacked most of the way through one of the posts with the K-bar, then knocked it the rest of the way down with the Rover's front bumper and rolled across the border.

Welcome to Guinea-Bissau, hoss. Hope you enjoy your visit.

He had gotten kind of turned around, so he pulled over to check the map. And it was a lucky thing too. While the hot

engine ticked, he heard another vehicle. He got out of the Land
Rover and moved down the trail.

Ahead was a beat-up pickup, painted jungle green, with four
soldiers in it, two inside, two in the back. They had AKs like
his, and they were cruising along slow, looking.

Platt realized that if he hadn't stopped, he might have run
right into them, and with four guns against his one, that could
have been real bad—especially if they had seen him first,
which they would have probably done, since they were looking and he wasn't.

He hadn't figured on a border patrol. He revised his opinion
up a little. Maybe these jungle bunnies were sharper than he'd
thought. Bad idea to underestimate the other side.

After the truck had time to get a couple of miles away, he
went back to the Rover. Better take it slow and careful from
here on in.

He figured he needed to get fairly close to the city, then
find himself a place to hide the Rover, 'cause he'd need it to
leave. And he'd have to hole up for a day, until tomorrow
night, because he definitely didn't want to be moving around
during the day, disguise or not. Tuesday night, good and dark,
he'd mosey on in and do his business.

As he drove through a field of high grass, the damp and
heavy air rumbled with distant thunder. He could smell the
approaching rain.

Oh, good. A storm, just what he needed to slow him down
even more.

On the other hand, a thunderstorm would probably keep the
local militia inside drinking bull pee or whatever it was they
drank, and that would be good. He wasn't lookin' to get shot
if he could help it.

He wiped sweat away from his forehead with the back of
his right hand. Damn, but it was muggy here.

He saw a cloud of mosquitoes or flies or something buzzing
in the air ahead of him, and he reached for the bug dope spray
in the bag on the passenger seat. Be another good thing the

rain would do, keep the bugs down. All he needed was to catch sleeping sickness or malaria or elephantitis from all this crap.

No two ways about it, he was gonna take a little more than the twenty million when he talked to Hughes. He sure had it coming.

Monday, January 17th, 9 p.m.
In the air over the Atlantic Ocean

"Banjul, huh?" Joanna said.

Seated next to her in the seat of the team's 747, Fernandez said, "Yep. It's in The Gambia, kind of an insert around the Gambia River, runs right into the lower half of Senegal. A little farther away than we wanted, right on the coast, but it's the only airport south of Dakar where we can put this bird down and not be noticed. The Company has a store there—we're switching to a couple of Hueys for the rest of the trip. So we'll go in at treetop level Tuesday night, land, do our thing, then come out. It worked great on that Chechnya caper, it sure ought to work out here in darkest Guinea-Bissau. I don't think their radar is exactly state-of-the-art. Even if they see us, they don't have much to throw at us or chase us with."

"Heads up, here comes the colonel," Joanna whispered.

"Sir," Fernandez said as John Howard stopped next to their seats.

"Sergeant, Lieutenant." Howard looked at them for a couple of seconds, then smiled.

"Something funny, sir?" Fernandez said.

"Not really. You know that joke you were remembering when I called you on the way back from Washington State? The one you laughed at?"

"I remember."

"I do believe I get it now, Sergeant. Carry on."

After the colonel left, Joanna looked at Fernandez. "What was that all about?"

Fernandez grinned widely. "I expect the colonel knows that you and I have been, ah . . . intimate."

"How would he know that? You bragging?"

"No, ma'am, as proud as I am of it, I didn't say a word. But I've been working for the man for a long time. He doesn't have a dull edge, and he knows me too well. Any time a man feels as good as I do, it shows. And I expect that it shows more when you're around, seeing as how you're the reason. Is this a problem?"

"Not for me. In fact, I'm going to take a run to the head. You want to come along?" She waggled her eyebrows like Groucho Marx in an old black-and-white movie.

"You know, you are an *evil* woman, Lieutenant Winthrop, teasing a man that way."

"You don't know the half of it, Sergeant. I'm just getting warmed up with you. Besides, who said I was teasing?"

"Brought your wavy knife, I see," Alex said.

Toni looked up and nodded. She had the *kris* in its wooden scabbard on her lap. "Guru is convinced the *kris* is magic. I figured it wouldn't hurt."

He nodded, then said, "I'm just going to have a few words with the colonel. Looks like everything is on schedule. We'll be at the airport in a few more hours. We'll transfer stuff to helicopters there, then on to the target."

"You couldn't talk the colonel into letting you go into the city on the mission, could you?"

He smiled, shook his head. "No. And the truth is, I'm not unhappy with us staying with the pilots at the copters until they get back. My recent success as a soldier in the field was more luck than skill. This is what Howard and his team do. I don't want to get in the way."

"We could stay in Banjul," she said.

"Do that, and we might as well have stayed in Washington."

"Didn't I say that in the first place?"

"Yep. But look, we came this far, we might as well go along for the ride."

"As long as we both go along for the ride," she said.

He smiled at her.

So far, he hadn't said anything to her about that other thing she had said. The "I love you" part. It had seemed the right thing to her at the time, but after she had done it, she'd been almost sick with fear. They had kissed each other for a few minutes in the front seat of a very small car, that was all. It was maybe too early to be hitting him with something that heavy. What if he didn't feel anything for her other than lust? She knew that was there, there wasn't any way to hide the evidence of that. And she wanted it, sex with him, and she would settle for that, for now, but she also wanted a lot more.

Then again, he hadn't said anything about it, and that meant he hadn't refuted it either. Or maybe he hadn't even heard it.

No news was good news—or at least it wasn't bad news.

She wouldn't push it. She would see what happened. The magic in the *kris* had gotten her this far. Maybe it would help take her the rest of the way. . . .

39

Domingos had some pressing state business he had to attend
to—probably a ribbon cutting at a new bodega or something—
so Hughes enjoyed his cigar and brandy in solitude. Well, save
for the brief appearance of a messenger who informed him
that the five o'clock plane had come, and that once again Platt
was not on it.

This was worrisome. Platt certainly wanted his money, and
the only reason Hughes could imagine that he hadn't hurried
here to collect it was that something had prevented him from
doing so. And the only things that came to mind that were
capable of stopping Platt from doing anything were serious
injury, death, or being arrested. And Platt hadn't called, another thing that bothered Hughes.

What if somehow Platt had run afoul of the law? What if
he had been captured?

Hughes held the cigar in his mouth without puffing on it.
He had considered this before, of course, although he had to
admit to himself he hadn't really thought it likely. And even

if he had been caught, Hughes did not think Platt would say anything about their venture; it would hardly be in his best interest to do so. Still, what if somehow he was made to speak? If the feds had Platt, and if they had squeezed him, then that would alter Hughes's plans considerably.

Going back to the U.S. would be out of the question. As soon as he stepped off the plane, the feds would swoop down on him like a hawk on a chicken, and he'd be in real trouble.

What to do?

The least risky proposition was simply to sit tight. Wait until Platt showed up here, or called. If he didn't do either in the next week or so, Hughes would have to risk some long-distance research and see if he could figure out what had happened to his operative. If Platt was in a hospital from a car wreck or some such, or even dead, well, so much the better. But if the authorities had somehow caught him, if he had slipped up, then one had to assume the worst.

The cigar was out. He reached for a match.

He wasn't due to return to the U.S. from Ethiopia until Thursday, so he had a couple of days. If Platt hadn't shown up by then, Hughes would put in a call to the senator and offer some reason why he had to stay in Africa for a few more days. Easy enough. And if Platt had been caught and had given him up, then here was where Hughes would stay. It would be ahead of schedule, and irritating to have been found out, but not a major setback, all things considered.

He lit the cigar. When he had his house built, he'd have to be sure to include in it a humidor, a walk-in humidor, to keep his own stock of Cubans nice and fresh. . . .

Tuesday, January 18th, 9 p.m.
Banjul, The Gambia

Rain fell on the corrugated metal roof, a constant, almost hypnotic drumming that felt relaxing despite the muggy interior of the staging shed. The hard rain almost drowned out the electrical generator droning on outside the building.

Michaels felt lulled by the rain and the heat. This was supposed to be the dry season, the monsoons were supposed to be over. What must the wet season be like then, if this was dry?

Howard had a map projected on a more-or-less-white concrete block wall. "This is the city of Bissau," he said. "On the north side of the Rio Géba where it turns into the bay." He waved a laser pointer in a circle of red around the Presidential Palace. "This is the compound."

Howard used a remote, and the viewpoint zoomed in. "This is the main building and this is where our target should be."

He fiddled with the remote, and the map was replaced by a computer-enhanced spysat photograph, the angle altered to give a view from what appeared to be only a few hundred feet above the buildings. "The CIA rerouted one of their fast-flying high-eyes to footprint the city for us, and we'd like to thank them for that, and for the use of the Hueys and this staging area."

Howard would have liked even more assistance from the Agency—like a geosynch spysat with full IR capabilities footprinting the area from now through the time of the assault—but this operation was strictly unofficial. The Agency had done all it could without risking calling attention to what Net Force was doing out here, and Howard appreciated their efforts. He nodded at a fit-looking gray-haired man in khaki shorts and a T-shirt, who smiled and waved.

There were thirty-four people in the room. Howard had brought four five-troop squads, not counting Fernandez and Winthrop. There was the CIA Liaison, four helicopter pilots, four ground-support techs, plus Toni and Michaels. The troops were already mostly dressed in their SIPEsuits.

Howard put the map up again. "We'll land here, about two miles from the target, where we will switch to local transport, again courtesy of the Company. Alpha Team will proceed to here and initiate our diversion, while Beta Team will proceed to the compound and prepare for the incursion. Look over your house plans one more time, Beta. We don't want anybody getting lost in there and winding up in the bathroom instead of the package's quarters.''

That caused a little nervous laughter.

''We would like to avoid casualties on either side if at all possible, so we will utilize flashbangs, puke gas, and pepper fog to neutralize threats. No one is to fire unless fired upon first, and then only if the other side is using armor-piercing rounds, which is highly unlikely. Our intelligence indicates that most of the soldiers in Bissau are armed with Kalashnikovs—when they are armed at all—and issue ammo is standard Soviet Bloc surplus.

''Let me be clear on this point. We are not at war with this country, and we don't want to leave bodies piled up all over the place, understood?''

There was a mumble of acknowledgment.

''We are set to collect the package at 0130 hours. Any questions so far?''

Nobody had any.

''After Beta Team collects the package, we will rendezvous with Alpha at the assembly point, then proceed to the landing site. Whatever our status on the ground, the Hueys will lift at 0230 hours and proceed on the prearranged flight path back to Banjul. If you miss the bus, you'll have a long walk home. Any questions?''

There were no questions.

''All right then. Finish suiting up and lock and load. We leave in one hour. Dismissed.''

The pilots and squads filed out into the rain, which was finally beginning to slacken. Michaels, Toni, Winthrop, and Fernandez stayed behind with the colonel.

''Got your gear?'' Howard asked Michaels and Toni.

He was referring to the Kevlar helmets and hardweave armor vests he had given them. They weren't going into combat, but he'd insisted that if they were going in the copters they must wear them. And he'd also issued them each a suppressed pistol, which he also wanted to see strapped on. There was always a chance the copter could blow a gasket or take small-arms fire and be forced to land. It was better to be armed than not when moving overland in hostile territory. And with a gun that didn't make a lot of noise.

"Got them," Toni answered for herself and Michaels.

"You know you really should stay here," Howard tried again.

"You've assured us the danger is minimal," Michaels said.

"Minimal is not the same as none," Howard said.

"I appreciate your concern," Michaels said. End of discussion.

"All right. We're set then. Winthrop will be with me on Beta Team, Sergeant Fernandez leads Alpha. Our projections run between eighty-eight-percent and ninety-three-percent success, if we've plugged in all the proper variables. This ought to be a piece of cake. In and out, quick and clean. By this time tomorrow, we should be well on our way home."

Michaels nodded.

"I'll see you at the transports in fifty-five minutes."

Tuesday, January 18th, 11 p.m.
Bissau, Guinea-Bissau

Platt hated this damned country. Being stuck in a mud hut that sat there and cooked in the hot sunshine all day hadn't helped his mood. Hell, even when it rained a frog-drowner like it had this afternoon, it still didn't get cool. Just muggier, so your sweat wouldn't even evaporate, it just rolled down your legs and soaked into your socks. It was like sitting in a steam bath with your clothes on.

He looked at his watch for the fiftieth time since it got dark.
He was about a mile from the pink palace, the Land Rover
parked inside a tin shed next to the mud house. The house's
owner, a white-haired old man, was tied up and lying on the
cot in the corner. The old guy hadn't seemed too fretted about
a man with a gun barging in. He'd damned near brained Platt
with his walking stick—he was a lot faster than he looked.
Another two inches and the party would have been over; as it
was, the stick had left a scrape over Platt's left ear.

These jigs weren't complete pushovers like he'd figured.
That bothered him. If the palace guards were up to snuff, that
could be a real problem.

After he'd gotten the stick away, Platt had trussed the old
man up like a hog. Near as Platt could tell, the old boy was
asleep. Couldn't get away, hell, might as well take a nap. In
the old man's place, Platt didn't think he'd feel so cool.

The idea of being taken out by a nigrah was . . . was unreal.
He had to be more careful.

He'd planned to wait until around midnight before he
headed for the palace, but Platt had had enough of this hanging
around. He was going now. They'd roll up the sidewalks
around here by eight or nine anyhow—if they'd *had* sidewalks.

He changed into a black T-shirt and black pants, with black
tennis shoes and black socks. What skin showed was stained
pretty dark, and it wouldn't show up too well at night. He
tucked a little flashlight into his back pocket and strapped on
the Browning 9mm, with two extra magazines in pouches on
the other side of the web belt, next to the sheath knife. He
had a screw-on suppressor for the pistol; he'd put that on when
he got there. Coiled over his shoulder was a half-inch hemp
rope with knots in it every two feet, and a steel grappling hook
on one end. He thought about taking the AK, but decided
against it and left it in the Rover. But he did hook the pouch
with the two old German hand grenades in it onto the web
belt. Things got nasty, he would go out with a bang. . . .

As ready as he was going to get, Platt rolled his shoulders and bent his neck left and right to stretch, waved at the sleeping old man, and started out. He was gonna move careful, so it might take him a couple-three hours to get where he was going.

If Hughes had company in bed, they were going to get a surprise along about 1:30 or 2 a.m. Platt was looking forward to it.

12:40 a.m.

Howard piled into the ancient pickup truck last, and dropped the piece of canvas that covered the back opening. The pickup was an old one-ton Chevy, and the owner had built a wooden frame over the bed and stretched canvas over the frame, so the thing looked more or less like a motorized covered wagon.

"Go!" Howard commanded.

One of Beta Team drove. The driver started the motor and the truck lurched off. When he shifted into second, the driver clashed the transmission gears together, and one of the troops said, "Hey, grind me a pound too!"

Howard glanced at Lieutenant Winthrop, whose face looked awfully pale in the darkness, then looked at his watch.

Alpha Team was already on the road in a similar dilapidated vehicle.

Howard had been assured that no matter how bad they looked, the trucks were mechanically sound, and would take them to and from where they wanted to go.

He sure hoped so.

The locals would have heard the copters coming down, no way around that, but local police response time to motor noises in the night wasn't likely to be real fast—if they bothered to come out and check at all. And as soon as Beta Team was another quarter mile farther up the road, its truck would stop, whereupon two soldiers would hop out and rig flashbangs on the road's shoulders. These devices would be controlled by a pressure strip set on the only road leading from town to the helicopters. If any local cops or troops came out to check on things, they'd would get a light and noise show that would make them stop and think. So would anybody else out driving this late, but that wasn't likely to happen. This was a narrow dirt road that dead-ended at a forest, and the people who lived off this path didn't own automobiles. The pressure strip would let a bicycle or motorcycle pass over it without firing the flash-bangs.

The day's heat hadn't abated much, and Howard felt the sweat soaking his clothes. They were wearing tropical-weight assault uniforms under the SIPEsuits, but in this kind of high-temperature, high-humidity weather, any-weight clothes were too much.

"You all right, Lieutenant?"

"Sir, I'm fine," she said.

Then she said, "Actually I'm a little nervous, sir."

He smiled at her. "Only a little? I personally am scared spitless. Pucker Factor of about twelve."

That got a little smile out of her. Yeah, she was a soldier, but she wasn't a combat trooper, she'd never been on anything other than sims or training exercises. She was a computer expert, one of the best, and she didn't have to go into the field. Net Force was not like RA, where if you wanted to advance in rank, sooner or later you had to have some field experience. But she'd wanted to do this, and Julio had vouched for her, so she was here.

"Really?" she said. "You?"

"If you don't feel fear, you can't be brave. Brave is when your bowels are like ice and you're terrified, but you go out and do the job anyway. I don't want troopers who are fearless. They're the first ones to get taken out when the situation goes hot. Fearless and stupid go together."

"Thank you, sir."

He smiled. "You'll do fine, Winthrop. You're wearing state-of-the-art combat armor; anything that might get thrown at you will probably bounce right off."

"That's not how Sergeant Fernandez tells it, sir."

Howard chuckled. "Well, of course, Julio is the exception that proves the rule. He's a good man, Fernandez. Best I have."

"I think quite highly of him myself," she said.

1 a.m.

Hughes got up and went to the bathroom. He shouldn't drink anything after ten at night. He knew better; he woke up every time he did having to go urinate.

He was a little peeved too. Monique hadn't shown up tonight, she wasn't answering her com, and nobody seemed to know where she had gone. Domingos said she had done that before, disappeared for a day or two. He suspected she either had a local lover or went off to do drugs. Some of the locals grew prime *ganja*—it wasn't hard to come by.

Ah, well. It wasn't as if Hughes needed her to be here—he'd done more screwing in the last few days than he had in months—but he didn't like surprises. That was the trouble with whores. No matter how high-priced they were, you couldn't depend on them. You needed to think of them like Kleenex. You used them, then you disposed of them, and the next time you felt a sneeze coming on, you plucked another one from the box.

He smiled at his metaphor, then waded through the thick carpet back to bed. The hum of the air conditioner would put him back to sleep soon enough.

1:15 a.m.

Getting into the compound had been harder than Platt had figured. The trees had been cut back from the walls, and there was all that broken glass on top too, but he'd managed to get over using the rope and grapple without slicing himself to ribbons.

Shit, every time he turned around, things were tougher than he'd expected. He'd been here before, on the inside, but he'd never figured he'd be going in over the wall the next time he came to visit.

He'd figured that once he was inside, all he'd have to do was keep from stepping on one of the sleeping guards, then make his way into the main building. But maybe the guards weren't going to be sleeping. He could get his ass handed to him if he wasn't careful.

He paused, then screwed the sound supressor onto the Browning's threaded barrel and tightened it. Gun would still make a fair *pop!* if you shot it—the suppressor wouldn't stop the noise coming out of the slide when it went back and the spent shell ejected—but with subsonic ammo, it wouldn't be like a bomb going off or anything. You could miss the noise if you weren't too close.

Getting in would be tricky, 'cause the guards in the house would sure as hell be awake and told to shoot first and don't ask questions. But there was a way in, something he had seen when he'd been here before. There was a trash chute coming out of the kitchen that led into a big metal trash container next to the kitchen exit. The chute was big enough to put a whole can of garbage into at once, and it was big enough for a man to get through too, if he didn't mind getting covered with old banana peels and coffee grounds and rotten fruit.

Platt headed for the garbage chute.

1:25 a.m.

Howard and Beta Team went in over the east wall. There was a grove of orange trees between the nearest building and the base of the wall where they came down, offering cover. Fortunately, according to the CIA, the President of this country did not like to hear the barking of dogs, so there weren't any roaming the grounds.

The team moved through the orange grove, got to the pre-arranged position, spread out, and went prone. The main building was right in front of them.

Howard looked at his watch.

He held up his hand, three fingers spread. "In three minutes, people," he said quietly.

1:30 a.m.

Julio Fernandez counted the seconds off aloud. "Five, four, three, two, *one*!"

Fernandez pressed the detonator stud on the IR control.

Two hundred yards away, a low-roofed warehouse stored full of cashews and palm kernels for export went up in a blinding white flash and a *boom!* that rocked the truck in which Fernandez and the others Alpha Teamers sat.

Flames spewed high, and bits of debris pattered back down, in a rain somewhat harder than the locals were used to.

A shower of nuts bounced off the truck's roof and hood.

"Now *that's* how to roast cashews," Fernandez said. "That ought to give 'em something to worry about. AMF, we're outta here! Roll!"

The driver cranked the truck and wheeled it out onto the road. They passed a wailing fire engine a mile away, and Fernandez waved at the firemen.

"Good luck putting *that* one out, boys."

1:30 a.m.

The warehouse flashed brightly, followed in a couple of seconds by the sound of the explosion. Lights went on in the main building, and guards rushed out, weapons held ready, excited voices jabbering away.

"Move in!" Howard commanded.

The two point men, Hamer and Tsongas, scuttled toward the half-dozen guards who were waving their assault rifles and looking puzzled. The point men wore backpack foggers, high-pressure tanks filled with military-grade pepper spray. They were within twenty feet of the nearest guards before they were noticed, and by then it was too late. As the guards turned to bring their weapons to bear on the threat, Hamer and Tsongas cut loose.

The pepper fog boiled out in a long white cloud that enveloped the unfortunate guards. Unlike Mace or even commercial five-percent pepper spray, whose effects a man might shrug off, pepper fog was impossible to ignore. It got into your breathing passages and eyes, and you couldn't stop your body's reaction. Your eyes swelled shut and you dropped to the ground, trying to find air you could breathe. For the next fifteen or twenty minutes, you weren't going to be doing much of anything except wishing you'd never been born.

Howard had gone through the training, he'd eaten the fog, and he knew how those guards felt.

The military stuff was designed to spew hard and settle out fast, but you wanted to wait a few seconds before you ran through the area you'd just fogged, and you wanted your goggles or spookeyes down when you did it.

"Go, go!"

The point men moved in to disarm the squirming guards, while two more troopers offered cover.

Howard and Winthrop headed for the door with the other six team members. He remembered to hold his breath. Two of Beta peeled off to cover their flanks, while two more ran into the building through the open front door, Howard and Winthrop right behind them, handguns drawn.

Nobody in the hall to stop them, Howard saw. The main staircase was just ahead. "Third floor! Go, go!"

With Winthrop next to him, Howard ran for the stairs.

1:31 a.m.

Platt was in the kitchen, scraping what smelled and looked like fermented mayonnaise off his arm, when things went wonky. He saw a bright light strobe the window next to the back door, and heard an explosion in the distance that rattled the hanging pots and pans.

What the hell was *that*?

He didn't have time to worry about it, though. A guard ran into the kitchen, spotted Platt, and raised his assault rifle to pot him.

Platt already had the Browning nine in his hand. He indexed the guard and shot him twice—*pop! pop!*—right in the center of mass. Wasn't too loud—

The guard stopped, looked down at his chest as if he was annoyed, then went back to swinging his AK around at Platt.

Man! Platt put the next two into the guard's face. The guy dropped like a boneless chicken. That ended that.

Goddamn pansy nine-millimeter! You couldn't get a decent .45 or .357 in these foreign countries—they restricted you to small-caliber if you were a civilian!

Platt scooted across the kitchen and opened the door to the electric dumbwaiter. The tiny elevator was going to be a tight fit. He hit the button for the third floor, then squeezed himself into the little box and let the door shut. The dumbwaiter groaned, not having been designed for this much weight, but it rose. He heard somebody else make it into the kitchen and start yelling in oogaboog as the dumbwaiter lifted, but by then they didn't know where he was.

Apparently the residents knew enough to stay in their rooms. Nobody tried to stop them as the went down the hall on the third floor.

Winthrop was glad. The H&K pistol in her hand didn't offer the comfort she thought it would. It felt like an alien device, despite her training, too barrel-heavy because of the silencer, the grip sweaty. She didn't particularly want to shoot anybody, though she thought she could if she had to.

"Third door on the left," the colonel said.

The two Beta Team troopers split, one going past the door, the other stopping on the near side. They turned so they were facing away from each other, covering both ends of the hall.

Howard reached the door and tried the knob. Locked. He nodded at her, pointed at the room. "I'll get the door, you go in."

She nodded in return, said, "Okay," through dry lips.

Howard raised his foot and kicked the door open. Winthrop dived in and rolled, just as she had done in VR so many times, and came up on one knee, the pistol pointed in front of her.

Thomas Hughes, dressed in white silk pajamas, sat up in bed, where he had obviously been sleeping until that moment.

"Who the hell are you? What do you want?"

The colonel stepped in behind Winthrop. "Mr. Hughes," he said. He smiled. "Commander Alexander Michaels at Net Force would like to have a word with you."

"I don't think so," somebody said.

Winthrop snapped her gaze to the glass door leading out to the balcony. A tall, dark, and muscular man stood there, holding an odd-looking device in one hand. She swung her pistol around to cover him.

"I wouldn't do that, darlin'," the man said.

Winthrop recognized him now that she heard the corn pone in his voice.

"Platt!"

"You look much better in person than you do in VR, honey. How about you put those guns down?"

"How about I just shoot you instead?" Winthrop said.

"Bad idea. Ask your jig friend there why."

She glanced at the colonel.

"He's holding some kind of a grenade," Howard said.

"Yep, a gen-u-wine World War Two *po*-tato masher. Shoot me and I drop it, and even if your armor stops most of it, you still probably get stung pretty good. Maybe a piece gets through and punches a hole in an artery and you bleed out. And old Tommy boy here, well, he surely gets turned into hamburger."

"I don't think so," Howard said. "I think if I shoot you, both you and that grenade will fall off that balcony behind you."

"Ah," Platt said. "But then I would die, and you don't want that, now, do you?"

"Why not?"

Damn, Winthrop thought. She knew Platt was right. And so did Colonel Howard. She'd heard Commander Michaels telling him all about the dead-man switches. But she also knew that the colonel didn't necessarily want Platt to know they knew . . . or that, even now, Jay Gridley was working furiously to defuse the things.

God dammit, Gridley, she thought. *Hurry up.*

"I'm surprised you haven't found my little surprises yet, boy," Platt said, "but then maybe you Net Force folks aren't as good as ole Tommy-boy here thought. Let's just say that if I don't make it back to my ride out of here—and the little ole computer with its satellite uplink—by a certain time, well, things will happen that will make those last assaults on the net look like kid's stuff.''

"What do you want?'' Howard said.

"Well, we need to come to some kind of . . . arrangement,'' Platt said.

He smiled.

40

At the helicopters, the pilots were relaxed, laughing and joking. Michaels and Toni weren't so animated. They stood a short ways off, swatting at the bugs that swirled around them. The bug dope was enough to keep the insects from landing, most of them, but not enough to keep them from buzzing close enough to be annoying.

Michaels was beginning to get worried. The others were supposed to be back by now.

Even as he thought this, the sound of a truck motor reached them.

Two of the pilots moved away from the copters, assault weapons held at the ready.

The truck rounded a curve a couple hundred yards out, and as soon as it did, it blinked its lights off and then on again.

"It's them," Toni said.

Michaels felt himself relax a little.

The truck pulled to a stop ten feet away from where Michaels stood, and Sergeant Fernandez stepped out. He frowned. "Beta Team is not back." It was not a question.

"We thought they were supposed to meet you, and you'd all come back together," Toni said.

"That's how it was supposed to go. We waited until 0150 hours as planned. The deal was, if for some reason they ran long, they'd meet us back at the Hueys by 0200. I don't like this. The colonel is never late. I think we have to give him a call."

"We're not supposed to break radio silence except in an emergency," Michaels said.

"Sir, we're supposed to lift in twenty-five minutes," Fernandez said. "It's an emergency."

Michaels nodded. "Yeah."

2:06 a.m.

Howard felt the com vibrate soundlessly against his left hip. That would be Julio calling. But he couldn't answer him right now. Their suits' long-range broadcast radio had been put on standby, to make sure nobody who might be listening for such things picked up stray signals. LOSIR was up, and GPS transponders were on, but that wouldn't be much help—they knew *where* he was, just not why he was still *there*.

Howard had his pistol trained on Platt, as did Winthrop. Platt, meanwhile, waved the grenade back and forth as if it was a spinning reel and he was fly-fishing for bass in a pond.

"Thing is, Colonel, we can't hang around here all night in this Mexican standoff," Platt said. "We don't leave pretty soon, El Presidente's boys are gonna come up here pokin' around, and we don't want to be here when they do."

"Put that thing away," Hughes said. "Are you crazy?"

"No, sir, what I am is pissed off. You owe me thirty million dollars and I want it."

"*Thirty* million?"

"Yeah, I figure I'm due a little extra, for all my trouble. Trouble you caused me."

"I don't know what you are talking about."

"Course not," Platt said.

From the hall, Martin called: "Colonel, is everything okay in there?" He couldn't see them, because the kicked-in door had shut behind him when Howard had come into the room.

"Affirmative!" Howard called back. "But listen up! I want you and Hull to go downstairs, collect the rest of Beta Team, and take the truck back to the rendezvous point ASAP!"

"Sir? What about you and the package?"

"We are involved in some . . . delicate negotiations in here, Martin. Get back to the rendezvous, you copy?"

"Yes, sir!"

"Good move," Platt said. "We'd better be going ourselves." He waved the grenade at the door. "We can leave through the kitchen. It's pretty quiet back there now."

"Maybe not," Howard said.

"Listen up, Colonel Sambo, here's the deal. I need Hughes because without him, I am up Poor White Trash Creek without a paddle. You want him for your own reasons. Let's go somewhere I can get what I want, then you can have him."

"Dammit, Platt—!"

"Shut up, Hughes. You ain't part of this discussion."

"You turn me over to them, why should I give you the money?"

"Oh, I dunno, maybe because if you don't, I'll poke out your eyes or cut off your family jewels?"

"I don't much like your deal," Howard said.

"Only one I'm offering. I got a ride out of this stinkin' country. I'm gonna take an account code with me or I ain't goin'. Grab that laptop there off the bedside table, would you, darlin'? We got to move. You object to that, Colonel?"

Howard shook his head. This guy was dangerous at the very

least, maybe crazy enough to let that grenade go and kill or maim them all.

"If that thing is from World War II, what makes you think it will still work?" Winthrop said. "Maybe I shoot you, it drops and fizzles out like a wet match."

"Maybe so," Platt said. "But you know them krauts, they build to last. You want to risk fat boy's ass on maybe it won't blow up?"

"Let's move," Howard said. "He's right about one thing, if we don't we're all for sure dead."

"Age before beauty," Platt said.

As Howard turned to leave the room, he reached down with his left hand, while it was hidden from Platt's view, and triple-tapped the panic button on his com.

2:10 a.m.

"Oh, shit," Fernandez said.

"What?" Michaels and Toni said together.

"My com just started a beeper pulse. The colonel has pushed his panic button. That means he's down or captured, he can't talk."

Michaels said, "Can we locate him from the signal?"

"Yes, it's a GPS pulse."

"Then let's go."

"We're supposed to lift in twenty minutes," one of the pilots said. "Sooner or later the local army is going to get its pants on and come looking for whoever caused all the trouble."

Michaels said. "We don't leave until we bring our people out."

"Sir, the colonel's orders—" the pilot began.

"Negative," Fernandez cut in. "If the colonel's been captured, then I'm in charge, and I say we're not leaving without Colonel Howard. Understood?''

The pilot looked at the ground.

Fernandez said. ''If the local army comes around, then you can take off. Otherwise, you wait until we get back.''

''I'm going with you,'' Michaels said.

''And so am I,'' Toni said.

''Not a good idea, sir,'' Fernandez began.

''Why does everybody keep saying that? Let's move, Sergeant. Time is running out.''

2:15 a.m.

The rest of Beta Team had left by the front gate, which was opened and unmanned. The guards who had been fogged were still on the ground, bound in plastic wrist and ankle cufftape.

Howard, Platt, Hughes, and Winthrop moved out. There was still a big commotion at the diversion fire, less than half a mile away, and nobody seemed to be standing around gawking at the presidential compound.

''He's crazy,'' Hughes said quietly to the colonel. ''He hates black people, or at least black men. He'll kill us all if he gets the chance.''

Platt moved over and tapped Hughes on the back of the head with the grenade he held.

''Ow!''

''Didn't I tell you to shut up? You burned all your goodwill up with me.''

''Why do they call it a potato masher?'' Winthrop said, trying to distract the man.

''Because of the shape,'' Platt said. ''See, narrow here, on the handle, but fat down here. You take your cooked potatoes and pound away at them, like this.''

He moved the grenade up and down, as if using it to smash things under the heavy end. "See?"

God, he was crazy. Look at him grin. And what was that stain all over his skin? He couldn't possibly think he was passing for a native, could he?

2:20 a.m.

"Randall, what are they doing?" Fernandez asked.

"Still moving, Sarge. Gotta be on foot, slow as they are going."

They were in the truck, running with the lights off, and the vehicle found every pothole in the dirt road, bouncing them around like Ping-Pong balls. Toni kept one hand on the wooden frame mounted on the back, the other hand on her *kris* handle. She had shoved the sheath into her belt when they'd gotten on the helicopters, although she didn't know how much luck it was bringing her at the moment.

Could be worse. She could be dead.

"Same direction as before?" Fernandez asked.

"Yep."

"Get us in front of them, Butler, half a mile or so, then shut it down."

"You have a plan?" Toni asked.

"Not really. The colonel's GPS unit is going somewhere at foot speed. If it's still attached to the colonel and he's free, he'll probably like a ride. If he's been captured and is being taken out to be shot or something, then he probably won't be too unhappy to see us. Either way, we need to know—hold on a second, somebody is calling. Go ahead."

"Sergeant Fernandez, this is Martin. Beta Team is at the rendezvous—except for Colonel Howard and Lieutenant Winthrop."

"What happened to them?"

"I don't know, Sarge. They went into the package's room and then things got real quiet. We could hear them talking, but couldn't make out what they were saying through the closed door. After a while, the colonel told us to take off."

"Did he give a reason?"

"Negative. All he said was, he was doing some kind of negotiation."

"Copy, Martin. Hold your ground as long as you can. We're going to collect the colonel and the lieutenant now. See if you can shoo away anybody who comes nosing around until we get back."

"Affirmative, Sarge."

Fernandez looked puzzled. "Doesn't make any sense."

"When we find Howard, we'll get him to explain it," Michaels said.

2:25 a.m.

"Where are we going?" Howard asked. The brush around the little trail was thick, still radiating damp heat from the day. You couldn't see two feet into the forest, and could barely see the trail, even with flashlights.

"Not too much further," Platt said. "A half mile or so. I have my ride stashed up ahead. We get there, Hughes gives me the bank code, I check it out using the laptop, we go our separate ways."

Platt saw Winthrop and Howard exchange quick looks.

"Well, in your shoes, I don't reckon I would much trust me neither. But I got nothing to gain by killing anybody here. And you got your guns and all, right? You get your big-time thief and most of the money back, I get paid what I'm owed and I'm gone, you don't never see me again. I'll even shut off my little surprises, once I'm safely out of here. Now don't that sound like a good deal all the way around? Except for fat boy here, but we don't really care what he thinks, do we?''

Howard didn't say anything, but what he was thinking was, *Dammit, Gridley, we're about out of time here. Move your ass!*

2:30 a.m.

''This doesn't make any sense,'' Michaels whispered to Toni. ''That's Hughes, in the white pajamas, and I'm pretty sure the big guy behind him is Platt, wearing some kind of disguise.''

''Yeah, and Howard and Joanna both have their pistols out, but it doesn't look like they are in charge.''

''The big guy's carrying a grenade in one hand, that's why,'' Fernandez said. ''Probably already armed. That's who is in charge, and that's why they don't plug him. He falls, the grenade goes *boom*. Jesus, it's dark out here. I wish we could use the spookeyes.''

''Why can't we?'' Michaels asked.

''Flashlights will cause cutouts, they shine in our direction. Safety feature, otherwise it's like looking into the sun.''

''Hostage scenario,'' Toni said. ''You have an SOP for this, don't you?''

''Yes, ma'am—only not one set up to cover being in a foreign jungle with enemy troops breathing down our necks and our ride about to take off. Standard negotiations for hostage situations are based on psychology—and hours or days to work. We don't have the time.''

Michaels, Toni, and Fernandez were in the bushes fifty yards ahead of the quartet moving toward them. The rest of Alpha Team was spread out behind the four on the trail.

''What do we do?'' Toni whispered.

Fernandez said. "Look for an opportunity. Push comes to shove, we take the bad guy down and hope for minimal casulties."

"How much danger are Howard and Winthrop in, given the suits they are wearing?"

"Some," Fernandez said. "They will surely pick up damage, cuts, but the armor will stop most of a low-yield explosive shrapnel. It's the guy in the PJs and the big brown guy who are gonna get shredded for sure."

Toni said, "No great loss—except that Hughes might have left us some electronic bombs of his own. We can't let him die until we know for sure he didn't. And if he did, maybe it was Platt who set them up, if there are any. Can we afford to let both of them die? Don't we need at least one of them alive?"

"Yeah," Michaels said. "But the clock is ticking. We don't move, everybody dies." At that moment his virgil vibrated.

It was Gridley. "Got 'em, Boss. Every last one of them."

"Good work, Jay," Alex said. "And just in time." Disconnecting, he looked around him. "Jay did it. Get ready to get our people out of there now." He stood and stepped out of the bushes.

"Alex, don't—!" Toni began.

Too late.

"Hold it right there, asshole!" Michaels yelled.

Behind him, Fernandez said to Toni, "I'll flank right, Commander, go left!"

The four people moving up the path stopped.

"Who the hell are you?" Platt said. "Get out here where I can—oh, hello! You're the Net Force honcho, aint'cha? What you doin' out here in the jungle, desk boy? Come to see how real men play?"

Howard made his move—he leaped, grabbed the hand holding the grenade, and squeezed it tight in both of his. "Shoot, Winthrop, shoot!"

Startled, Joanna pointed her pistol and fired, but Platt spun, swung the colonel around one-handed like swinging a small child, and the bullet from Joanna's pistol *spanged!* off the colonel's back armor.

A beat later, another bullet from somewhere boomed and whistled past, not hitting anything Michaels could see.

Jesus! Everybody dancing around wouldn't leave Fernandez or Toni a clear shot, Michaels knew. And if bullets started bouncing off armor, no telling where they might go—or who might catch one in an unprotected spot.

"Cease fire!" Fernandez yelled. He must have realized the danger too.

Things went into slow motion. . . .

—Platt pulled a knife from his belt even as he danced around in a circle with Howard holding on to his other hand—

—Michaels ran toward the two struggling men, moving as if his feet were mired in thick mud—

—Platt slashed at Howard's arm and drew blood—

—Michaels got to the wrestling men, saw Platt grin, turn the knife in his direction, and cut at him, forcing Michaels to jump back—

—Platt turned back to Howard, raised the knife to Howard's throat, to a gap in the armor. Slow, oh, so slow . . .

"Adios, black boy," Platt said. He didn't even raise his voice.

Michaels's gun was still in its holster; he was the only one close enough to shoot and hit Platt. He pulled it, fired without aiming—he couldn't miss this close—but Platt saw him reach, spun Howard around, and once again the bullet hit the colonel's armor—

Damn—

"John!"

—Michaels turned, saw Toni. She had already tossed something at Howard—

—the *kris*—

Reflexively, Platt batted at the thing he saw twirling in toward him, missed, but that meant his knife was away from Howard's throat—

—Howard let go of the grenade hand, snatched the wavy-bladed knife from the air, turned, twisted into Platt, stabbed as Platt stabbed—

—Platt snarled as his knife hit Howard's armor and skidded off—

—The *kris*'s point slipped between Platt's ribs, the blade sinking in until the hilt almost touched the center of the big man's chest—

Platt moaned, blew out a breath, stabbed again, hit more armor. The knife actually dug in a little—then the blade snapped in half.

"Fuck," Platt said. He fell to his knees, dragging Howard down with him, pulling the *kris* from Howard's grasp.

Hughes screamed, "Jesus, Jesus, don't shoot me! Don't shoot me! Please!"

Platt toppled to the side, and when he did, he let go of the grenade.

—The grenade—

Michaels dropped the gun, dived, rolled, came up with the bomb, and threw it into the trees to his left. He hoped like hell none of the troops had circled back into that area, or that it didn't hit a tree and bounce right back—

"Down!" he yelled. "Down, down—"

He dropped.

Howard was still on his feet, staring at Platt.

One . . . two . . . three . . .

Boom!

The grenade went off, and metal sleeted through the trees and bushes, punching holes in leaves and bark.

Something burned along Michaels's arm. He frowned. What—!

A long time passed, a couple of thousand years, Michaels figured. Toni grabbed him, and he realized he was still alive. His ears rang.

He hugged her with his good arm, and watched his other arm bleed from the shrapnel gash on it. It didn't hurt, but it was putting out what seemed a goodly amount of red.

"Don't shoot!" Hughes said. He started to blubber, big tears streaming.

"Shut up," Howard said quietly.

Hughes shut up.

Howard moved to stand next to Michaels, holding his own arm, which was also bleeding. "Commander. You okay?"

"Yep. You, Colonel?"

"Better, now. Nice of you to drop by."

"We were in the neighborhood."

They looked down at Platt, who was still breathing. Platt said, "Damn. I can't believe it. A *nigrah* . . ."

Howard didn't say anything.

Platt stared at Howard. "I hate this fuckin' country," he said. "Kilt by a goddamned *nigrah*—"

Platt's last breath escaped and he collapsed.

Howard stared off into the forest. "He was right about the Germans."

"Excuse me?" Michaels said.

"I'll tell you about it later, Commander."

Behind them, Joanna Winthrop and Julio Fernandez were locked in a tight embrace.

"Well," Michaels said, "I hate to break this party up, but it would be a good idea for us to take our leave now."

"Amen, Commander. Amen."

Michaels bent, and with some difficulty, pulled the *kris* from Platt. He wiped it off on the man's shirt, then gave it back to Toni. "I think you are right, Toni. This is definitely a lucky thing to have around."

"Let's go, people! We got a helicopter to catch!"

They went.

EPILOGUE

In his own bed, Michaels woke up slowly and rolled from his right side onto his back. The left arm was still little sore, but the medic had used skinstat glue and bonded the six-inch-long gash into a thin line they said would leave minimal scarring. A nice conversation piece at informal parties, they'd told him. Not everybody nearly gets blown up by an antique hand grenade.

The ride back from Guinea-Bissau had been relatively uneventful. The locals had never gotten around to finding the helicopters, at least not until after they were in the air. The flight from Banjul couldn't have been smoother. True, the director hadn't been thrilled with the operation, but nobody in Guinea-Bissau was going to complain about it, given that their President had received a hundred million dollars in stolen money. They might even let him keep it, the director had said, because maybe it was better that he was beholden to the U.S. government, given the unstable political situations over there. Better he felt as if he owed them a favor, should they need to collect it. But that was up to State, of course.

All in all, the director wasn't too upset. And everybody in the regular FBI and Net Force was happy to hear the great silence from the offices of Senator Robert White after his chief of staff was indicted for all those horrible crimes. White was too rich to have been involved in Hughes's little scheme, but there would be a little tar from that brush on his nice suit. Maybe he might even get unelected next time around. There was a nice thought.

Colonel Howard's arm needed a little work, but it would heal almost as good as new, so he was told. And apparently the colonel had picked up some kind of rare bacterial infection a while back that had been sapping his strength lately. It had been missed during his initial exam, but picked up while the knife wound was being treated. Once it was diagnosed, the medics were able to start Howard on antibiotics, and he'd been delighted to find out that the disease would be cured in a couple of weeks and he'd feel a lot perkier. Not that Michaels thought the colonel particularly needed that—he'd looked pretty damned perky when he'd been wrestling with the sociopathic racist bodybuilder.

So, despite a few glitches, things had turned out pretty well. . . .

"Alex?"

He looked up. Toni, naked and gloriously beautiful, stood at the foot of the bed beaming down at him. "Hmm?"

"You want some coffee? I can go and make you some."

He smiled at her. "Maybe later," he said. "I've got something else in mind just at this moment."

"Oh? And what might that be?"

"Come here and I'll show you."

She did, and then he did.

That turned out pretty well too.

And the coffee didn't get made until almost noon.